# WHEN IS
# JUDGEMENT
# DAY?

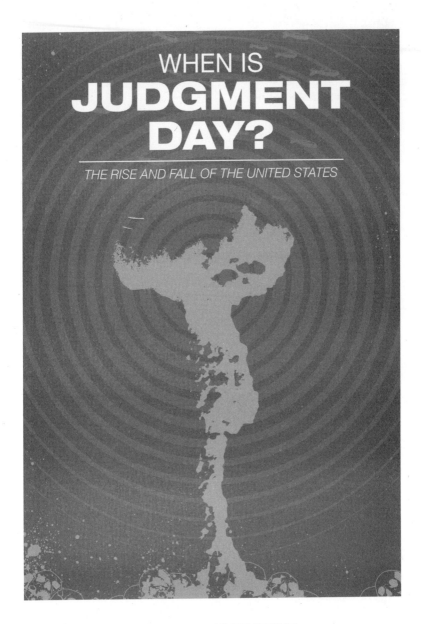

# WHEN IS
# JUDGMENT
# DAY?

*THE RISE AND FALL OF THE UNITED STATES*

## STEPHEN JOHNSTON

OFFICIAL DISCLOSURE

A DIVISION OF ANOMALOS PUBLISHING HOUSE

CRANE

Official Disclosure
A division of Anomalos Publishing House, Crane 65633
© 2008 by Stephen Johnston
All rights reserved. Published 2008
Printed in the United States of America
08 1
ISBN-10: 0981509134 (paper)
EAN-13: 9780981509136 (paper)

Cover illustration and design by Steve Warner
All Bible verses are quoted from the New King James Version
unless otherwise specified.

A CIP catalog record for this book is available from the Library of
Congress.

# CONTENTS

Foreword . . . . . . . . . . . . . . . . . . . . . . . . . . . . . . . . . . vii

Preface . . . . . . . . . . . . . . . . . . . . . . . . . . . . . . . . . . . ix

1. When Is Judgment Day? . . . . . . . . . . . . . . . . . . . . . 1

2. The Prophecy Regarding Israel . . . . . . . . . . . . . . . . . 17

3. Peace in the Middle East . . . . . . . . . . . . . . . . . . . . . 45

4. The Church Age . . . . . . . . . . . . . . . . . . . . . . . . . . . 63

5. The Rapture . . . . . . . . . . . . . . . . . . . . . . . . . . . . . 93

6. Signs of the Rapture . . . . . . . . . . . . . . . . . . . . . . . . 105

7. The Immanency of the Rapture . . . . . . . . . . . . . . . . . 129

8. The Seven Seals and the Tribulation . . . . . . . . . . . . . . 155

9. The United States of America in Prophecy . . . . . . . . . 181

10. The Seven Trumpet Judgments . . . . . . . . . . . . . . . . . 207

11. Is Israel Just Dirt? . . . . . . . . . . . . . . . . . . . . . . . . . . 221

12. The Revived Roman Empire . . . . . . . . . . . . . . . . . . . 233

13. The Seven Bowl Judgments . . . . . . . . . . . . . . . . . . . . 251

14. The Destruction of Babylon .................... 269

15. The Resurrection ............................ 279

16. The Millennial Reign of Christ. ................ 295

17. Eternity .................................... 303

    Notes ...................................... 309

    Bibliography ................................ 313

# FOREWORD

**W**hen is Judgment Day? shows Messiah Yeshua fulfilled the Law and the Prophets. "Think not that I am come to destroy the law, or the prophets: I am not come to destroy, but to fulfill" (Matt. 5:17). Students of prophecy recognize how Leviticus 23 anticipates the Rapture and the Day of the Lord. The feasts of the spring months—Passover, Unleavened, First-fruits, and Pentecost—were historically fulfilled in the same order as listed in Leviticus 23. Death, burial, resurrection, giving of the Holy Spirit. Mr. Johnston argues that it is consistent to believe the remainder of these feasts will be fulfilled in order. He argues that we are now in verse 22 of Leviticus 23 and awaiting the Rapture of the church and the Day of the Lord on the Feast of Trumpets, the next prophetic feast. The Feast of Trumpets, Atonement, and Tabernacles will be fulfilled by the Rapture, Second Coming, and Millennial Reign.

Mr. Johnston believes the Law, as stated in Deuteronomy 30:3, the Prophets, as stated in Ezekiel 38:8, and our Lord, as stated in Matthew 24:14 declared the nation of Israel would be scattered, gathered, and back in the land as a nation prior to the Rapture of the

Church. He also believes the seven churches in Asia Minor, as stated in Revelation chapters 2–3, were actual churches, but also a preview of church history. He believes we are in the final age of lukewarm apostasy, represented by the church of Laodicea.

Mr. Johnston also argues the disciples of the Apostle John, Polycarp and Irenaeus believed the Second Coming of the Lord would not occur until the sixth millennium of human history,—the 21st century (II Peter 3:8).

*When is Judgment Day? The Rise and Fall of the United States* is a must-read for everyone interested in end-time events. Serious students of prophecy will find Mr. Johnston's book stimulating and a necessary addition to their studies.

Thomas Horn

# PREFACE

*When Is Judgment Day?* is a systematic doctrinal study concerning end-time events prophesied in the scriptures. A truthful doctrinal conclusion must correctly interpret and consider all scriptures on a given subject. The contemporary apostate postmodern church rejects propositional absolute truth. Jesus defined a disciple as someone who "knew the truth" (John 8:31–32). By definition, refusing to acknowledge or defend the revealed truth of God is unbelief and in opposition to truth. However, one must not go to the other extreme and assume end-time events do not have specific sequential conditions. "Quickly" and "at hand" may be near from God's perspective, but not necessarily near from man's perspective, and without intervening events. "...For the day of the Lord is at hand." (Zeph. 1:7). "...I am coming quickly" (Rev. 2:20). When Christ comes he will come quickly.

The Rapture of the Church is the next major prophetic event following the First Advent of Christ. However, this does not mean there are not signs or conditions precedent. Much confusion has been caused by man's failure to recognize that immanency does not necessarily mean "soon." To teach that Jesus regarded the Second Coming as immediately at hand would be to represent him as in error, since almost two-thousand years have already elapsed since that time.

The editors of the New King James Bible were so enthusiastic about end-time events they took it upon themselves to add the word "eagerly" to "waiting for the Savior" in I Corinthians 1:7, Philippians 3:20, and Hebrews 9:28. I Corinthians 1:7 is actually speaking of the unveiling of our Lord at the Second Coming. Hebrews is also talking about the Second Coming, not the Rapture. James 5:7 states the coming of the Lord is near, but when one reads further the believer is encouraged to look at the Old Testament prophets as an example of patience. In other words, "near," is not necessarily soon.

The Rapture of the church has three conditions precedent: (1) the establishment of Israel as a nation, as stated in Daniel 9:27. (2) The completion of the church age as outlined by the seven churches in Revelation 2–3. (3) Apostasy in the last days, as stated in I Timothy 4:1. Since Israel is a nation again, since we are in the final phase of church history as stated in Revelation 3:14, and since the post modern church has become apostate as stated in I Timothy 4:1, these three conditions appear near completion. We can now say the Rapture is imminent, could happen without delay, and could happen without major conditions precedent. People who say the Rapture could have occurred in the first century should not be surprised when people do not take the Day of the Lord to be relevant. However, to those who have an ear, we can now say with more specific assurance, maranatha! Our Lord, come!

Stephen B. Johnston, B.S., J.D.

# CHAPTER 1

# WHEN IS JUDGMENT DAY?

## The End of the World

The purpose of this book is to present a systematic analysis of the end-time Biblical expectation of cosmic cataclysms in which God destroys the ruling power of evil, disposes usurpers, redeems the universe to its rightful owner, and resurrects the righteous to life in a Messianic Kingdom. This book will discuss the need for a biblical method of literal interpretation of scriptures. It will cover the imminent return of Christ and the signs of his coming. It will delineate the distinctions between the Rapture (removal of the Christian Church to heaven) and the Second Coming of Christ. It will compare the distinctions between Israel and the Church. The purpose of chapter 1 is not to present a detailed systematic theological discussion of eschatology (the study of end-times), but to merely define terms and present a framework for the study of end-time events.

## The Day of the Lord

Judgment Day is part of what the Bible calls the Day of the Lord. The Day of the Lord is a period of time at the end of time when God's will and purpose for mankind and his word will be fulfilled. It includes the Tribulation, the Second Coming of Christ to earth, a one-thousand year reign of Christ on earth, and the creation of a new heaven and a new earth.

One of the weaknesses of modern Christian theology is the failure to develop a systematic study of Israel in regards to end-time events. Israelology refers to a subdivision of systematic theology incorporating theological doctrines concerning the people of Israel as distinguished from the church. It is important to understand the purpose and plan for Israel versus God's purpose and plan for the church. Without an understanding of the unconditional covenants with Abraham, and his descendants, one cannot understand prophecy and God's word. One of the main failures of Catholic, Greek Orthodox, and reformed theology is lack of understanding of doctrines concerning the people of Israel as described in Old Testament prophecies regarding end-time events. Even some Pre-Tribulation authorities who have a full understanding of the church in prophecy fail to develop systematic doctrines concerning the people of Israel. The doctrine of diaspora (scattering) and gathering of Israel in the last days is often underestimated as a sign of the end and a condition precedent to the Rapture of the church. To say the return of Christ is imminent without making a specific reference to time is irrelevant. Without the proper definition of biblical idioms and the proper prophetic outlines, the understanding of end-time events becomes suspect and disorganized. Unfortunately, this can cause disillusionment, division, and lack of confidence in end-time prophecies.

Bible prophecy is not meant to be used to make speculative predictions of the future and date setting, but rather is to be used as a promise about the assurances of the future and to orient the believer to understand signs of the end. The Bible contains over five hundred specific prophecies that have been fulfilled in specific ways, all with 100 percent accuracy. There is no denying that truth. Prophecies of Jesus Christ, Israel, and world empires are found throughout the Old and New Testament. The Bible distinguishes itself from all other religious literature through its use of prophecy. Only God knows our history from beginning to end and is outside the dimension of time. Satan and false prophets are limited to time and space and do not know the future, other than what they have learned from God's word. God's veracity, sovereignty and immutability ensure that his word will be fulfilled. The seal of proof of the veracity of the Gospel and the source of assurance to believers as to their hope of resurrection and eternal life with God is defined by the fulfillment of prophecy. The understanding of prophecy should not merely be considered an intellectual exercise. God gave us prophecy to motivate us to focus on spiritual things, holy living, evangelism, and to eagerly anticipate the return of Jesus Christ. Prophesy is not just a fixation on end-time events, it is the biblical perspective of God's plan of redemption from beginning to end. It is the source of orientation to the plan, purpose, and meaning of life.

Fulfilled prophecy is one of the most powerful proofs that the Bible is the word of God. Since all the prophecies regarding the first coming of Christ were fulfilled, and since Christ was victorious over death, we can be sure all prophecies of his second coming will also be fulfilled. We can be sure the Bible is God's revelation to man, since only God is outside of time and knows the beginning from the end. For every one prophecy on the first coming of Christ there are seven prophecies regarding the second coming of Christ to rule and reign in an earthly kingdom for a thousand years in Zion.

## Tribulation

The Tribulation in bible prophecy is the seven-year period of time between the Rapture of the church and the second coming of Jesus Christ. The Tribulation is described in the book of Daniel, in chapter 9, and an expansion of the description is found in Revelation 6–19.

The Tribulation is described in days, months and years to ensure no mistake is made in assigning its length of time. Christ refers to this period and specifically the book of Daniel in Matthew 24:15 and 29. The seven-year period of Daniel's seventieth week is a time span to which a host of terms are used by the prophets. These terms include Tribulation, great Tribulation, the time of Jacob's distress, the day of darkness and gloom, and the wrath of the Lamb. The book of Joshua was the anticipatory model of the Tribulation. Joshua is the Hebrew name of Jesus, and means "salvation is of Yahweh." Joshua is the story of the disposition of the land from usurpers and the redemption of the land to its rightful owner. Jericho and Babylon both fall after the blowing of seven trumpets. Two spies are sent in to save those who will believe.

The seventieth week found in Daniel 9, is a seven-year period we call the Tribulation. This is a period where God personally intervenes in the lives of people on earth. God's purpose for the Tribulation is the redemption of the universe to the kinsmen redeemer, Jesus Christ or the second Adam, a time of judgment for the wicked, a warning for those willing to repent, and a severe testing of Jacob to cause a remnant from Israel to turn to their Messiah.

## God's Disclosed Purpose of the Tribulation

1.  To turn Israel to their Messiah. "…that hardening in part has happened to Israel until the fullness of the Gentiles has come in. And so all Israel will be saved, as it is written: 'The Deliverer will come out of Zion, and he will turn away ungodliness from Jacob. For this is my covenant with them, when I take away their sins" (Rom. 11:25–27).
2.  To make an end of wickedness and wicked ones (Isa. 13:9).
3.  To bring about a worldwide revival. This purpose is given and fulfilled in Revelation 7:1–17.

## Daniel's Seventieth Week

The term "the seventieth week of Daniel" comes from chapter 9 of the book of Daniel. Daniel is given dream which covers 490 years consisting of seventy weeks. This dream covers the history of the Jews until the first and second coming of the Messiah. However, there is a gap or parenthesis between the sixty-ninth and seventieth week. The Hebrew word, translated weeks in English, is *shabua*. It means a "unit of seven." This unit of seven can mean days, months or years. In this case, we know it means "units of seven years" because a time-specific prophecy was given of sixty-nine weeks or 483 years from the rebuilding of Jerusalem and the wall until the time of the Messiah. From history we know it took exactly 483 prophetic years (360 days) from the command of Artaxerxes Longimanus on March 5, 444 BC, to rebuild the city and the walls until Christ. The last seven years, the seventieth week, is described in Daniel 9:27. The gap between the sixty-ninth and seventieth weeks is what the Apostle Paul calls the Church Age. (Eph. 3:1–5) The Church Age was a mystery to the Old Testament prophets and was not revealed by God until the time of Christ. In Daniel 12:4, Daniel was told to "shut up the words and seal the book until the time of the end," when it would begin to be understood.

## The Gap between the Sixty-Ninth and Seventieth Week of Daniel

The gap between the sixty-ninth and seventieth week is clearly apparent in verse twenty-six, because it describes the fall of Jerusalem in 70 and 150 AD, which occurred over thirty-seven and 120 years respectively after the death of Christ. The dispersion and gathering of Israel between AD 70 and 1948 had to occur in the gap in verse 26. Jesus explains this gap in Matthew 24:2 : "...I say to you, not one stone shall be left here upon another, that shall not be thrown down...Therefore when you see the 'abomination of desolation' spoken of by Daniel the prophet, standing in the holy place (whoever reads, let him understand)" (Matthew 24:15). What Jesus is saying is that the temple will be destroyed in AD 70 and the people will be scattered, but they will return and build the temple again in the seventieth week. Old Testament prophetic scriptures often have a gap or an unseen skip in time. This skip in time hides the church age or the period of time we are presently living in. The church age is a parenthesis or mystery which was not revealed to Old Testament prophets.

Dwight Pentecost makes the following comments about gaps in prophetic scripture in his book *Things to Come*:

"The post tribulation rapturist (Rapture of church at end of Tribulation) joins with amillennialism (no literal one thousand year rule of Christ) in asserting:

a.  That the seventieth week of Daniel's prophecy was fulfilled historically in the years immediately following the death of Christ. Some hold that Christ was cut off at the end of the sixty-ninth week and that the seventieth week followed immediately after his death. Others hold that Christ was cut off in the middle of the seventieth week so that the last half of the week followed his death. Some go so far as to assert that the entire present age is the seventieth week. The fallacy of this consecutive view is seen in the fact that only spiritualizing the prophecy can the results of Messiah's work, as outlined in Daniel 9:24, be said to have been fulfilled. The nation Israel, to whom the prophecy was addressed, simply has not experienced a single one of the prophesied benefits of Messiah's coming as yet. Since this interpretation depends on a method of interpretation that is unacceptable, the view must be rejected.

b.  Opposed to the view that the sixtieth and seventieth weeks are chronologically consecutive is the view that the period is separated by an indefinite period of time. There are several considerations to support this view.

(1) The interval between the "acceptable year of the Lord" and the "day of vengeance of our God" (Isa. 61:2—a parenthesis already extending more than nineteen hundred years). (2) The interval between the Roman Empire as symbolized by the legs of iron of the great image of Daniel 2 and the feet of ten toes. Confer also Daniel 7:23–27; 8:24, 25. (3) The same interval found between Daniel 11:35 and Daniel 11:36 (4) A great parenthesis occurs between Hosea 3:4 and verse 5, and again between Hosea 5:15 and 6:1. (5) A great parenthesis occurs also between Psalm 22:22 and 22:23 and between Psalm 110:1 and 110:2 (6) Peter in quoting Psalm 34:12–16 stops in the middle of a verse to distinguish God's present work and his future dealing with sin (1 Per. 3:10–12). (7) The great prophecy of Matthew 24 becomes intelligible only if the present age be considered a parenthesis between Daniel 9:26 and 9:27. (8) Acts 15:13–21 indicates that the apostles fully understood that during the present age the Old Testament prophecies would not be fulfilled, but would have fulfillment "after this" when God " will build again the tabernacle of David" (Acts 15:13). (9) Israel's yearly schedule of feasts showed a wide separation between the feasts prefiguring the death and resurrection of Christ and Pentecost, and the feasts speaking of Israel's gathering and blessing. (10) Romans 9–11 definitely provides for the parenthesis, particularly the future of the olive tree in chapter 11. (11) The revelation of the church as one body requires a parenthesis between God's past dealings and his future dealings with the nation Israel. (12) The consummation of the present parenthesis is of such a nature that it resumes the interrupted events of Daniel's last week. (246–247)

## The Rapture of the Church

The church age begins on the Feast of Pentecost in Acts 2. The Holy Spirit descends on believers from heaven. The church age will end on the Feast of Trumpets when living believers are raptured to heaven and given a glorified body. They will remain with Christ until the Second Advent when they will return to earth for the one-thousand-year reign in the millennium. In chapter 4, verse 17 of I Thessalonians, the Bibles states: "For the Lord Himself will descend from heaven with a shout, with the voice of an archangel, and with the trumpet of God. And the dead in Christ will rise first. Then we who are alive and remain shall be caught up (Raptured) together with them in the clouds to meet the Lord in the air…" In John 14:3 and 4 it goes on to say, "And if I go and prepare a place for you, I will come again and receive you to myself; that where I am, there you may be also. And where I go you know, and the way you know." We are going to heaven at the Rapture. At the Second Advent, Christ comes down to rule for a thousand years.

## The Second Advent

At the end of the seven-year Tribulation, Christ will come to rescue Israel, vanquish his enemies, and reign in righteousness upon this earth for one-thousand years. "I will return again to my place till they acknowledge their offense. Then they will seek my face; in their affliction they will diligently seek me" (Hosea 5:15). "I will bring the one-third through the fire, will refine them as silver is refined, and test them as gold is tested. They will call on my name, and I will answer them, I will say, this is My People; and each one will say, 'The Lord is my God'" (Zech. 13:9).

## Millennial Reign

"Blessed and holy is he who has part in the first resurrection. Over such the second death has no power, but they shall be priests of God and of Christ, and shall reign with Him a thousand years" (Rev. 20:6). Christ was the first fruit of the first resurrection. Church age believers will be resurrected at the Rapture. Old Testament Saints and Tribulation martyrs will be resurrected at the Second Advent. Jews and Gentiles will rule with Christ on earth for one-thousand years.

## Premillennialism

In Christian eschatology, or the study of end-times, premillennialism is the belief that Christ will physically return to earth a second time and will reign for one-thousand years. The doctrine is called premillennialism because it views the current church age as prior to Christ's kingdom. The Apostle John was given specific information related to end-time prophecy from God. John relayed specific teachings to the early church fathers.

In his book *History of the Christian Church,* Philip Schaff states, "The most striking point in the eschatology of the ante-Nicene age is the prominent chiliasm,[1] or millenarianism, that is the belief of a visible reign of Christ in glory on earth with the risen saints for a thousand years, before the general resurrection and judgment. It was indeed not the doctrine of the church embodied in any creed or form of devotion, but a widely current opinion of distinguished teachers, such as Barnabas, Papias, Justin Martyr, Irenaeus, Tertullian, Methodius, and Lactantius" (Volume II, page 614). What he is saying is the disciples of John, such as the early church believers, were premillennialists. Papias's belief in Premillennialism is especially significant since he was a disciple of Polycarp, who in turn was a disciple of the Apostle John, who in turn penned the statements about a one-thousand-year reign of Christ in the book of Revelation. This Revelation in turn came from God the Father.

This tradition was passed down from the Apostles to the early church fathers to the Montanists, Donatist, the Britons, the Celtic churches of Ireland, the Paulicians, the Albigenses, the Waldenses, the Anabaptist, the Plymouth Brethren, the Baptists, and contemporary premillennial teachers. These believers were persecuted and almost entirely wiped out by the Roman Catholic and Reformed State churches that did not believe in premillennialism and were determined to destroy anyone who disagreed with them.

## Ante-Nicene

The First Council of Nicaea, Asia Minor, was convoked by the Roman Emperor Constantine I in AD 325. It was the first ecumenical conference of bishops of the early Christian church, and resulted in an attempt to establish a uniform creed. A precedent was established for a state church to attempt to speak for God. The Nicene Creed correctly stated that God the Father and Jesus Christ are one. However, it was not for man to attempt confirm what the scriptures had already clearly stated. The council promulgated twenty church laws, called canons. These laws included the invalidity of baptism by Paulian believers, the changing of the Passover feasts to Easter, and the prohibition of kneeling during the liturgy. The Nicene Council established Emperor Constantine as head of the state Christian Church as well as the Supreme Pontiff of the Babylonian Priesthood, which initially moved from Babylon to Pergamos, and finally Rome.

## Allegorical Interpretation

The early orthodox disciples of John were premillennialists. However, when the visible church became supported by the Roman Empire and Christianity was mixed with pagan religions, theologians began to undercut prophecy and considered it subject to error, allegorical, and non-literal. The essential heart of the entire question in regards to prophecy is one's view of interpreting scriptures. For the most part, those who believe the Bible to be literal are premillennialists. In *Understanding End-Times Prophecy*, Paul Benware states, "The curse of the allegorical method is that it obscures the true meaning of the Word of God. Most of the objectivity in biblical interpretation is lost, since one allegorical interpretation is as valid as another" (27).Amillennialism teaches that there will be no literal millennium on the earth following the second coming of Christ. It tends to spiritualize or allegorize all prophecies concerning the Kingdom and attributes prophecies related to Israel to the church. This is called Replacement Theology, and teaches that the promises made to Israel in the Bible are fulfilled in the Christian Church. Prophecies concerning the blessing and restoration of Israel to the Promised Land are spiritualized or allegorized into promises of God's blessing for the church. This is a slippery slope and ends in a dead, lifeless theology. Those who hold the amillennial point of view concede that it was first suggested by Augustine, who molded the doctrines of the Roman Catholic Church and the reformed church more than any other man. In *History of the Christian Church, Volume II*, Reformed Theologian Schaff states, "From the time of Constantine and Augustine chiliasm took its place among the heresies, and was rejected subsequently even by the Protestant reformers as a Jewish dream" (619). Augustine defined any doctrine that disagreed with what the state church that Rome taught as heresy. He did not define heresy as something that disagreed with scripture. Augustine was influenced by Clement of Alexandria and his student, Origen, who trained Dionysus. Together these three established the Alexandrian emphasis on spiritualizing the scriptures. Augustine is widely regarded as the major influence behind Western church theology. Besides Amillennialism, Augustine established the doctrines of purgatory, extreme predestination, the depravity of man, and salvation through church sacraments, such as baptismal regeneration. Many people today see Augustine (Aurelius Augustinus) as a saint and as the greatest thinker since the Apostle Paul. However, it is interesting how Revelation 2:14–15 describes this period in church history:

> But I have a few things against you because you have there those who hold the doctrine of Balaam, who taught Balak to put a stumbling block before the children of Israel, to eat things sacrificed to idols, and to commit sexual immorality. Thus you also have those who hold the doctrine of the Nicolaitans, which thing I hate.

This describes a literal church called Pergamos. The Nicolaitans created a caste system of bishops, priests and laymen instead of making all believers priests and brothers in the name of Christ. The word *pergamos* means mixed marriage. The seven churches in Revelation 2 and 3 represent literal churches and characteristics of churches in the church age. They also are a type of periods in church history in chronological order. Pergamos represents the general state of affairs in the visible church from 312 to 606 AD. Chapter 3 of Revelation calls this historical phase the Church of Laodicea. The influence of Augustine has continued to this day and has contributed to the current apostasy. Postmillennial theology, which states that Christ will come at the end of a millennial kingdom, and amillennial theology are in error. There is no possibility that the church will Christianize the world before the King comes back to rule with a rod of iron. Scripture does not teach that the world will be Christianized. It teaches that the world is heading for destruction and that if Jesus does not come back in the flesh no flesh will be saved.[2] Liberal theologians are replacing the literal rule of Jesus and the literal role of Israel with the church. They have robbed the prophets of their prophecies with replacement theology and do not teach what God inspired the prophets to tell the world. They rob God of all the future events he foretold by his prophets and replace them with a strange doctrine of Western market-driven Christianity on earth that is not taught in the Bible. Many of those who lead this movement have no clue that we are in the end-times because they deny the truth of God's word. Other than a minority of true believers, the church has become a sanctuary for unbelievers and biblically illiterate Christians.

## Judgment Day

There are several types of judgment in the future, each with a specific purpose. It is incorrect to speak of one specific event as Judgment Day. The church age believers will be judged for the good works in heaven during the Tribulation period. Old Testament saints and Tribulation martyrs will be judged for their good works at the Second Advent.

## White Throne Judgment

Unbelievers will be judged at the white throne and consigned to the lake of fire on their day of judgment at the end of the millennial reign. Upon death, unbelievers are sent to Hades until Judgment Day:

> And I saw a great white throne and the one who sat upon it, from whose face the earth and the heaven fled, and a place was not found for them. And I saw the dead, the great and the small, standing before the throne, and books were opened; and another book was opened, which is the book of life; and the dead were judged from the things written in the books according to their works. And the sea gave up the dead which were in it, and death and Hades gave up the dead which were in them, and each of them was judged according

to his works. And death and Hades were cast into the lake of fire. This is the second death, the lake of fire. And if anyone was not found written the book of life, he was cast into the lake of fire. (Rev. 20:11–15)

In his book *James and Peter,* Harry Ironside describes the Day of the Lord as follows:

"(W)hen at last the day of grace is ended the day of the Lord will succeed it … The day of the Lord follows (the Rapture). It will be the time when the judgments of God are poured out upon the earth. It includes the descent of the Lord with all his saints to execute judgment on his foes and to take possession of the kingdom … and to reign in righteousness for a thousand glorious years" (98–99).

In his book *Things to Come,* Dwight Pentecost states:

This judgment includes not only the specific judgment upon Israel and the nations at the end of the Tribulation that are associated with the Second Advent, but, from a consideration of the passages themselves, include judgments that extend over a period of time prior to the Second Advent. Thus, it is concluded that the Day of the Lord will include the time of the Tribulation. Zechariah 14:1–4 makes it clear that the events of the Second Advent are included in the program of the Day of the Lord. II Peter 3:10 gives authority for including the entire millennial age within this period. If the Day of the Lord did not begin until the second advent, since that event is preceded by signs, the Day of the Lord could not come as a "thief in the night", unexpected, and unheralded, as it is said it will come in 1 Thessalonians 5:2. The only way this day could break unexpectedly upon the world is to have it begin immediately after the Rapture of the church. It is thus concluded that the Day of the Lord is that extended period of time beginning with God's dealing with Israel after the Rapture at the beginning of the Tribulation period and extending through the second advent and the millennial age unto the creation of the new heavens and new earth after the millennium. (230–231)

# CHAPTER 2

# THE PROPHECY REGARDING ISRAEL

The issue of Israel is one of the major points of division in evangelical theology today. "An evangelical theologian's view of Israel will determine whether he is a Covenant Theologian or a Dispensationalist."[3] There are many systematic theological reference books which have systematized all areas of biblical truth; however, they seldom develop Israel as part of their system. Arnold Fruchtenbaum's *Israelology* is a rare exception. It must be remembered that three-quarters of the Bible has to do directly with Israel. Jesus said, "Do not think that I came to destroy the law or the prophets. I did not come to destroy but to fulfill" (Matt. 5:17). The book of Revelation makes over 500 references to Jewish idioms. Revelation chapters 5–19 are an expansion of the seventieth week of Daniel 9. Many evangelical theologians fail to understand that as a condition precedent to the Rapture of the Church, the chosen people of God had to be back in the land of Israel as a nation. "In the latter years you will come into the land" (Ezek. 38:8). "Then he shall confirm a treaty with many for one week (seven years); but in the middle of the week (seven years) he shall bring an end to sacrifice and offering." (Dan. 9:27). The Old Testament is not meant to be understood only in an allegorical sense. When the Old Testament prophets speak of the Messiah literally coming to Zion to rule and reign, Messiah Yeshua will literally come to reign.

## The Garden of Eden

In the Garden of Eden, Adam and Eve were able to confer directly with God. They understood that God had created the world, that he was sovereign, and that they were responsible to him. When sin entered the human race through Adam, fellowship with God was broken. God had a problem with his own essence. God's mercy and love wanted to forgive Adam and have fellowship. However, justice and righteousness demanded punishment. Because God is not in a time zone, he was not caught off guard and the problem of reconciliation was solved in eternity past. Grace would provide God's righteousness at Christ's expense on the cross. In the interim, animal sacrifices would temporarily cover man's sin until God would come in the appearance of man and die. John 3:16 states that "For God so loved the world that he gave his only begotten Son, that whoever believes in Him should not perish but have everlasting life." God revealed his plan of salvation through one who would come from a woman.[4] This anticipated the virgin birth of Christ. God apparently revealed to Adam the principle of blood sacrifice as a means of atoning for sin. Adam and Eve knew God as a gracious and loving god, but also as a God of righteousness and judgment.

By the time Noah and his family emerged in the Bible, the human race had largely departed from God to the point where God himself said that Noah and his family were the only ones worthy of deliverance from judgment. When the worldwide flood came as a tremendous demonstration of the sovereign power of God, Noah saw the world of his day wiped out and he and his sons committed to the tasks of beginning anew. Noah had a clear revelation that God works in the world and is involved in history through his providence.

## Abrahamic Covenant

God made an important announcement to Abraham about the future. To him the special purpose of God was made known to him in the calling out of a people to be the express channel of his revelation. Abraham, Isaac, and Jacob were committed the promises of the Abrahamic covenant, including the promise of a great nation and the promise that through them One would come who would be a blessing to the whole world.

Scripture charts a new course for God's people, beginning with Abraham. The choice of Abraham marked a new narrowing of the redemptive purpose of God. Genesis 12:1–3 states:

> Now the Lord had said to Abram: "Get out of your country, from your kindred and from your father's house, to a land that I will show you. I will make you a great nation; I will bless you and make your name great; and you shall be a blessing. I will bless those who bless you, and I will curse him who curses you; and in you all the families of the earth shall be blessed."

This is the Abrahamic Covenant in which God unconditionally declares that "I will bring to pass the promised blessings… I will make you a great nation…I will bless you…you will receive personal honor and reputation." Abram (whose name God changed to Abraham) settled in Hebron in the land of Canaan.

## The Promised Land Covenant

Genesis 13:14–16 states, "And the Lord said to Abram, after Lord had separated from him: 'Lift your eyes now and look from the place where you are-northward, southward, eastward, and westward; for all the land which you see I give to you and your descendants forever.

And I will make your descendants as the dust of the earth; so that if a man could number the dust of the earth, then your descendants also could be numbered.'" God unconditionally promised the Holy Land to Abraham and his descendants forever. The land into which God led Abram was Canaan, the people were Canaanites. Under King David, the land prospered as the nation Israel. When Israel rejected its Messiah, the Kingdom of God on earth was postponed. Israel was dispersed in AD 70 AD. In AD 150, when the Romans put down a Jewish revolt, they expelled Jews from Jerusalem and changed the name of Israel to Palestine. However, just as the diaspora, scattering of the Jews was predicted by the prophets, so the regathering was predicted. God gave the holy land to Abraham and his descendants forever.

Today's problems in the Middle East all center upon a dispute over a land that was promised to Abraham and his heirs. On that promise, Jews, Muslims, and Christians basically agree. The dispute concerns the identity of Abraham's heirs who were to inherit the Promised Land. Abraham had at least eight sons: Ishmael, by Hagar, his wife Sarah's maid; Isaac, by his wife Sarah; and six other sons by Keturah, whom he married after Sarah's death. Which of these sons' descendants qualify? Do they all get a share? In addition, because of Augustine's fathering of Replacement Theology, Christians believe the church replaced Abraham as the true heirs of Abraham's blessings. Fortunately, the Bible gives a clear answer, and establishes who the Promised Land rightfully belongs to.

## The God of Abraham, Isaac, and Jacob

The terms *Israel* and *Israelite* are found approximately 2,300 times in the Old Testament, and in every case they refer to those racially descended from Abraham, Isaac and Jacob. One of the main causes for contemporary confusion in understanding prophecy is the failure to take Israel-related prophecies literally. Attempts to transfer promises given specifically to Israel to Arabs or the church have been a major obstacle in understanding God's prophetic purposes as a whole. Once prophecies about Israel are distinguished from prophecies concerning the church or the Gentiles, the main programs of God as outlined in prophecy begin to be clear.

In Genesis 28:13, God's word declares, "And behold, the Lord stood above it and said: 'I am the Lord God of Abraham, your father and the God of Isaac; the land on which you lie I will give to you and your descendants.'" In Exodus 3:14–15, God said to Moses, "I Am WHO I Am." And he said, "Thus you shall say to the children of Israel, "I AM has sent me to you." Moreover, God said to Moses, "Thus you shall say to the children of Israel, 'The Lord God of your father, the God of Abraham, the God of your fathers, the God of Abraham, the God of Isaac, and the God of Jacob, has sent me to you. This is my name forever, and this is my memorial to all generation.'"

Islam claims that, as the firstborn, Ishmael had the right of inheritance to the Promised Land. Ordinarily that would have been true, but God had promised Abraham that Sarah, his wife, would bear him a son who would be his heir. Ishmael was not the son of God's promise, but of Abraham's and Sarah's unbelief. Sarah gave her handmaid to have a son by proxy, because she did not believe she could have children, and she did not believe God would fulfill his pledge. This lack of faith has caused much bloodshed in the Middle East.

Fourteen years after Ishmael's birth by Hagar, Isaac was born in Hebron to Abraham and Sarah. Ishmael mocked his half-brother, Isaac. In anger, Sarah banished him and his mother from the land God had given to Abraham and to his heirs. From that time onward, Ishmael was no longer part of Abraham's household but lived far away "in the wilderness of Paran" (Gen. 21:21).

Abraham, Isaac and Jacob all died and were buried in Hebron. Ishmael never lived there as an adult. Arabs never lived in Hebron in any numbers until after the seventh-century Muslim invasion of Israel. The PLO claims that Hebron, a city with no connection to Islam, belongs to Muslims and insists that every Jewish resident be removed. In fact, Hebron is one of the most revered places to every Jew. Despite several failed peace plans the disputed claims go on. However, the Messiah of Israel will soon come, settle the dispute, and establish who the land belongs to.

The amillennial interpretation, which does not believe in a millennial reign after the second coming of Christ, tends to deny any future literal fulfillment, though it sometimes recognizes the possibility of spiritual revival of Israel in the present age. In contrast, the premillennial interpretation pictures the second coming of Christ as bringing in a kingdom of glorious release and freedom for Israel, the seating of Christ on the throng of David, Israel's occupation of the Promised Land, and Israel as the object of God's special divine grace. Accordingly, the question as to whether or not Israel still has a future as a nation becomes an important aspect of the interpretation of the prophetic account.

## Who Speaks for God?

Part of God's essence is his veracity and omnipotence. Therefore, God cannot tell a lie and he does what he says he will do. Those who speak for God speak the truth. Deuteronomy 18:22 states, "When a prophet speaks in the name of the Lord, if the thing does not happen or come to pass, that is the thing which the Lord has not spoken; the prophet has spoken it presumptuously; you shall not be afraid of him." As an example of this idea, we know that Muhammad was a false prophet because he lost his first battle with the Arabs from Mecca after he had predicted victory. In his book *The Islamic Invasion*, Robert Morey makes the following comments, "He was struck in the mouth by a sword, lost several teeth, and almost died. Some of his followers fell away as a result of this incident. They felt they had been deceived because they had gone forth in battle expecting a glorious victory. They had been told they were being led by a prophet of Allah and this prophet was beaten in battle and severely wounded" (83).

The Bible teaches us that God's chosen people are the descendents of Abraham, Isaac, and Jacob. God was not only going to use Israel as a means of redemption and revelation, but their very history and prophecy were to be a type which would reveal God in his general dealings with mankind. Looking at the history of Israel in the Old Testament through the lens of their relationship to the Gentiles is also a spiritual analysis of the human experience as the people of God seek to live in a temporal world.

## The New Eternal Covenant

The Prophet Jeremiah describes how God has made an eternal covenant with Israel and they will live forever with God:

> Behold, the days come, saith the LORD, that I will make a new covenant with the house of Israel, and with the house of Judah:
> Not according to the covenant that I made with their fathers in the day that I took them by the hand to bring them out of the land of Egypt; which my covenant they brake, although I was an husband unto them, saith the LORD:
> But this shall be the covenant that I will make with the house of Israel; After those days, saith the LORD, I will put my law in their inward parts, and write it in their hearts; and will be their God, and they shall be my people.
> And they shall teach no more every man his neighbour, and every man his brother, saying, Know the LORD: for they shall all know me, from the least of them unto the greatest of them, saith the LORD: for I will forgive their iniquity, and I will remember their sin no more.

Thus saith the LORD, which giveth the sun for a light by day, and the ordinances of the moon and of the stars for a light by night, which divideth the sea when the waves thereof roar; The LORD of hosts is his name:

If those ordinances depart from before me, saith the LORD, then the seed of Israel also shall cease from being a nation before me for ever.

Thus saith the LORD; If heaven above can be measured, and the foundations of the earth searched out beneath, I will also cast off all the seed of Israel for all that they have done, saith the LORD. (Jer. 31:31–37; King James Version)

Through the prophet Jeremiah, God is saying that as long as there is a sun and a moon he will be faithful to Israel, no matter what they do. In addition, God's word says the sun and moon will last for ever.

While the eternal city of Jerusalem will not be dependent on the sun and moon for light, they will still exist. Revelation 21:23 states, "And the city had no need of the sun, neither of the moon, to shine in it; for the glory of God did lighten it, and the Lamb is the light thereof." Neither the sun nor the moon will ever really be destroyed, since God has promised that they, as well as all the starry heavens, will endure forever.[5] It is just that their light is no longer needed to illumine the holy city, for the city itself radiates light to all the surrounding regions. The sun and moon will continue to serve their present functions with respect to the nether regions of the earth, serving there as lights by day and night, respectively. For those who believe the church replaced Israel and became heirs of God promise to Abraham, they need to look at the sun and moon and stand corrected.

Despite the faithlessness of the nation Israel, God confirms that he will be faithful to her. God reputation and name is at stake. God is setting the stage for Judgment Day. Judgment day is near. The Arabs led by Allah believe they are the true descendants of Abraham. The orthodox Muslims believe the end is near and the final battle is coming soon. The world will soon find out who is speaking for God.

The Old Testament prophet Zechariah says the following about Judgment Day:

> Behold, the day of the Lord is coming, and your spoil will be divided in your midst. For I will gather all the nations to battle against Jerusalem; the city shall be taken, the houses rifled, and the women ravished. Half of the city shall go into captivity, but the remnant of the people shall not be cut off from the city. Then the Lord will go forth and fight against those nations, as he fight in the day of battle. And in that day his feet will stand on the Mount of Olives, which faces Jerusalem on the east. And the Mount of Olives shall be split in two, from east to west, making a very large valley; half of the mountain shall move toward the north and half of it toward the south. (Zech. 14:1–4)

There will not be peace in the Middle East until the King of Kings comes to rule, brings peace on earth for a thousand years, and makes a new covenant with Israel.

## Was the History of Israel Told in Advance?

In Amos 3:7–8, the prophet Amos makes this amazing statement, "Surely the Lord God does nothing, unless he reveals his secret to his servants the prophets. A lion has roared! Who will not fear? The Lord God has spoken! Who can but prophesy?" Every major event in the history of Israel was prophesied by God and told to his prophets.

## The Prophecy of Egyptian Bondage

Abraham, Isaac, and Jacob, although promised the land as a perpetual possession of their seed, never actually possessed the Promised Land. Instead, as God predicted in Genesis 15:13 and 15, "Know of a surety that thy seed shall be a stranger in a land that is not their, and shall serve them; and they shall afflict them four hundred years; and also that nation, whom they shall serve, will I judge; and afterward shall they come out with great substance." This prophecy of Israel's relationship to Egypt was fulfilled in Genesis 46 when Jacob and his family followed Joseph to the land of Egypt to avoid the famine in the Promised Land. The sojourn of the children of Israel in Egypt for 430 years increased the people of Israel from seventy to approximately two million. Israel spent four-hundred years enslaved first under the Hyksos rulers who displaced the native Egyptian kings and were also enslaved when the Egyptian kings resumed control.

## Miracles at the Time of Moses

Miracles are only used very sparingly by God. There are only a few brief periods where God actively used miracles in the history of Israel to bring about his will. The first outbreak of miracles was during the Exodus and the conquest of Canaan. Moses and Joshua were leading God's people through a great period of transition in their earthly pilgrimage, and miracles paved the way. Those miracles stopped as suddenly as they began. In their place, God gave his people his written word: the Pentateuch, the early historical writings, some of the wisdom literature, and the Psalms of David. During the reign of Amenhotep II, God used ten plagues upon Egypt. These plagues are a precursor of some of the plagues God will use to regain possession of the world during the seventieth Week of Daniel, detailed in the Book of Revelation.

The book of the Law prophesied of the eventual diaspora (scattering) of the children of Israel. Deuteronomy 28:64 states, "Then the Lord will scatter you among all peoples, from one end of the earth to the other, and there you shall serve other gods, which neither you nor your fathers have known—wood and stone." However, God promised to gather Israel in the last days, in Deuteronomy 30:1 and 3: "Now it shall come to pass, when all these things come upon you, the blessing and the curse which I have set before you, and you call them to mind among all the nations where the Lord your God drives you...that the Lord your God will bring you back from captivity, and have compassion on you, and gather you again from all the nations where the Lord your God has scattered you."

## Miracles at the Time of Elijah

A second outbreak of miracles occurred in the days of Elijah and Elisha, and those miracles likewise stopped as suddenly as they began. This was also an age of transition. The miracles were designed to draw attention to the ministry of God's two witnesses, who were making a last ditch attempt to bring the nation back to God. Unfortunately, these warning signs were not listened to. God prepared to hand the northern tribes over to the Assyrians. Before he did that, however, he replaced the miracles with his written word: the later histories and the written prophecies of Isaiah, Jeremiah, and the early prophets. Jeremiah warned Judah they would spend seventy years in captivity, and Jeremiah 25:11–12 states, "'And this whole land shall be a desolation and an astonishment, and these nations shall serve the king of Babylon seventy years. Then it will come to pass, when seventy years are completed, that I will punish the king of Babylon and that nation, the land of the Chaldeans, for their iniquity,' says the Lord."

Elijah was raptured and taken to heaven. The body of Moses was also taken to heaven.[6] Moses and Elijah returned to earth and had a prophecy update with Christ.[7] Elijah will come back as a prophet in the near future. "Behold, I will send you Elijah the prophet, before the coming of the great and dreadful day of the Lord" (Mal. 4:5). "Now when they finish their testimony, the beast that ascends out of the bottomless pit will make war against them, overcome them, and kill them. And their dead bodies will lie in the street of the great city which spiritually is called Sodom and Egypt, where also our Lord was crucified. Then those from the peoples, tribes, tongues, and nations will see their dead bodies three and a half days, and not allow their dead bodies to be put into graves. And those who dwell on the earth will rejoice over them, make merry, and send gifts to one another, because these two prophets tormented those who dwell on the earth. Now after the three and a half days the breath of life from God entered them, and they stood on their feet, and great fear fell on those who saw them" (Rev. 11:7–11). Apparently Moses and Elijah will be seen dead on Ted Turner's CNN. The reason people hate the two prophets so much is because they just completed a three-and-a-half year ministry, which unbelievers around the world resented. "And I will give power to my two witnesses, and they will prophesy one thousand two hundred and sixty days (three-and-a-half years—the first half of Daniel's seventy weeks)…And if anyone wants to harm them, fierce proceeds from their mouth and devours their enemies. And if anyone wants to harm them, he must be killed in this manner. These have power to shut heaven, so that no rain falls in the days of their prophecy; and they have power over waters to turn them to blood, and to strike the earth with all plagues, as often as they desire" (Rev. 11:3,5,6). The lack of rain in Europe may cause the Antichrist and the Vatican to move to Babylon and the Tigris and Euphrates rivers.

## Miracles at the Time of Daniel

The Babylonians came in 605 BC. During this invasion, Nebuchadne-zzar the Babylonian, took Daniel and various young Judean nobility to Babylon, as well as Jewish slaves. A third and brief outburst of miracles took place in Babylon in the days of Daniel and his friends. These miracles included being protected in a lion's den, standing in a furnace, and the appearance of the "Son of God" in the furnace (Dan. 3:25).

The Babylonian captivity lasted, as foretold, for seventy years, from 605 BC until 535 BC. There were several miracles during the early part of Daniel's public ministry. These stopped almost at once and were replaced by additions to the word of God by the writings of the exilic prophets, the final historical books, and the postexilic prophets. The final book of the Old Testament was written by Malachi between the years of approximately 432 and 425 BC. This is almost a century after Haggai and Zechariah began to prophesy in 520 BC.

Daniel was a young man of royal blood, of the tribe of Judah, who was deported to Babylon by Nebuchadnezzar. He lived in exile through the reigns of a half-dozen Babylonian kings and two Medo-Persian kings. He lived in Babylon throughout the entire period of the captivity. The prophecies of Daniel are in specific detail and some are time specific. For example, the specific day the Messiah would present Himself was given in Daniel 9.

The visions in Daniel 2 and 7 provide a history of the world and the four major coming Gentile kingdoms:

1. Babylon (612–529 BC): Represented by the head of gold and a lion having the wings of an eagle.
2. Medo-Persia (539–331 BC): Represented by the silver upper body and a bear.
3. Greece (331–63 BC): Represented by the belly and thighs made of bronze and a leopard with four wings and four heads.
4. Rome (63 BC–AD 476 and Tribulation): Represented by legs of iron, feet of clay and iron, and an unspecified beast with iron and bronze claws.

There is a gap of time in the statue of Daniel 2. The church age of approximately two-thousand years is inserted as a parent at the point where the feet are attached to the legs. This gap is shown in many other prophetic passages in the Old Testament. They could not see the mystery of the church, which was not revealed until the time of the Apostle Paul. We now can see there is a gap of over two-thousand years in the statue at the point of the feet, otherwise he would have very long feet. The feet of clay are a ten-nation confederacy, which is called the revival of the Roman Empire. This is described in Daniel 8:24.

## Daniel's Seventy Weeks

The seventy weeks (seventy units of seven or 490 years) prophesied in Daniel 9:24–27 are the framework within which the seven-year Tribulation (or the seventieth week) occurs. The prophecy of the seventy weeks was given to Daniel by God while Daniel was living under Babylonian captivity.[8] Daniel was concerned for his people who were nearing the end of their seventy-year captivity. In his vision he was reassured that God had not forgotten his chosen people. The angel Gabriel told Daniel that God would bring Israel back into its land and would one day set the millennial Messianic kingdom. What was unexpected for Daniel was the revelation that all of this would not be fulfilled at the end of the current seventy-year captivity in Babylon but after a future seventy-week period described in 9:24–27.

The fulfillment would take place in two different parts. In part one there would be sixty-nine weeks (483 years) from the decree to rebuild Jerusalem and the wall until the Messiah. We know in this context the idiomatic Hebrew term "week" means unit of seven years, because it was exactly 483 years until Jesus Christ presented Himself as the Jewish Messiah. However, because Israel rejected their Messiah, there is a gap between the sixty-nine weeks and the seventieth week. This gap has lasted over two-thousand years. Because Israel was dispersed and ineffective, God inserted a spiritual race, the church as the body of Christ, to act as the voice of God. When the fullness of the Gentiles is complete, the Holy Spirit will remove the church to heaven. At this time the gap will be closed and Israel will complete the seventieth week of Daniel.

"For I will be like a lion to Ephraim, and like a young lion to the house of Judah. I, even I, will tear them and go away; I will take them away, and no one shall rescue. I will return again to My place till they acknowledge their offense. Then they will seek My face; in their affliction they will diligently seek Me" (Hosea 5:14–15).

The prophet Ezekiel, like Daniel, was carried off to Babylon as a captive. He prophesied there for about twenty years. Also, like Daniel, he was aware from the prophecies of Jeremiah; that the captivity in Babylon would last seventy years. All three prophets were contemporaries of each other. Then the Lord appeared to Ezekiel in a vision and gave him this prophecy, "This shall be a sign to the house of Israel. Lie thou also upon thy left side, and lay the iniquity of the house of Israel upon it: according to the number of the days that thou shall lie upon it thou shalt bear their iniquity. For I have laid upon thee the years of their iniquity, according to the number of the days, three hundred and ninety day: so shalt thou bear the iniquity of the house of Israel. And when thou has accomplished them, lie again on thy right side, and thou shalt bear the iniquity of the house of Judah forty days: I have appointed thee each day for a year" (Ezekiel 4:3–6,38–39). In this prophecy we are given a sign and a clear interpretation that each day represents one biblical year. Ezekiel was told that Israel would be punished for 390 years and for forty years. As prophesied, at the end of the seventy years of captivity in Babylon, in the spring of 536 BC, in the month Nisan, under the decree of the Persian king Cyrus, a small remnant of the house of Judah returned to Jerusalem.

The vast majority were content to remain with the Persian Empire, a pagan government, as colonists. Once one deducts the seventy years of the Babylonian captivity from the total decreed punishment of 430 years for Israel's and Judah's sin (390 years plus forty years equals 430),; there is a total of 360 years of further punishment beyond 536. BC, the end of the Babylonian Captivity.

Israel did not repent of its sin at the end of the seventy years in Babylon. The larger part of the nation failed to repent of their sin and disobedience, which caused God to send them into captivity. The majority simply settled down as colonists in what is now Iraq-Iran.

Grant Jeffrey makes the following calculations in his book, *Armageddon* "'And if ye will not yet for all this hearken unto me, then I will punish you seven times more for your sins'" (Lev. 26:18, 21, 23–24, 27–28). 360 years x 7 = 2,520 biblical years (360 days). 907,200 days. Converting to 365.25 day years is 2,483.8 calendar years. 536 BC plus 2,483.8 years is May 14th, 1948, when Israel became a nation again."

What Jeffrey is saying is that Israel owed God a balance of 360 years of judgment for not following God's commands. Because they refused to repent, under Levitical law, God multiplied the punishment seventy times. This became a total of 2,520 years. Jewish prophetic years, consisting of 360 days, when converted to Gentile years equals 2,483.8 years. The completion of Israel's discipline come out to 1948, when the nation of Israel came into existence, after over two thousand years.

## Miracles at the Time of Jesus

By far, the most spectacular period of miracles was associated with Christ and his apostles. This was yet another transition period when God first offered the kingdom to Israel, withdrew the offer when the King was rejected, and began to prepare the way for the church. This period of miracles was ceased as suddenly as it began at about the time of the destruction of the Jewish temple and the dispersal of the Hebrew people. It was replaced by the written New Testament.

Miracles are only used by God to get attention; then they cease and are followed by long periods of time devoid of spectacular miracles because he would never have us rely on them. He would have us rely on his word. We are to take his word at the truth and be content with that.[9] When we put our trust in Christ through his word, we put our faith in the supernatural. The Bible is itself a supernatural book and much more reliable than voices and visions. The fact of the matter is that miracles can be counterfeited.

In Matthew 24:1, Jesus prophesied that the temple in Jerusalem would be destroyed and not one stone would be left standing. This is what happened in AD 70 and the Jews were dispersed throughout the world. But Jesus also said in Matthew 24:15 that the Antichrist would desecrate the temple as described in chapter 9 of Daniel. How can the people be dispersed and the temple destroyed and then the temple be desecrated? The answer is that the Jews are to be returned to the land as a nation again in the last days. This is what will happen in the seventieth week of Daniel after the Rapture of the church. "For then there will be great Tribulation such as has not been since the beginning of the world until this time, no, nor ever shall be. And unless, those days were shortened, no flesh would be saved; but for the elect's sake (Tribulation Saints) those days will be shortened … Immediately after the Tribulation of those days the sun will be darkened, and the moon will not give its light; the stars will fall from heaven, and the powers of the heavens will be shaken. Then the sing of the Son of Man will appear in heaven, and then all the tribes of the earth will mourn, and they will see the Son of Man coming on the clouds of heaven with power and great glory" (Matt. 24:21–22, 29, 30). At the end of the seven-year Tribulation, or the seventieth week of Daniel, Christ will come to the earth and establish his one thousand-year literal reign on earth.

## Miracles at the Time of the Great Tribulation

Following the Rapture of the church, two prophets of God, Moses and Elijah will perform miracles for three-and-a-half years during the first half of the Tribulation. Two of Satan's men will counter them with signs and lying wonders. Moses and Elijah will then be killed and removed from the earth. The Antichrist will receive a death blow and will come back to life as a false Messiah. Many people will be fooled. The Antichrist will rule the world for three-and-a-half years and then Christ will come again to take charge. "I saw one of his heads as if it had been mortally wounded, and his deadly wound was healed. And all the world marveled and followed the beast. So they worshiped the dragon (Satan), who gave authority to the beast (Antichrist) and they worshiped the beast, saying, 'Who is like the beast? Who is able to make war with him?'" (Rev. 12:3).

As a condition precedent to the return of the Lord the Diaspora (dispersion of Israel), the gathering of Israel must occur as prophesied. "Then they shall know that I am the Lord their God, who sent them into captivity among the nations, but also brought them back to their own land, and left none of them captive any longer" (Ezek. 39:28). "In that day the Lord will defend the inhabitants of Jerusalem; the one who is feeble among them in that day shall be like David, and the house of David shall be like God, like the Angel of the Lord before them. It shall be in that day that I will seek to destroy all the nations that come against Jerusalem. And I will pour on the house of David and on the inhabitants of Jerusalem the Spirit of grace and supplication; then they will look on Me whom they have pierced; they will mourn of Him as one mourns for his only son, and grieve for Him as one grieves for a firstborn" (Zech. 12:8–10).

## Replacement Theology

Replacement Theology teaches that the church is the replacement for Israel, and that the many promises made to Israel in the Bible are to be fulfilled in the Christian church, not in Israel. The Prophecies in scripture that concern the blessing and restoration of Israel to the Promised Land are spiritualized and allegorized. Scripture does not teach that the world will be Christianized. It teaches that the world is heading for destruction and that if Jesus does not come back in the flesh no flesh will be saved.[10] The Apostle Paul specifically says that God has not cast away his people.[11] Paul explains that the hardening of Israel will continue only until the fullness of the Gentiles is complete.[12]

"When you are in Tribulation, and all these things come upon you in the latter days, when you turn to the Lord your God and obey his voice (for the Lord your God is a merciful God), he will not forsake you nor destroy you, nor forget the covenant of your fathers which he swore to them" (Deuteronomy 4:30–31).

Emperor Constantine I called the first Council of Nicaea in AD 325. The emperor of Rome established himself as the head of the Christian church and the Babylonian religion. At this time it became unpopular to believe that a Jewish Messiah would some day come and replace a worldly empire such as Rome. As the persecution of Christians ended and unbelievers began to hold positions of authority in the new state-church, biblical principals began to become fuzzy and unclear. In time, Augustine of Hippo, the famous North African that converted to Christianity in AD 386, devised a system of eschatology that twisted the scriptures to mean what was acceptable to the worldly church of his day. Augustine, who had originally been orthodox, changed his position in later years and became what is now called amillennial, meaning to belief in no literal millennial reign of Christ. Christendom canonized Augustine's evil ideas by establishing him as an official saint. Theologians throughout the Roman Empire accepted his false doctrine. The Chiliasts (*chiliasm* is Greek for one-thousand) were branded as holding "aberrant and heretical views."[13] Augustinian Replacement Theology, along with other false theologies became the cornerstone of the Roman Catholic concepts. In the later developments in the Eastern Orthodox Church, the European Reformation and the Anglican split, and Replacement Theology continued essentially untouched. It was an important part of the standard

Christian view of Israel, the world, and prophecy. Though this view evolved, it had no basis in what the Apostles taught. On the contrary, instead of being biblical this view became anti-biblical. Cursing Israel, in reality, is cursing God's chosen people. Roman persecution, the Holocaust, the Russian persecutions, and the Spanish Inquisition used this type of theology in order to destroy the Jew. How can anyone claim a devotion to biblical Christianity and support this view but not recognize the slippery slope and the inevitable dangers?

## Why Do Some People Deny Prophecy?

Why did the majority of the Jewish people, who knew the teachings of their prophets, reject Jesus of Nazareth as their Messiah when he came? Why did they ignore the portraits of the suffering Messiah? Jesus Himself pointed out to them Old Testament predictions concerning his life and ministry which were being fulfilled during his lifetime.

First of all, the Jews did not take the prophecy regarding a suffering Messiah literally. They took the portrait of the Messiah who would come as the reigning King very literally. However, they had degenerated in their own religious convictions to the point where they did not believe they were sinful. They believed they were keeping the laws of Moses; therefore, they saw no need for a suffering Messiah to deliver them from their sins. Since they were not serious Bible students they did not distinguish between the first and second advents. They did not see a need for a savior.

## Signs of the Times

The religious leaders of his day were the number one skeptics. They came to Jesus and asked Him to show them a sign from heaven. They wanted some sensational miracle which would give them proof that Jesus was their promised Messiah. They wanted Him to

suddenly step out of the sky as the conquering Messiah (as he is rev-
eled in Zechariah 14) and take over all the kingdoms of the world
and defeat the Roman empire.

Jesus had already given them important signs to prove who he
was. He had healed many persons and had raised at least one from
the dead. They did not, however, consider this sufficient evidence
to prove his claim of being the Messiah. Jesus said, "You know how
to interpret the appearance of the sky, but you cannot interpret the
signs of the times" (Matt. 16:2–3).

Jesus said that the signs leading up to his coming were just as
clear as the face of the sky. Let us examine some of the prophetic
signs the Jewish religious leaders refused to see:

1.  The Messiah would be born of the seed of a woman (No human
    father) (Gen. 3:15).
2.  Descendant of Abraham. (Gen. 12:1–3)
3.  Tribe of Judah to the family of David. (I Chron. 17:11–15)
4.  Born in Bethlehem. (Mic. 5:2–5)
5.  Born of a virgin. (Isa. 7:14)
6.  Present himself as the Messiah on March 30, 33 AD (Dan.
    9:25)
7.  Die for the sins of the world. (Isa. 53:5)
8.  On the third day following his death he will rise again. (Matt.
    12:40)

Will we repeat history? Will we fail to take the prophets literally and seriously? Will we be indifferent? Will we allow those who
claim to be religious leaders to explain those things away and not
investigate for ourselves? For every one prophecy of the first advent
of Christ there are seven prophecies of the second coming. For those
who are serious students of the Bible we can see God has a different
purpose and plan for Israel. They will turn to God at the end of the
Tribulation when they are surrounded by the armies of the world

and have no one else to turn to. As for the church, we will be removed at the end of the church age through the Rapture. Everything
is laid out in the Bible to those who have ears and to those who take
the prophets seriously.

## The Dispersion of Israel

What has and is happening to Israel is significant to the entire prophetic picture. Men who have studied events that were to occur
shortly before the great holocaust known as Armageddon are amazed
as they see them happening before their eyes. Too few Bible scholars
pay any serious attention to the proven prophetic content of scripture. Some 3,500 years ago, at a time when the Jewish people were en
route from Egypt to possess the Promised Land of Palestine, Moses
predicted that they would be chastened and disciplined as a nation
for not believing their God and rejecting his ways. Prophets such as
Isaiah, Jeremiah, Ezekiel, and Amos predicted the great world-wide
exile of the Jewish people and the destruction of the Jewish nation.
Just before his arrest and crucifixion Jesus warned that Jerusalem
would fall.

Because of Israel's failure to follow God's laws and because of
their rejection of the promised Messiah, God dispersed his chosen people to the uttermost parts of the world. "And the Lord will
scatter you among the peoples, and you will be left few in number
among the nations where the Lord will drive you" (Deut. 4:27).
"The whole land will be a burning waste of salt and sulfur, nothing
planted, nothing sprouting, no vegetation growing on it. It will be
like the destruction of Sodom and Gomorrah, Admah and Zeboim,
which the Lord overthrew in fierce anger" ( Deut. 29:23). The land
of Israel became a sparsely populated wasteland, as recently as the
late 1800s. In 1867, American writer Mark Twain wrote the following about Israel in his work *Innocents Abroad:*: "Palestine sits in
sackcloth and ashes...the spell of a curse that has withered its fields

and fettered its energies…Palestine is desolate and unlovely…It is a hopeless, dreary, heartbroken land" (126).

"The Lord will drive you and the king you set over you to a nation unknown to you or your father. There you will worship other gods, god of wood and stone. You will become a thing of horror and an object of scorn and ridicule to all the nations where the Lord will drive you" (Deut. 28:36–37). The people of Israel, known today as Jews, have been expelled from their homeland by the Assyrians, Babylonians, and Romans. The Jews, perhaps more than any other group of people, have been subject to hatred, scorn and persecution throughout the world. From the Hasmonaean Period, more than two-thousand years ago, until 1948, the Jews did not have sovereign control over any part of their homeland. Nor had Israel been a united and sovereign country for nearly 2,900 years, until 1948.

Leviticus 26:31–32 states, "I will turn your cities into ruins and lay waste your sanctuaries, and I will take no delight in the pleasing aroma of your offerings. I will lay waste the land, so that your enemies who live there will be appalled." This prophecy has been clearly documented throughout history. Each time the people of Israel were forced out of their homeland and other cultures moved in and took advantage. Upon their prophesized return to their homeland during the nineteenth and twentieth centuries, the Jews had ongoing skirmishes with the Arab people living there. These Arabs continue to live in parts of the land of Israel to this day.

"I tell you the truth, not one stone here will be left on another; every one will be thrown down" (Matt. 24:1–2). Approximately forty years after Jesus was crucified by the Romans, the Temple was destroyed. In the year AD 70, the Romans destroyed Jerusalem. A fire was accidentally set in the temple, fire caused the gold-leafed ornamentation on the Temple ceiling and ceremonial items to melt. The melting gold flowed down the walls and settled into crevices within the building stones. In fulfillment of the prophecy of Jesus, not one stone was left standing on another as the temple building stones were separated to recover the gold.

Luke 21:24 says, "They will fall by the sword and will be taken as prisoners to all the nations, Jerusalem will be trampled on by the Gentiles until the times of the Gentiles are fulfilled." Jesus said that the Jews soon would be forced out of Jerusalem and that the city would be destroyed. He said Jerusalem would be trampled upon by the Gentiles, and that the Jews would be scattered to all nations. All of this took place when the Romans destroyed Jerusalem and the temple in the year AD 70, and again in the year 135. During the two destructions, the Romans killed an estimated 1.5 million Jews. Hundreds of thousands of Jews were taken as slaves to other countries, mostly throughout Europe and parts of Asia.

The worldwide scattering of Jews began when the Romans exiled them from Jerusalem and the surrounding area between 70 and 135. However, intense persecutions during the past nineteen centuries drove many to move as far south as South Africa, as far east as China, and as far west as Chile and California. During the past two centuries, many Jews across the world returned to their ancient homeland and re-established sovereignty for Israel.

## The Prophecy of the Regathering of Israel

The same prophets who predicted the worldwide exile and persecution of the Jews also predicted their restoration as a nation. It is surprising that so many people could not see that since the first part of these prophecies came true, it should follow that the second part would come true. Not only would God disperse Israel, he would regather them. It appears that only a few of the serious Bible scholars anticipated the prophesied events of the re-establishment of Israel in the promised land. Throughout history there has been a group of men who diligently studied the prophetic content of the Bible and took it both seriously and literally. Many commentaries dating back to AD 1611 clearly understood that the Jews would return to Palestine and re-establish their nation before the Messiah would come. These men held this position in spite of the mocking and ridicule from the majority of Christendom.

Contrary to popular opinion, the doctrine of the Rapture of the church was not invented by John Neson Darby in the Nineteenth Century. Men such as Increase Mather (1639–1723), John Asgill, (1659–1738), Morgan Edwards (1722–1795), John Darby (1800–1882), John Cumming (1807–1881), James Grant 1790–1853), all believed in a Pre-Tribulation Rapture and that Israel would be re-gathered prior to the return of Christ. In more recent times, Eugene Blackstone, Cyrus Scofield, John Walvoord and H. A. Ironside all predicted that Israel would once again be a nation prior to the return of Christ. Despite the fulfillment of prophecy, as predicted by these men, many of them are ridiculed for their belief in God's word and their literal interpretation of prophecy. Despite the overcoming of all obstacles and the miraculous return of Israel, the majority of professing Christendom refuses to acknowledge that Abraham's covenants are unconditional, that God has a future for Israel, and that we are in the last days. It appears nothing changes, man continues to refuse to listen to God's prophets, even though they speak for God and tell history from beginning to end.

"The Lord your God will bring you back from captivity, and have compassion on you, and gather you again from all the nations where the Lord your God has scattered you" (Deut. 30:3). "Thus says the Lord God: 'When I have gathered the house of Israel from the peoples among whom they are scattered, and am hallowed in them in the sight of the Gentiles, then they will dwell in their own land which I gave to My servant Jacob" ( Ezek. 28:25). "After many days you will be visited. In the latter years you will come into the land of those brought back from the sword and gathered from many people on the mountains of Israel, which had long been desolate; they were brought out of the nations, and now all of them dwell safely." (Ezek. 38:8). "It shall come to pass in that day (Millennium) that the Lord shall set his hand again the second time to recover the remnant of his people who are left…" (Isa. 11:11).

During the Babylonian captivity the Jews were not dispersed throughout the world. After that captivity some even returned and rebuilt the temple. After the Roman captivity, however, the Jews were scattered throughout the world as prophesied. In 1948, after over two-thousand years of dispersion they re-established their nation and the Hebrew language. The Jewish survival is a phenomenon, unparalleled in history. However, Jewish history, with all of its tragedies and triumphs, has been accurately foretold by God's prophets. What is amazing is not that God foretold history in advance, but that he is not limited to time and space. This is simple for God. What is interesting is that people, throughout history, fail to listen to God even though he makes no mistakes and they have not vague or indefinite in their predictions.

Noah was ignored, and the people perished in the flood. Isaiah was ignored and even sawed in half. Jeremiah was ignored and thrown in a pit. The land of Israel was overrun by the Assyrians and the Babylonians. Christ was ignored and hung on a cross. Israel was destroyed by the Romans. Prophecy scholars are ignored today. The world is about to be judged. To anyone but the Biblically illiterate, we are in the last days. The Day of the Lord is at the door! Will history repeat itself?

## Will a Temple Be Rebuilt?

The first temple was built by King David's son Solomon. The glory of God filled the Holy of Holies. Because of the sin of Israel the Shekinah departed from the temple.[14] This temple was destroyed in 568 BC, when Judah went into captivity. After the Babylonian captivity, a second temple was built by Zerubbabel in 515 BC This temple was completely reconstructed from its foundations upward by Herod the Great in 20 BC This was not a Third Temple because sacrificial offerings continued during the remodeling. As Christ predicted, this temple was destroyed in AD 70. There was not one stone left in place.

A temple will be built during the seven-year Tribulation as prophesied in the Olivet Discourse Matthew 24 and Daniel's seventieth week in chapter 9 of Daniel.

Too much credit is given to the Antichrist for enabling the temple to be built. God sends Moses and Elijah at the time of the end to protect Israel and the temple during the first three-and-a-half years of Daniel's seventieth week . No one is going to touch the temple as long as they are alive. Once they are killed, the Antichrist has the power to break his seven-year treaty and desecrate the holy of holies for three-and-a-half years. A fourth temple will be built by God during the Millennial reign of Christ.[15] The millennial temple will have memorial sacrificial offerings in remembrance of the death of Jesus Christ and to atone for the sins of Jewish believers living during the millennial kingdom. However, in the eternal state, when all believers will have a glorified body and God the Father and Son dwell in Zion, there will no longer be a need for a temple.

The fact that Orthodox Jews in Israel today have the plans and the capability to reconstruct a temple is another sign of the endtimes. As soon as the Rapture occurs, the Antichrist will broker a seven-year peace treaty, Moses and Elijah will appear, and the temple will be constructed. The construction of the this temple is one of the reasons Iran, Libya and the Sudan are motivated to join Russia and Germany to invade Israel. For Israel to build a temple on the temple mount will be an affront to the Muslim nation. This invasion described in Ezekiel 38 and 39 will cause the decimation of the United States, Russia, and Israeli armies, and will cause a vacuum for the rise in power and the ultimate worldwide domination of the Revived Roman Empire and the Beast.

# CHAPTER 3

# PEACE IN THE MIDDLE EAST

## Has God Rejected Israel?

The scriptures clearly declare that God has promised a full and final restoration of Israel, both in relation to her land and in relation to God Himself. Of that final restoration, the Apostle Paul, a minister to the Gentiles, declares:

> Has God cast away his people? Certainly not! For I also am an Israelite, of the seed of Abraham, of the tribe of Benjamin. God has not cast away his people whom he foreknew. Or do you not know what the Scripture says of Elijah, how he pleads with God against Israel, saying, "Lord, they have killed Your prophets and torn down Your altars, and I alone am left, and they seek my life"? But what does the divine response say to him? I have reserved for Myself seven thousand men who have not bowed the knee to Baal. Even so then, at this present time there is a remnant according to the election of grace. For if you were cut out of the olive tree which is wild by nature, and were grafted contrary to nature into a good olive tree, how much more will these, who are the natural branches, be grafted into their own olive tree. For I do not desire, brethren, that you should be ignorant

of this mystery, lest you should be wise in your own opinion, that hardening in part has happened to Israel until the fullness of the Gentiles has come in. And so all Israel will be saved, as it is written: "The Deliverer will come out of Zion, and he will turn away ungodliness from Jacob; For this is My covenant with them, When I take away their sins" (Rom. 11:1–5, 24–27).

Jeremiah 31:35–36 declares, "Thus says the Lord, Who gives the sun for a light by day, and the ordinances of the moon and the stars fro a light by night, who disturbs the sea, and its waves roar (The Lord of Hosts is his name); If those ordinances depart from before Me, says the Lord, then the seed of Israel shall also cease from being a nation before Me forever."

In Revelation 21:23, the Bible says, "And the city had no need of the sun, neither of the moon, to shine in it: for the glory of God did lighten it, and the lamb is the light thereof" In his book *The Revelation Record*, Henry Morris makes the following comments:

> Since "God is light" and "in Him is no darkness at all" (I John 1:5) and since Christ Himself is "the light of the world" (John 9:5), it would be unfitting for the city (New Jerusalem) ever to be darkened or for night to fall there.

Neither the sun nor the moon will ever really be destroyed, of course, since God has promised that they, as well as the starry heavens, will endure forever...It is just that their light is no longer needed to illumine the holy city, for the city itself radiates light to all the surrounding regions. However, the sun and moon will continue to serve their present functions with respect to the nether regions of the earth, serving there as lights by day and night, respectively (456).

Praise the Lord!
Praise the Lord from the heavens;
Praise Him in the heights!
Praise Him, all his angels;
Praise Him, all his hosts!
Praise Him, sun and moon:
Praise Him, all you stars of light!
Praise Him, you heavens of heavens,
And you waters above the heavens!
Let them praise the name of the Lord, for he commanded
and they were created.
He has also established them forever and ever.
(Ps. 148:1–6)

And there shall be a time of trouble. Such as never was since
there was a nation, even to that time. And at that time your
people shall be delivered. Every one who is found written in
the book. And many of those who sleep in the dust of the
earth shall awake, some to everlasting life, some to shame
and everlasting contempt. Those who are wise shall shine
like the brightness of the firmament, and those who turn
many to righteousness like the stars forever and ever. But
you, Daniel, shut up the words, and seal the book until the
time of the end; many shall run to and fro, and knowledge
shall increase. Many shall be purified, made white, and refined, but the wicked shall do wickedly; and none of the
wicked shall understand, but the wise shall understand.
(Dan. 12:1–4, 10)

The scriptures clearly state that Abraham's seed will live forever. If
you could destroy the sun, moon, and stars you could destroy Israel,
but you cannot. They will all live forever. God goes on to say that in

the last days Israel will come under severe persecution, but they will be rescued. The wicked will not understand this, but in the last days the book of Daniel will be opened and the wise will understand.

For Satan to be defeated, it is not enough for individual Jews to survive. Israel must exist as a nation in her own land. If Satan can destroy Israel, he believes he can stop the return of the Messiah for the rescuing of God's chosen people. The essence of his plan is to make a preemptive attack on Jews and thereby prevent his own doom. Satan is the most intelligent creature ever made. He knows he must destroy Israel, and he has tried to do that many times. In the middle of the Tribulation, when's Satan's access to heaven is denied, he realizes time is of the essence and he will attack Israel with a vengeance. "Now when the dragon saw that he had been cast to the earth, he persecuted the woman (Israel) who gave birth to the male Child. But the woman was given two wings of a great eagle, that she might fly into the wilderness to her place, where she is nourished for a time and times and half a time (three-and-a-half years), from the presence of the serpent. And the dragon was enraged with the woman, and he went to make war with the rest of her offspring, who keep the commandments of God and have the testimony of Jesus Christ" (Rev. 12:13–14,17). Satan has a huge intelligence, but he has no wisdom. He will follow God's script to the letter, not knowing that his fight is doomed.

Some believe that you should not spit into the wind, tug on superman's cape, or mess with a mother bear's cubs. These are a good idea for most people. But they do not apply to God. In the coming future, God will put the superman ruler the Antichrist and the false prophet in the lake of fire. Satan will be chained in darkness by a single un-named angel. In the millennial reign of Christ, bears, lions, and tigers will eat grass. It is important for a wise man to understand that he should not be contrary to God or his chosen people. Do not call Him a liar. Do not say that God's arms are too short to accomplish his plans. He has, he is, and he will do exactly what he determines to do.

## Christendom's Opposition to Israel

We can certainly understand opposition to Israel from Satan, the Antichrist, the False Prophet and the Muslims. What is harder to understand, however, is opposition from within the Christian church. Many reputable leaders within the Christian church seem to have no fear of the God of the Bible. They are not afraid to flaunt their denial of God's covenants to Israel in the face of the Creator of the universe, who calls himself "the God of Israel" over 200 hundred times and has declared that they are his people by an everlasting covenant.

Despite repeated promises and oaths made by God, most Calvinists and many of those who call themselves "reformed" insist that Israel has been replaced by the church. For example, in 2002, the faculty of Calvinistic Know Seminary in Fort Lauderdale, Florida (Founded by James Kennedy) issued an "Open Letter to Evangelicals and Other Interested Parties." This was signed by seventy-one prominent evangelical leaders, including R. C. Sproul and Michael Horton. Their statement denied that the physical descendants of Abraham, Isaac, and Jacob have any special blessing or place in prophecy, much less any claim upon the land of Israel. Their document declares "The inheritance promises that God gave to Abraham...do not apply to any particular ethnic group, but to the church of Jesus Christ, the true Israel...The entitlement of any one ethnic or religious group to territory in the Middle East called the "Holy Land" cannot be supported by Scripture." This common view, known as Replacement Theology, is supported by such men as Rick Warren, Bill Hybels, Ken Gentry, Gary DeMar and Hank Hanegraaff.

## What Does God Think About Replacement Theology?

"God is not a man, that he should lie, nor the son of man, that he should repent. Has he said, and will he not do it? Or has he spoken,

and will he not make it good" (Num. 23:19). "For You have magnified Your word above all Your name" (Ps. 138:2). "For the Lord's
portion is his people; Jacob is the place of his inheritance. He found
him in a desert land and in the wasteland, a howling wilderness; he
encircled him, he instructed him, he kept him as the apple of his
eye" (Deut. 32:9–10). "For when God made a promise to Abraham,
because he could swear by no one greater, he swore by Himself, saying, "surely blessing I will bless you and multiplying I will multiply
you." And so, after he had patiently endured, he obtained the promise. For men indeed swear by the greater, and oath for confirmation
is for them an end of all dispute. Thus God, determining to show
more abundantly to the heirs of promise the immutability of his
counsel, confirmed it by an oath, that by two immutable things, in
which it is impossible For God to lie, we might have strong consola-
tion, who have fled for refuge to lay hold of the hope set before us"
(Heb. 6:13–18). "The Gentile shall know that the house of Israel
went into captivity for their iniquity; because they were unfaithful to
Me, therefore I hid My face from them. I gave them into the hand of
their enemies, and they all feel by the sword...Now I will bring back
the captives of Jacob, and have mercy on the whole house of Israel;
and I will be jealous for My holy name" (Ezek. 39:23–25). "And
he did not do many might works there because of their unbelief"
(Matt. 13:58).

God is not a man that he should lie. He magnifies his word
higher than his reputation. His reputation is important to Him, but
most of all his integrity, veracity, and righteousness requires that he
upholds his word and he cannot lie. He not only promised Abraham, but he also gave an unconditional covenant to Abraham, Isaac,
and Jacob that they would inherit the promised land. As prophesied, Israel was dispersed as punishment for their sins. However, as
God gave his word they were given part of their land back in 1948.
his arms are not too short that he cannot save Israel and give them
all that he has promised. Those who do not believe that God will

honor his covenant to Abraham rob God of his power and glory. Their lives will lack the blessings they could have had except for their unbelief. God will bless those who bless Israel and curse those who curse Israel. If you deny the word of God's prophets and you deny the covenants of Israel, you deny much of God's word. Some people do not understand why prophecy enthusiasts talk so much about Israel. They get tired of hearing about Israel. However, it is important to understand that 75 percent of the Bible is about Israel. The covenants were given to the church. If God is not going to be faithful to Israel, what assurances do we as Christians have that he will be faithful to the church? We are only grafted into the olive tree as wild limbs.

In Joel 3:1– 2, God declares, "For behold, in those days and at that time, when I bring back the captives of Judah and Jerusalem, I will also gather all nations, and bring them down to the Valley of Jehoshaphat; and I will enter into judgment with them there on account of My people, My heritage Israel, whom they have scattered among the nations; they have also divided up My land." Very soon, God is going to gather all nations to the battle of Armageddon and discipline the wicked for dividing up the land of Israel. President Bush claims to be a Christian, yet he continually attempts to divide up the land that God gave to Israel. President Bush listens to Reformed theologians who believe that Israel is no longer the apple of God's eye.

Many of the United States advisers put pressure on Israel to be a good neighbor and to give away large portions of its land to Muslims for the sake of peace. Time after time America has sold out Israel to the Arabs because we obtain 60 percent of our oil from the Middle East and we are afraid to make enemies with the Arabs. Unfortunately, it is too late. The handwriting is on the wall. As soon as the church is removed through the Rapture, Russia, Iran, Germany, Turkey, Sudan and Libya will attack Israel, and God will personally get involved.

## Will the Jews and the Arabs Find Peace?

Unfortunately, the mistake continues to be made of calling true Muslims "extremists." Was Muhammad an extremist? How can the founder of Islam be an extremist? Muhammad plundered, murdered, and raped in the name of Allah to the glory of Islam. When Muslim leaders say that Islam is "a religion of peace," they do not define what this means for non-Muslims in their religion. To Muslims, peace equates to the entire world coming under the protection of Islam. To accomplish this requires a jihad that will extend the territory of Islam over non-Islamic lands. To Muslims, peace equates to submission, surrender, or subjugation of the infidels. In his book *Why I Left Jihad*, Walid Shoebat, an ex-Muslim terrorist, states, "In Islam, conceding to peace means that the Islamic Umma, nation, is weak. So as soon as Islam becomes the dominating force, it switches into war gear. Of course, there are Muslims who reject many of the classical sources and truly focus on the peaceful verses of the Qur'an, seeking to re-interpret the verses because they truly do not want to engage in violence. These 'liberal' Muslims seem to 're-write' Islam rather then correctly interpret it. They are peaceful despite Islam, not because of it" (36). This peace can be brought about through intrigue, commerce, threats, terrorism, warfare, lying, or whatever it takes. Once a country or land falls under Islam control, it becomes their property. Once Israel fell under control of Muslims, it became the property of those Muslims. To Muslims, Jews in Israel are foreign invaders of Muslim territory. Muslims are filled with hate and believe the Jews are stealing land from the Palestinians and mistreating the Palestinians who lived under Arafat's control until his death. The truth is that the Israelis face an enemy with whom they cannot negotiate, because the enemy's primary goal is not the land. The enemy wants all Jews dead and Israel eliminated from the face of the earth.

In truth, much of the land called Israel was purchased from Arabs by Jews. They started purchasing it in the nineteenth century when it was worthless swamp and desert land. The balance of Israel was government owned land and given to them under the British mandate or retained after the Arab attacks. The condition of the Palestinian Arabs has nothing to do with Israel. These Arabs voluntarily left Israel and have been refused sanctuary by Egypt and Jordan. They have been given hundreds of millions of dollars from America and many other governments, but Yasser Arafat stole their money and deposited in Switzerland or spent it on terrorist attacks on Israel. In *A Cup of Trembling*, Dave Hunt states, "Under Arafat the PLO. became the world's best known, best-armed, wealthiest guerrilla organization. Upward of $1 billion a year...swelled its treasury during the peak oil-rich years. President Reagan characterized the entire organization as a "gang of thugs" (200). It is a myth that the Palestinians are the underdogs in a conflict with Israel. The PLO Palestinians are a terrorist front group for Muslim countries which finance their guerrilla warfare against Israel and Western Culture. The ultimate goal is not more land and a Palestinian State, the true goal is the making of a worldwide Muslim culture. People who believe there can be peace in the Middle East if only the two parties can get together are uninformed. The Jews want peace and the Islamists want only the death of the Jews. The only way a lion and lamb are going to play together is when the Jewish Messiah comes and reigns.

The world condemns Israel for taking over the "Palestinian nation." However, there is not and never was a nation called Palestine. Prior to 1967, Arabs in the West Bank were Jordanians and they lived under Jordanian rule. They acknowledged King Hussein as the country's leader. When the Jews captured Jerusalem, they were suddenly Palestinians. The Arab leaders removed the star from the Jordanian flag and instantly made a Palestinian flag.

The same is true of Gaza, which was part of Egypt and whose people accepted Nasser and then Anwar Sadat as their leader—until the Jews formed the state of Israel. After the nation Israel was formed, magically, the people were no longer Egyptians, but Palestinians!

The "Palestinian nation" is a fiction of the Islamists. The local Arabs never wanted a Palestinian state. Yet Arafat made it his battle cry and it became a successful political strategy. However, this is not a political war, it is a religious holy war. The issue is, who is God? Is it Allah or the God of the Judeo/Christians?

According to Islamic law, once a place has been conquered by Allah through Islam, it must remain Allah's property in perpetuity. Otherwise, the command of Allah to conquer the world would be negated and the Muslin religion would be repudiated as inferior. Therefore, regardless of the city's spiritual significance, it has now become Islamic property that cannot be relinquished to the infidel or inferior religions without the honor of Allah being affected.

This was the concern of Muslims in 1967 when Israeli forces retook East Jerusalem and the Temple Mount. The Qur'an depicts the Jews (and Christians) as inferiors, so for the Jews to control life in the city and govern Muslim access to their mosque on the Temple Mount is an affront to Islam. For this reason, Yasser Arafat said, "I will continue to liberate all Islamic and Muslim holy places."

The Qur'an teaches that Muslims are not permitted to make peace with non-Muslims or with a non-Muslim country until its inhabitants surrender to Islam. They can agree to a ceasefire or a truce for a limited period of time, but never to an unconditional peace. Muslims can lie to their enemies in the midst of a jihad and declare a peace, yet they have no intention of keeping a peace treaty. In *Behind the Veil, Volume II*, Joseph Abd El Shafi states, "They were to offer the besieged nations three options: convert to Islam, surrender and pay the poll tax, or prepare for the holy war (Jihad), as stated in Surah 9:29 of the Qur'an" (20).

In *Why I Left Jihad*, Shoebat states, "What the West does not understand about Islamism is that jihad has states. If Muslims have the upper hand, then jihad is waged by force. If Muslims do not have the upper hand, then jihad is waged through financial and political means. Since Muslims do not have the upper hand in America or Europe, they talk about peace in front of you while supporting Hamas and Hezbollah in the back room. The whole idea of Islam being a peaceful religion emanates from that silent stage of jihad" (35–36).

The Arab refugees claim the land of Israel as their own under the assertion that they are descended from the original Palestinians who lived in there before the Israelites invaded and conquered it. The Jews, they insist, are unlawfully occupying their hereditary land and must leave. One repeatedly hears the complaint that the obstacle to peace is Israeli occupation" of the West Bank and the Gaza Strip. If that is the case, why was the Palestine Liberation Organization created in 1964, when Israel had nothing to do with those territories, which were then completely under Arab control? The Palestinian refugees are mere pawns of the Arabs who seek to destroy Israel.

## How Old is the Middle East Conflict?

The media has led many people to believe the Middle East conflict began with Israel's invasion and occupation of Palestinian land. However, the conflict in the Middle East has persisted for thousand of years and has involved many nations. The Land of Israel, originally called the Land of Canaan, is a land bridge situated in the middle of the fertile crescent between the continents of Europe, Asia, and Africa to the west, the land of Mesopotamia and the Orient to the east. Israel has been invaded over thirty times from ancient to modern times. In AD 70, the Roman army destroyed the city of Jerusalem, and in subsequent years Jews were banned from entering the city.

The events that led up to the establishment of the Jewish state began with a Jewish immigration prompted by the Zionist movement in 1897 to what was then known as Palestine. While the waves of persecution and expulsion that came upon European Jews led them to move to Palestine to live alongside Arabs (then under Turkish rule), a resident Jewish population always existed in the land throughout the past nineteen centuries. The resident Jews have long endured oppressive conditions, just as Jewish communities today still exist in Arab Muslim countries hostile to them.

By 1920, a growing Arab nationalism originating from Turkish rule was destined for a conflict with the growing Jewish population and its nationalistic Zionist ambitions. The reawakening of Arab nationalism seeking to throw off Turkish rule and the growing Jewish efforts of reestablishing Israel were destined to fight each other as two opposing religions.

On May 14, 1946, the British gave the eastern four-fifths of the Land (known then as Transjodan) to the Arabs and the Hashemite Bedouin tribe. This created the Hashemite Kingdom of Jordan. Thus, the new state of Israel was left to occupy only 23 percent of Palestine while the Arabs received the remaining, greatest portion of the land. The League of Nations had originally intended this territory to be for the resettlement of Palestinian Arabs, not the development of an independent Arab state of Jordan.

After a brief war, the United Nations stepped in and established a temporary peace partitioning Palestine into two separate Jewish and Arab states. At this time the term "Palestinian," the Anglicized form of the Latin name of Israel's ancient enemies, the Philistines, was applied equally to both the Jewish and Arab populations. Failing to overrun the infant Israel, the attacking Arabs occupied what land they could. In 1950, Jordan annexed the biblical territories of Judea and Samaria to the west of the Jordan River (the original dividing line between Israel and Jordan) and created the modern term for their area, "the West Bank." Egypt took the Gaza Strip on the coastal plain north of their country. The 1948 Israeli victory displaced Palestinian Arabs who voluntarily left the Israel controlled land. Any of the Arab countries surrounding Israel could have easily absorbed the Palestinian Arabs, but all (but Jordan) refused. They did not want the economic and social burden of caring for an indigent people, but they also wanted to create a problem for Israel. Most of the displaced Palestinian Arabs took up residence in the Palestinian nation of Jordan in the Jordanian-occupied area of the West Bank while others chose to remain in Israeli-controlled land. In *Jerusalem in Prophecy*, Randall Price states, "Until the Arab-Palestinian refugee situation was created in 1948, the term Palestinian applied to both Arabs and Jews living in the Land of Israel, then called Palestine. The 'Jerusalem Post' was called the 'Palestine Post.' The Israeli Philharmonic Orchestra was called the Palestine Philharmonic Orchestra" (240) In 1967, Israel captured the West Bank. Arafat's PLO claimed the liberation of the West Bank as its purpose. However, the PLO was started before the 1967 war. Arafat was a proxy for oil money from Arab countries given for the purpose of Guerrilla warfare and the ultimate extermination of Israel as a country. In *A Cup of Trembling*, Hunt states, "The PLO's vow expressed in its charter-to exterminate the entire nation of Israel-has never been renounced and can never be so long as Islam continues to teach "that Holy Land" was given by God not to the Jews but to the Arabs" (68).

## Who Where the Philistines?

The term *Palestine* derives from the word *Philistine*. The name was given to the non-Semitic ethnic group, originating from Southern Greece, closely related to the early Nycenaean civilization. They inhabited a smaller area on the southern coast called Philistia, the border of which approximated the border of the modern Gaza Strip. When Chaldean troops commanded by the Babylonian empire carried off significant numbers of the population into slavery, the distinctly Philistine character of the coastal cities ceased to exist, and the history of the Philistine people effectively ended. During the time of Abraham, and later Joshua, the promised land was called Canaan. The people who lived there were called Canaanites, which included Hittites, Jebusites, Amorites and other related clans. Five city-states in south Canaan formed an alliance and were defeated by Joshua's army and the Lord's "stones from heaven." ,However, more died from hail than from the swords of Israel.

Greek and Roman writers used the terms *Palestine* and *Palestinian* to refer to the land of Israel and its Jewish inhabitants. Herodotus and Aristotle both used these terms in this way. The Arabs originated as nomadic tribes in the modern Arabian Peninsula and emerged in Palestine only after the Islamic invasion of the Land in the seventh century AD However, most of the Muslim rulers during the 1,174 years of Islamic dominance were not Arab. The Seljuk's, whose rule lasted from AD 1071–1099, were Turkish mercenaries.

The Muslim commander Saladin, whose defeat of the Crusaders began the Ayyubid period (AD 1187–1260), was Kurd. The Mamluks (AD 1260–1516) were descendants of Turkish and Caucasian slave soldiers from the Caucasus. Suleiman the Magnificent, whose capture of Jerusalem began the Ottoman period, last period of Islamic rule (AD 1516–1917), and who rebuilt the walls of the Old City to their modern appearance, was a Turk. While it is true that the Jews did not establish their independence until the twentieth century, that is also true of the Arab Nations: Saudi Arabia (1913), Lebanon (1920), Iraq (1932), Syria (1941), Jordan (1946), and Kuwait (1961). None of these nations, can make a historical claim to certain borders on the basis of antiquity.

## What Is Islam?

Islam is the world religion founded by an Arabian visionary named Muhammad who lived from AD 570 to 632. Muhammad claimed he received supernatural revelations from God through the angel Gabriel. Because Muhammad was illiterate, these revelations were written down by others and compiled into a book called the Qur'an. Muhammad was not sure if he was talking to an evil spirit. However, his wife convinced him it was an angel. She exposed her breasts and the being left. She decided that because the Jinn was shy, that proved he was good. In *Behind the Veil, Volume II*, El Shafi states, "Muhammad was afraid that the one who used to appear to him in the cave was one of the Jinn…But his wife assured him that he was not one of those that the harm of Satan could afflict him. It is the opinion of Ibn Hisham, in his famous book, *Fiqh Al-Sira*, that the being was an angel because he felt embarrassed by Khadija's actions. Had he been a devil he would not have been embarrassed" (22) During Muhammad's life he had twenty-two wives and concubines, which included his son's wife and also a nine-year-old girl. El Shafi goes on to say, "In their interpretation of Surah 4:54, Muslim commentators stress that the permission given to Muhammad to marry a large number of woman was a special privilege and a gift from God for his prophet. Verse 4:54 of the Qur'an states, 'Or they envy people for what Allah bestowed on them from His goodness'" (36).

Islam is not a religion such as Christianity, Judaism, or Buddhism, in that it is not merely a spiritual belief. It is a complete way of life, having its own unique ruling, social, economic, and judicial systems and foreign policy. To claim that the religion of the terrorists is not that of Islam is not correct. Throughout the history of Islam, the religion has been spread by conquest from the fertile crescent to Western Europe, killing or enslaving those who refused to convert to Islam. No one ever imagined calling Islam a religion of peace until that lie was invented as part of the political correctness of our day. Appropriately, there is a sword on Saudi Arabia's flag. Muslims are required to raise the banner of jihad in order to make the word of Allah supreme in this world. The imams boldly preach jihad in the mosques, while the followers of Islam are determined to conquer under cover of the popular lie that Islam is a peaceful as any other religion.

Most of today's Muslims have forgotten, if they ever knew, that their ancestors were unwillingly forced into Islam under the threat of death. This is Islam as it was at the beginning, always has been whenever possible, and still is. In AD 732, in perhaps the most important battle in European history, Charles Martel defeated an invading Muslim army of several hundred thousand jihad warriors at Tours, France. He killed their commander, Abd el-Rahman. That was nearly thirteen hundred years ago. Now through a more passive invasion Islam has become the second largest religion in France, with about 6 million Muslims and fifteen hundred mosques. Worldwide, there are 1.3 billion followers of Islam. Muslims are divided into 90% Sunnis and 10% Shiites.

The word *Allah* is derived from the Arabic words *al*, which means "the," and *ilah*, which means "god," to indicate a particular deity—"the god" or "the idol." It is believed that Allah was used in Muhammad's time as the personal name for a vague high god who was one of the astral deities associated with the moon. Early on, Muhammad worshiped the three Meccan goddesses Al-Lat, Al-Manat, and Al-Uzza as deities because he believed them to be daughters of Allah. Muhammad, however, later renounced this worship, declaring his thinking had been corrupted by Satan. The belief that this teaching had been part of an earlier version of the Qur'an was the basis of Salman Rushdie's 1989 novel *Satanic Verses*. Its publication led the late Iranian Muslim cleric Ayatollah Khomeni to offer a $3 million bounty for the assassination of the book's author and publisher. The Khomeni was incensed that Rushdie mentioned a period in Muhammad's early life in which he purportedly accepted more than one God. This, Khomeni believed, was blasphemy.

Beginning in AD 610, Muhammad claimed to have received angelic revelations that Allah was the supreme god and had a message of warning. From its inception, Islam stated that its duty is to destroy infidels (non-Muslims) and subjugate the tolerated minorities, mainly Jews and Christians, under Islamic rule. The Arabic word *jihad* literally means "struggling" or "striving" and generally indicates holy efforts in the cause of Allah, especially the spreading of the faith of Islam, whether by missionary or military means.

The explosion of technology and the material prosperity of the West has kept Islam at bay for the last hundred years. However, with the growing demand for oil, and the resultant cash flow to Muslim countries, Islam has made a resurgence. In the sixteenth century, gold, spice, and land inspired Europe to colonize new frontiers. In the twenty-first century, black gold, or oil, will cause a newer, increasing focus towards the Middle East and create new alliances. In time the world will turn against Israel and against the God of Israel. In time we will find out who is the true God, Allah (the moon god) or Yahweh, the God of Israel. A confrontation is about to occur. Many believe World War III has already begun.

There are two reasons for the hatred of Jews and Israel. First, the Jews are God's chosen people and are under God's judgment for their rebellion against Him and the rejection of their Messiah. Secondly, anti-Semitism is inspired by Satan. If Satan can succeed in destroying the Jewish people, he believes he can show God to be weak, prevent the fulfillment of the prophetic restoration of Israel, and prevent his own doom. In polls across the European Union, most Europeans rate Israel as "the greatest obstacle to peace" in the world. Most countries are intimidated by Arab oil, and find little reason to support a small country like Israel.

# CHAPTER 4

# THE CHURCH AGE

## Distinguishing Between the Church and Israel

The church is a separate entity from Israel and remains distinct from Israel. The church was a mystery to the Old Testament prophets and was revealed to the Apostle Paul. "For this reason I, Paul, the prisoner of Jesus Christ for you Gentiles, if indeed you have heard of the dispensation of the grace of God which was given to me for you, how that by revelation he made known to me the mystery (as I wrote before in a few words, by which, when you read, you may understand my knowledge in the mystery of Christ), which in other ages was not made known to the sons of men, as it has now been revealed by the Spirit to his holy apostles and prophets" (Eph. 3:1–5).

The church started on the Feast of Pentecost[16] and will conclude on the Feast of Trumpets.[17] First I Corinthians 12:13 identifies the manner in which the church is being built—it is the work of the Holy Spirit in baptizing believers into the one Body of Christ. At the moment of regeneration, the Holy Spirit places believers into union with Christ. Ephesians 1:22–23 identifies the church as the Body of Christ, stressing the union with Christ that all believers are brought into at the moment of conversion. The picture of the church as the bride of Christ is seen in Ephesians 5:23 where an analogy is drawn that compares the husband and wife relationship in marriage to Christ and his bride the church. As in the Oriental wedding custom, the bride receives the promise of future blessing with her husband at the engagement (betrothal). The Holy Spirit was the deposit or the token of pledge. The Groom is currently building a home for his bride in heaven. Today the church is awaiting her groom return and to be taken to heaven. "If I go and prepare a place for you, I will come again and receive you to Myself; that where I am, there you may be also" (John 14:3 & 4). At the end of the church age, believers will be caught up to heaven, or (Raptured. "Then we who are alive and remain shall be caught up together with them in the clouds to meet the Lord in the air. And thus we shall always be with the Lord" (I Thessalonians 4:16 & 17).

Christendom includes true believers and mere professors, the wheat and the tares growing up together.[18] However, the true church is made up of Jews and Gentiles who genuinely know Christ as their Savior and have been born again. Beginning on the day of Pentecost in Acts 2 and continuing to the Rapture, all believers are part of Christ's body, the church. The groom has gone away to the Father's house to prepare a place to which he can bring his bride. While he is away the bride's faithfulness is tested by the separation. She is to remain faithful while constantly watching for his return. When the Father gives the signal, the shout will go forth and the church age will be completed at the Rapture—all true believers will be caught up to heaven. The rest of Christendom will be left behind to enter into the Tribulation period as Satan's harlot (False religion) that will help facilitate the great delusion of Antichrist in the form of the world church. A ecumenical and apostate church will pave the way for a one-world religion: the worship of Antichrist and reception of the mark of the beast.[19] The Antichrist will use "Christendom" and the world ecumenical movement to gain world domination, but at some point he will turn against the Babylonian religion and cause the world to worship himself and Satan.

The English word *church* is derived from the Greek word *kuriakon,* and the neutral adjective of *juries* ("Lord"), meaning "belonging to the Lord. Church also translates to the Greek word ekklesia, which is derived from *ek,* meaning "out of," and *kaleo,* which means "to call." Hence, the church is "a called out group."

Some Christians believe the church is synonymous with the kingdom and that the church inaugurates the kingdom. This is a misunderstanding of the word *kingdom,* which means "royal dominion." It is a designation both of power and the form of government. The church is not the kingdom. The church exists in this present age, whereas the kingdom, which is future, will be inaugurated at the Second Coming of Christ. Jesus came to offer the kingdom to the Jewish nation, hence, the proclamation "the kingdom of heaven is at hand" (Matt. 4:17). When the kingdom was rejected, it was held in abeyance, to be introduced at his Second Advent. Jesus announced he would build his church after the offer of the kingdom war rejected .[20] When the church is complete it will be removed and the seventieth week of Daniel will commence, ending in the second coming of Christ to rule and reign for a thousand years.

## The History of the Church As Revealed in Revelation 2–3

An overview of the church age is presented in Revelation 2–3. This overview proceeds from Pentecost to the Rapture as indicated by the often-repeated phrase, "He who has an ear, let him hear what the Spirit says to the churches." These seven historical churches of the first century provide a pattern for the types of churches that will exist throughout church history and show a sequential historical overview. Why are there seven churches? Seven is the Biblical number of completion. "Seven churches in Asia" refers to what we now call Turkey. Why were these churches selected? Why were the Churches of Colossae and Antioch not included? John was told to write what he saw in a book. This again emphasizes the fact that John actually saw the things he wrote down; he did not dream them up. At the time John wrote these messages, there were probably several hundred small congregations of Christians throughout Asia Minor. The seven churches to whom these letters were sent were not the largest or best known of their day. The churches at Rome and Antioch, for example, no doubt had bigger congregations and more prominent people as members. Why were these churches selected? No other churches could have so perfectly painted the picture they are intended to portray.

First, they are to be applied locally. The cities of the seven churches are given in the order of an ancient Roman postal circuit. Thus, the Book of Revelation could be easily circulated among the churches addressed. Secondly, they apply to churches today. Every problem, difficulty, and challenge facing the church is addressed in these seven letters. Thirdly, they apply personally to each of us. "Let he that hath an ear, hear what the Spirit says." (This phrase is repeated in Revelation 2 and 3 when Christ is outlining church history.) This applies to anyone who has an ear. Fourthly, the letters apply prophetically. For us today, most of the events are history because we are approaching the end of the church age. One must be careful not twist scriptures through allegories and spiritualization to make them mean whatever the interpreter wants. However, God does use types and analogy. For example, Jesus is called the Lamb of God. He was crucified on the Passover and rose again on the Feast of Firstfruit. This was not an accidental coincident. The seven churches of Revelation just happen to describe the future events in church history. If you change the order of these churches they do not correspond to chronological events. The seven churches are: Ephesus, Smyrna, Pergamos, Thyatira, Sardis, Philadelphia and Laodicea. The last church, Laodicea is marked by apostasy, and that clearly describes the church in the last days.

## The Last Days of the Church

The New Testament clearly speaks about the last days for the church in the epistles. The New Testament pictures the condition within the professing church at the end of the age by a system of denials. They are as follows:

-Denial of God (2 Timothy 3:4,5)
-Denial of Christ (2 Peter 2:6)
-Denial of Christ's return (2 Peter 3:3,4)
-Denial of the faith (I Timothy 4:1,2)
-Denial of sound doctrine (2 Timothy 4:3,4)
-Denial of the separated life (2 Timothy 3:1–7)
-Denial of morals (2 Timothy 3:1–4)
-Denial of authority (2 Timothy 3:4)
-Denial of creation work of God (2 Peter 3:5)

### 1. The Church of Ephesus (AD 33–170)

The church of Ephesus speaks of the period of church history from AD 33 to 170 AD In the year 97, when John wrote the Book of Revelation, the church was already under attack. By the time John penned Revelation, the purity of the church had been compromised to such a degree that they were in a position to hear the Lord say, "Unless you repent, I am not going to stay in your midst" (Rev. 2:5). The word *Ephesus* means "darling," and refers to romantic love—an area needing adjustment within the Ephesian Church. While the Ephesian church labored, it was theologically discerning how they lost their first love and had become flat in their love for Christ. The dominant historical characteristic of this ear was correct doctrine, circumspect conduct, and zealous labor for the Lord, but they had lost their first love: their passion for Christ. As their love for Christ began to wane, they more and more served out of a sense of duty.

In their own estimation, their acceptance by the Lord depended on their performance for Him. This opened the door to legalism.

## 2. The Church of Smyrna (AD 170–312)

The word *Smyrna* means "myrrh," a fragrance which is only released when crushed. Smyrna was characterized by works, Tribulation, and poverty, but it was rich with spirituality. In AD 155, the pastor of the church at Smyrna was a man named Polycarp, the last man personally discipled by John. Polycarp, along with many other believers at this time, was put to death for their faith. "...the devil shall cast some of you into prison, that you may be tried; and you shall have Tribulation ten days" (Rev. 2:10). In the years AD 100–313, there were ten Roman Emperors who launched such massive attacks against the believers that between 5 and 7 million Christians were killed during their rule. Despite persecutions the church prospered spiritually. It has been estimated that 10 percent of the people in the Roman Empire became Christians. The Devil decided to try a new tactic. The suffering of the church at Smyrna was prophetic of the great era of persecution under ten Caesars. The motives of the church were purified during this long and difficult period. Millions of Christians met cruel martyr deaths rather than renounce Christ or swear allegiance to Caesar as Lord. Today, in modern times, churches under persecution often prosper, while many churches in the West existing under relative freedom and material prosperity become lukewarm. Lukewarm is not outwardly hostile to Christianity, but it lacks in any meaningful belief system. It is, in effect, a mixture of hot and cold and results in a temperate lifestyle. This is not much different than the religious apathy of the secular world.

Soon after the apostolic age, great changes began to occur in many of the churches. Some of these changes included a drift toward ritualism, the rise of a clergy class, a lack of spirituality, and a developing laxity in discipline and church membership standards. Montanism was in reality a crusade to restore churches to their spiritual simplicity, to get back to basics. Montanus laid great emphasis upon the work of the Holy Spirit in the life of believers and the churches, and declared that the clergy had no franchise on the Gospel. He was an enemy of worldly philosophy and religion. Apart from emphasizing the ministry of the Holy Spirit, the Montanists held the following beliefs and practices: a regenerate church membership, believer's baptism by immersion only and the re-baptizing of those who came to them from established churches, the holiness of life, the opposition of second marriages, laxity in fastings, and flight in persecution. They believed in Trinitarian theology, the complete word of God, accepting all the Scriptures of both the Old and New Testaments, and premillennial eschatology. These chiliastic views were held by Justin Martyr, Irenaeus, and Tertullian. The spirituality and life of Montanist churches so contrasted with the formality and deadness of the mainstream churches that friction sometimes occurred. The Montanists were named because of the preaching of a man named Montanus. In most church histories the Montanists are classified as heretics, as were all groups that held doctrines that did not agree with the writer of the history book, most of which were either Catholic or liberal Protestant. However, a careful study of their beliefs and practices reveal they were not only orthodox but the first general stand against the drift away from church purity and spirituality. In his book *The Reformers and Their Stepchildren,* Leonard Verduin states, "The one thing the prevailing Church had against the 'heretics' was their refusal to go along with 'Christian sacralism.' This was their sin, their one and only sin. And it was this sin, and this sin only, that set the wheels of the Church's discipline going. This 'Donatism' was never absent from the medieval scene. In the twelve centuries that went before the Reformation it has never lacked for attempts to get away from the State-Church Priests and to reinstitute the apostolic congregational structurization" (35).

Another orthodox group that lived during this period were

the Novatians. The Novatians were named because of the leadership of a man name Novatian who became a Christian in about AD 250. Novatian was ordained to the ministry of the church at Tome by the Pastor, Fabian. The edicts of Decuis Trajan brought severe persecution to the churches. The doctrines of the Novatian's are well recorded by their own writings. They stood for: the purity of church membership, without great ceremony, on Biblical authority (as opposed to the authority of a man). The Novatians received persecution from within and from beyond the church, however, they survived into the sixth and seventh century. Some authorities have traced them up to the Reformation and the rise of the Anabaptist movement. On the count of the purity of their lives they were called the Cathari, or "the pure." The fourth Lateran Council decreed that these heretics should be punished by death. And they were. Because they baptized those who came from other communions they were sometimes called Anabaptists by their critics, but never by themselves. In his book *Church History*, Bruce Shelley states, "A presbyter and highly respected theologian, Novation, argued that the church had no power to grant forgiveness to those guilty of murder, adultery, and apostasy. It could only intercede for God's mercy at the Last Judgment…Soon Novatianits built up a network of small congregations and considered the Catholic churches polluted as a result of their lenient attitude toward sinners. They may have been right, for the Catholic churches now offered unlimited forgiveness to all who sinned" (76).

### 3. The Church of Pergamos (AD 312–606)
Satan changed his tactics in AD 312. Instead of attacking the church through persecution, he moved unbelievers to a position of authority over the visible state-church and attacked from within.

The name *Pergamos* is derived from two Greek words: *pergos*, which means "tower" or "elevation" and *gamos*, which means "married." Combined, the words mean "married to the tower." This speaks of a time when the church was elevated to a place of power and was married to the world. The church and the state were united under Constantine and his successors. This age marks the creation of the Greek and Russian Orthodox theology type. This was the merger of Christianity and pagan worship that originated at the tower of Babel in old Babylon. This period of church history covers the time period from Constantine to Boniface III, who declared himself the universal bishop. The church compromised its position more and more in order to gain favor and power. A church hierarchy began to develop, with the Bishop of Rome claiming increasing prominence because of his proximity to the ruler of the empire. He sought to strengthen his claim with the declaration of apostolic succession, alleging that his office in Rome was linked directly to apostles and that Peter was the foundation of the church, rather than Christ.

As the church at Pergamos compromised with the world's paganism and immorality, its symbolic counterpart—the historical church in the fourth and fifth centuries—committed spiritual adultery in an impure alliance with the Roman Empire.

"I know thy works, and where thou dwells, even where Satan's seat is… (Rev. 2:12)" The Greeks believed Pergamos was the birthplace of Zeus. Pergamos has a 150-foot high structure dedicated to Zeus in the middle of the city. Babel, or Babylon, was built by Nimrod and was the seat of the first great apostasy.[21] The city continued to be the seat of Satan until the fall of Babylonian and Medo-Persian Empires. He then shifted his Capital to Pergamos in Asia Minor, where it was in John's day. When Attalus, the Pontiff and King of Pergamos, died in 133 BC, he bequeathed the Headship of the Babylonian Priesthood to Rome. When the Etruscans came to Italy from Lydia (the region of Pergamos), they brought with them the Babylonian religion and rites. They set up a Pontiff who was head of the Priesthood. Later, the Romans accepted this Pontiff as their civil ruler. Julius Caesar was made pontiff of the Etruscan Order in

74 BC. The Emperors of Rome continued to exercise the office of "Supreme Pontiff" until AD 376, when the Emperor Gratian, for Christian reasons, refused it.

In his book *Dispensational Truth*, Clarence Larkin states, "The Bishop of the church at Rome Damascus was elected to the position. He had been Bishop twelve years after having been made Bishop in AD 366. He was made Bishop through the influence of the monks of Mt. Carmel, a college of Babylonian religion originally founded by the priest of Jezebel" (140). In AD 378, the Head of the Babylonian Order became the ruler of the Roman Church. Thus, Satan united Rome and Babylon into one Religious System.

The Church of Pergamos represents the period of church history from AD 312 (Constantine)–600. This period is summarized by Christ in Revelation 2:14–15, "I have a few things against you because you have there those who hold the doctrine of Balaam, who taught Balak to put a stumbling block before the children of Israel, to eat things sacrificed to idols, and to commit sexual immorality. Thus you also have those who hold the doctrine of the Nicolaitans, which thing I hate."

Balaam was a priest who was hired by a Moabite King, Balak, to curse Israel. He could not curse Israel, so he told the Moabites to seduce the men of Israel with Moabite women and introduce idol worship. The doctrine of Balaam in Pergamos is the objectionable marriage between the world and the Babylonian religion. The Nicolaitans were those who taught there was a special priest cast with special knowledge and rituals. *Nicos* meaning "conquest" and *laity* meaning "people of the church." The Nicolaitans introduced a separation between clergy and laity into the church. In Matthew 23:8–12, Jesus said, "But you, do not be called 'Rabbi'; for One is your Teacher, the Christ, and you are all brethren. Do not call anyone on earth your father; for One is your Father, he who is in heaven. And do not be called teachers; for One is your Teacher, the Christ. But he who is greatest among you shall be your servant. And whoever exalts himself will be abased, and he who humbles himself will be exalted" (Matthew 23:8–12). The State Church of Pergamos created the Episcopal form of church hierarchy. This Episcopal structure is found in the Roman Catholic and Orthodox churches. For most of the history of Christianity after 312, Episcopal government was the predominant form.

The Donatists were named (again, by their enemies) after Donatus, who died in AD 355 . He was a North African pastor and one of the leaders of the schism that began in Carthage in 311. A large group in the church protested at the ordination of Caecilianus as Pastor. This ordination was presided over by Felix of Aptunga, a man who had wavered badly during the Diocletian persecutions. Both Felix and Caecilianus were considered to be traitors, men who had surrendered the Scriptures to be burned in Imperial persecutions. The protesting group ordained Majorinus as their pastor, and then, following his death shortly thereafter, ordained Donatus in 316. Donatus at first appealed to Emperor Constantine, but to no avail. The Emperor ordered their suppression, a move which fired them into a great separatist movement which covered the whole of North Africa and lasted until the Muslim conquest of that region. The doctrines of the Donatists were very similar to the Novatians in that they believed in church purity; separation of church and state; scriptural baptism; and independence of the local churches. The Council of Milevi in AD 416 passed the following edict against the Donatists: "Whosoever denies that newly born infants are to be baptized let him be accursed." The Donatists rejected the Catholic liturgy and set up for themselves a more congregational way. Augustine labeled the Donatists heretics. The Donatists suffered great persecution, and were the first Christians to feel persecution at the hands of the State-Church. In AD 377, Gratian published edicts against Donatists, depriving them of their buildings and prohibiting their assemblies. They were noted for the fact that they patiently bore suffering for Christ, and did not retaliate with any persecutions of their own against Catholics. By the end of the fourth century, their teachings had spread abroad to Italy and Spain. In *Church History*, Shelley states, "The Donatist name arose from Donatus, an early bishop of Carthage (313–355) who led the protest against Catholic practices. Donatist charges centered on the fact that certain Catholic bishops had handed over the Scriptures to be burned during the persecution under Diocletian. Such an act, the Donatists insisted, was a serious sin of apostasy. Donatists believed the Church consisted only of true believers. Augustine rejected the Donatist's view of a pure church. Until the day of judgment, he said, the church must be a mixed multitude" (127)

The old British churches were of great antiquity, originating around the close of the apostolic age, and remained isolated from the mainstream of religious change. With the impending collapse of the Roman Empire, Britain was abandoned and its Roman garrisons sent home to Rome in AD 410. The churches, along with much of the population, were soon pushed back into Wales and Western Britain by the invading Saxons around AD 449. At approximately this time a Briton Christian named Patrick took the Gospel to Ireland. Patrick was an Anabaptist, not a Catholic. The issue over the date of Ester demonstrates that the Britons received their Christianity from Syria, possibly from the Montanists, and not from Rome. They rejected Catholic baptism, and practiced congregational rule. Although these ancient churches were consigned to obscurity, they still played a role in subsequent events.

The Celtic churches of Ireland came about largely through the efforts of Patrick who preached in Ireland from AD 432 until 465. In 521, a man named Columba was born to parents belonging to one of these Celtic churches. In 563, he began to do missionary work among the Picts in Scotland. From Columba's efforts, other mission bases were founded and in turn evangelized parts of Scotland, England, Normandy, Denmark and parts of Germany. Columba died in 597.

### 4. The Church of Thyatira (AD 606–1520)

We now come to the period of time which begins in AD 606 and goes through to a lesser extent until the present. The following four churches: Thyatira, Sardis, Philadelphia, and Laodicea all represent churches on the earth today. How do we know this? Because Jesus talks about his coming and about the Tribulation to these four churches.

Prophetically speaking, the major characteristics of Thyatira fit the church era that spanned the Middle Ages. During this time the dominant church fabricated a system that, like Jezebel, bound the people to image worship, superstition, and priest craft. Even secular historians categorize this period as the Middle Ages. If the first century was the beginning and 606–1520 was the middle, is the twenty-first century the end?

In the period of church history characterized by Thyatira we see a church emerge in the year AD 606, with a man who established himself as a universal bishop, or pope. This church exerted major influence on society during the medieval times and to a lesser extent on the church after 1517 through Martin Luther and the Reformers. This church still exists in present day. Jesus makes the following critique in Revelation 2:20, "Notwithstanding I have a few things against thee, because thou suffers that woman Jezebel, which calls herself a prophetess, to teach and to seduce may servants to commit fornication, and to eat things sacrificed unto idols."

The Church at Thyatira was floundering because of a woman who called herself a prophetess and persuaded people to eat food sacrificed to idols. Her influence upon the church was reminiscent of one of the most ungodly women in Israel's history. In I Kings 21, we learn that Jezebel, daughter of Ethbaal, king of the Zidonians, was given to King Ahab of Israel in marriage. Since Ethbaal was the high priest of Ashtaroth, goddess of sensuality and fertility, Jezebel's background adversely influenced God's people. Jezebel devised a plan for her husband, the King, to have a man falsely accused, killed, and appropriate his property. Thus, Ahab and Jezebel inherited land in a power play and an inquisition. This is exactly what happened in church history during the period delineated as the Church of Thyatira from 600 to 1500 AD. In *Revelation Unveiled*, Tim Lahaye states, "The Church Age of Thyatira produced what is known in history as the Dark Ages. "Dark" indicates that the program of merging paganism with Christianity, begun under the church of Pergamum, increasingly emphasized paganism, which is darkness" (65).

During the Inquisition Period from 600 to 1500, the Catholic Church amassed great amounts of wealth through political power plays. In addition, the Catholic Church sold salvation and forgiveness for money, and assumed the role of spiritual harlotry. Several of the popes and clergymen had bastard children through relations with prostitutes. Through the selling of salvation , the Catholic Church became extremely wealthy with land holdings and a banking system. Vast amounts of money, property, treasures were accumulated for 900 years through keeping people in spiritual darkness.

Eventually, men like John Wycliffe, Hugh Latimer and John Hus said it was not right that one had to go through a priest to get his sins forgiven. They taught that purgatory and the selling of indulgences were an abomination. To a large extent, the church of this period bought into the deception of Jezebel and followed after imagery and idolatry. Much of the false doctrine of the Roman Catholic Church has remained to this day. Her tremendous physical wealth has as well. In his book *A Woman Rides the Beast*, Dave Hunt states, "Most of Rome's wealth has been acquired through the sale of salvation. The practice continue to this day, blatantly where Catholicism is in control, less obviously here in the United States. In addition to such perversions of the gospel which have led hundreds of millions astray, there are the further abominations of corrupt banking practices, laundering of drug money, trading in counterfeit securities, and dealings with the Mafia, which the Vatican and her representatives around the world have long employed" (75).

During the darkest days of the papal stranglehold on Christendom there existed a group of Bible-believing Christians that stood tall for the faith once delivered unto the saints. The Paulician churches were the most maligned of all the enemies of the Roman system. In his classic, *The Rise and Fall of the Roman Empire*, Gibbon notes that the faith of the Paulicians stemmed from the first century and was a branch of Antiochan Christianity. They managed to survive for such a long period of time largely due to the fact that Armenia is a very isolated and mountainous region located mainly in modern Turkey, but also extending into present-day Iran and the former Soviet Union. The name *Paulician* did not come into general use until the seventh century and was applied because of the emphasis placed by these people on the epistles of Paul, and their adoption of Pauline names for their leaders. The Paulician movement rose to prominence during the seventh century, but existed long before they were called by that name. When the Paulicians rejected the Roman dogma of the primacy of Peter, they were accused of rejecting the writing of Peter, which was a false charge. It is apparent the first century churches of Armenia remained in the backwaters of mainstream Christianity for many years, relatively unchanged in their New Testament simplicity.

The greatest impact of the Paulician movement was seen in its spread into Eastern Europe. The Gospel was preached all over Asia Minor. During the severe persecutions of the ninth century, many Paulicians fled to the Balkans, where many churches were established. Byzantine persecutions sent many westward into Serbia where the Serbian Orthodox Church pushed them into Bosnia in the twelfth century. In 1203, Pope Innocent II tried to eradicate these Bible-believing Christians in Bosnia, who were now often called *Cathari*, meaning "pure ones." In 1291, a Dominican and Franciscan Inquisition was launched against them, the end result of which was to once again weaken the barrier against the onslaught of Islam, and by 1400 much of this area fell under the control of the

Ottoman Turks. Paulicians also found their way into Europe, and particularly Southern France in the Languedoc region. They had a profound influence in the revival of the ancient Christians there. When Bogomils from the Balkan countries fled to Europe, they met many believers, such as the Albigenses, of like faith.

The name *Albigenses* is taken from the French town of Albi, on the river Tarn. Albi was a major center of Catharist activity. These people rejected the Catholic concept of the church and formed simple congregations with pastors in the place of leadership. They accepted the scriptures over tradition. The Albigenses were some of the most persecuted people on Earth in their day. Almost twenty-thousand innocent people were slain in just one attack on the town of Beziers. Women and children were not spared. Campaigns of terror were conducted in 1215–1233. The business of inquisition was entrusted to the Dominicans, called "the hounds of the Pope." The Albigenses were all but eliminated from the South of France. Many who did escape fled to Italy and Germany where they sowed the seeds of the Anabaptist movement in Europe. Some returned to their home of Bulgaria, where the Bogomils exist to this day. In *Church History*, Shelley states, "The spread of the Waldenses and Albigenses, however, called for stricter measures. In 1215, the Fourth Lateran Council, under Innocent III's leadership, provided for the state's punishment of heretics, the confiscation of their property, excommunication for those unwilling to move against the heretic, and complete forgiveness of sins for those cooperating" (211).

Many historians attempt to fix the beginnings of the Waldenses with one of their leaders, Peter Waldo, who died in 1218. This is, in fact, not the case. The Waldenses are of ancient origin dating back to the time of Sylvester (AD 325) and to the disciples of the Apostles. The Waldenses are closely linked to the Albigenses. The name derives from the Italian word *Valdesi,* or the French word *Vaudois,* meaning "valley." It was applied because the usual residence of these Bible believers was in the fertile valleys of the high mountain ranges where they would be protected by the natural land barriers of the Church of Rome, their deadliest enemy. They were noted for their memorization of large parts of the Bible, their poverty, and their preaching. They believed the scriptures ought to be available to all people. Many of them knew the New Testament, or great sections of it, by heart. They opposed any spiritualized interpretation of the Bible, taking it literally. They rejected Rome's claim to be the true church, believed preaching should be the right of every Christian, and denied the right of a priest to bind, loose, consecrate, or bless. An edition of the Walden Ian Olivetan Bible was influential in the translation of the English Geneva Bible, the Bible ultimately replaced by the Authorized Version of 1611. Churches calling themselves Waldensian exist in many cities of Italy today and have their headquarters in Piedmont, the major city being Turin. They represent the largest evangelical group in Catholic Italy. Unfortunately, the Waldenses fell into the Protestant camp after the reformation. Today's Waldenses are modernistic, ecumenical, and more of a social Gospel organization than a Gospel preaching group.

Brother Dolcino was a member of the Apostolic Brethren, a sect which rose in Piedmont. He was caught, tortured, and burnt to death. He believed in a PreTribulation Rapture. Dolcino wrote three circular letters. In AD 150, the Rapture idea was preached by the Shepherd of Hermas. In 270, Victorinus, the Bishop of Pettau and a Catholic leader, preached it. A PreTribulation Rapture is also taught in 350 by works written under the name Ephraim the Syrian.

### 5. The Church of Sardis (AD 1520–1750)

Looking at church history, we now come to the Reformation. The age of Medieval Catholicism became so dark that when Sergius II became Pope (904–967), he ushered in what history calls the Rule of Harlots during which time his mistress publicly accompanied him to the papal palace. Sergius' grandson, Jon X, continued this legacy until he was actually killed in his bedroom while committing adultery. Next came Benedict IX, who assumed the position of pope at twelve years of age through the practice of simony-selling positions within the church to the highest bidder. Benedict IX was so corrupt that the citizens of Rome drove him out of the city, replacing him with Clement III, who was appointed by Henry II. Clement II was not a Roman because, in the word of Henry II, "I appoint no one from Rome because no priest can be found in this city who is free from the pollution of fornication and simony." In *A Woman Rides the Beast*, Hunt makes the following comments, "For centuries the priesthood was largely hereditary. Most priests were the sons of other priest and bishops. More than one pope was the illegitimate son of a previous and supposedly celibate pope. For example, Pope Sylverius (536–537) was fathered by Pope Hormisdas (514–523), and John XI (931–935) by Sergius III (904–911). No wonder Pope Pius II (1458–1564) said Rome was 'the only city run by bastards.' Pius himself admitted to fathering at least two illegitimate children, by different women, one of them married at the time. The rule of celibacy literally created prostitutes, making Rome the 'Mother of Harlots,' as the Apostle John foresaw" (164).

The church of Sardis symbolized the Reformation Era. During this period of history the church was reformed, but not revived. Some essential doctrines were reclaimed, such as the truth that people can be justified with God only by faith, but the changes did not shake loose the elaborate rituals and human traditions of the medieval church. Complacency and a new legalism set in, and only a few tasted the power of the Holy Spirit for Christian living.

In 1330, a man named John Wycliffe was born in England. He was an Oxford scholar and Catholic priest, and he began to write about the need to get away from papal edicts and back to the Bible. He began to publicly question doctrines such as transubstantiation and continual sacrifice so much that he was excommunicated by the powers in Rome. Although he himself was safe at Oxford, his disciples—men like John Hus and Hugh Latimer—were burned at the stake. Their death, however, caused a spark of Reformation which would burn throughout England.

In the year 1483, in Eiselben, Germany, a coal miner and his wife gave birth to a baby boy they named Martin. Martin was frightened in a storm one day and prayed to St. Anne, the patron saint of coal miners, "If you save me from this lightning, I will become a monk." True to his word, Martin enrolled in seminary. After two years, he earned his Doctorate, but the more he studied theology, the more he knew he could never obtain righteousness. He became ill on a trip to Rome. While recovering in an Alpine monastery, one of the monks, sensing his struggle, told him to read the book of Habakkuk. Martin took his advice and when he came to the fourth verse of the second chapter, he read, "The just shall live by faith". He finally understood. He discovered that "the just shall live by faith" is the theme of Romans, Galatians and Hebrews. Martin Luther discovered that man cannot obtain salvation by good works or by performing ritual. He discovered that many of the traditions and current practices of the Roman Catholic Church were not based upon biblical teachings. The gospel is the good news that man is saved by the shed blood of Jesus Christ on the cross and is appropriated by grace through faith. However, upon arriving in Rome, with his heart full of excitement, Martin was shocked by the buses and hypocrisy. Returning to Germany, he realized he had to take a stand. In 1517, he nailed a parchment to the university door in Wittenberg containing ninety-five theses challenging the Pope. Three-and-a-half-years later, Rome answered, "Retract or die."

After several exchanges, Martin Luther gave his classic reply: "Here I stand, I can do no other, so help me God."

Within a few years the Reformation swept across Europe. Luther in German, Zwingli in Switzerland, Knox in Scotland all called for a return to the bible. Austria and Hungary were also early hotbeds of the Reformation. Luther's stand gave rise to the birth of the Jesuits, an order dedicated to enforce Papal power.

The sect known as the Anabaptists came to prominence at the time of the protestant reformation, although they are known to have been in existence long before that time. The name *Anabaptist* means re-baptizer, and is a title given to this ancient group of Baptists by their enemies because of their practice of re-baptizing all who came into their ranks from the Catholic Church. *Anabaptist* was a title of slander and reproach.

One of the marks of the Baptists at this time was their willingness to live simple lives, in contrast to the opulence of the Catholic and Protestant clergy. Luther called the Baptist *Rottengeister* or "clique-makers" because of the threat their beliefs and practices presented to the monolithic church -state system. In 1525, an edict of the City of Zurich was written by Zwingli against the Anabaptists prohibiting them from preaching without permission. It is clear that the Anabaptist had an apostolic heritage. They were called Christians in the first century;[22] Montanists; Novatians; Donatists; Paulicians; Albigenses; Waldenses; Anabaptists; and today Brethren and Baptists, and non-denominational believers. Throughout church history, there has always been a remnant of believers who remained truthful to the gospel and biblical teachings. These believers were often called heretics and given various names such as Waldenses, Albigneses and Anabaptists. However, despite being called various names, they shared a common belief in the scriptures and a common persecution by the institutionalized Christian church. "And I saw the woman, drunk with the blood of the saints and with the blood of the martyrs of Jesus. And when I saw her, I marveled with great amazement" (Rev. 17:6).

In *The Road to the Holocaust*, Hal Lindsay shows that the persecution of European Jews did not begin with the Third Reich. This persecution began with Replacement Theology taught by the Roman Catholic, Orthodox, and Reformed Churches. Anti-Semitism is the mark of people who do not read their Bible or decide to intentionally distort scriptures to meet their theological bias.

The Replacement Theology of Augustine, as taught by the Roman Catholic Church, the Orthodox Church and the Reformed Church is unbiblical and undermines the prophets and the warning against end-times judgment.

Anti-Semitism began in Christianity with the statements of the early liberal theologians, including Eusebius, Cyril, Chrysostom, Augustine, Origen, Justin, and Jerome. These men published papers and historical pamphlets attacking Jews. Poisonous streams of venom came from the mouths of spiritual leaders to virtually illiterate congregants, sitting benignly in their pews, listening to their pastors. They labeled the Jews as "Christ killers, plague carriers, demons, children of the devil, and money-hungry Shylocks.

In 1095, Pope Urban II preached the call for Crusade at Claremont, appealing to the French to recover the Holy Land for Christianity. Crusaders under Godfrey killed Jewish men, women, and children in Palestine.

Jerusalem was captured by the Crusaders on July 15, 1099, with most of the Jewish population, which numbered between twenty and thirty thousand. They were slaughtered that very day. The Jews who were not burned alive in the synagogue were sold into slavery in Italy.

In 1306, France drove one-hundred-thousand Jewish people out of the country. At the time of the Black Death (1348–1350), Jewish people in Germany were accused of poisoning the wells and the springs of the Christians. Martin Luther wrote several anti-Semitic pamphlets which helped set the stage for Adolph Hitler's anti-Semitic Holocaust. *The Encyclopedia Judaica*, Volume 3, states that Martin Luther preached that Christians should burn Jewish synagogues. Jewish homes should be broken down and destroyed. Passport and traveling privileges should be absolutely forbidden to Jews. It is interesting that a few years after writing this tract, Martin Luther died. Anti-Semitism is sin. Jesus Christ told us to "Love your neighbor as yourself" (Mark 12:31). Anti-Semitism does not come from the Bible, it comes from hell. Fortunately, Godly men such as William Blackstone and John Darby would read the Bible and discover that God had not abandoned Israel forever, and God was about to restore the Jews to their promised land.

### 6. The Church of Philadelphia (1750–1900)

"I know your works, see, I have set before you an open door, and no one can shut it; for you have a little strength, have kept My word, and have not denied My name. Indeed I will make those of the synagogue of Satan, who say they are Jews and are not, but lie, indeed I will make them come and worship before your feet, and to know that I have loved you. Because you have kept My command to persevere, I also will keep you from the hour of trial which shall come upon the whole world, to test those who dwell on the earth" (Rev. 3:8–10).

In this next phase of church history, we see a stirring in the dead denominationalism which had strayed from the simplicity of the Gospel. William Carey goes down in history as the father of the modern missionary movement. The church suddenly woke from her lethargy, and Carey set the example that one does not have to be skilled, gifted, or special to be used in the work of the Lord. God is simply looking for men who are willing to go.

The church at Philadelphia speaks of the missionary church in history led by men like Carey in India, Hudson Taylor in China, D. L. Moody in America, and C. H. Spurgeon in London that evangelism was taking place, and missionaries were being sent out. The letter to Philadelphia is one of only two letters of the seven in which Jesus has nothing critical to say.

During the winter of 1827–28, four Christian men, Jon Nelson Darby, Edward Cronin, John Bellett, and Francis Hutchinson, who had been concerned for some time about the condition of the professing church, agreed after much prayer and conference to come together on the Lord's Day. They remembered the Lord Jesus in the breaking of bread, as the early Christians did, counting on the Lord to be with them. Their first meeting was held in Francis Hutchinson's house in Dublin, Ireland. Over a period of time they started a movement which became known as the Plymouth Brethren. These students of the scriptures did not feel at home nor find spiritual food and fellowship in the Anglican Church of Ireland and were not accepted in the relatively few dissenting and independent churches of the day. In 1830, John Darby left the Anglican priesthood and devoted himself full time to forming and feeding small gatherings both in Ireland and England. It was about this same time that Lady Powerscourt opened her Irish mansion for a series of Prophetic Truth Conferences, which continued for several years. Before long, Darby became the acknowledged leader of these meeting to which many clergymen were attracted.

During the first twenty years these groups, known as assemblies, were established worldwide. In their New Testament simplicity they preferred to designate themselves as "brethren," but they became known as the "Plymouth Brethren." During his more than fifty years of leadership among the Brethren, Darby traveled to France, Germany, Holland, Switzerland, Italy, Jamaica, Canada, America, Australia, and New Zeeland.

During his travel he wrote deep theological material in the form of personal and pastoral letters, published and unpublished papers, tracts, magazine articles, and book manuscripts. His books, most of which were written over one hundred years ago, are all in print today; there are forty-four volumes averaging nearly 400 pages each.

In no uncertain terms, the Brethren proclaimed the scriptures to be absolutely inspired by God and the sole authority for faith and practice. It was mainly through Darby's ministry and writings that the sovereignty of God, election, assurance, acceptance, and unconditional eternal security were built into the movement's foundation.

The popularization of the term "Pre-Tribulation Rapture" is associated with the teaching of John Nelson Darby, the rise of Premillennialism, and the rise of dispensationalism in English-speaking churches at the end of the nineteenth century. In 1908, the doctrine of the Rapture was further popularized by an evangelist named William Eugene Blackstone, whose book, *Jesus Is Coming*, sold more than 1 million copies. Although Blackstone was a Gentile, he had a major influence on the Zionist movement and the encouragement of the Jews to return to Israel in fulfillment of prophecy.

In 1888, Scofield attended the Niagara Bible Conference where he met Hudson Taylor, the pioneer missionary to China. The two became life-long friends, and Taylor's approach to Christian missions influenced Scofield to found the Central American Mission in 1890. Scofield soon became a leader in dispensational Premillennialism, a forerunner of twentieth-century Christian fundamentalism. Dispensationalism emphasized the distinctions between the New Testament church and Israel of the Old Testament. It was largely through the influence of Scofield's notes that dispensationalist and Premillennialism became influential among fundamentalist Christians in the United States. The first known appearance of the theological use of the word *rapture* in a reference Bible was the Scofield Reference Bible of 1909. Lewis Sperry Chafer (1871–1952), a student of Scofield, became a well-known American premilleniarian, dispensationalist, founder of Dallas Theological Seminary, writer, and conference speaker.

After 1945, the operations of the Dallas Theological Seminary were given to John Walvoord. Chafer died of a heart failure while on a conference Bible tour in Seattle, Washington, in 1952. John Walvoord and Charles Ryrie became the leading theologians in the Pre-Tribulation movement. In 1957, Dr. John Walvoord authored a book, *The Rapture Question*, that gave theological support to the Pre-Tribulation Rapture; this book eventually sold over 65,000 copies. In 1958, J. Dwight Pentecost authored another book supporting the Pre-Tribulation Rapture, *Things to Come: A study in Biblical Eschatology*, that sold over 215,000 copies.

In 1979, Tim LeHaye, along with Henry Morris, established the Institute for Creationist Research in Santee, California. Tim LeHaye founded the Pre-Tribulation Research Center along with Thomas Ice in 1998. A fiction series by LaHaye and Jerry Jenkins called *Left Behind* has sold millions of copies and has been made into movies. Hal Lindsey has also been a prolific Pre-Tribulation writer selling over 15 million books. The number of Pre-Tribulation writers is geometrically expanding. There have been more end-time prophecy books written in the last fifty years than in the entire church age.

Just as the Old Testament prophets predicted, God would return Jews to the promised land in the last days. The modern return to Israel began as early as 1871, when a few Jews began to trickle back into the land. By 1882, about 25,000 Jews had settled there. At the First Zionist Congress led by Theodore Herzl in 1897, the goal of reclaiming the land for the Jewish people was officially adopted. The gather, however, was very slow. By 1914, the number of Jews in the land was only 85,000.

During World War I, the British sought support from the Jews for the war effort. In return, the British foreign secretary, Arthur J. Balfour, issued what has since become known as the Balfour Declaration on November 2, 1917. This declaration was contained in a letter from Balfour to Lord Rothschild, who was a wealthy Jewish entrepreneur. In that letter, Secretary Balfour gave approval to the Jewish goal of reclamation. "His Majesty's Government views with favor the establishment in Palestine of a national home for the Jewish people…"

The United Nations approved a national homeland for the Jews, and British control of the land ended on May 14, 1948. At that time it was populated by 650,000 Jews—or 6 percent of the world's Jewish population—and several hundred thousand Arabs. By the year 2001, thirty-8 percent of the 13.2 million Jews in the world were back in the land of Israel. Current projections indicate that by the year 2030 half of the Jews in the world will be back in the land of Israel.

Mark Hitchcock makes the following observation in his book *Seven Signs of the End-Times*:

> According to Scripture, Israel will experience two (and only two) international, worldwide returns from exile. The first worldwide regathering will be a return in unbelief in preparation for the judgment of the Tribulation. The second, worldwide regathering will be a return in faith at the end of the Tribulation, in preparation for the blessing of the Millennium (one-thousand-year reign) of Christ. (14–15)

"The it will happen on that day that the Lord will again recover the second time with his hand the remnant of his people, who will remain, from Assyria, Egypt, Pathros, Cush, Elam, Shinar, Hamath, and from the islands of the sea. And he will lift up a standard for the nations and assemble the banished one of Israel, and will gather the dispersed of Judah from the four corners of the earth." (Isa. 11:11–12)

During the prophetic period of church history known as Philadelphia, the church sensed its need for spiritual revival when God sent men like Wesley, Whitefield, Edwards, Finney, Spurgeon, and Moody across England and America. Revivals swept across the English speaking countries and out of this great spiritual awakening rose many universities and churches dedicated to Christ. Unfortunately, missionary zeal began to wane after World War I, and though some evangelistic movements continued to flourish, many of the schools and churches that arose during this era have long since abandoned their Christian heritage. The Philadelphia type of church is still present in the world and it will be here until the Rapture, but it is not the dominant force in the professing Christian church today.

### 7. The Church of Laodicea (1900–200?)

"I know your works, that you are neither cold nor hot. I could wish you were cold or hot. So then, because you are lukewarm and neither cold nor hot, I will spew you out of My mouth. Because you say, I am rich, have become wealthy, and have need of nothing and do not know that you are wretched, miserable, poor, blind, and naked: I counsel you to buy from Me gold refined in the fire, that you may be rich and white garments, that you may be clothed, that the shame of your nakedness may not be revealed: and anoint your eyes with eye salve, that you many see" (Rev. 3:15–18).

The destination of the letter is to *Laodicea*, which means "people ruling." This is set in contrast to God ruling in the church. It is a church ruled by men rather than the Holy Spirit. The Holy Spirit is not present and is not guiding the church. This becomes a clear description of much of Christendom today. Jesus describes the church today as being rich in worldly goods but self-deceived. It is spiritually poor, blind, and naked. This is an accurate description of the modern Apostate church today.[23]

I Timothy 4:1 warns, "But the Spirit says expressly, that in later times some shall fall away from the faith, giving heed to seducing spirits and doctrines of demons." During the period between the time Paul wrote I and II Thessalonians, some one wrote a fake letter from Paul warning that the Rapture had already occurred. Paul sent a second letter with the following statement, "now we beseech you, brethren, by the coming of our Lord Jesus Christ, and by our gathering together unto him, that you be not soon shaken in mind, or by trouble, neither by spirit, nor by word, nor by letter as from us, as that the day of Christ is at hand. Let no man deceive you by any means: for that day shall not come, except there come a falling away first, and that man of sin be revealed, the son of perdition" (II Thess. 2:1–3).

In his book *The Footsteps of the Messiah*, Arnold Fruchtenbaum makes the following comments, "In this passage two things are to occur before the Tribulation can begin, one of which is the falling away. The Greek word here is *apostosia* which can be translated as the apostasy. Thus, it was inevitable that the church would become apostate in the closing days of its history" (51–52).

Fruchtenbaum continues, "One type of deed that will be performed by apostates is mockery...They will mock the fundamentals of the faith such as the verbal inspiration of the Scriptures, the virgin birth, the substitutionary death of Christ, and his physical resurrection from the dead ... If the present age of the apostasy had a definite beginning (and this is impossible to determine), it might well have been January 20, 1891. On that day a man named Charles Augustus Briggs gave his inaugural address at the Union Theological Seminary in new York City. At that time, Union was a Presbyterian seminary training ministers for Presbyterian pulpits. In this inaugural address Briggs made six points, some of which involved destructive heresies: 1) there are three great fountains of truth: the bible, the church, and reason. Thus, reason and the church became equal in authority with the Scriptures; 2) not only were some of the Old Testament prophecies not fulfilled, but they were also reversed; 3) he questioned the Mosaic authorship of the five books of Moses; 4) he questioned the unity of Isaiah; 5) he stated that those who dies unsaved would have a second chance; 6) sanctification is not complete at death. Briggs was not the first modernist, But this address was the first public affirmation of modernism in a theological seminary in the United States" (55).

Near the turn of this century the scholars at many theological seminaries, particularly in Europe, began to introduce what they called "higher criticism" of the scriptures. They were eager to examine the historicity and accuracy of the Biblical documents by using research methods developed in secular education. Many of the leading critics possessed, at best, a lukewarm relationship with Christ, and this was reflected in their hazy views of scripture. The more open skeptics began to deny outright the supernatural aspects of the Biblical faith. This was all done in the name of scholarship. Before long they had demythologized Jesus into a mere man. This Satanic infection spread like wildfire through the seminaries in Europe and the United States, and by the 1920's it was echoing from the pulpits of American churches. The western world was caught up in scientific and philosophical rationalism and the church got sucked into the vortex because so many of its leaders had never experienced a deep faith in Jesus Christ. The sad truth is that thousands of churches around the world today call themselves Christian, but Christ is nowhere to be found in them. Tragically, most of the unbelieving world look at them, and want no part of their false religion.

Today, the teaching of absolutes is out of the church, just as in the secular schools. Instead of teachers who teach facts, you have facilitators to keep a dialogue going. Little do people realize that a technique called the Hegelian Dialectic is being used on them to get rid of the old-fashioned notion of truth. Humanists believe they can bring peace on earth without the return of Christ. The Gospel has been replaced by a more seeker-friendly message. Preachers avoid anything to hot or too cold. They preach a bland, lukewarm message designed not to be divisive or offensive. Churches today are market driven and designed to address the demands and supposed needs of the people rather than the absolutes of the Bible.

Offensive topics such as being born again, and hell, fire, and brimstone are avoided. Modern church leaders believe that people will not respond unless they have their personal needs met. Their pain, loneliness, hurts, and self-fulfillment become the focus. If we can make them comfortable and happy they will stay in the church. These new church services create a non-challenging, comfortable environment for the seeker (the unsaved visitor). The congregation will purposely dress down, avoiding ties, suits and dresses to that the average person can feel comfortable being there. Because time is money, twelve minutes is saved per service by putting scriptures on a screen rather than believers opening their own Bibles. Church is seen as a competitive entertainment businesses and services are ramped up to meet the needs of the masses with short attention spans or what is clinically referred to as attention deficit. The seeker or sinner-friendly church movement theology suggest that the church needs to be conformed to the image of the world. But, Christ and his apostles write that we are to be conformed to the image of Christ. The word *church* means "a called out group." Although this Laodicean luke-warmness is the predominant characteristic of the church age today, there will always be a remnant of believers who love and follow the Lord. Time is of the essence. The period of church history called the Church of Laodicea is coming to a close. Judgment Day is knocking on the door.

# CHAPTER 5

# THE RAPTURE

## What is the Rapture?

When over three hundred Bible references to the Second Coming are examined, it becomes clear there are two phases to Christ's return. The passages have too many conflicting activities connected with his return to be merged into a single coming. Just as we know there are two comings of Jesus Christ, we also know the Second Coming can be sub-divided into to two stages. At the completion of the church age, prior to the seven-year Tribulation, Christ will come suddenly in the air to rapture living Christians and at the same time resurrect dead Christians. He will take the church to his Father's house where we will appear before the judgment seat of Christ and participate in the marriage supper of the Lamb.[24] The second stage of the Second Coming will involve Christ and, accompanied with his bride (the church), will physically come to the earth where he will rescue Israel and establish the Millennial reign for a thousand years.

The Greek word for "caught up" is *harpazo*. The familiar word *Rapture* does not appear in the Greek New Testament, for it is a Latin word. Those who translated the Greek New Testament into Latin used *Rapture* to describe "snatched up" or "caught away" because it suggests a joyous exaltation. A more pejorative term is used in Revelation 19:20, when the Antichrist and the false prophet are thrown alive into the lake of fire burning with brimstone. The scriptures predict that the church will be raptured, or caught up to heaven, at the coming of the Lord for them. The word "rapture" is from *rapere*, found in the expression "caught up" in the Latin translation of I Thessalonians 4:17: "The we who are alive and remain shall be 'caught up' together with them in the clouds to meet the Lord in the air. And thus we shall always be with the Lord." John 14:3 states, "And if I go and prepare a place for you, I will come again and receive you to myself; that where I am, there you may be also." Hebrews 11:6 states, "By faith Enoch was transferred or removed so that he did not see death, 'and was not found because God had removed him'; for before his translation he had this testimony, that he pleased God." Enoch was a picture of God removing a believer prior to judgment or the worldwide flood of Noah's day. "Then it happened, as they continue on and talked, that suddenly a chariot of fire appeared with horses of fire, and separated the two of them; and Elijah went up by a whirlwind into heaven" (II Kings 2:11). Like Enoch, Elijah was translated to heaven without dying. Later, we see Elijah at Christ's transfiguration.[25] And according to Malachi 4:5, Elijah will return to the earth to minister during the first three-and-a-half years of the Tribulation. Rapture, or the Greek word harpazo, is used in Revelation 12:5, where Christ is called the "male child" who "was caught up to God and to his throne." This picture looks back to Christ's ascension in Acts 1:8–11, where Christ ascended to heaven in a cloud.

The Rapture was unknown until it was revealed to the church by the apostles, especially Paul. All believers living when the Rapture occurs will not experience physical death. During the Rapture, every living believer will be instantly transformed from mortal to immortal bodies, which will be like the glorified body of Christ. This will occur whether a Christian believes in the Rapture or not, for it comes with the package. Those raptured will be caught up in the air to meet the Lord and the resurrected church age believers who have died. At that time, we will be taken into God the Father's presence to temporary dwelling places the Lord Jesus is presently preparing.

## What Is The Pre-Tribulation Rapture?

The next major event in God's prophetic calendar is the Rapture of the church. While this event resembles the Second Coming of Christ, Pretribulationists distinguish the Rapture from the Second Coming. In the Rapture, Christ will return in the air for the entire Christian Church. Dead believers will be resurrected and then caught up in the air, where they will join with living believers who have been transformed and lifted bodily out of the world.

None of this will be visible to the unbelieving world, which will be left behind following the Rapture. All that unbelievers will know is that suddenly every Christian in the world will have disappeared. The Rapture will not only mark the end of what is called the church age, it will also usher in the most terrible period of time the world has ever known: the great Tribulation. Thus, the Rapture taking place prior to the Tribulation is what is called the PreTribulation Rapture.

A powerful, evil world leader known as the Antichrist will then gain control of things. People who become believers during the Tribulation will suffer terrible persecution; many thousands of them will be martyred. The world will experience numerous natural catastrophes (wars, famines, plagues, earthquakes and tsunamis) along with the war that will finally end all wars. At the end of the seven-year Tribulation period, the armies of the world will gather at a place in Israel called Armageddon. At this time, Christ will return (this is the second phase of the Second Coming) with the armies of heaven (believers who were raptured), destroy the wicked, and set up an earthly kingdom for one-thousand years (the millennium). Chapters 4–18 of the book of Revelation support the PreTribulation Rapture. Church history is revealed in chapters 2 and 3, and then the church is not shown on the earth, until the second coming in chapter 19.

## Why Was Pre-Tribulation Rapture Not Taught Until John Darby?

Contrary to popular belief, John Darby did not invent the doctrine of pre-Tribulation. The pre-Tribulation Rapture was taught by the apostles, especially Paul and John. This tradition was handed down through the centuries. However, Roman civil and religious authorities did not appreciate the fact that the prophetic books of the Old Testament and the Book of Revelation referred to the Roman Empire and the State Church of Rome as the seat of the Antichrist and the religious mother of harlots.

Replacement theology was systematized by Augustine and became Orthodox Church doctrine in the fourth century. This theological perspective taught that the church became heir to the promises made to Israel, Christ is now reigning by means of the church, and there would be no Tribulation or literal millennial reign. From the fourth century until now, most Christians do not believe in the premillennial return of Christ. If you do not believe in a literal Tribulation and a literal millennial reign, you could not possibly believe in a PreTribulation Rapture. However, despite the Replacement theology of state churches and most liberal historians, a remnant of true Bible believers, labeled as heretics, survived throughout history in the underground church, often died as martyrs, but remained true to biblical principals.

Chiliastic or pre-millennial eschatology was taught by Justin Martyr, Irenaeus, and Tertullian. Tertullian was a noted convert to Montanists ideals, Montanists were conservative Christians living in North Africa, circa AD 150, who helped to refine conservative Bible teachings and left a legacy in North Africa, which would later give rise to the Donatists. The Donatists, Paulicians, Albigenses, Catharist, Waldenses and Anabaptists all had members who were pre-millennial in their eschatology.

A document known as the Epistle of Barnabas was written to the early churches. It was alleged to have been written by Barnabas, the first missionary to accompany the Apostle Paul. Many early church leaders, including Origen and Jerome, believed this document to be genuine. However, it has never been part of the Bible and may not have been written by Barnabas of the Bible. This letter speaks of a pre-millennial return of Christ around the year AD 2000. In AD 150, the Shepherd of Hermas speaks of the pre-tribulational concept of escaping the Tribulation.

A specific Pre-Tribulation doctrine was written between AD 374 and 627 under the pseudonym Ephraem the Syrian. The Apostolic Brethren, taught by Brother Dolcino in 1304, believed in a Pre-Tribulation Rapture. Francisco Ribera, a Spanish Jesuit and doctor of theology, wrote a commentary on the book of Revelation in 1591. He taught a Pre-Tribulation Rapture would occur forty-five days before the end of a three-and-a-half year Tribulation.

Paul Benware, in his book "understanding *End-Times Prophecy,* makes the following comments:

> As early as 1687, Peter Jurieu, in his book *Approaching Deliverance of the Church* (1687), taught that Christ would come in the air to rapture the saints and return to heaven before the battle of Armageddon. He spoke of a secret Rapture prior to his coming in glory and judgment at Armageddon. About fifty years later, Philip Doddridge's commentary on the New Testament (1738) and John Gill's commentary on the New Testament (1748) both used the term *rapture* and speak of it as imminent. It is clear that these men believed that this coming will precede Christ's descent to the earth and the time of judgment. The purpose was to preserve believers from the time of judgment. (247)

Frank Marotta, a brethren researcher, believes that Thomas Collier made a reference to a pre-tribulational Rapture in 1674, but rejects the view, thus showing his awareness that such a view was being taught. In 1742, a Baptist named Morgan Edwards predicted a distinct Rapture three-and-a-half years before the start of the millennium. John Darby claims to have first understood his view of the Rapture as the result of Bible study during a convalescence from December 1826 until January 1827. He is the fountainhead for the modern version of the doctrine.

The doctrine of the Rapture was further spread through annual Bible conferences such as the Niagara Bible Conference from 1878–1909, turn of the century publications such as William Blackstone's *Jesus Is coming*, and the *Scofield Reference Bible* (1909). Many of the greatest Bible teachers of the first half of the twentieth century helped spread the doctrine such as Arno Gaebelein, C. I. Scofield, R.. A. Torrey, Harry Ironside, and Lewis Chafer.

In virtually every major metropolitan area in North America a Bible institute, Bible college, or seminary was founded that expounded dispensational Pre-Tribulationism. Schools like Moody Bible Institute, The Philadelphia Bible College, Bible Institute of Los Angeles (BIOLA) and Dallas Theological Seminary taught and defended these views. These teachings were found primarily in independent churches, Bible churches, Baptists, and a significant number of Presbyterian churches. Around 1925, Pre-Tribulationism was adopted by many Pentecostal denominations such as the Assemblies of God and the Four-Square Gospel denomination. Pre-Tribulationism was dominant among Charisma tics in the 1960's and 1970's. Hal Lindsey's *Late Great Planet Earth* (1970) furthered the spread of the Pre-Trib Rapture as it exerted great influence throughout popular American culture and then around the world.

Although still widely popular among Evangelicals and Fundamentalists, the dominance of Pre-Tribulationism first began to wane in some academic circles in the 1950s and 1960s. As the result of a shift toward greater social concern, there was a decline among Pentecostals, Charismatics, and Evangelicals as well.

## Why Is Pre-Tribulational Rapture Eschatology a Minority Position?

First it must be understood that in Christianity, as well as other religions of the world, most followers are not conservative or strict Fundamentalists. For example, the Qur'an clearly teaches that Muslims are to conquer the world and kill all Christians and Jews who do not submit. However, most Muslims are not overtly militant. During the first three centuries, Premillennialism was orthodox. During the Middle Ages, only one person out of 2,500 was literate. There were no printing presses and books were firmly in control of the state and state religion. As the power of secular Rome declined in Western Europe, the power of the Catholic Church was the major unifying cultural influence. The Catholic Church, with a centralized administration through its network of bishops, controlled religious thought. Dissenters from accepted theology were subject to death, loss of property, and destruction of any written material. During the dark ages, the common man was not allowed to have scriptures in his own language. Men were not allowed to preach unless officially sanctioned by the state church.

Things began to change in 1455 with Johann Gutenberg's invention of the printing press and movable type. Also, the freedom of the middle class began to increase with the emergence of modern city-states and the decline of the power of the church in Rome. However, it must be remembered that as late as 1700 in England, John Asgill was thrown into prison, lost his property, and had his books burned for teaching the doctrine of a pre-tribulational Rapture. The doctrine of a pre-tribulational Rapture is not politically correct and will not be the majority opinion by the Christian church until the Rapture actually occurs. Satan is the ruler of this world. He is a liar and a deceiver and the majority will not accept truth as taught in the Bible until Christ comes to restore the World to the Kingdom of God.

## What Is the Most Effective Way to Teach the Pre-Tribulational Rapture?

Most realtors will tell you the most important factor when investing in real estate is location, location, location. If Donald Trump wants to find a property to build a high rise building, he does not want a pasture in South Dakota zoned forest and grazing. He wants prime commercial property in a metropolitan community. Most theologians understand the battles in theology are won or lost in definition of terms. The primary issue in regards to the Rapture is how you define God's covenants with Abraham and Israel. If one believes in Replacement Theology, they will not accept the doctrine of the Rapture.

The trouble with many PreTribulation advocates today is that they do not know where the battle is. In his book *The Rapture Question*, John Walvoord states, "It is not too much to say that the Rapture question is determined more by ecclesiology than eschatology" (16). What he is saying is that the doctrines concerning the church bear more on the Rapture question than the doctrines of prophecy. Charles Ryrie expresses a similar conviction in his book *What You Should Know About the Rapture*, "Actually the question boils down to whether or not the church is a distinct entity in the program of God. Those who emphasize the distinctiveness of the church will be Pre-Tributationists, and those who deemphasize it will usually be post-Tributationists" (62). Another way to say it is, those who do not see a distinction between Israel and the church will not see the Tribulation period. If you do not see the Tribulation and the pre-millennial return of Christ, you could not possibly be a pre-tributationists. That is why most Christians today do not see a Rapture, because they believe in Replacement Theology and see Israel as having no special standing and no unfilled promises from God."

Many fine supporters of the Pre-Tribulation doctrine are ineffective in their efforts to gain supporters because they are using the wrong weapons. If a nine-year-old boy is hunting small birds in his backyard, he does not need much fire power. However, a big game hunter deep in a jungle with ferocious wild animals and numerically superior hostile savages would need superior fire power and lots of ammunition.

If you are speaking at a prophecy conference and the audience consists of Bible students with a working knowledge of the Old Testament verse by verse as students of J. Vernon McGee or Chuck Smith you will have no problem going over the finer points distinguishing between the Rapture, the Second Coming, and the immanency of the Rapture. However, if you are in front of a hostile audience of Reformed theologians or unbelievers you are going to need some bigger guns.

When it comes to the Rapture, the lead dog should not be the immanency of the Rapture Many theologians attempt to establish the immanency of the Rapture through a word study. The immanency of the Rapture is difficult to establish through word study alone. For example, several thousand years ago Zephaniah stated, "The Day of the Lord is at hand" prior to even the first advent. If one attempts to establish a point of doctrine out of word-study alone, "at hand" would imply immanency. However, we know that a condition precedent for the "Day of the Lord" was the death, burial and resurrection of Christ. The "Day of the Lord" was not immanent, if one means near in time, during the time of Zephaniah. Therefore, we can not base doctrine upon word-study alone, without considering all relevant passages.

The two primary arguments for the Rapture of the church are (1) The distinctions between Israel and the Church. If one understands the Church and the dispensation of Israel are mutually exclusive, one is likely to see the Rapture in the scriptures. If one believes the Church replaced Israel as to its eternal blessings, one is not likely to see the Rapture in the scriptures. This is more a question of ecclesiology, rather then eschatology. (2) The wrath of God directed to earth dwellers after the church is removed. Prior to going to war, it is normal protocol to remove embassy family members, prior to acts of war. It is also logical that Christ will remove his bride, the Church, prior to God wrath upon the world.

We can discern what God considers important for us at this time by the amount of space he allocates in the scriptures. Very little information is devoted to the Rapture and heaven in the Bible. However, throughout the Bible we learn of the character of God and specifically Jesus Christ as presented in the law, by the prophets, and in the New Testament. Three-quarters of the Bible is devoted to the history of the Jews. Only a third of the Bible addresses the church. The bulk of the Bible addresses Israel and the unconditional promises made to Israel. It is crucial that one understands that the Christian church is merely a gap in time, until God once again addresses Israel. The church is a parenthesis inserted between the sixty-ninth and seventieth week of chapter 9 of the Book of Daniel. Once a person understands that the church is only on earth for a season, the removal of the church through the Rapture makes logical sense. If you try to teach the Rapture without establishing that Israel and the church are mutually exclusive, you will have little success. That God directs his wrath towards the earth is a major argument in favor of the Rapture of the church. Before a country declares war it often removes embassy staff from an opposing country. A large portion of the word of God describes the judgment of God on the wicked and the escape from God's wrath by the righteous. Before God judges the world, he will remove the church to heaven. "In my father's house are many mansions; if it were not so, I would have told you, I go to prepare a place for you, and if I go and prepare a place for you, I will come again and receive you to myself; that where I am, there you may be also" (John 14:1–4).

One reason prophecy has become as popular as it has in the latter days is because more information has been revealed and people can see the end is near. For example, what were the Middle Ages in the middle of? They were in the middle of the beginning and the end of the church age. It is interesting that many of the church fathers who knew the Apostle John personally believed Christ would come in approximately two-thousand years. While we are told that no one knows the date of the Rapture and the Day of the Lord, we are given signs of the end-times and one must be biblically illiterate to not see we are in the last times.

## What Is a Paradigm Shift?

A paradigm shift is a change from one way of thinking to another. It is a revolution, a transformation, a new foundational system of thought. For example, scientific advancement is often not gradual, but is of a series of peaceful interludes punctuated by intellectually violent revolutions in which one conceptual worldview is replaced by another. The Ptolemaic system, the theory that the earth is at center of universe, shifted to the Copernican system, the theory that the sun is at the center of the universe. Johann Gutenberg's fifteenth century invention of movable type was an agent of change. Books became readily available, smaller and easier to handle and cheaper to purchase. Masses of people acquired direct access to the scriptures. Attitudes began to change as people were relieved from church domination. The introduction of the personal computer and the Internet have impacted both personal and business environments, and is a catalyst for a paradigm shift. We are shifting from a mechanistic, manufacturing, industrial society to an organic, service-based, information-centered society. The printing press helped break Christianity from the state church dominion. With increased knowledge of the scriptures, believers came to understand the true Gospel again, prophecy in regards to Israel and its restoration, and a resulting understanding of the Rapture. Unfortunately, television and entertainment are causing a new paradigm shift in reverse. People have stopped reading, and have become mere depository folders for the dissemination of mass media information. Most Christian bookstores today have a dwindling supply of sound Old Testament scholarly commentaries. Self-improvement books offering purpose-driven church growth information have become popular. They are crafted to attract materialistic people desiring more success in a materialistic world. A growing trend in today's post-modern churches is a trend towards the view where evil on earth is conquered through the good will of men. In the view of the dominionist leaders pushing this agenda, the church will bring in a paradise on earth before the return of Christ.

It would not be productive to give a talk on barbecuing pork ribs to a conference attended primarily by orthodox Jews, Arabs, or vegetarians. Similarly, it is not productive to discuss the finer points of a pre-tribulational Rapture to people who believe in Replacement Theology. In order to affect a paradigm shift or a revolution in one's thinking, an agent of change must attack the core or base beliefs in a person's way of thinking. This is why Satan attacked the Book of Revelation and convinced people to allegorize away its meaning and ignore the Old Testament's covenants in regards to Abraham and Israel. To counteract Replacement Theology, pre-tribulational believers need to study and document the distinctions between Israel and the church and show that the prophetic scattering and regathering of Israel is a sign of the coming Rapture.

# CHAPTER 6

# SIGNS OF THE RAPTURE

## What Are the Signs of the Coming of Christ?

Due to the invention of the printing press, the translation of the Bible into the language of the people, and the resulting Protestant Reformation, serious study of the scriptures by the common man resumed. One of the areas that received renewed emphasis was the study of prophecy and the Second Coming. Except for the doctrine of salvation, the Second Coming is mentioned more than any other subject in scripture. It is therefore understandable that prophetic teaching, evangelism, missions, and holy living would return. Historically, that is exactly what happened during the last three centuries—as the Bible had its greatest distribution.

Any time a person sets a specific date of Christ's return, we know they are a false prophet. According to our Lord's statement in Matthew 24:36, we cannot know "the day or the hour." However, the scriptures do provide signs of the last days. The Bible declares the following as signs of the last days before the Day of the Lord.

## What Are Doctrines of Demons?

I Timothy 4:1–5 states, "Now the Spirit expressly says that in latter times some will depart from the faith, giving heed to deceiving spirits and doctrines of demons, speaking lies in hypocrisy, having their own conscience seared with a hot iron, forbidding to marry, and commanding to abstain from foods which God created to be received with thanksgiving by those who believe and know the truth, for every creature of God is good, and nothing is to be refused if it is received with thanksgiving; for it is sanctified by the word of God and prayer." In his book *Exploring the Future*, John Phillips states, "The Bible clearly teaches that we can expect an invasion from the pit in the last days. People will be led astray by evil spirits and occult teachings. The shadows of these things are already darkening the world. Nothing but the restraining presence of God the Holy Spirit is holding back the flood-tide of this evil...It has long been know, for instance, that Adolph Hitler consulted horoscopes and that Nazi Germany had its Federal Commission for Occultism, the first time that a modern state officially recognized the existence of the occult and created a government department to oversee it" (227). Once the church is removed at the Rapture, Satan will be unrestrained in ruling the world with cosmic thinking.

Hitler was ahead of his time. He and his occult society included judges, lawyers, doctors, university professors and industrialists. They were members of a secret society of Satanists who practiced the black arts and communicated with demons. One of the secret aims of the Nazi leaders was to impose a new world religion on mankind once the war was won. In this religion the swastika would replace the cross, Hitler would be the messiah, and demons would guide the destinies of mankind. He and his fellow conspirators came close to succeeding but failed. Hitler's link to the occult is well documented by several books. Three such books are *Hitler And The Occult* by Ken Anderson, *The History of Nazi Occultism*, by Alan Baker, and *Hitler, The Occult Messiah* by Gerald Suster.

Hitler used the Roman Catholic Church to assist him in his rise to power. However, his plan was to turn on the church and to make the occult and the worship of man as the new religion. In 1 Timothy 4:1, the Apostle Paul states, "Now the Spirit speaks expressly, that in the latter times some shall depart from the faith, giving heed to seducing spirits, and doctrines of devils." The Greek word for *depart* means "to apostatize." It indicated a widespread turning away from the truth of God toward the end of the age.

God revealed to Paul that people would turn their backs on Christian faith and embrace religious teachings and secular philosophies sponsored by lying spirits. Christian ethics are being replaced through a secularization of mankind which in turn results in outright occultism. The preparation of the world for the coming Antichrist, the supreme occultist, is proceeding and was prophesied by the scriptures. Perhaps nothing has made this more possible than the publication of Charles Darwin's *The Origin of Species by Means of Natural Selection or the Preservation of Favored Race In the Struggle For Life.* This book launched the theory of evolution. Darwin's theory of the survival of the fittest underlies the political theories of both Nazism and communism. In Mein Kampf Hitler used the word evolution many times with reference to lower human types. The name Mein Kampf, is German for "Human Struggle", and refers to the survival of the stronger and the elimination of the weak.

[26]Professor Adam Sedgwick, a Cambridge geologist, saw right through Darwin's book as soon as it was published. He described it as "a dish of rank materialism cleverly cooked and served up merely to make us independent of a creator." He and Thomas Carlyle both shared the fear that if Darwin's theories were generally accepted the human race would inevitably be brutalized (Ibid., page 113). After two world wars and the global communist menace, we can see how right they were. Darwin's theory of the survival of the fittest underlies the political theories of both Nazism and communism.

In *Exploring the Future*, John Phillips has the following to say about today's culture:

> Secular humanists have a fourfold goal. The want a world religion based on science in which man is his own god, in

which the state is supreme, and in which the best of all religion is synthesized into a common faith. They want a new economic system based on socialism or communism. They want a new world order in which war and poverty are abolished and there are no social problems. They want a new race in which man takes charge of the destining and evolution of the human race, using genetic engineering to breed a new kind of man. Education must serve the interest of this new order, which means that children must be indoctrinated from the age of two through college. The mass media, courts, educational system, churches and government agencies must all be enlisted to speed up the process. They see Biblical Christianity as old-fashioned, and patriotism and traditional beliefs as obstacles that must be systematically attacked and uprooted. (231)

As the impact of the Bible and Judeo-Christian beliefs subsides in Western culture, people are becoming increasingly influenced by eastern religions, astrology, psychic phenomena, and spiritism. These things are accepted by millions without question as being of divine origin. Paul's warning that the last days of the church age will coincide with massive demonic activity in society is carelessly ignored. An increasing number of books, films, TV programs, and news articles deal with New Age and the occult. Few people realize that occultism is at the root of Mormonism, one of the world's fastest-growing religious cults. Joseph Smith and other prominent founding fathers of Mormonism had recourse to the spirit world. Joseph Smith was an occultist who used what he called a peepstone to help him translate his Bible.

A big part of the developing occult is what is known as the New Age movement, a strange blend of Indian gurus, holistic medicine, tarot cards, superstition, astrology and Yoga. The common vision is that a new age is coming, an age of peace and mass enlightenment, the age of Aquarius. No beliefs are universally held, although certain Hindu concepts of God as an impersonal, infinite consciousness and power seem to be generally accepted. Most also hold to the Hindu doctrine of reincarnation. Evolution replaces orthodox Judeo-Christian beliefs of sin and judgment.

A demonic attack upon marriage, a divinely instituted ordinance, is underway in today's culture.

In his classic *Earth's Earliest Ages,* a work on spiritism and occult religion, G. H. Pember spoke of the "strange doctrines" spiritists have and their tendency to reject marriage, "In spite of the Lord's express declaration to the contrary, Spiritualists teach…those who are not spiritual affinities being joined together are unable to agree and live in union. This they affirm to be the cause of all misfortune in wedded life…Many…declare that marriage should last only so long as the contracting parties may be disposed to live together, in short that God's first ordinance, like every other restraint, is to be snapped asunder as soon as it becomes wearisome" (316–317).

Pember wrote his book near the end of the nineteenth century when spiritism was making its first inroads into western society. In today's culture, more people are living together unmarried. Many are having children out of wedlock. Those who become married, due to social pressure, believe marriage is a contract between two people and can be broken if it appears not to benefit either party. They do not see marriage as an oath to God to take for better or for worse until death. Those professing to be Christians appear to divorce as much as non-Christians.

In concluding his summary of end-time demonic teachings, the Apostle Paul indicated that in the last days there would be an attack on eating meat. Vegetarianism seems to be common in today's new age, occult and modern thinking. Among professing Christian churches, the Seventh Day Adventists encourage vegetarianism. It is interesting that Hitler was a vegetarian who often was in a state of near-starvation while taking hallucinogenic drugs.[27] The combination of low blood sugar from not eating and drugs caused Hitler to make monumental drug-related trips into the demonic world. It is interesting that Hitler as well as the Antichrist will apparently not have much interest in marriage. It will not be surprising if the coming world ruler is a vegetarian. "Forbidding to marry, and commanding to abstain from foods which God created to be received" (I Tim. 4:3). "He shall regard neither the God of his fathers nor the desire of women, nor regard any god; for he shall magnify himself above them all" (Dan. 11:37). It is interesting the Karl Marx was against religion, marriage and private property. Paul anticipated Godless communism.

Throughout the Western world today, there is a reaction against food additives and steroids. The danger comes when people drift from a quest for more wholesome food into vegetarianism and then into eastern mysticism. It is common sense to be concerned over excess preservatives, excess sugar and over-processed food. However, many health food stores go too far by promoting eastern mysticism, vegetarianism, yoga, and the occult. Just as rat traps often use real cheese, Satan mixes some truth with his lies. In fact, most rat poison is 99 percent food. Satan has been deceiving for a long time and knows all the tricks. In fact much of what is called *New Age* is actually Babylonian. It is nothing new, but is in fact thousands of years old.

## Who Are Lovers of Self?

II Timothy 3:1–7 states:

But know this, that in the last days perilous times will come: for men will be lovers of themselves, lovers of money, boasters, proud, blasphemers, disobedient to parents, unthankful, unholy, unloving, unforgiving, slanders, without self-control, brutal, despisers of good, traitors, headstrong, haughty, lovers of pleasure rather than lovers of God, having a form of godliness but denying its power. And from such people turn away. For of this sort are those who creep into households and make captives of gullible women loaded down with sins, led away by various lusts, always learning and never able to come to the knowledge of the truth. Now as Jannes and Jambres resisted Moses, so do these also resist the truth: men of corrupt minds, disapproved concerning the faith; but they will progress no further, for their folly will be manifest to all, as theirs also was." Self-love is native to the human heart. No one has to teach a baby how to throw a temper tantrum to get his own way. However, a healthy society imposes restraints on selfishness. It recognizes the need to teach children respect for authority. A healthy society teaches children respect for parents, teacher and the law. Regardless, contemporary society has institutionalized love of self. Children are not punished and not taught respect for authority. Today's culture may be described as a generation addicted to drugs, given to self-indulgence, contemptuous of the law, and totally without regard for social values. In other words, we have become the kind of end-time generation described by Paul.

Love for self and love for money are born twins. There is an alarming propensity in America today for people to incur large amounts of debt and then fail to pay their debts and file for bankruptcy. A man's word once meant something. Today, a person's word is basically worthless.

Paul said, too, that in the last days people would be "boastful, proud, abusive" (II Tim. 3:2). Our generation has given birth to hard rock, heavy metal, and rap. Our movies promote bad language and immoral life styles. Today's music lyrics and movies glorify sin, rebellion, and self-promotion. The words boastful, proud, abusive sum up much of the culture today. Today's society glorifies sex, hate, and drugs and attacks patriotism, decency, and moral purity. We are truly in the last days.

Next, Paul said that in the end-times people will be "disobedient to parents, unthankful" (II Tim. 3:2). The apostle foresaw an attack on the family unit and home life in the last days. Today there is a soaring divorce rate, which has undermined the stability of the home and the authority of parents. Nearly half the marriages in this country end in divorce. Most states have no-fault divorce laws, which encourage throw-away marriages. More and more people of all ages are living together and having children or women are living alone and having children from different men.

Vice saps a nation's moral fiber, promotes apathy, weakens character, and destroys the will to resist. The enormous drug traffic in the United States and the western world and the wholesale promotion of sexual excess and perversion are all parts of a cleverly orchestrated plot to produce a decadent society, to demoralize youth, and to lure people into compromising situations so they can become enslaved by their passions and controlled by Satan.

Paul also wrote that people would be "without natural affection, trucebreakers" (II Tim. 3:2). Paul foresaw a time when people would be callous and without either hear or principle. The atrocities committed by the Nazis and the communists illustrates the utter heartlessness of their regimes. In the last days people will become heartless towards destroying babies, old people and anyone who stands in their way of pleasure or self-interest. Currently, atrocities and genocide are committed in many parts of the world where one group decides to go on a rampage of ethnic or religious cleansing.

Some of the evil things we see in our society today can be associated with the fact that men lack self-control of their passions. Society has surrendered to men of unprincipled, unbridled lust. Society is becoming increasingly tolerant of perversion as a lifestyle. Homosexuals are not only condoned but portrayed as merely an alternate lifestyle. Homosexuals do not reproduce—they recruit. Homosexuals are becoming more aggressive in their assertion of projecting their decadent immorality upon mainstream culture.

Cable TV networks bring foul language, nudity, and every form of sex into thousands of American homes. American courts make it almost impossible to restrain all types of perversion and obscenity into the lives of families and children.

## Who Are Scoffers?

"Knowing this first: scoffers will come in the last days, walking according to their own lusts, and saying, 'Where is the promise of his coming? For since the fathers fell asleep, all things continue as they were from the beginning of creation.' For this they willfully forget: that by the word of God the heavens were of old, and the earth standing out of water and in the water, by which the world that then existed perished, being flooded with water. But the heavens and the earth which now exist are kept in store by the same word, reserved for fire until the day of judgment and perdition of ungodly men" (II Pet. 3:3–7).

Until modern times, a paradigm known as didactic logic was founded upon absolute value. While the Greeks were not without fault, they did believe in the view of black and white and pre-set rights and wrongs. Today, the humanistic paradigm is known as dialectic and is built upon the view that feelings and human relationships must determine what is right and wrong. A rational person is one who will compromise for the common good.

Classical philosophy from the time of the Greeks was based upon the fact two contradictory statements could not both be true. The Biblical paradigm is based upon the thesis God said this or God said that. It requires faith, obedience, accountability, and responsibility under a higher authority.

Immanuel Kant, a German philosopher who lived from 1724 to 1804m formulated an alternative way of thinking which now holds sway in the modern world. Kant found no personal basis for accepting absolutes. Kant believed that no one could know something without experience. Another German philosopher named

Hegel took the ideas of Kant and began to press them forward. He believed that one idea (thesis) working against another fact (antithesis) would produce a new fact (synthesis). This philosophy was the basis of Darwin's theory of evolution. It was the basis of Sigmund Freud's justification of pleasure seeking, the communistic ideas of Karl Marx, and the fascism of Adolph Hitler.[28] The end result is an openly immoral lifestyle portrayed by entertainment celebrities such as Hugh Heffner and Howard Stern. These people see gross immorality as nothing more than choice diversification. Ethnic cleansing by Stalin and Hitler were merely the natural selection of superior life forms.

Through the Middle Ages, belief in a Creator God was the normal course of reasoning among people in Judeo-Christian cultures. However, with the advent of the industrial revolution, the power of the monarchs and the state-church subsided and the emerging middle class gained power. Religiously, Britain contrasted sharply with continental Europe. Britain was a Protestant country, having divorced itself from Catholicism in the early sixteenth century. Prior to the eighteenth century, attacks on religion and the church were dangerous. By the late eighteenth century, seeds of discontent within the British intellectual community were beginning to take root. Many secular socialists concluded that the Bible was the greatest single obstacle to the achievement of socialistic aims. They decided the best way to challenge the ruling class was to generate disbelief in the Bible and change public opinion.

One organization that was established to challenge authority and undermine the Bible was the Lunar Society. The founder of the Lunar Society was a man named Erasmus Darwin (1731–1802), who was also the grandfather of Charles Darwin. Erasmus Darwin's contribution to the emerging view of evolution was a two-volume work written in 1794–96 called *The Zoonomia*. Although Charles Darwin was born seven years after his grandfather died, the ideas of Erasmus Darwin deeply influenced his life. *Zoonomia* expressed the essence of the theory that his grandson announced to the world fifty years later. English Physician Erasmas Darwin speculated on evolution, but did not develop his theories. However, his grandson, Charles Darwin, expanded his laws of organic life, and the rest is history. The Western world has been totally influenced by the idea that man evolved by accident, rather than being created by a divine creator. Another challenge to the biblical view of creation was put forward by James Hutton (1726–1797). Hutton proposed that the earth had been molded not by sudden violent events, but by a slow and gradual process—the same processes that can be observed in the world today. This theory became known as "uniformitarianism." Today, Hutton's proposal is considered a turning point in history. It was geologists more than biologists who paved the way for evolutionary theory.

Today, children in American schools are taught how they are animals, that there is no God, that there should be no restraint in seeking pleasure and there is no right or wrong. The evolutionary theory is taught as fact. This theory says that the universe was made by a random explosion and that man is an accident with no purpose.

The United States was founded on the Biblical scheme of thinking. The United States Supreme court made a long line of rulings such as Vidal v. Girard's Executors in 1844. This ruling said, "Such a case is not to be presumed to exist in a Christian country." The Declaration of Independence states that all men are created with certain unalienable rights from God. Fisher Ames who wrote the First Amendment stated that the Bible should always remain the principle text book in America's classrooms.[29] John Jay, the original Chief Justice of the United States Supreme Court, said it is the duty of all wise, free, and virtuous governments to help and encourage virtue and religion. Robert Morris, Pennsylvania Governor, who penned the United States Constitution, advocated that "education should teach the precepts of religion and the duties of man towards God" (David Barton, "The Myth of Separation" p.23).

Prior to 1830, few schools in America were not based upon the Bible as their main text book. In 1830, a humanist named Horace Mann began an attack of schools in America and was determined to get the Bible out of education. Although Hutton had a Quaker background, he rejected the belief in a literal worldwide flood. He argued that the earth's history could best be explained by examining the earth's layers rather than accepting the Bible. This was just as Peter predicted, "Scoffers will come in the last days, walking according to their own lusts, saying, 'Where is the promise of his coming?' For since the fathers fell asleep, all things continue as they were from the beginning of creation" (II Pet. 3:3).

Charles Lyell (1797–1875), who is remembered for his significant contributions to the development of uniformitarianism geology, was born the year James Hutton died. He was a lawyer, a politician, an amateur geologist, and the author of *The Principles of Geology*. In 1826, at the age of 29 and with no formal science background, he was elected a fellow of the Royal Society, an elitist institution founded by the Lunar Society. Charles Lyell believed that if the Bible was considered the truth, there was no way of peacefully challenging the monarchy in Britain, for sovereignty was supposed to descend from God to the King; but if the Bible could be shown to be inaccurate, particularly in respect to the flood, the whole foundation on which the monarchy based its power would be shattered. Lyell was firmly convinced that his book "Principles of Geology" had shaken the faith in the Deluge far more efficiently by never having said a word against the Bible directly.

Charles Darwin was keenly influenced by *Principles of Geology* and published his book *On the Origin of Species* in 1859. Charles Darwin (1809–1882) stands in most people's minds as the father of evolution. Indeed, the terms Darwinism and evolution have become relatively synonymous.

Much of the changes in schools was made possible by the theory of evolution being strongly accepted after the writings of Charles

Darwin. Since Darwin popularized that theory in 1859, the idea infected other areas of men's thoughts including law, morals, theology, and education. John Dewey is recognized as the Father of modern education. Dewey developed ideas of evolutionary democracy, education, and law. His ideas were based on the premise that nothing is constant. He stated change is for the better, without regard to right or wrong (positivism). He had no absolute standards, and instead based his reality on a relative perception based on human desire. Relativism denies absolutes. Relativism is a destructive ideology that sheers man away from truth a little at a time. The German writer, Engels, wrote that if you could remove a people from their roots, they could be easily swayed to your point of view.

Humanism denies the Salvation of God and replaces it with salvation by men. John Dewey helped popularize the teaching of evolution since the idea of constant change reinforced his perceived foolishness of God and the Bible. Dewey believed in neither God nor the bible. Since man evolved from slime, there could have been no fall of man from the perfection of Adam. With no fall of man, there would be no need for salvation. Thus, evolution strikes at the root of Christian faith and accountability to God. Evolution make the whole of scripture meaningless. And the scripture makes evolution meaningless.

John Dewey declared it was wrong to believe in something that cannot change. He explained that the Constitution as it had been interpreted was a stumbling block. John Dewey mocked the beliefs of the founders. Progressive humanists such as Dewey and Langdell mocked and ridiculed those in education who believed in absolutes and traditional values.

Roscoe Pound (1870–1964) strengthened the new philosophy of positivism that had been birthed by Langdell at Harvard. Pound, as a college professor at four different law schools and as Dean of Harvard and the University of Nebraska, helped to make positivism the new way of thinking if one wanted to graduate. Humanists pushed until professors were able to teach evolution as fact and ridiculed anyone who disagreed. Moral relativists who teach us to be tolerant, nonjudgmental, and open-minded rarely take it to people who disagree. Their tolerance is one way. Today, almost every university student believes that truth is relative.[30] However, if truth cannot be known, then the concept of moral truth becomes incoherent. Every debate ends with the barroom question, "says who?" Instead of morality constraining pleasures, pleasure-seeking defines today's morality. Those who believe in relative morality argue that we should respect another's point of view. However, if we have a point of view that is opposed to a lack of absolutes, we are considered immoral and judgmental. Contemporary relativists have become sociopaths with no conscience. Liberals preach that fundamental respect for others is morality of the highest order. However, they often turn legislation to enforce their neutral, unbiased and tolerant viewpoint. This includes making it illegal to talk about God as creator or stating certain behavior is immoral.

At the time of the Scopes Monkey Trial in 1925, most public schools taught the divine creation theory. According to Phillip Johnson, in his book *Darwin on Trial,* the atheist lawyer Clarence Darrow declared, "It is bigotry to only teach one view of origins" (173). The evolutionists lost and it remained illegal to teach evolution in many states until the 1960's. Today times have changed and evolution is now universally taught in schools as fact and it is presumed to be illegal to teach creation science in public schools.

John Dewey and other humanists have been successful in introducing strong ideas about accepting multi-values with the denial of absolute values. Standard educational materials in the United States and Europe now teach that students need to be raised up so they can be better citizens of the new world economic order. Country, family, and God are no longer the goals to be achieved but are instead seen as causes of bigotry, narrow-mindedness, prejudice, and intolerance.

In 1962, the United States Supreme Court removed the long-standing tradition of school prayer in public schools through their ruling in the case Engel v. Vitale. This was another example of the God-given rights declared in the first amendment being used by an evolutionary humanist court to legislate their relativist dialectic intolerance in the name of tolerance.

David Barton, in his book *The Myth of Separation*, makes the following observations:

> There now have been two distinctly differing philosophies under which the Constitution has been interpreted: first, the philosophy of natural and Divine law (introduced by the Founders), and second, the philosophy of legal relativism and positivism (introduced by contemporary Courts)... Following the judicial rejection of natural law and the embracing of relativism, the United States has become number one in the western world in violent crime, divorce, and illegal drugs and teenage pregnancies; and number one in the industrial world in illiteracy. By removing Divine law, the Court removed the source of our previous national stability. (145)

John Dewey and other humanists were adamantly opposed to anything that would support the Christian faith in children. They introduced strong ideas about accepting multiple values that oppose absolute values. John Dewey was instrumental in the founding of the ACLU and what became the National Education Association. In his book *Trial and Error*, George Grant describes how the ACLU's founder and member of the Communist Party Roger Baldwin summed up his expectations, "We want to look like patriots in everything we do. We want to talk about the Constitution and what our forefathers wanted, and show that we are really folks that stand for the spirit of our institutions" (26). Laws are being changed to accommodate conformity and one-worldliness without regard for what is right or wrong. Changes are being made regarding to what extent government is involved in our lives. Changes are being made to restrict our free society and to make us into a socialist one-world state. This is why multi-culturalism is the buzzword. It is to prepare us for the one-world system.

In II Peter 3:3, the Apostle Peter anticipated that scoffers would come in the last day, walking according to their own lusts, and saying, "Where is the promise of his coming?" Evolution is a bankrupt belief system that is morally and intellectually bankrupt.

Unbelief is a state of the soul and is sin. The Apostle Paul states in chapter 1 of Romans that creation clearly reveals God and that man is without excuse for disregarding the very existence of God. Romans 1:18 states, "For the wrath of God is revealed from heaven against all ungodliness and unrighteousness of men, who hold the truth in un-righteousness." There is a continuous revelation of the wrath of God in nature, but one must have ears that hear and eyes that see.

If there is no God, life has no purpose. Life is meaningless, absurd, and without ultimate significance. If there is no God, there is neither right nor wrong. There is no accountability. Adolph Hitler would be correct in killing millions of people whom he construed to be inferior. However, the truth is man does have a conscience and only sociopaths operate without a conscience. Because there is a God, life can have purpose, meaning, and significance.

In 1931, the publication of Edwin Hubble's *Law of Red Shifts*, proved that the universe is, indeed expanding. Following this publication, Albert Einstein accepted its professed "necessity for a beginning" and stated he had made the greatest mistake of his life to deny that the universe had a beginning. Einstein was forced to accept "the presence of a superior reasoning power,"[31] but did not accept the doctrine of a personal God with accountability.

Evolution is a belief system which believes in a process of self-transformation with no outside agency of any kind. According to this paradigm, simple organisms randomly developed into complex organisms. However, we have discovered that single-celled organisms are not simple. They are structurally complex and require complex genetic sequencing called DNA. If life evolved over billions of years, we should be able to identify living things in the process of change. However, intermediary fossils are glaringly absent. Also, the entire evolutionary paradigm collapses without the required billions of years of random selection. Einstein stated that thousands of experiments cannot prove a theory, but one experiment can disprove a theory. The truth is that many facts have been discovered that show the universe is not billions of years old and that complex design reveals a designer. The Apostle Paul was right when he declared man can find God in nature if he has eyes. Peter was right that when he warned that scoffers would come in the last days.

A case for man as the creator has been fabricated from an analogy found in quantum mechanics. Quantum particles have an associated wave. This wave represents the probability of finding the particle at a particular point in space. Before the particle is detected there is no specific knowledge of its location—only a probability of where it might be. In this sense, the act of observation is said by some to give reality to the particle. What is true for a quantum particle, they suggest, may be true for the universe. However, this is in truth an erroneous leap of faith. The observer does not give "reality" to the particle, but rather the observer chooses what aspect of reality he wishes to discern, either position or momentum. This only shows man's limits. In truth the observer is irrelevant not God.

Some incorrectly make the assumption that Einstein's general relativity theory stated that everything is relative and therefore, there are no longer any absolutes. This is not correct. The general relativity theory states that the relationship between time and space is influenced by matter and its motion. It is important to remember that energy cannot be destroyed. Only its form is changed. Something outside time and space had to create matter.

A man caught speeding by a radar gun cannot use quantum physics as a defense in court. He would probably find little sympathy with a judge if he stated that internal components in the atoms of his automobile, such as electrons, do not appear to follow meaningful, well-defined trajectories. Since the electrons in his car are random, truth is relative and he should be able to drive as fast as he wants. Just as a human judge would not accept Einstein's theory of relativity or quantum physics as a defense against law breaking, so our creator will not allow these as a defense on Judgment Day.

II Thessalonians 2:3 states, "Let no one deceive you by any means: for that Day will not come unless the falling away (apostasy) comes first, and the man of sin is revealed, the son of perdition, who opposes and exalts himself above all that is called God or that is worshiped, so that he sits as God in the temple of God, showing himself that he is God."

Apostasy, of course, has existed in some measure as long as the church. However, the mushrooming, widespread incidence of the apostasy among those who claim to be Christians is a specific sign of the last days just prior to the Rapture and going into the Tribulation. In Matthew 24, Christ mentions that one of the signs of his coming would be religious deception by professing Christian leaders. The words, Christs, prophets, elect signs, and wonders indicate that the deception would be among professing Christians. "Many will come in my name, saying, "I am the Christ, and will deceive many...For false Christs and false prophets will arise and show great signs and wonders, so as to deceive, if possible, even the elect" (Matt. 24:5 and 23).

What is a departure from which marks one as an apostate? As defined by Paul, the Gospel declares the death, burial, and resurrection of Christ according to the scriptures. "For I delivered to you first of all that which I also received: that Christ died for our sins according to the Scriptures, and that He was buried, and that He rose again the third day according to the Scriptures" (I Cor. 15:3–4). The entire word of God is foundation to the faith or the Gospel.

If you had lived in Europe prior to about 1890, or in the United States before about 1935, you would not have had to spend much time, in practice, thinking about your presuppositions. Prior to this period, most people accepted that there were absolutes. One could tell someone to "be a good girl" and while they may not follow the advise, they understood what you meant. To say the same thing to a modern girl today would be to make a nonsense statement. The blank look you might receive would not mean that your standards had been rejected, but that your message was meaningless.

The rejection of absolutes began in Germany and spread outward. They affected the main continent of Europe first, then moved on to England, and then across the Atlantic to America. Secondly, it spread through society, from the real intellectual and the more educated, down to the society in general. Thirdly, it started with philosophers, spread to scientists, then eventually to theologians.

Society has felt the brunt of a shift from absolutes to a mindset of relative morality. Drug addiction, children out of marriage, and homosexuality are all an expression of an obliteration of the distinction between right and wrong.

In the entertainment industry, movies and television are usually divided into two classes: good and bad. The term "good" means "technically good" and does not refer to morals. The good pictures are the serious ones, the artistic ones. The "bad" are simply escapist, romantic, pictures only viewed for entertainment. If we examine them, however, we will notice that the "good" pictures are actually the worst pictures. They are created by men propagating the modern philosophy of Godlessness and meaninglessness. The products they produce are tools for teaching their beliefs.

The Reformers had to battle the Catholic Church in regards to what was theologically right and wrong. However, modern theologians do not accept the concept of right and wrong. They believe that man's knowledge of God is evolving and depends on the experience of the individual. Christian experience replaces the authority of scripture, creeds and the church. Theological liberalism originated in Germany.

Engels wrote that if you could remove a people from their roots, they could be easily swayed to your point of view.[32] Since man was considered to have evolved from the slime, there could have been no fall of man from the perfection of Adam. With no fall of man, there would be no need for salvation. Thus, evolution undermined the root of Christian faith. Evolution and God's word are mutually exclusive. Evolution makes the whole of scripture meaningless.

Liberal theologians have concerned themselves with building the kingdom of God and promoting the applied liberalism known as the social gospel. This emphasized the need to modify the corrupt society that in turn was corrupting man. Modernists talked of the kingdom where men would live as brothers in a spirit of cooperation, love and, justice. It was believed the church must turn from saving individual sinners and focus of the saving of collective society. Achieving a better life on earth replaced the concern for afterlife, and it was expected that Christ and Christian values would conquer the world. Modernists believe progress can be made in the advancement of political democracy, the movement toward world peace, and the end of racial discrimination. Many believe we need to turn to a one-world government and one uniform church embracing all of man's beliefs.

The largest Christian movement of the twenty-first century is clearly the seeker-friendly, purpose-driven explosion of churches. Many of the books sold today in Christian bookstores are fluffy books dealing in self-improvement or motivational books for living a more abundant life while in the flesh. The self-improvement gurus that write the books and offer the purpose-driven church growth movement seminars have crafted them to attract materialistic people who want more success in life.

Most of those attracted by these authors and the seeker-friendly, purpose-driven churches share a worldview where evil on earth is conquered through the good will of men. In the view of the dominionist leaders, pushing the church's agenda the will bring in a paradise on earth before the return of Christ. They teach or imply that the church will make the world a paradise and only after that happens will Jesus come.

This seeker friendly, purpose-driven church movement is founded upon world corporation marketing strategies and pop psychology concepts that are known to be successful to reach large numbers of people. The movement has become a clearinghouse for those who believe in the basic goodness of man, for those who think all paths lead to God, for those who hold a theology that does not take the prophetic scriptures in any real literal sense, for those who do not know the scriptures, for those who pick and choose words of scripture out of context to make them say what they want them to say, and for those who think sins of the flesh are really just sickness and addictions.

In many ways, seeker-friendly churches are a social replacement for those who attend or once attended Catholic and liberal mainline denominational churches. Like the liberal mainline churches, the seeker-oriented teaching lacks depth on Sunday, so people out of mainline churches feel very comfortable.

These churches teach nothing they think is negative, because they want the church to be a place where the unsaved seeker is comfortable and not threatened. There are no altar calls, soul-searchings, or prayers that anyone might consider a threat. Hell, sin, and salvation are not discussed at the main Sunday service.

However, the scriptures do not teach that the world will be Christianized before Jesus returns. It teaches that the world is heading for destruction and that Jesus will physically come back. Modern theology is replacing the literal rule of Jesus with the church and the literal role of Israel with the church. The is replacement theology, which takes Christ and Israel out of prophecy. They rob the prophets of their prophecies. Many church leaders have no clue we are in the end-times, because they believe all prophecy was fulfilled in AD 70 and the church on earth has replaced Israel.

Many modern churches do not teach how mankind is sinful and can only be changed by a rebirth in Christ. Many modern churches have become sanctuaries for unbelievers and biblically illiterate baby Christians. The Christian church is being infiltrated from within by new age philosophers and humanistic psychologists. This self-esteem Christianity encourages all sorts of eastern concepts such as meditations and reincarnation.

Revelation states that the last period of church history will be described as a period of compromise and lack of moral integrity. The last days of the church will be a period where one cannot tell believers from unbelievers. "I know your works, that you are neither cold nor hot. I could wish you were cold or hot. So then, because you are lukewarm, and neither cold nor hot, I will spew you out of My mouth. Because you say, 'I am rich, have become wealthy, and have need of nothing and do not know that you are wretched, miser-able, poor, blind, and naked'" (Revelation 3:15–17). The Christian Church in the West has never had so much material wealth, but at the same time it has never been so spiritually poor, blind, and naked. We are truly in the last days. Evolution has replaced Christianity as the state religion. Today, men scoff at the Bible and consider it out-of-date and irrelevant. We are in the last days, and the Day of the Lord is about to hit this world as a thief in the night.

## Is the Increase in Knowledge a Sign?

But thou, O Daniel, shut up the words, and seal the book, even to the time of the end: many shall run to and fro, and knowledge shall be increased. (Dan. 12:4)

The book of Daniel was not to be fully understood until "the time of the end." At the time of the end, many would run to and fro through the scriptures, comparing text with text, and understand these prophecies. We have reached that time.

During the first two centuries (AD), believers understood that Christ would come and rule for a thousand years. In the third century, Constantine merged the church and the state and made Christianity the state religion. It became unpopular to envision the need for Christ to come and displace man's rule with the Kingdom of God. Origen started a slippery slope changing the interpretation of scriptures from literal to vague allegories and a spiritualization decided upon by the expositor. This had the dangerous result of making scriptures arbitrary and capricious. Augustine used this method and created a new concept called replacement theology. This dogma maintained that Israel has lost her blessings and was replaced by the church. The Jewish people had no further purpose or plan in God's plan.

Augustine replacement theology became official doctrine of the Roman Catholic Church. When the Reformation came, Augustine's Amillennialism became the dominant position by the Reformed Church. While there were always believers who remained premillennial, they were severely persecuted.

It was not until the nineteenth century that Premillennialism came back strong. During the early twentieth century, the Scofield Bible became a standard for conservative bible scholars. However, in the last day, interest in prophecy, except for the serious student, has waned. Today, most Bible bookstores carry fluffy books dealing with self and popular psychology, rather than serious commentaries on the Bible.

While the vast majority of the world will be without God and without hope when Jesus returns, the Bible says that many people will have their eyes opened and prepare themselves. "Many shall be purified, and made white, and tried; but the wicked shall do wickedly: and none of the wicked shall understand; but the wise shall understand" (Dan. 12:10).

The primary application of "knowledge increased" (Dan. 12:4) is in reference to people understanding the prophecies of the book of Daniel. However, many Bible scholars believe that this prophecy also applies to an increasing knowledge of science, medicine, travel, and technology.

We are living in "The Information Age," making this sign seem even more obvious. Even the most skeptical mind must admit that knowledge is exploding in all directions. It is said that 80 percent of the world's total secular knowledge has been brought forth in the last decade and that 90 percent of all the scientists who have ever lived are alive today. The speed of travel has gone from that of the horse and buggy to space ships and jet airplanes within the last hundred years. Information can now be dispersed on the Internet at the speed of light, making television and newspaper news somewhat obsolete. One can be almost anywhere in the world and have access to the internet. One can Google such words as "end-times," "Rapture" and "Tribulation" and find out amazing details about end-time prophecy. Twentieth century technology has increased exponentially. We used to be in awe of how much information could fit on a CD Rom disk. Now a DVD can hold up to four times as much volume. Just as Daniel was told, at the "time of the end, knowledge shall be increased."

# CHAPTER 7

# THE IMMANENCY OF THE RAPTURE

## Is the Rapture Imminent?

We do not find the word "imminent" in scripture. The Greek word on which the theological term is built is *engus*, which means "near," but is most generally translated as "at hand." James states, "Therefore, be patient, brethren, until the coming of the Lord…for the coming of the Lord is at hand (engiken)…Behold, the Judge is standing at the door! (James 5:7,9) The idea seems to be that he has taken a position nearby and could enter at any moment (Phil. 2:30; Mark 1:15; Luke 10:9,11). It is only necessary for him to open the door and make his appearance. It may happen in a few minutes (Matt. 26:45–47) or in a few thousand years (1 Peter 4:7 & II Peter 8–14). The latter case definitely included predicted intervening events; thus the argument for no intervening events cannot be made strictly by word study alone. For example, Zephaniah 1:7 & 14 states, "For the day of the Lord is at hand…The great day of the Lord is near; It is near and hastens quickly." This statement was made by Zephaniah prior to the First Advent. What Zephaniah is saying is that the final judgment of the world is certain and from God's perspective it is near. God is not in a time zone, and from the perspective of eternity, judgment of the world is near. The failure to recognize that from man's perspective immanency does not necessarily mean "soon," has caused much confusion. To teach that Jesus regarded the Second

Coming as immediately at hand would be to represent him as in error, since almost two thousand years have already elapsed since that time.

The Bible does not teach the imminence of Christ's return without markers or signs, but merely states that Christ will come again, and soon. We are to watch and be ready for his return. This seems to imply nearness, but in reality is an exhortation of mental priority and a proper orientation or focus upon Christ.

Many pretribulational scholars have taken one definition of the word *engus,* or the phrase "at hand," and have attempted to make the word a statement of doctrine. They define "at hand" as not a positive affirmation that the person or thing will immediately appear, but only that no known or predicted event must intervene. They use one possible lexical meaning of a word as its only meaning. They do not differentiate between a word and a term.

A term is a word used in a specific context. It therefore has only one meaning, whereas the same word may have several. The word "trunk" may mean the stem of a tree, a box, or the nose of an elephant. An exegetical error can occur when one tries to prove their point from word studies alone. The error arises when the meaning of a word in one context is illegitimately transferred in totality or is argued that one use of a word is the only acceptable use of a word. In other words, it is an error to establish a doctrine from one definition of a word. The Rapture of the church was imminent in the first century if by "imminent" one means certain or a proper object of focus. However, the Rapture was not imminent in the first century if by definition one means near.

Simply because Jesus told Peter that is was none of his business if John should remain until he returns, many people of that day jumped to the conclusion that the Lord would return before John died. He was only exhorting Peter that he was to get his immature, childish eyes off others and concentrate on his own relationship with

Christ. Some Thessalonians were wont to wait for the Lord, forsaking any productivity, being content only to be a leech, and to wait for the Lord's return. Thus, Paul was admonished that if a man does not work, he should not eat.

The weakness in the immanency argument is the material fact that Israel had to be in the land before the Lord could come again. The times of the Gentiles had to be fulfilled first. Knowing this, and also knowing that Israel was not a nation again until the Balfour Agreement and her later settlement in 1948, the doctrine of imminence (if understood as near) was invalidated as soon as the dispersion of Israel occurred in AD 70 It remains, then, that the doctrine of the imminent return of Christ was invalid for the space of about 1900 years. Israel had to be back in the land in order for the Lord to execute his second coming, as well as other significant preceding events.

This assertion is upheld by the prophecy of Ezekiel, in the Old Testament, concerning one of these events where it is told that an alliance of Islamic powers along with Russia come against the Israeli people and upon the mountains of Israel in the later years.[33] This has not yet happened. In order for this to be fulfilled, Israel must be resurrected from the dead as a nation and restored to her previous location—the land of Israel, and the city of Jerusalem. Israel is the only nation in history to come back from the dead, and therefore is testimony to the credibility of the prophetic scriptures, and the existence of God. Jerusalem, however, is still trodden of the Gentiles.

The supporting scripture for the restoration of Israel is in chapters thirty-six and thirty-seven of Ezekiel. This includes the restoration of Israel, the valley of the dry bones coming to life, and the binding of the two sticks to make Israel one entity. The attack against Israel follows this, and so we are to watch for an amalgamation of nations to come against the tiny nation of Israel.

## What Does Maranatha Mean?

*Maranatha* was a greeting used by first century Christians. It is an Aramaic expression made up of three Aramaic words: *mar*, which means "Lord," *ana*, which means "our," and *tha*, which means "come." When one puts it together, *Maranatha* means "Our Lord, come." *Maranatha* is used once in the Bible by Paul as part of a curse. In I Corinthians 16:22, Paul said, "If any man love not the Lord Jesus Christ, let him be Anathema. Maranatha." The word *anathema* means "banned," so Paul was saying to let him be banned from our Lord's coming. When believers in the early church would make this statement, they were actually petitioning the Lord to come. Just as Abraham sought a New Jerusalem, we as Christians are to look for the coming of Christ to take us to heaven. In the Lord's prayer, Christ told us to pray, "thy kingdom come." We are to look for his appearance with confident hope and assurance. When a young woman's fiancée goes off to war, that woman is expected to wait faithfully for her betrothed. She is expected to look forward to her lover's safe return. We as Christians are to wait faithfully for the anticipated arrival of our bridegroom. Now that prophecy has been fulfilled in these last days we can truly say, "Our Lord, come."

## Is The Rapture Soon?

Many prophecy experts present a dichotomy when it comes to the immanency of the Rapture. They use two mutually exclusive or contradictory statements. They say the Rapture has always been imminent, but we are in the "end-time." You cannot have it both ways. Either the Rapture has always been imminent or we are in the "end-time." Their dilemma comes from being too stiff or wooden in the reading of scriptures that emphasize different perspectives of God's truth. The expression "shortly come to pass," found in Revelation 1:1, translates from a Greek expression which carried the idea of "in" or "with" speed. However, words can take on special meaning, depending upon the immediate context or the type of literature. In context, dealing with prophecy, the time factor becomes quite elastic. Idioms such as "shortly" or "at hand" can be used to convey certainty of God's plan or to highlight that the event described is the next major event on God's prophetic horizon. In addition, if Revelation 2 and 3 provide a historical preview of church history, then some events, such as the persecution of the church, took place soon, but other things, such as the Second Coming, would take longer.

Jon Courson, in his book *Bible Commentary Revelation, Volume 1*, points out:

> The word "shortly" is "en tachei," meaning "must come to pass with rapidity." It is the same Greek word from which we get the word "tachometer"—the instrument used to determine the speed of an engine. Thus, the Lord is telling us in this verse that when end-time events begin to happen, they will increase their RPMs, and happen with greater rapidity. (2)

Once end-time events begin to happen, an increase in speed and severity occurs. We know this from the description of the seven seals, trumpets, and bowl judgments. John Courson uses the example of the road from Medford, Oregon to San Diego, California. Going south on I-5 he does not see one road sign that says San Diego until he passes Chico. The further south he gets the more frequent the signs. Finally, he sees the sign, "Welcome to San Diego."

## Preterism

Preterism is the eschatological teaching that all bible prophecy is history. Most of it took place in AD 70 with the destruction of Jerusalem by the Romans. The Tribulation was the persecution of the saints and Nero was the Antichrist. At the heart of the doctrine is that prophecy was declared and destines to be fulfilled within the generation of Christ's earthly ministry. All references in the Bible to the "last days" refer to the last days of Israel, which means that today she has no more relevance than the Canary Islands. The "New Jerusalem" is the church now and forever. It will Christianize the world.

Preterism was not taken seriously until the seventeenth century, since the Book of Revelation was written in approximately AD 95, after the destruction of the temple in AD 70. It should not be taken seriously now. Preterism is just another teaching that is filled with doctrinal error. It takes our eyes off our "blessed hope"—the glorious return of our Lord. Satan is hardly bound at this time, but we can be sure he will be when Christ returns to rule.

## Pending Rapture

The expressions "awaiting eagerly" and "eagerly wait" in I Corinthians 1:7 and Philippians 3:20 are translations of the Greek word *apekdechomai*, meaning to expect, to look for, or to wait for. It is used as a suitable expression for Christian hope. This is not in the sense of being anxious, but with faith being those that are focused and with anticipation and confidence.

The *Scofield Reference Bible* has an excellent footnote to Matthew 4:17, "From that time Jesus began to preach, and to say, Repent; for the kingdom of heaven is at hand." The Bible expression "at hand" is never a positive affirmation that the person or thing said to be at hand will immediately appear, but only that that person or thing has the quality or immanency. When Christ appeared to the Jewish people, the next thing, in the order of revelation as they understood it, should have been the setting up of the Davidic kingdom. Yet God had predicted the rejection and crucifixion of the King.[34] The long period of the mystery-form of the kingdom, the worldwide preaching of the cross, and the out-calling of the church was as yet locked up in the secret counsels of God (Mt. 13:11,17; Eph. 3:3–12).

One would be correct in saying the next major event in the prophetic calendar is the Rapture of the church. It would be correct to say that we are to look forward in anticipation to the coming of the Lord. However, it is an incorrect statement to say that there are no prerequisites or that there are no end-time signs and that the Rapture could have come at any moment in the church age. While it may be said that the return of Christ may be near, based upon the fulfillment of signs, it would be incorrect to say that has always been the case.

Even if the Rapture is near, it may not necessarily happen at any moment. Just as Christ died on the Passover, it appears the Rapture and the Day of the Lord will occur on the Feast of Trumpets. The Rapture will apply to the church and the Day of the Lord will apply to those Jews on earth that are not part of the church and go through the seven-year Tribulation. Confusion on this point has caused skeptics to become dull to anything prophetic. As a result, most people today are ignorant of the fact several major prophetic events have been silently fulfilled, without notice. This is because many people have become dulled by misinformation and false date setting by false prophets."

## Why Is There a Gap Between the Spring and Fall Feasts of the Lord?

The first four Feasts of the Lord are celebrated in the spring. These feasts were literally fulfilled by four prophetic events. The first four major events on the prophetic calendar are the death, burial, resurrection of Christ, and the outpouring of the Holy Spirit to the church. Students of prophecy will recognize how these events historically fulfilled the feasts of the spring months—Passover, Unleavened Bread, Firstfruits, and Pentecost—listed in the same order in Leviticus 23. The Hebrew word *moedim*, translated as "feasts," means appointed times. These appointed times in the Jewish calendar were given to the children of Israel from God, through the prophet Moses. The idea is that the sequence and timing of each of these feasts have been carefully orchestrated by God himself. The first "Feast of the Lord" is Passover. It is the foundational feast. The six Feasts that follow are built upon it. Passover occurs in the spring of the year, on the fourteenth day of the Hebrew month, Nisan (March/April). The first four feasts representing the death, burial, resurrection, and the outpouring of the Holy Spirit upon the church, occur during the spring.

There is a four-month gap and then the last three feasts occur in the fall during the month of Tishri (September/October). These feasts are Rosh Hashanah, (Rapture/Day of the Lord), Yom Kippur (Israel Repents/Second Advent) and Tabernacles (Millennial Kingdom).

## Are There Any Conditions Precedent to the Rapture?

In his book *The Rapture Question*, John Walvoord makes the following statement, "The hope of the return of Christ to take the saints to heaven is presented in John 14 as an imminent hope. There is no teaching of any intervening event. The prospect of being taken to heaven at the coming of Christ is not qualified by description of any signs or prerequisite events" (73). This is not a totally correct statement. There are many signs with regards to the end of the church age. The primary sign is the Diaspora and gathering of the nation Israel.

In Matthew 24:2, Jesus said, "…Assuredly, I say to you, not one stone shall be left here upon another, that shall not be thrown down." Jesus refers to the destruction of the temple and the Diaspora in AD 70 and then he speaks of Israel being back in the land in the last days. This is a gap of almost two-thousand years, which is a condition precedent to the Rapture. Christ refers us to chapter

9 of Daniel for the details. It is true that the seventieth week of Daniel, which is also the seven years of Tribulation, comes after the Rapture. However, this period is initiated by the coming Antichrist brokering a peace treaty with Israel. Since this is the first event in the Tribulation, we can conclude that Israel must be in the land prior to the Rapture. Therefore, one condition precedent to the completion of the church age was the gathering of Jews and the creation of the nation of Israel in 1948.

John Walvoord, sort of recognizes the dilemma of an imminent Rapture and a re-gathering of Israel in his book *Church in Prophecy.* He makes the following observation:

> According to the interpretation followed by many pre-millenarians, Israel's consummation will involve a covenant for seven years with a Gentile ruler in the Mediterranean area. This covenant anticipated in Daniel 9:26–27 is between "the prince that shall come" and the "many," referring to the people of Israel. It is transparent that in order for such a covenant to be fulfilled, the children of Israel had to be in their ancient land and had to be organized into a political unit suitable for such a covenant relationship. Prior to the twentieth century, such a situation did not exist and tended to support unbelief on the part of some that Israel would never go back to their ancient land and could never have such a covenant. The fact of Israel's return and establishment as a nation has given a sound basis for believing that this covenant will be literally fulfilled as anticipated in Daniel 9:27. If the Rapture occurs before the signing of this covenant, as many premillennial scholars believe, it follows that the establishment of Israel in the land as a preparation for this covenant is a striking evidence that the Rapture itself may be very near. Of the many signs indicating the end of the age, few are more dramatic and have a larger Scriptural

foundation that the revival of Israel as a token of the end of the age. (173–174)

Walvoord approaches the concept that Israel must be back land as a condition precedent for end-times, but is unwilling to state it as such, because it conflicts with his understanding of the eternal immanency of the Rapture. He is aware of the dichotomy, but accepts it simply as a mystery.

## What Was the Teaching of the Early Church?

Tim LaHaye, at a Pre-tribulation Study Group, presented a paper in Dallas, Texas in 2000. In his paper he provided several quotes about what the early church Apostolic Fathers believed. "..they expected the return of the Lord in their day. They believed the time was imminent because their Lord had taught them to live in a watchful attitude. Concerning the Ante-Nicene Fathers, he says: "By tradition they knew the faith of the Apostles. They taught the doctrine of the imminent and premillennial return of the Lord. Many authors can be cited to prove that a belief in the soon return of Christ existed throughout the first three centuries." One of the examples of this belief sited was the Epistle of Barnabas (written perhaps around AD 130 by an unknown author). Actually, the Epistle of Barnabas teaches that Christ will return around the year 2000. It also teaches that the first six-thousand years of human history would be the equivalent of six days, and that the millennial reign of Christ would be the seventh or the last one-thousand years of history prior to a new earth. Many church fathers such as Irenaeus believed the Epistle of Barnabas was inspired. Irenaeus also held to the belief that Christ would return around the year 2000. In his work *Against Heresies*, he states, "For the day of the Lord is as a thousand years; (II Peter 3:8) and in six days created things were completed: it is evident therefore, that they will come to an end at the sixth thousand year. (Book 5, Chapter 28).

## Is Diaspora and the Gathering of Israel a Rapture Prerequisite?

The term *diaspora* is the transliteration of a Greek word meaning "to scatter or sowing of seeds." The Septuagint version of Deuteronomy 28:25 stated, "thou shalt be a dispersion (diaspora) in all kingdoms of the earth." The word came to refer to the Jews who were exiled from Judea by the Babylonians and the Romans in AD 70 and 136 respectively.

In the Olivet Discourse, Jesus referred to chapter 9 of Daniel when he described the coming Jewish diaspora and ultimate gathering. Just as the Passover is the foundational feast of the Feasts of the Lord, Daniel 9:26 is the foundational cornerstone for prophetic events.

Daniel 9:26 says, "And after the sixty-two weeks Messiah shall be cut off, but not for Himself. And the people of the prince who is to come shall destroy the city and the sanctuary. The end of it shall be with a flood, and till the end of the war desolations are determined."

The word translated as "weeks" in the King James bible is the Hebrew word *shabua*, which means "units of seven." In this context, it refers to units of seven years. The translation of "weeks" has made Daniel 9 much more difficult than it should have been. Within the text of Daniel 9 we can determine weeks are a period of seven years. We know this because there are exactly sixty-nine weeks or 483 years until Messiah Yoshua. Verse 24 tells us that the total vision covers a period of 490 years (Seventy times seven). Verse 25 declares that there will be 483 years (seven and sixty-two times seven or 69 x 7=483) from the command to restore Jerusalem and build the wall or moat until the Messiah.

Verse 26 states, "and after the sixty-two weeks the Messiah shall be cut off, but not for Himself." Since Verse 25 explained how the sixty-two followed the seven, we know the idiom sixty-two includes the seven. Therefore, the Messiah will be separated out of the flock or out of the Jewish nation on what we now call Palm Sunday. On March 30, AD 33, Jesus Christ presented himself to Israel as the Messiah. He was subsequently crucified on the Passover.

"And the people of the prince who is to come shall destroy the city and the sanctuary. The end of it shall be with a flood, and till the end of the war desolations are determined" (Dan. 9:26).

History records that Jewish war against the Romans erupted in 66 AD and lasted three and a half years until 70 AD This conflict resulted in the destruction of Jerusalem and the great Herodian temple by the Roman forces under the leadership of Prince Titus, the son of Roman Caesar Vespasian. The battle resulted in a massive loss of Jewish life via starvation, crucifixion, and the sword. "The end thereof" was indeed "with a flood."

In AD 132, when the Bar Kockhba rebellion broke out, "the people of the prince that shall come" (referring to the Romans under whom Christ was crucified) completed the war of destruction. Around AD 130, the Roman emperor Hadrian built a new Roman colony named Aelia Capitolian in Jerusalem. He also erected a temple to Jupiter Capitolinus on the Holy Hill. As prophesied, Israel was broken up and the remnant of Jews in Jerusalem were dispersed into the Roman Empire. Subsequently, the Romans forbade both Jews and Christians to re-enter a Jerusalem that was plowed under with salt. They renamed the province as Palestine, from which we get the popular term used today.

The prophecy in Daniel 9:26 fits only one disaster in Jewish history after the nation returned from captivity in Babylon, and that disaster was the war which engulfed the Jews in AD 66–73, almost forty years after the death of Jesus. The disaster unfolded in four stages exactly as prophesied.

### Stage One: Invasion

The Jews revolted in AD 66. The Romans, at first overpowered, chose the expedient course of withdrawing their forces from Palestine. Soon, however, the Roman general Vespasian began a campaign of recon quest in the north. His advance was slowed by stiff opposition, seasonal delays, and political instability back in Rome. In AD 70, however, after he had made himself emperor, a Roman army under the leadership of his son Titus reached Jerusalem.

### Stage Two: Flood

The end of Jerusalem indeed came with a flood. After a siege of about three months, the people of the city were greatly weakened by food shortages. Eventually, the Romans successfully stormed the Temple and the lower city. Both were destroyed rapidly by a great conflagration. A month later, the upper city, which was the last bastion of the rebels, fell in a single day. The legions poured in like a flood through breaches in the walls met little effective opposition.

### Stage Three: Destruction

The Romans then proceeded to raze the city. They tore down every building except three towers and the western wall, which Titus left as a monument to his victory. No trace of the Temple complex remained. Fire in the temple caused gold to pour between the large cut stone blocks. Not one stone was left of the temple in search of gold, just as Christ had predicted in the Olivet Discourse.

### Stage Four: Desolation

The English word "desolations" is the translation of the Hebrew word *shamem*. The Hebrew word means to stun, stupefy, to grow numb, to destroy, lay waste, to be astonished, to be desolate, be ravaged, be depopulated. According to Josephus, the toll of Jewish casualties in this war exceeded 1 million.[35] Ninety-seven thousand were taken alive and many died in Roman arenas.

## The Diaspora Was Prophesied By Both the Law and the Prophets

"Then the Lord will scatter you among all people, from one end of the earth to the other, and there you shall serve other gods, which neither you nor your fathers have known-wood and stone" (Deut. 28:64).

"For I have laid on you the years of their iniquity, according to the number of the days, three hundred and ninety days; so you shall bear the iniquity of the house of Israel. And when you have completed them, lie again on your right side; then you shall bear the iniquity of the house of Judah forty days. I have laid on you a day for each year. " Ezek. 4:5–6. The total dispersion was to last 430 years, or 390 plus 40).

However, according to Jewish law, if they did not repent, their sentence was to be multiplied seven times, until they did repent. "And if you will not yet for all this hearken unto me, then I will punish you seven times more for your sins" (Lev. 26:18–28). Hosea 5:14–15 states, "For I will be like a lion to Ephraim, and like a young lion to the house of Judah. I, even I, will tear them and go away; I will take them away, and no one shall rescue. I will return again to my place till they acknowledge their offense. Then they will seek my face; in their affliction they will diligently seek me." The total number of years decreed is 430 years of punishment. Four-hundred and thirty years, less seventy years time served in Babylon, leaves 360 years. 360 years times seven equals 2,520 biblical years or 2,483.8 calendar years.

Grant Jeffrey makes the following amazing observation in his book *Armageddon*:

The end of the captivity in Babylon, according to the Bible and other historical sources-including Flavius Josephus, is recorded as having occurred in the spring of 536 BC This date is the starting point for our calculations: 2,520 biblical years x 360 + 907,200 days. Converting this figure into our calendar year of 365.25 days and dividing 365.25 into 907,200 days we reach a total of 2,483.9 calendar years. (In these calculations we must keep in mind that there is only one year between 1 BC and AD 1). Therefore, the end of Israel's worldwide captivity would occur after a total of 2,483.8 years had elapsed from the Spring of 536 BC. (40)

The nation of Israel miraculously appeared right on schedule, on May 14, 1948. The gathering of Israel is a condition precedent to the Rapture. The stage has been set for the immanency of the Rapture. This is because the two first events during the seventieth week of Daniel are the signing of a seven-year peace treaty brokered by the Antichrist, and will result in the invasion of Russia, Iran, and their allies.

"Then he shall confirm a covenant with many for one week; but in the middle of the week, he shall bring an end to sacrifice and offering. And on the wing of abomination shall be one who makes desolate" (Dan. 9:27). One of the first events described during the final seven years of Jewish history is the signing of a peace treaty. If Israel is not a nation it cannot sign a peace treaty. Therefore, the Jews had to return to the land of Israel prior to the commencement of the last seven years of their history.

The second event that happens at the beginning of the last seven years of Jewish history is the Magog invasion. Therefore, Israel must be a nation. Also Russia, Iran, and their allies must be a threat to Israel. "Son of man, set your face against God, of the land of Magog, the prince of Rosh, Meschech, and Tubal, and prophecy against him...After many days you will be visited. In the latter years you will come into the land of those brought back from the sword and gathered from many people on the mountains of Israel, which had long been desolate; they were brought out of the nations, and now all of them dwell safely. Then those who dwell in the cities of Israel will go out and set on fire and burn the weapons, both the shields and bucklers, the bows and arrows, the javelins and spears; and they will make fires with them for seven years" (Ezek. 38:2, 8–9).

The first event of the seven years of the Tribulation is a peace treaty brokered by the prince to come of the Romans who sacked Israel to begin the Diaspora. This requires two conditions It requires a completion of the Diaspora. It requires that the Roman Empire be revived. It also requires that the Revived Roman Empire have two legs or two parts. The Revived Roman Empire must include both Europe and an Eastern leg. "Its legs of iron, its feet partly of iron and partly of clay ... And as the toes of the feet were partly of iron and partly of clay" (Dan, 2:33 and 42). The two legs are the East and West part of the Roman Empire. The ten toes are a coming confederation of kings or leaders who submit to the coming world ruler. "The ten horns are ten kings who shall arise from this kingdom. And another shall rise after them; He shall be different from the first ones and shall subdue three kings" (Dan. 8:24).

"And the ten horns which you saw are ten kings who have received no kingdom as yet, but they receive authority for one hour as kings with the beast" (Rev. 17:12).

We can determine how Russia (Magog) and her allies invade Israel at the beginning of the Tribulation because it takes seven years to burn their weapons. "...and they will make fires with them for seven years" (Ezek. 39:9). We know the Magog invasion is in the last days after the Rapture. This is because the Church Age is a mystery to the Old Testament prophets.[36] "After many days you will be visited. In the latter years you will come into the land of those brought back from the sword and gathered fro many people on the mountains of Israel" (Ezek. 38:8). As a condition precedent to the "Day of the Lord," God had to restore Israel as a nation, place oil in the Middle East to finance the armament of Iran, and allow communism to make Russia a military threat.

Since the Tribulation is only seven years the Magog invasion is at the beginning at a time of a pseudo peace. This invasion is described with the four horsemen in chapter 6 of Revelation. It is also mentioned as "Nation against nation" in Matthew 24:7, and as the "Northern army" in Joel 2:20.

Since a peace treaty with Israel and the Magog invasion of Israel are the first two immediate events of the Tribulation, Israel needs to be back in the land prior to the Rapture to set the stage for the prophetic world events. Therefore, the creation of the nation Israel was a condition precedent to the Rapture, and should be construed to be a marker that we are in the last days prior to Judgment Day.

## What are the Cornerstones for the Rapture?

The construction of any building starts with establishing corner stones. When putting a puzzle together one needs to establish the edges and then fill in towards the middles. If we explore a theory such as the Rapture of the church, we need to first establish a theory and then find appropriate corner stones.

The English term *rapture* is derived from the Latin word *rapere* and the Greek word *harpazo* which together means "to seize, snatch, or seize away."

In Acts 1:9, Christ was raptured to heaven, "Now when he had spoken these things, while they watched, he was taken up, and a cloud received him out of their sight. Just as Christ was raptured to heaven, those in Christ and alive at his coming, will be raptured as well.

The four prophetic cornerstones of the Rapture of the church are:

1.  Daniel 9:26–27 shows a gap of approximately two thousand years between the sixty-ninth and the seventieth week of Daniel.

    Verse 26 completes the sixty-nine units of seven years leading up to the death of the Messiah. Verse 27 describes the last seventy units of seven, or the seventieth week of Daniel. Between the death of the Messiah and the seventieth week of Daniel is the church age.

2.  Ephesians 3:1–4 explains that the church age was a mystery to the Old Testament prophets: "For this reason I, Paul, the prisoner of Jesus Christ for you Gentiles—if indeed you have heard of the dispensation of the grace of God which was given to me for you—how that by revelation he made known to me the mystery (as I wrote before in a few words by which, when you read, you may understand my knowledge in the mystery of Christ)."

3.  The church will be Raptured at the close of the church age, "Then we who are alive and remain shall be caught up together with them in the clouds to meet the Lord in the air. And thus we shall always be with the Lord" (I Thess. 4:17).

4.  The history of the church age is described in Revelation 2 and 3. Clarence Larkin makes the following observations in his book *Dispensational Truth*:

"The Book of Revelation was written in AD 96. The writer was the Apostle John. He was told to write the thing which he 'saw; and 'heard.' The Book therefore is a divinely given book, and is the 'Revelation of Jesus Christ' (Rev. 1:1) and not of John. It is the most important and valuable prophetic book in the Bible" (128).

Some pretribulational dispensationalists are so focused on the centrality of Christ in their understanding of the unfolding plan of redemption in the Bible they seem to denigrate the revelation of God in the Old Testament. The superior light of the revelation of God in Christ caused a shadow of insignificance to fall over the less clear revelation of Him in the Old Testament. This has created in the minds of some dispensationalists, a discontinuity between the two testaments that has become a defining characteristic of their understanding of the Bible. However, three quarters of the Bible have to do with Israel. What must be understood is that the law and the prophets revealed Yeshua Messiah on every page. While in a more subtle way, the Old Testament should in no way be dismissed as less relevant. In fact, without an understanding of Jewish idioms, many of the code words used in the book of Revelation become sealed in a shroud of mystery.

All through the Old Testament there are scattered references to things which are to come to pass in the Last Days. The book of Revelation reveals the Divine Program, or order, in which these events are to happen. It is the book of consummation and its proper place in the sacred canon is where it is placed, at the end of the Bible. The book is addressed to the "seven churches which are in Asia." Asia is not meant to be the great continent of Asia, or even the whole of Asia minor, but only its western end. Neither were the seven churches named the only churches in that district. These seven churches then must be representative or typical churches, chosen for certain characteristics typical of the character of the church of Christ from the end of the first century down to the time of Christ's return for his church. These characteristics are descriptive of seven church periods clearly defined in church history.

## How Long Will the Church Age Last?

The seven churches representative of church history are:

1. Ephesus the Apostolic Church: From AD 33 to 170, a period of 137 years.
2. Smyrna, the Church of the Roman Persecution: From AD 170 to AD 312, a period of 142 years.

3.  Pergamum, Church of the Age of Constantine: From AD 312 to 606, a period of 294 years. The prophet Balaam encouraged the Moabites to compromise the children of Israel. This was repeated in the church age when the Babylonian religion was merged with the Christian state church of Rome.

4.  Thyatira, Church of the Dark Ages: From AD 606 to 1520, a period of 914 years. "You suffer the woman Jezebel who calls herself a prophetess; and she teaches and seduces my servants to commit fornication" (Rev. 2:30). During the Dark Ages, the state church of Rome departed from the Bible and taught Mariology, indulgences, and praying for the dead.

5.  Sardis, The Church of the Reformation: From AD 1520–1750, a period of 230 years. The reformed church returned to salvation by faith, but ignored Christian living and a walk of holiness.

6.  Philadelphia, the Church of the Missionary Movement: From AD 1750–1900, a period of 150 years. He that has the key of David, he that opens and none shall shut, and that shut and none opens. The missionary movement went to India and Africa. "I also will keep thee from the hour of trial" (Rev. 3:10). John Darby established the systematic doctrine of the Rapture, which through William Blackstone and others, resulted in the nurturing of the Zionist movement.

7.  Laodicea, the Church of the Apostasy: From AD 1900–Present. "Lukewarm, neither cold nor hot, lukewarm" (Rev. 3:160). The contemporary post-modern church of today may be described as neither openly hostile to Christianity nor on fire for the Lord. It is largely indifferent. This church says it is rich, but in God's eyes is wretched, miserable, poor, blind and naked. This perfectly describes much of the Christian Church today.

In Matthew 24:36, Jesus declared at the Olivet Discourse, "But of that day and hour no one knows, no, not even the angels of heaven, but My Father only."

The word "knows" is derived from the Greek word *eido*, which means to know or understand. The Greek word is from the root *eidon*, but here it is written in the present active indicative. This means that no one knew at that time, but it is still possible that one may know at a later date. Jesus adds in the next sentence, "But as the days of Noah were, so also will the coming of the Son of Man be." Jesus said that the unbelievers did not know about the flood until it happened, "so also will the coming of the Son of Man be" (Matt. 24:37). The Apostle Paul confirms that the world will be blissfully ignorant when the Day of the Lord comes, but Christians are not supposed to be ignorant.

I Thessalonians 5:4–5 states, "But you, brethren, are not in darkness, so that this Day, should overtake you as a thief. You are all sons of light and sons of the day. We are not of the night nor of darkness. Therefore let us not sleep, as others do, but let us watch and be sober."

If a Christian Bible student was transported back to the days of Noah he could estimate the time of the flood. One could observe Noah during the 120 years it took to build the ark. As the ark neared completion one could estimate with a fair amount of accuracy the speed of progress and the amount of work needed to be completed. Once Noah went in the ark, the flood would then come in seven days. "For after seven more days, will cause it to rain on the earth forty days" (Gen. 7:4).

Just as in the days of Noah, a Bible student can observe that we are in Laodicea, the last phase of church history. Israel is a nation again. Apostasy is rampant. If we take the number of years of the first six stages of church history, we can observe what appears to be a parabolic curve: 137, 142, 294, 914, 230, 150. In mathematics, a parabola is the transliteration of a Greek word, used to describe something bowl-shaped. It is a plane curve generated by a point moving so that its distance from a fixed point is equal to its distance from a fixed line. The parabolic curve is seen with considerable frequency in the physical world, and is often used in the fields of engineering and physics.

Using a parabolic curve we might estimate the final phase of church history to last approximately 130–140 years. This would place the Rapture at between 2030–2040. This would only be a crude estimate, because the seven periods of church history are speculative and subject to arbitrary dating. The margin of error could be plus or minus 2%, and would depend totally on God's undisclosed will. This would mean The Day of the Lord could come today or fifty years from now. How is this different from saying the Rapture is Imminent? The difference is that the word "imminent" has no significance if you say it could happen at any time during the two-thousand years between the first and second advent. But if you say the year 2008 is in the last days because Israel is a nation again, then this has relevant meaning and is prophetic, based upon sound Biblical footing.

Once the church age is completed, the Tribulation commenced, the time of the Second Advent could then be set to occur in seven years or at the end of Daniel's seventieth week. This would compare to the day of the flood. At the time of Noah, we could only estimate based upon Noah's progress on the Ark, but once he entered the Ark and the door was closed, the flood was set to come in seven days.[37]

## Why Estimate the End of the Church Age?

If you were hired as an engineer by a hydro-electric company to study and monitor the structural strength of a large water dam above a large metropolitan city, you would have a legal and moral obligation to perform your duties without negligence.

1. You would be negligent if you presented yourself as an expert, but in fact had no qualifying skills.
2. You would be negligent if you never observed the dam, because you liked to spend-time with your family and enjoy life.

3. You would not be performing your duties if you said, "A major break in the dam is imminent, but I have no idea when this will happen and I will not look."
4. You would be negligent if there were large cracks in the dam, it was about to break, and you said "Dams never break" or "It will break after we are all dead."
5. You would be negligent if you calculated false dates that the dam would break, and based these calculations upon faulty techniques.
6. You would be a good public servant and would be considered to have discharged your duties if you: diligently and eagerly examined the dam for danger, estimated the amount of danger, and warned people of immediate pending danger.

Setting specific dates for the end of the world cannot be based upon God's word, since no one knows. However, we are given signs which are meant to warn us that we are in the last days. The fulfillment of last day events should motivate us to holy living and motivation to warn others of pending judgment. Study of end-time events should not be an intellectual pursuit to cause division and to cause us to fail to show love to those who do not agree. If you say, "The Rapture could come today, but I have no basis to believe today is any different from any other day in the last two-thousand years," your message is hollow and its relevancy would be suspect. However, if you say "I have Biblical evidence to show that we are in the last days, the Rapture is imminent, and there is a large probability it will occur in your life time," your message has meaning and relevancy. In fact, if true, you have a moral obligation to warn others. You also have a strong incentive to get your life in order and focus on Godly things versus temporal things.

The doctrine of immanency, which states there are no intervening events and the Rapture could happen at any time from the first Century on, is both unscriptural and tends to cause a dullness in people in regards to end-time events. If a person calls wolf too many times when there is not wolf, he should not be surprised when people do not respond when there truly is a wolf. People who say the Rapture could have occurred in the first century should not be surprised when people do not take the Day of the Lord as relevant in their lives.

Surely the Lord God does nothing, unless he reveals his se-cret to his servants the prophets. (Amos 3:7)

...If you warn the wicked, and he does not turn from his wickedness, nor from his wicked way, he shall die in his in-iquity, but you have delivered your soul. (Ezek. 3:19)

In other words, if you warn people and they do not listen, you are not accountable to God for not telling them.

Blessed is he who reads and those who hear the words of the prophecy, and keep those things which are written in it; for the time is near. (Rev. 1:3).

## The Doctrine of Immanency of the Rapture

1. A truthful doctrinal conclusion must correctly interpret and con-sider all scriptures that the Bible presents on a given subject.
2. "Quickly" and "at hand" may be near from God's perspective, but not necessarily near from man's perspective, and there can be intervening events. (Zeph. 1:7)
3. 3. Immanency is something which could happen without delay and without conditions precedent.
4. 4. The Rapture of the Church has three conditions precedent: (1) The establishment of Israel as a nation (Dan. 9:27). (2) The

completion of the seven stages of Church history as delineated in Rev. 2 & 3. (3) Apostasy in the Last days. (I Tim. 4:1)

5.  Since these conditions were not met in the first century, the Rapture was not imminent in the first century.

6.  Currently the church age is almost complete and these conditions are almost entirely completed. (Rom. 11:25)

7.  The Rapture of the church is now imminent. (I Thess. 4:17)

# CHAPTER 8

# THE SEVEN SEALS AND THE TRIBULATION

## What is the Tribulation?

In Bible prophecy, the Tribulation is the seven-year period of time between the Rapture of the church and the second coming of Jesus Christ. The most extensive biblical comments on the Tribulation are found in the writings of John, specifically in Revelation 6–19. In these chapters, John provides a detailed exposition of the Tribulation days. Daniel's seventy weeks[38] are the framework within which the Tribulation or the seventieth week occurs. Some of those descriptive terms found in the book of Daniel, the books of the prophets, and the book of Revelation include: Tribulation, great Tribulation, day of the Lord, day of wrath, day of distress, day of trouble, day of darkness and gloom, and wrath of the Lamb.

The book of Joshua is the anticipatory model of the Tribulation. In the book of Joshua, the Captain of the Lord's Host (Jesus Christ), not Joshua, was the actual leader. The battle plan was to redeem the land to its rightful owner from the usurper kings in the land. Two spies were sent in and resulted in the salvation of a family living in the promised land. After blowing seven trumpets, the walls of the enemies' capital city fell down. During the Tribulation, the land of Israel will be redeemed to its rightful owner. God will send in Moses and Elijah as two spies. After seven trumpet judgments, Babylon will be destroyed. In the end, Christ will return to reign and rule in Zion.

The Law (Pentateuch) constitutes the first part of the Hebrew Scriptures. Joshua is the first book in the second part of the Hebrew canon called the Prophets. The name Joshua, or Yehoshua, is the given Hebrew name of Jesus. Yehoshua means "Salvation is of God" or "Yahweh delivers." Yehoshua is normally translated to "Joshua" in English. Jesus would have been referred to by the shorter name Yeshu "Salvation," at least in Jerusalem and the rest of Judea. Yeshua was translated by the early Pauline Christians as *Iesous* in Greek. This became "Iesus" in Latin, and Jesus in German. The English name "Jesus" came from the German spelling and pronunciation.

Redemption out of Egypt occurred through the Passover and was anticipated in the book of Exodus. Moses gave the Israelites a redeemed position. Redemption into the Promised Land occurred in the Book of Joshua. Redemption became experiential based upon the conquest and possession of the land. Christ redeemed the universe by his death on the Cross as the kinsman redeemer and the second Adam. The giving of the Holy Spirit on Pentecost was the down payment. However, escrow does not close until Israel is back in the land and calls for their Messiah to save them. The Tribulation is the redemption of the land to the rightful owner.

> For I will be like a lion to Ephraim, and like a young lion to the house of Judah. I, even I, will tear them and go away; I will take them away, and no one shall rescue. I will return again to My place till they acknowledge their offense. Then they will seek My face; in their affliction they will diligently seek Me. (Hosea 5:14–15)

"Why do the nations rage, and the people plot vain thing? The kings of the earth set themselves, and the rulers take counsel together, against the Lord and against his Anointed, saying, "Let us break their bonds in pieces and cast away their cord from us. He who sits in the heavens shall laugh; the Lord shall hold them in derision. Then he shall speak to them in his wrath. And distress them in his deep displeasure; Ye I have set My king on My holy hill of Zion." I will declare the decree; the Lord has said to Me, You are My Son, today I have begotten You, ask of Me, and I will give You the nations for Your inheritance. And the ends of the earth for Your possession. You shall break them with a rod of iron; You shall dash them in pieces like a potter's vessel. Now therefore, be wise, O kings; be instructed, you judges of the earth. Serve the Lord with fear, and rejoice with trembling. Kiss the Son, lest he be angry, and you perish in the way. When his wrath is kindled but a little. Blessed are all those who put their trust in Him" (Ps. 2).

> The Lord said to My Lord, "Sit at my right hand, till I make your enemies your footstool." The Lord has sworn and will not relent, "You are a priest forever according to the order of Melchizedek." The Lord is at Your right hand; he shall execute kings in the day of his wrath. (Ps. 110:2,2,4,5)

In chapter 5 of the Book of Revelation, John is in heaven and sees the seven seals on the deed to the earth. "And I saw in the right hand of Him who sat on the throne a scroll written inside and on the back sealed with seven seals; Then I saw a strong angel proclaiming with a loud voice, 'Who is worthy to open the scroll and to loose its seals.' And no one in heaven or on the earth or under the earth was able to open the scroll, or to look at it. But one of the elders said to me, 'Do not weep, behold the lion of the tribe of Judah, the root of David, has prevailed to open the scroll and to loose its seven seals.' And I looked, and behold, in the midst of the throne and of the four living creatures, and in the midst of the elders, stood a Lamb as though it had been slain, having seven horns and seven eyes which are the seven Spirits of God sent out into all the earth. Then he came and took the scroll out of the right hand of Him who sat on the throne. Now when he had taken the scroll, the four living creatures and the twenty-four elders fell down before the Lamb, each having a harp, and golden bowls full of incense which are the prayers of the saint. And they sang a new song, saying; 'You are worth to take the scroll, and to open its seals; for you were slain, and have redeemed us to God by your blood. Out of every tribe and tongue and people and nation. And have made us kings and priest to our God; and we shall reign on the earth'" (Rev. 5:1–3, 5–10).

God's basic purpose of the Tribulation is to make an end of wickedness, bring the nation of Israel to repentance and bring a worldwide revival. It is important to note that more people, 7 billion, will be alive at the beginning of the seven-year Tribulation than have existed since Adam. At the time of Christ there were only 300 million people alive. During medieval times there were only 400 million people. During the first three-and-a-half years of the Tribulation Moses and Elijah will be warning the earth that Judgment Day has arrived. Also during the Tribulation, angels will be flying throughout the world warning of coming judgment. Unfortunately, most people will not make it through to the end of the seven-year period. Most will perish.

Contrary to popular opinion among prophecy students, the Holy Spirit will not be taken out of the world when the church is raptured. Although widely accepted, this is an erroneous idea that was caused largely by footnotes in the Scofield Reverence Bible. It interpreted the "restrainer" of 2 Thessalonians 2:3–8 as the Holy Spirit. What is removed is the restraining power of the Holy Spirit through the church. However, the Holy Spirit will be poured out upon the nation Israel, and especially 144,000 out of the tribes of Israel. We know that the outpouring of the Holy Spirit on the day of Pentecost was only a partial fulfillment of chapter 2 of Joel . We know this because Joel 2 mentions the coming great and terrible day of the Lord. "I will pour out my spirit in those days. And I will show wonders in the heavens and in the earth: Blood and fire and pillars of smoke. The sun shall be turned into darkness, and the moon into blood, before the coming of the great and terrible day of the Lord" (Joel 2:29–31). "And I heard the number of those who were sealed. One hundred and forty-four thousand of all the tribes of the children of Israel were sealed" (Rev. 7:4). Also, many Gentiles will become believers in the Tribulation. "These are the ones who come out of the great Tribulation, and washed their robes and made them white in the blood of the Lamb" (Revelation 7:14).

Another false opinion is that tongues stopped when the scriptures were completed. This popular fable is based on an improper interpretation of I Corinthians 13:10, "But when that which is perfect has come, then that which is in part will be done." Intellectuals opposed to the latter-day sign of speaking in tongues use this verse to say tongues stopped when the book of Revelation was finished. However, Christ is what is complete, not the Bible. If it was the Bible, then based upon verse eight, knowledge and prophecy would have also stopped with tongues. Speaking in tongues is speaking in a language you never learned. Acts 2, which is quoting from the book of Joel, shows this was a sign of the dawn of apostolic power in the early church and a sign of end-times. The Apostle Peter said it applied to the Day of Pentecost, the day the church age officially started. But he also said it applied to end-times and mentioned wonders in heaven above and signs in the earth beneath; hail, fire and brimstone. The prophet Joel is not only referring to the end of the church age, but also the seven-year Tribulation—when the Holy Spirit will be poured out on the 144,000 Jewish believers described in Revelation 7. He was not talking about zealots who come to your door and deny Jesus is God, with their mistranslation of the Greek New Testament. Unfortunately, during the apostasy of the end-times, all sorts of strange activities have been associated with the unscriptural use of tongues and false signs. One of the major signs of end-times is false television prophets who attempt to use the church and false signs to fill their pockets with money and power. Ultimately, the Antichrist and the False Prophet will cause the world to worship the Antichrist and will offer as proof false miracles and a pseudo resurrection as proof of their false religion.

## What are the Seven Seals?

In the ancient world, seals were used to close up a scroll of writing. After hot wax was dripped on the papyrus, the sender's signet ring was pressed into the wax to form a mark. This mark showed that the message or legal deed had not been opened. Revelation 5 indicates that the scroll or deed to the universe was sealed, and only the Lamb of God was qualified to open the seals and restore the earth to its rightful owner God. Before Christ comes to claim earth and dispose of Satan, the Antichrist, and the false prophet (the false trinity), he fires heavy artillery from his command post in heaven. As Christ opens the seals to the deed of the universe, the Russian invasion is launched. The consequences are hail, fire and brimstone and almost 1.75 billion human casualties. The seventh seal consists of seven more intense trumpet judgments. The seventh trumpet judgment consists of seven more intense bowl judgments. During the sixth and seventh bowl judgments, the battle of Armageddon and the destruction of Babylon occur. The first four seals are represented by the four horsemen of the apocalypse, or the unveiling of Jesus Christ. All four of the horsemen represent movements that will be a work in the end-time.

### The First Seal

First Seal (Revelation 6:1–2). The first seal is also called the white horse judgment. This first judgment is what is called a "cold war." This is a period where the Antichrist begins to conquer and revive the Roman Empire by forming a ten-nation European confederacy. The rider on the white horse is a movement or wave of false messiahs that will appear after the Rapture of the church to heaven. The disappearance of the true believers will pave the way for an outbreak of counterfeit Christs, false messiahs who will claim to have the answers for the world's chaos. But out of this movement of false messiahs, one man will stand head and shoulders above the rest. He will be the ultimate fulfillment of the rider one the white horse, the ultimate pseudo messiah. He will be the one who later, in Revelation 13:1–10, is called the beast out of the sea.

The anticipatory model for the Antichrist is Antiochus Epiphanies, the evil ruler who gained control of Syria. This was one of the four subdivisions of the Greek Empire after the death of Alexander the Great. Alexander's empire was divided among four surviving generals. Ptolemy took Egypt and Seleucus Nicator took Syria. Chapter 11 of Daniel describes the wars and intrigues between Egypt and Syria at this time.

Antiochus rises to power through his craftiness and his ability to convince people. He has been described by ancient historians as "vile" or "contemptible."[39] Often his behavior was eccentric, if not actually mad. He was given to the most degraded and unnatural vices. He was unscrupulous, cruel, of a savage temper, and fond of the company of the lowest of men. He was erratic and cunning, but not devoid of courage. He came to the throne "peaceably" and "obtained the kingdom by flatteries," as had been foretold in Daniel. This becomes a double fulfillment in that the Antichrist comes to power in the same manner. Antiochus signed a peace treaty with the youthful Egyptian king to lull Ptolemy into a false sense of security. His army starts out small, but he builds it up in time. This sounds a lot like the coming world ruler. "Then he shall confirm a covenant with many for one week; but in the middle of the week he shall bring an end to sacrifice and offering. And on the wings of abominations shall be one who makes desolate, even until the consummation, which is determined, is poured out on the desolate. (Daniel 9:27).

For many will come in My name, saying, "I am the Christ," and will deceive many. And you will hear of wars and rumors of wars. See that you are not troubled; for all these things must come to pass, but the end is not yet. For nation will rise against nation, and kingdom against kingdom. And there will be famines, pestilences, and earthquakes in various places. Therefore when you see the "abomination of desolation," spoke of by Daniel the prophet, standing in the holy place (whoever reads, let him understand), then let those who are in Judea flee to the mountains. (Matt. 24:5–8, 15–16)

There are incredible parallels between Matthew 24:4–14 and Revelation 6–7. The parallels are so close that Matthew 24 is often referred to as the "mini apocalypse," or the miniature book of Revelation. As Billy Graham says in his book *Approaching Hoof Beats: The Four Horsemen of the Apocalypse*, "Who, therefore, is the rider on the white horse? He is not Christ, but a deceiver who seeks to capture the hearts and souls of men and women. He is one who seeks to have people acknowledge him as Lord instead of the true Christ."(78)

At the beginning of his career, the Antichrist will slip unobtrusively onto the stage of world events. The clear mention of him in the Bible is in Daniel 7:8, where he is called "al little horn." His first appearance will be inconspicuous. Revelation 6:2 describes the rider on the white horse as having a bow and wearing a crown. His bow has no arrows! This symbolism seems to indicate he will win a bloodless victory at the beginning of his career. Like Adolph Hitler, the Antichrist will rise to power and enlarge his power base through guile and intimidation rather than violence. However, once Russia, the United States, and China have been removed from the picture, the Antichrist and the Revived Roman Empire will fill in the vacuum created by the elimination of the first three super powers.

You might be asking how the Antichrist will be able to pull this

# THE MEANING OF THE JEWISH HOLY DAYS
### THE SET FEASTS OF JEHOVAH

| Crucifixion Messiah | Resurrection Christ | Church Age | Leviticus 23 | Rapture & Day of the Lord | 2nd Coming | Millennial Kingdom |
|---|---|---|---|---|---|---|

**Crucifixion Messiah**

**Resurrection Christ**

**Church Age**

**Leviticus 23**

**Rapture & Day of the Lord**

**2nd Coming**

**Millennial Kingdom**

Pesach — Passover — 1 Cor. 5:7

First Fruits — 1 Cor. 15:20,23

Shevuoth — Church Age — Pentecost — Acts 2:1

4 month harvest period — John 4:35

Rosh Hashana — Trumpets or New Year — 1 Cor. 15:51

Yom Kippur — Day of Atonement — Zech. 12:10–13:9

Succoth — Tabernacles Feast of Booths — Zech. 14

Dispersion Jews

THE CHURCH

Mt. 28:19–20

The promise of the Father

Behold the Lamb of God

He is RISEN

He ASCENDED

1 Th. 4:17

The meeting in the air

7 years — Jacob's Trouble

1000 years — Christ reigns

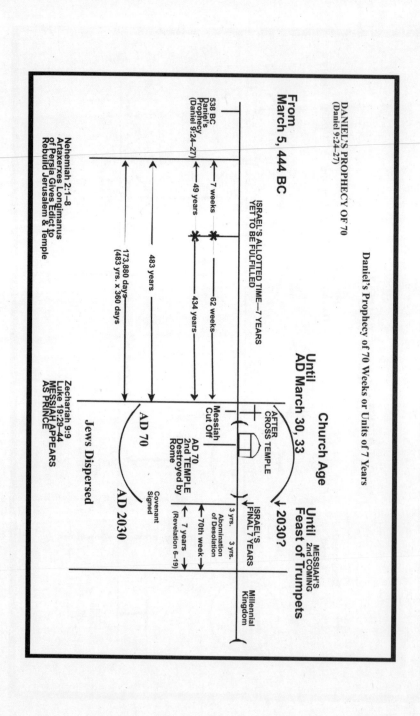

Daniel's Prophecy of 70 Weeks or Units of 7 Years

DANIEL'S PROPHECY OF 70
(Daniel 9:24-27)

From
March 5, 444 BC

538 BC
Daniel's
Prophecy
(Daniel 9:24-27)

7 weeks
49 years

ISRAEL'S ALLOTTED TIME—7 YEARS
YET TO BE FULFILLED

62 weeks
434 years

483 years

173,880 days
(483 yrs. x 360 days)

Nehemiah 2:1–8
Artaxerxes Longimanus
of Persia Gives Edict to
Rebuild Jerusalem & Temple

Until
AD March 30, 33

Church Age

Until
Feast of Trumpets

MESSIAH'S
2nd COMING

AFTER
CROSS TEMPLE

Messiah
Cut Off

AD 70
2nd TEMPLE
Destroyed by
Rome

2030?

ISRAEL'S
FINAL 7 YEARS

3 yrs.    3 yrs.
Abomination
of Desolation
70th week
7 years
(Revelation 6-19)

AD 70

AD 2030

Covenant
Signed

Jews Dispersed

Millennial
Kingdom

Zechariah 9:9
Luke 19:29–44
MESSIAH APPEARS
AS PRINCE

# Actual Churches & Preview of Church History
## Revelation 2 & 3

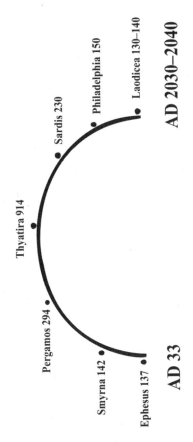

Pergamos 294

Thyatira 914

Smyrna 142

Sardis 230

Ephesus 137

Philadelphia 150

Laodicea 130–140

AD 33

AD 2030–2040

Actual Churches & Preview of Church History

1. Ephesus AD 33–170          = 137 Years
2. Smyrna AD 170–312          = 142 Years
3. Pergamos AD 312–606        = 294 Years
4. Thyatira AD 606–1520       = 914 Years
5. Saris AD 1520–1750         = 230 Years
6. Philadelphia AD 1750–1900  = 150 Years
7. Laodicea AD 1900–2030–2040? = 130–140 Years

# Map of Israel,
# the West Bank, the Gaza Strip,
# and the Golan Heights

GOLAN
HEIGHTS

Hafia

Mediterranean
Sea

Tel Aviv-Yafo

WEST
BANK

Jerusalem

GAZA
STRIP

Be'er Sheva

Dead Sea

JORDAN

EGYPT

off. The answer is that he will be energized and empowered by Satan himself. He will have the full power of the evil one behind him like no man who has ever lived. Revelation 13:2 says that during the second half of the Tribulation, "And the dragon (Satan) gave him (Antichrist) his power and his throne and great authority." The Antichrist will possess all the qualities of all the great leaders who have ever lived rolled into one man. He along with the False Prophet will be given supernatural powers beyond anything any one unbeliever has ever had. At the midpoint of the Tribulation, the mask of peace will come off, and the world will be plunged into the terrible darkness of the Great Tribulation and the ultimate reign of the world dictator.

### The Second Seal

Second Seal (Revelation 6:3–4). The second seal is the red horse judgment. The color of the horse appears to indicate blood and death since the passage says that "it was granted to take peace from the earth, and that men should slay one another; and a great sword was given to him." This rider brings destruction through war. Here we have one of the few instances in the Tribulation when God instigates his judgment by pitting nation against nation. This is where Russia, Iran, Germany, and others make a power play in the Middle East, with the intention of capturing most of the world's oil, control the Suez canal, and destroy Israel. This is the Magog invasion delineated in Ezekiel 38:7, Joel 2, and the Olivet Discourse in Matthew 24.

> Blow ye the trumpet in Zion, and sound an alarm in my holy mountain: let all the inhabitants of the land tremble: for the day of the LORD cometh, for it is nigh at hand;
>
> A day of darkness and of gloominess, a day of clouds and of thick darkness, as the morning spread upon the mountains: a great people and a strong; there hath not been

ever the like, neither shall be any more after it, even to the years of many generations.

A fire devoureth before them; and behind them a flame burneth: the land is as the garden of Eden before them, and behind them a desolate wilderness; yea, and nothing shall escape them.

The appearance of them is as the appearance of horses; and as horsemen, so shall they run.

Like the noise of chariots on the tops of mountains shall they leap, like the noise of a flame of fire that devoureth the stubble, as a strong people set in battle array.

Before their face the people shall be much pained: all faces shall gather blackness.

They shall run like mighty men; they shall climb the wall like men of war; and they shall march every one on his ways, and they shall not break their ranks:

Neither shall one thrust another; they shall walk every one in his path: and when they fall upon the sword, they shall not be wounded.

They shall run to and fro in the city; they shall run upon the wall, they shall climb up upon the houses; they shall enter in at the windows like a thief.

The earth shall quake before them; the heavens shall tremble: the sun and the moon shall be dark, and the stars shall withdraw their shining:

And the LORD shall utter his voice before his army: for his camp is very great: for he is strong that executeth his word: for the day of the LORD is great and very terrible; and who can abide it?

Therefore also now, saith the LORD, turn ye even to me with all your heart, and with fasting, and with weeping, and with mourning:

And rend your heart, and not your garments, and turn

unto the LORD your God: for he is gracious and merciful, slow to anger, and of great kindness, and repenteth him of the evil.

Who knoweth if he will return and repent, and leave a blessing behind him; even a meat offering and a drink offering unto the LORD your God?

Blow the trumpet in Zion, sanctify a fast, call a solemn assembly:

Gather the people, sanctify the congregation, assemble the elders, gather the children, and those that suck the breasts: let the bridegroom go forth of his chamber, and the bride out of her closet.

Let the priests, the ministers of the LORD, weep between the porch and the altar, and let them say, Spare thy people, O LORD, and give not thine heritage to reproach, that the heathen should rule over them: wherefore should they say among the people, Where is their God?

Then will the LORD be jealous for his land, and pity his people.

Yea, the LORD will answer and say unto his people, Behold, I will send you corn, and wine, and oil, and ye shall be satisfied therewith: and I will no more make you a reproach among the heathen:

But I will remove far off from you the northern army, and will drive him into a land barren and desolate, with his face toward the east sea, and his hinder part toward the utmost sea, and his stink shall come up, and his ill savour shall come up, because he hath done great things. (Joel 2:1–20; King James Version)

Joel 2:22 reverses the order of "fig tree and the vine" from Chapter 1:12. This is a common Jewish idiom or code in which the reversing of words orient us to show if we are looking forward to the cross or looking back after the cross. Chapter 1 of Joel refers to a literal locust judgment during the time of Joel. Chapter 2 is an end-time prophecy looking back to the time of Joel. Instead of a locus invasion, it is an invasion of people from the north.

### The Third Seal

"When he opened the third seal, I heard the third living creature say, 'Come and see.' And I looked, and behold, a black horse, and he who sat on it had a pair of scales in his hand. And I heard, a voice in the midst of the four living creatures saying, 'A quart of wheat for a denarius (a days wages), and three quarts of barley for a denarius; and do not harm the oil and wines'" (Rev. 6:5–6).

After the red horse and the outbreak of war, food shortages cannot be far behind. This is the way it has always been. Hunger is one of the wretched results of war. The fact the rider holds a pair of scales refers to weighing food for a day's wages. This reveals food is in short supply and that a man can only earn enough food for himself for one day of work. He cannot provide for his family, afford a home, or afford luxuries. The world will experience runaway inflation. However, the wealthy seem to prosper for a while. They are still able to buy oil and wine. During the first part of the Tribulation, the gulf between rich and poor will grow even wider. Food will be so expensive that only the wealthy will have enough. Famine will relentlessly hammer the middle and lower classes. However, as the judgments become more severe, eventually everyone will be effected. The rulers will hide in caves, just as in the book of Joshua.

### The Fourth Seal

Fourth Seal (Revelation 6:7 & 8). The fourth seal is also called the ashen horse judgment. This is the most severe of the four judgments:

"And authority was given to...over a fourth of the earth, to kill with sword and with famine and with pestilence and by the wild beasts of the earth." This is the result of World War III and the Russian invasion. People die not only because of the actual war, but also because of the aftermath and resulting disease, famine and natural calamities. The beasts of the earth could also include microcosm and rodents carrying disease.

### The Fifth Seal

Fifth Seal (Revelation 6:9–11). The fifth seal judgment is not a judgment, but a statement in which martyrs of the Tribulation cry out to God for revenge upon those unbelievers who killed them on earth.

### The Sixth Seal

Sixth Seal (Revelation 6:12–17). The sixth seal judgment is very severe. Six things happen: 1) a great earthquake; 2) the sun is blacked out: 3) the moon becomes like blood; 4) the stars fall to the earth; 5) the sky tears apart like a scroll; and 6) every mountain and island are moved out of their places. Rather than such events leading to repentance and prayer to God for deliverance, they lead to further rebellion against God. The people pray to the rocks and mountains to "fall on us and hide us from the presence of him who sits on the throne, and from the wrath of the Lamb." This is where the Russian invasion is stopped in its tracks and comes to a swift conclusion. Hail, fire, and brimstone represent volcanic action. It is a trademark of Moses, who is used by God in the first part of the Tribulation. Stars falling in Revelation 6:13 is a sign of asteroid activity and/or nuclear war.

For in My jealousy and in the fire of My wrath I have spoken: Surely in that day there shall be a great earthquake in the land of Israel, so that the fish of the sea, the birds of the heavens, the beasts of the field, all creeping things that creep on the earth, and all men who are on the face of the earth shall shake at My presence. The mountains shall be thrown down, the steep places shall fall, and every wall shall fall to the ground. I will call for a sword against God throughout all My mountains," says the Lord God. "Every man's sword will be against his brother. And I will bring him to judgment with pestilence and bloodshed; I will rain down on him, on his troops, and on the many peoples who are with him, flooding rain, great hail stones, fire, and brimstone. Thus I will magnify Myself and sanctify Myself, and I will be known in the eyes of many nations, Then They shall know that I am the Lord. You shall fall upon the mountains of Israel, you and your troops and the peoples who are with you; I will give you to birds of prey of every sort and to the beast of the field to be devoured. You shall fall on the open field; for I have spoke," says the Lord God. "and I will send fire on Magog and on those who live in security in the coastlands, then they shall know that I am the Lord. (Ezek. 38 and 39)

This eliminates Russia, Iran, Turkey, Germany, and very possibly the United States. There is worldwide destruction from asteroids, volcanoes, tsunamis, war, famine, and disease. One quarter of the world's population eliminated. Moses and Elijah have miraculous power to fend off all threats to Israel and the temple construction during the first half of the Tribulation. "And I will give power to my two witnesses, and they will prophesy one thousand two hundred and sixty days, clothed in sackcloth and if anyone wants to harm them, fire proceeds from their mouth and devours their enemies. And if anyone wants to harm them, he must be killed in this manner. These have power to shut heaven, so that no rain falls in the days of their prophecy; and they have power over waters to turn them to blood, and to strike the earth wish all plagues, as often as they desire" (Rev. 11:3, 5–6).

Hail, fire, brimstone, and water turning to blood is a specialty of Moses. Elijah prefers the old trick of no rain. The normal response from unbelievers is anger at God, because they know where the true source of power is coming from. At the beginning of the church age, on the Feast of Pentecost, Peter warned of this day, "I will show wonders in heaven above and signs in the earth beneath: blood and fire and vapor of smoke. The sun shall be turned into darkness, and the moon into blood, before the coming of the great and notable day of the Lord" (Acts 2:19–20). Wonders in heaven are asteroids and signs in the earth beneath are volcanoes. In the days of Noah, water came from the sky and from under the earth. In the Day of our Lord, destruction will come from beneath the earth and from the sky.

### The Seventh Seal

Seventh Seal (Revelation 8:1). The seventh seal judgment is the next series of seven judgments known as the trumpet judgments. The seventh trumpet judgment is the seven bowl judgments. At the conclusion of the seventh trumpet, or the sixth and seven bowl judgments, the battle of Armageddon occurs, and the city of Babylon, the throne of Satan, falls. Christ finishes the series of seven seal judgments by appearing in the clouds and comes to redeem the land and set up his millennial kingdom.

## What Apocalyptic Events Will Occur?

World War III, and its aftermath at the commencement of the Tribulation, will eliminate 1 billion, 750 million men, women, and children.[40] Within the first forty months of the Tribulation another

1 million 570 million people will die.[41] This is before the Antichrist becomes the total dictator of the world, and the battle of Armageddon.[42] By the end of the seven years of Tribulation there will be very few people left of the original 7 billion world population. It will not be a very pretty sight. Cities, mountains, rivers, and the world's oceans will be laid to waste from war, famines, disease, asteroids, earthquakes, and tsunamis.

World War III started on September 11, 2001, when Muslims hijacked commercial airliners, struck the twin tower of the World Trade Center in New York City, and killed three-thousand people. Muslims resort their traditional sneak attacks on civilians when they know they cannot win with traditional warfare techniques. The Arab and Muslim world has suffered several frustrating disappointments. National ambitions were partially frustrated by the Western takeover of the Middle East after World War I, which, in the Arab view, prevented the realization of the aims of Arab nationalism that had begun to crystallize during the last years of the Ottoman Empire. In particular, the rise of Israel is a sore point and a focus for anti-Western resentment. Much of the Arab and Muslim world, burdened by high population growth and lack of a middle class, has failed to industrialize and lags far behind the West in standard of living, quality of life, and democratic institutions. Literacy rates are low and population explosions hamper economic growth. Muslims blame oil-greedy countries in the West for repressive regimes that they claim have stifled growth, even in the oil-rich Arabian peninsula and Persian Gulf area. Islamists have leveraged on this discontent and frustration to build populist movements that often have an extremely destructive and reactionary philosophy.

Islamist doctrine is not a passive philosophy, but a program for action. One of their favorite "military" tools is the suicide attack on civilians. People who die in such attacks are considered to be holy martyrs. Islamists were responsible for suicide attacks on the United States forces in Lebanon in the 1980s. They have been involved in plots to assassinate Arab leaders in different countries, and they instigated and carried out the attack on the United States on September 11, 2001. Shi'a Islamists came to power in Iran in 1979 and formed an Islamic Republic.

## The Frustration of Iran

The world is on the eve of almost total destruction. The crisis increased on January 9, 2006 when Iran broke the seals that UN inspectors had placed on two nuclear plants and restarted its nuclear program. Iran's president, Mahmoud Ahmadinejad, has openly expressed his desire to establish centrifuge capacity to enrich uranium. Iran has received shipments from North Korea of surface-to-surface missiles known as BM-25. These missiles have a range of 1,550 miles, putting Europe and Israel within firing range. Iran is currently building an arsenal of over twenty-five nuclear bombs. It is also putting long-range missiles in place that have a range of eight-thousand miles. This arsenal is more than required to destroy Israel. Iran's ultimate aim is to destroy the United States. Very shortly, the United States or Israel will be forced to stop Iran's nuclear armament program.[43]

This will force Iran and other Muslim countries to join forces with Russia and invade Israel. The Muslims need a nuclear umbrella to wage war in the Middle East and Russia needs Arab Oil. Today, Iran is the mother of Islamic terrorism. Tehran openly provides funding, training, and weapons to the world's worst terrorists, including Hezbollah, Hamas, the Palestinian Islamic Jihad, and the Popular Front for the Liberation of Palestine. It also has a relationship with al Qaeda. Iran has given sanctuary to major al Qaeda terrorists. Through its 900 mile border with Iraq, Iran is flooding its neighbor with money and fighters. It is infiltrating troublemakers into Afganistan, supporting terrorism against Turkey, sustaining Syria, and had a hand in the Khobar Towers bombing in Saudi Arabia.

In *Iran The Coming Crisis*, Mark Hitchcock makes the alarming observation, "Iran's new president is motivated by an apocalyptic, end-of-days Messianism that many fear is giving him a dangerous sense of divine destiny. He believes the apocalypse will occur in his own lifetime, and he's not even fifty years old. Many of his statements suggest that he believes his reign is destined to bring about the end-times. This is quite a vision for a mere mortal" (75).

Iran's President Ahmadinejad believes that only great Tribulation, increased violence, and increased conflict will bring about the coming of the return of a messianic, hidden, Twelfth Imam. Ahmadinejad believes he can accelerate the Imam's return through the "creation of chaos on the earth." This kind of end-of-days theology is what drives and compels Ahmadinejad. It is apparently no accident that the word "mad" appears in his name.

## Why Will Russia Take the Lead?

Vladimir Zhirinovsky, a Russian politician, explains current Russian politics in his book, *The Last March to the South*.

> I see Russian soldiers preparing for their last march to the south. I see Russian commanders tracing on their maps the routes to the final destination. I see airborne planes in our southern regions. I see submarines coming to the surface at the shores of the Indian Ocean. I see our marines landing on these shores where the soldiers of the Russian army are already marching, and armored vehicles moving along with tremendous masses of tanks. This last revision of the world has to be done as form of shock therapy-suddenly, swiftly, effectively. Our army is capable of this, all the more so since this is the only way of survival for the nation. And it will be the basis for the rejuvenation of the Russian army. The new military can be reborn only in the course of a military

operation. An army degenerates in the barracks. It needs a goal, a great task. It needs to exercise its muscle. This would be purification for all of us. (239)

This coming invasion is described in chapter 2, verses 2–11 of Joel:

A people come, great and strong, the like of whom has never been; nor will there ever be any such after them A fire devours before them, and behind them a flame burns; the land is like the Garden of Eden before them, and behind them a desolate wilderness; surely nothing shall escape them. Their appearance is like the appearance of horses and like swift steeds, so they run. With a noise like chariots. Over mountaintops they leap, like the noise of a flaming fire that devours the stubble, like a strong people set in battle array. They run like might men, they climb the wall like men of war. Every one marches in formation, and they do not break ranks. They do not push one another; every one marches in his own column. And when they lunge between the weapons, they are not cut down. They run to and fro in the city, they run on the wall. They climb into the houses, they enter at the windows like a thief.

The earth quakes before them, the heavens tremble; the sun and moon grow dark, and the stars diminish their brightness. For the day of the Lord is great and very terrible. We are on sound footing by equating the invasion of Joel 2 with the Magog Invasion (Russia and her allies) delineated in Ezekiel 38 and 39, for the following reasons:

1. It takes place at the beginning of the Tribulation (verse 1)
2. It is from the north

3.  Completed prior to Battle of Armageddon in Joel 3
4.  Not a battle from antiquities, because it is the strongest military force in history (verse 2)

## What Is the Magog Invasion?

The Magog Invasion is described in Ezekiel 38 & 39. *Gog* is a demonic leader. *Rosh* is a Hebrew word that can be translated as "Chief" and it can also be translated to mean the people and the territory of the ancient people of Russia, the Slavs of the southern steppes, and the root from which Russia eventually got its name. The Rus were simply a southern Slavic tribe living on the Ros River. The primary identity involved in Ezekiel 38 and 39 is the land of Magog which most ancient authorities clearly identify as the Scythians, which, in turn, are the ancestors of the present-day Russians. The allies of Russia will be: Iran, called Persia, until 1935, Cush (Sudan and Ethiopia), Put (Libya, Algeria, and Tunisia), Togarmah (Turkey), and Gomer (Germany). The origins of these people are described in chapter 10 of Genesis. The seventy ethnic races of the world came from the three sons of Noah: Shem, Ham and Japheth. Japheth had eight sons: Gomer, Magog, Madai, Tubal, and Meshech are all sons of Japheth. Ashkenaz (Germans) and Togarmah (Kurds) were sons of Gomer. Iranians are from Madai, though they are Aryan and not Arabs. They have, however, become Muslims. From Gomer came the Teutonic: Goths, Vandals, Franks, Lombards, Anglos, Saxons and Jutes.

At this time the European Union is dividing into inner and outer circles. Germany, France, Belgium, the Netherlands, and Luxembourg now form an inner ring of five key nations committed to relinquishing their sovereignty. If they come together as one entity and join the Russian invasion, their power would be eliminated. A vacuum would be created for the Antichrist to build the Revived Roman Empire starting with a loose confederacy of nations which might include Italy, Spain, and Britain. Based upon Daniel 7 and Revelation 17, the Antichrist power will come from a Confederacy of ten nations.

## When is the Magog Invasion?

We know the Magog invasion is at the beginning of the seven years of the Tribulation because the weapons recovered from Russia and her allies are used by Israel for fuel for seven years. "The those who dwell in the cities of Israel will go out and set on fire and burn the weapons, both the shields and bucklers, the bows and arrows, (missile launchers), the javelins and spears (hand held weapons), and they will make fires with them for seven years" (Ezek. 39:9). We know the invasion is in the first part of the Tribulation, because Israel is living in a false sense of peace after signing a peace treaty brokered by the Antichrist. "Then he shall confirm a covenant with many for one week (seven years); but in the middle of the week he shall bring an end to sacrifice and offering, and on the wing of abominations shall be one who makes desolate, even until the consummation which is determined, is poured out on the desolate" (Dan. 9:27). The Tribulation starts with a seven-year peace treaty brokered by the Antichrist. In the middle of the seven-year period, after the Russians and apparently the United States are removed from the picture, the Antichrist takes over the world, invades the Middle East, and desecrates the temple in Jerusalem by building an image to himself.

We also know the Magog invasion is during the first part of the seven-year Tribulation, because there is only a brief moment of peace after the Rapture and then World War III breaks out. "After many days you will be visited. In the latter years you will come into the land of those brought back from the sword and gathered from many people on the mountains of Israel, which had long been desolate; they were brought out of the nations, and now all of them dwell safely. You will say, I will go up against a land of unwalled villages.

I will go to a peaceful people, who dwell safely, all of them dwelling without walls, and having neither bars nor gates, to take plunder and to take booty, to stretch out your hand against the waste places that are again inhabited, and against a people gathered from the nations, who have acquired livestock and goods, who dwell in the midst of the land" (Ezek. 38:8, 11–12). The Magog Invasion will occur in the latter days after the Rapture. This Russian invasion of Israel does not take place in the church age, because it is too specific in detail and the church age was a mystery to Ezekiel and the Old Testament Prophets. Also, there will be no peace in Israel until a pseudo peace treaty is brokered by the Antichrist, which will allow the construction of a temple in Jerusalem next to the Mosque of Omar.

This period of time is described by Christ in the Olivet Discourse, "And Jesus answered and said to them: 'Take head that no one deceives you, for many will come in my name, saying, I am the Christ, and will deceive many. And you will hear of wars and rumors of wars. See that you are not troubled; for all these things must come to pass, but the end is not yet. For nation will rise against nation; and kingdom against kingdom. And there will be famines, pestilences, and earthquakes in various places. All these are the beginning of sorrow" (Matt. 24:4–8).

# CHAPTER 9

# THE UNITED STATES OF AMERICA IN PROPHECY

## America Discovered

On October 9, 1492, Christopher Columbus discovered North America and touched ground on the Bahaman Islands in the Caribbean Islands. "Christopher" literally means Christ-bearer. For a long time, Columbus had been convinced that God had given him a special, almost mystical mission: to carry the Light of Christ into the darkness of undiscovered heathen lands, and to bring the inhabitants of those lands to the holy faith of Christianity.

Indeed, he found confirmation of his call almost everywhere he looked. He quoted in his journal such lines of scripture as those in Isaiah which meant so much to him: "Listen to me, O coastland, and hearken, you peoples from afar. The lord called me from the womb, from the body of my mother he named my name...I will give you as a light to the nations, that my salvation may reach to the end of the earth" (Isa. 49: 1 & 6).

On a crisp October night in 1517, a black-garbed Augustinian monk made his way undetected to a castle church. The place was an insignificant medieval German town named Wittenberg. With swift, determined strokes he nailed one of the most inflammable documents of the age to the church door, which served as the village bulletin board. Whether Luther recognized the fact or not, the

Reformation was launched. What he did was publish the Ninety-five Theses, which revealed how the Roman Catholic Church had departed from God's word.

On January 21, 1525, a dozen or so men slowly trudged through the snow. After prayer, several men were baptized. With this simple act, the Anabaptism movement was born and the Swiss Brethren Church was constituted. For the first time in the course of the Reformation, a group of Christians dared to form a church after what was conceived to be the New Testament pattern. The Brethren emphasized the absolute necessity of a personal commitment to Christ as essential to salvation and a prerequisite to baptism. They became known by their critics as Anabaptists, or re-baptizers, because of their practice of re-baptizing all who came into their ranks from the Catholic Church, who were baptized prior to becoming old enough to believe. The sect known as the Anabaptists came to prominence at the time of the protestant reformation, although they are known to have been in existence long before that time.

The main line of the Protestant theology is a one-sided interpretation of the Pauline teaching of justification by faith; although including this doctrine in its foundation, sixteenth-century Anabaptism definitely shows a different orientation. With the Reformers there is indeed an imbalance between the positional truth and experiential truth. In other words they struggled with dead orthodoxy, in which their deeds did not match their words. Also, the state churches continued certain sacraments and lethargy brought over from Catholicism, which had little meaning. The Anabaptists, were continually persecuted by the Church of England and the Lutheran Church for re-baptizing adult believers.

## Who Were the Pilgrims?

The immigration of the Pilgrims to New England occurred in stages. That they had to go somewhere became apparent soon enough.

Theirs was the position of the Separatist: they believed that the reforms of the Anglican church had not gone far enough, that, although the break with Catholicism in 1535 had moved some way toward the Puritan belief in an idea of religious authority grounded solely in Scripture, by substituting king for pope as the head of the church England was only recapitulating an unnecessary, corrupt, and even idolatrous order. One of their great hopes was for the propagating and advancing the Gospel of the kingdom of Christ in those remote parts of the world

The most obvious difference between the Pilgrims and the Puritans is that the Puritans had no intention of breaking with the Anglican church. The Puritans were nonconformists, as were the Pilgrims. Both groups refused to accept an authority beyond that of the revealed word.

## Who Wrote the United States Constitution?

Until the time of the Constitutional Convention, the states had never actually functioned as a nation in the true sense of the word; they had always been individual states. Although joined together in the single purpose of the Revolutionary War, they had not been required to relinquish any rights as individual states. The states were more like a confederation of several small, independent, neighboring nations on the same continent than a single, unified nation. It was against this background that delegates were selected and sent to the Constitutional Convention. As a result of the War, the states recognized the need for a central government to perform functions they individually were not able to perform: for example, national defense.

The men chosen as delegates were not random selections. There were clearly written laws within each state prescribing the qualifications of those who would serve in public affairs. Every delegate who attended the Constitution Convention did so in a legal manner.

He fulfilled the requirements mandated by his own state's constitution. These qualifications were not denominations qualifications, such as Baptist or Lutheran, but they were simply general Christian qualifications, requiring beliefs common to any orthodox Christian denomination.[44]

The Delaware constitution required the following: Every person who was chosen to be a member of either house or appointed to any office or place of trust needed to make and subscribe the following declaration, to wit: "do profess faith in God the Father, and in Jesus Christ his only Son, and in the Holy Ghost, one God, blessed for evermore; and I do acknowledge the holy scriptures of the Old and New Testament to be given by divine inspiration."[45]

The Pennsylvania constitution contained similar requirements: "I do believe in one God, the Creator and Governor of the universe, the rewarder of the good and the punisher of the wicked, and I do acknowledge the Scriptures of the Old and New Testament to be given by divine Inspiration."[46]

The North Carolina provision said the following: "No person, who shall deny the being of God, or the truth of the protestant religion, or the divine authority either of the Old or New Testaments, or who shall hold religious principles incompatible with the freedom and safety of the state, shall be capable of holding any office, or place of trust or profit in the civil department, within this state"[47]

## What Was the Purpose of the United States?

From humble origins, God blessed America. Within a relatively short period, thirteen original colonies became a mighty continental country stretching from the Atlantic Ocean to the Pacific Ocean. The three primary purposes of the United States were to (1) support missionary activity throughout the world (2) Defeat Germany in World War II and (3) assist Israel in its fight against the Muslim world.

No other country in the history of the world has sent more missionaries throughout the world than the United States. No other country has done more to militarily support Israel than the United States of America. God blessed America and it prospered. After World War II, the United States was the unquestioned leader of the World from both a monetary and a military standpoint.

In the proceeding of the Constitutional Convention, Benjamin Franklin said, "Sir, I have lived a long time; and the longer I live, the more convincing proofs I see that God still governs in the affairs of men. If a sparrow cannot fall to the ground without our Father's notice, is it possible that we can build an empire without our Father's aid? I believe the Sacred Writings which say that "except the Lord build the house, they labor in vain that build it."[48] Franklin went on to move that a member of the clergy be invited to participate in the meetings from day to day, so that he participants might invoke the wisdom and guidance of the Father of lights. "Else," he said, " we shall succeed no better than did the builders of Babel."

James Madison, one of the framers of our Constitution, said, "We have staked the whole future of American civilization not upon the power of government, far from it. We have staked the future of all our political institutions upon the capacity of mankind for self-government; upon the capacity of each and all of us to govern ourselves, to control ourselves, to sustain ourselves according to the Ten Commandments of God."[49] George Washington, our first President, said, "The propitious smiles of heaven can never be expected on a nation that disregards the eternal rules of order and right which heaven itself has ordained."[50] He was speaking of the Ten Commandments and the laws of God as found in the Bible. The United States was built on a moral and spiritual foundation. Though all the founders were not Christians, all of them understood that a just society with freedom for all must be governed by the laws of God, who alone has the right to determine what is right and what is wrong.

General Douglas MacArthur wrote, "History fails to record a

single precedent in which nations subject to moral decay have not passed into political and economic decline. There has been either a spiritual awakening to overcome the moral lapse, or a progressive deterioration leading to ultimate national disaster."[51]

## Where Did We Go Wrong?

The West, with its history of democratic principles and moral values, is struggling desperately. We no longer seem capable of controlling ourselves in our pursuits of pleasure, ease, and material gain. The "good life" has brought corruption, greed, and a self-destructive narcissism. Crime and violent acts flourish in our cities, and our police departments seem helpless in their efforts to control the rampage. We glorify the criminal in our newspapers, television programs, and movies, while the victims are graphically depicted in the process of suffering and dying. Torture, abuse, blood, guns, and knives are constantly used to entertain a culture that willingly watches more violence while it complains of the rise of crime in our society.

How did all this happen? Two major factors in American life have contributed to the present moral decline: the theory of evolution and secular humanism. The theory of evolution finds its roots in the Babylonian religion of pantheism. Pantheism is basically the worship of creation rather than the creator. It puts man on par with plants and animals and removes accountability to a God who determines right from wrong. Secular humanists have the following beliefs:

1. The universe is self-existing and not created.
2. Man is a part of nature and that he has emerged as the result of a continuous process.
3. The traditional dualism of mind and body must be rejected.
4. Religion is a man-made invention.

5. Humanism asserts that the nature of the universe must be determined by science and not the supernatural.

Since Humanism and the theory of evolution has taken over the judicial, legislative, academic, and religious segments of our country, we can no longer be called a Christian nation. In 1973, the *Humanist Manifesto II* was published. Especially enlightening are these words from the very first tenet of this manifesto, "But we can discover no divine purpose or providence for the human species. While there is much that we do not know, humans are responsible for what we are or will become. No deity will save us; we must save ourselves."[52]

Without God, our country has lost is purpose, meaning, and direction. Without a belief in God, there is no basis for absolutes and no concern for right and wrong. People become sociopaths. They become mentally insane. One is clinically insane if they have at least three of the following symptoms:

1. Deceitfulness, as indicated by repeated lying, or conning others for personal profit or pleasure.
2. Impulsive behavior or failure to plan ahead.
3. Irritability and aggressiveness, as indicated by repeated physical fights or assaults.
4. Reckless disregard for safety of self or others.
5. Consistent irresponsibility, as indicated by failure to sustain steady work or honor financial obligations.
6. Lack of remorse, being indifferent to or rationalizing having hurt, mistreated, or stolen from another.
7. Failure to conform to social norms with respect to lawful behaviors as indicated by repeated arrests.

This definition of mentally ill describes a growing number of young people today who are sociopaths with no sense of right or wrong, empathy, discipline, or respect for authority.

## How Did the United States Become a Home of Sociopaths?

America changed from a Christian country with belief in absolutes to a Godless country and the philosophical position of Nihilism. *Nihilism* comes from the Latin *nihil*, meaning "nothing." Nihilists generally assert there is no reasonable proof of the existence of a higher ruler or creator, a "true morality" does not exist, and secular ethics are impossible. Therefore, life has no truth and no action can be preferable to any other. Nihilism is often associated with Friedrich Nietzsche. In the United States and in western culture, a competing alternative to Nihilism is Hedonism. Hedonism is the philosophy that pleasure is the most important pursuit of mankind. The name derives from *hedone*, the Greek word for pleasure. The basic idea behind hedonistic thought is that all actions can be measured on the basis of how much pleasure and how little pain they produce. The hedonist strives to maximize pleasure. Utilitarian John Mill proposed the greatest amount of happiness for the greatest number of people. Both Nihilism and Hedonism have led to young people in America leading purposeless, hopeless lives and with the resulting unhappiness. Unhappiness has in turn become a primary cause for the huge increase in drug and alcohol abuse.

## Who Was John Dewey?

John Dewey is recognized as the Father of modern education. Dewey was a major influence in what is called modern education today in America. Contemporary systems of education and democracy are based on the concept of evolution and natural progression. The education theories of Dewey would not have been so acceptable to people had it not been for the previous acceptance of Darwin's theory of evolution. Evolution praises change and declares the highest good is positive change. Darwin's theory helped strengthen the ideas of relativism and positivism which had been around for generations but were reinforced by John Dewey.

The foundational premise of progressive liberals is that nothing is constant. They think the only constant good is change for good, or in other words, positivism. Things should not be measured from any absolute standards, but from a relative perception based on human desire. Relativism denies absolutes. God is absolute. The word of God teaches absolutes. Evolution is diametrically opposed to God's word. Since man has evolved, there could have been no fall of man from the perfection of Adam. With no fall of man, there would be no need for salvation. Thus evolution strikes at the root of Christian faith. Evolution makes the whole of scriptures meaningless. John Dewey was strongly opposed to anything in public education that would encourage children's faith in God. Dewey was one of the founding fathers of the National Education Association and the ACLU.

Allan Bloom, author of the landmark critique of American education, *The Closing of the American Mind*, starts his analysis thus: "There is one thing a professor can be absolutely certain of: almost every student entering the university believes, or says he believes, that truth is relative" (25). Relativists believe that all people have a right to their own opinion, except those who hold that some opinions are better than others. Moral relativism takes the position that there are no right and wrong answers, and no one has the right to judge. Moral relativism is the unofficial creed of much of American culture, especially in the areas of education, law, and public policy. However, relativism itself is a dichotomy, saying there are no absolutes is in itself an absolute statement. Judging others for judging, is in itself judgmental. Unfortunately, the quintessential relativist is a sociopath with no conscience.

## How Did We Become Godless?

Since Darwin popularized his theory in 1859, the idea of evolution has infected other areas of men's thoughts including law and its interpretation, society and its rules of conduct, economics, and more. John Dewey helped popularize the teaching of evolution since the idea of constant change reinforced his idea of how God and the Bible were foolishness. Dewey believed in neither God nor the Bible. He ridiculed those who put their trust in traditional understanding of law and mocked the beliefs of the Founders.[53] Roscoe Pound and Louis Brandies were also influential in promoting the turning of evolutionary principals into law. As a professor and as a dean, Roscoe Pound had a significant effect on Harvard and other law schools. Harvard was originally founded as a missionary school, but has become a bastion for a new paradigm in progressive education. The old paradigm known as didactic was built upon the view of absolutes and classical logic. The new humanistic paradigm known as dialectic is built upon the view that feelings and human experience must determine what is right and wrong. The old school of thought focused on truth, feelings, or one's ability to justify what seems to be right. God's word is didactic, and it is written in absolutes. This goes back to Satan's original deception of Eve, "'Is that really what God said? You will not die. There is nothing wrong with that fruit.' Now the serpent was more cunning than any beast of the field which the Lord God had made. And he said to the woman, 'Has God indeed said, "You shall not eat of every tree of the garden?"'" (Gen. 3:1). Satan convinced Eve not to rely on absolutes, but to experience for herself how good the fruit was and that she could be like God.

In his book *The God Who Is There*, Francis Schaeffer makes the following observations:

> The present chasm between the generations has been brought about almost entirely by a change in the concept of truth…young people from Christian homes are brought up in the old framework of truth. Then they are subjected to the modern framework. In time they become confused because they do not understand the alternative with which they are

being presented. Confusion becomes bewilderment, and before long they are overwhelmed. This is unhappily true not only of young people, but of many pastors, Christian educators, evangelists and missionaries as well...In America the crucial years of change were from 1913 to 1940 and during these relatively few years the whole way of thinking underwent a revolution. (13–14)

What Schaeffer is talking about is the paradigm shift from absolutes to relativism and from creationism to a Godless evolutionary system.

## In What Way Did the American Culture Change?

In approximately 200 hundred years, America went from a country of God-fearing pilgrims on a mission to save the world, to a Godless country with a growing population of immoral perverted sociopaths with no concept of absolute ethical values.

In *Slouching Towards Gomorrah*, Robert Bork makes the following comments about American culture:

A pornographic culture is not one in which pornographic materials are published and distributed. A pornographic culture is one which accepts the ideas about sex on which pornography is based...Our popular culture has gone far beyond propagandizing for fornication. That seems almost innocent nowadays. What America increasingly produces and distributes is now propaganda for every perversion and obscenity imaginable. If many of us accept the assumption on which that is based, and apparently many do, then we are well on our way to an obscene culture. The Upshot is that American popular culture is in a free fall, with the bottom not yet in sight. (138–139)

Bork goes on to say:

Young males, who are more prone to violence than females or older males, witness so many gory depictions of killing that they are bound to become desensitized to it. We now have teenagers and even sub teenagers, who shoot if they feel they have been "dissed" (shown disrespect). Indeed, the newspapers bring us stories of murders done for simple pleasure, the killing of a stranger simply because the youth felt like killing someone, anyone, That is why, for the first time in American history, you are more likely to be murdered by a complete stranger than by someone you know. This is why our prisons contain convicted killers who show absolutely no remorse, and frequently cannot even remember the names of the persons they killed. (143)

Bork presents clinical studies showing the homicide rates in three countries increased dramatically ten to fifteen years after the introduction of television. Studies reflect that exposure to television violence is a causal factor in about half of the 21,000 homicides per year in the United States and half of all rapes and assaults.[54]

The fixation of self first became obvious with rock 'n' roll, which evolved into hard rock. The extrovert, hedonist, criminal, or exhibitionist can rise to heroic stature in rock. Now we have moved on to rap, which is even less constrained. Its performers do not just sing about criminals; some of them are criminals. Today's culture glorifies the criminal lifestyle. Tattoos, pants hanging off the butt, and hand signs all reflect prison and gang mentality.

What we hear in rap is paralleled elsewhere in popular culture in varying degrees. That the movies feature sex, violence, and vile language is not news. Car chases ending in flaming crashes, the machine gunning of masses of people, explosions of helicopters, the liberal production of corpses, language previously not heard even in semi-polite society, these are now standard fare. Many in Hollywood insist upon a liberal lacing of foul language in their films because they regard brutality and obscenity as signs of authenticity. Because they live a purposeless, meaningless life, they assume this fictional world is reality. Hollywood divides cinema and television into two classes good and bad.

Though it cannot begin to match rap, TV undermines authority in gentler way. Hedonism, or the pursuit of pleasure, with no bounds, is promoted. Businessmen are depicted negatively. Politicians, military personnel, and clergy are often cast in a poor light. Perhaps popular culture is inevitably vulgar, but today's entertainment is sinking to lower depths in free fall with no end in sight.

## What Is the ACLU?

The ACLU is the American Civil Liberties Union. It was founded by Roger Nash Baldwin, a card-carrying member of the Communist Party. Roger Baldwin did not believe in God, the Bible, Christianity, the death penalty, or quick punishment of evil. The ACLU believes that we are animals, and that we are not made in God's image. It believes that Man has no purpose and there are no absolutes. The ACLU does not want Christ in Christmas or God in the Boy Scouts. They think there is no such thing as a lie and that there is situation ethics. They think a person who commits murder should not be killed. They think children should not be spanked. They think men in prison who spit or attack guards in prison should have a time out and should not be unreasonably disciplined.[55]

What does God say about the ACLU? "The fool has said in his heart there is no God, the are corrupt, they have done abominable works. There is none who does good" (Ps. 14:1). "Whoever sheds man's blood, by man his blood shall be shed: for in the image of God he made man" (Gen. 9:6). "He who spares his rod hates his son, but he who loves him disciplines him promptly" (Prov. 12:24). "You shall not murder, commit adultery, steal, lie, or covet your neighbor's wife" (Exodus 20). "You shall not make any cutting in your flesh …nor tattoo any marks on you: I am the Lord. For everyone who curses his father or his mother shall surely be put to death. He has cursed his father or his mother. His blood shall be upon him. If a man lies with a male as he lies with a woman, both of them have committed an abomination. They shall surely be put to death. Their blood shall be upon them" (Lev. 20).

The ACLU has apparently won the cultural battle in the United States. God has been removed from education and government. Criminals who murder are rarely killed. Children are encouraged to question and disrespect their parents. Children are rarely spanked or punished. Unfortunately, crime and lawlessness have become a way of life to millions of Americans. Crime is the only thing they know, and they have learned how to do it and get away with it at an early age. Many of our major cities are not safe for either tourist or residents. America has growing areas called "Dead Zones." These are areas where anarchy has broken out and the police have lost control. Sections of urban America have been written off as "anarchic badlands." In many areas, youth gangs control the streets instead of governmental authority.

High crime and lawlessness have not caught God off-guard. The Apostle Paul warned, "Know this, that in the last days perilous times will come: For men will be lovers of themselves, lovers of money, boasters, proud, blasphemers, disobedient to parents, unthankful, unholy, unloving, unforgiving, slanderers, without self-control, brutal, despisers of good, traitors, headstrong, haughty, lovers of pleasure rather than lovers of God" (II Tim. 3:1–4).

Children today are taught Nihilism in public schools. They are told that human existence is without objective meaning, purpose, comprehensible truth, or essential value. Many high school and college students today have become mentally insane. They have become sociopaths, not knowing right from wrong. Two boys named

Eric and Dillon murdered seven people and wounded twenty-four students at Columbine High School. Since then, others have followed suit. Eric and Dillon stated that they believed in Darwinism, and that they were superior to the other students. They believed they were merely acting out what they had been taught at Columbine. Not to worry, all is not hopeless. Jesus is coming soon. He will bring not the world's peace, but true peace.

## Why Do We Have So Many Drug Addicts?

*The American Journal of Psychiatry* conducted a study and reported that 36 percent of medical students reported using cocaine at some time during their lives, 17 percent during the past year, and 6 percent n the past month! *USA Today* reported that Los Angeles is the new drug capital of the United States, surpassing Miami, Florida. Recently, Los Angels led the country in drug seizures. Street gangs, with eighty-thousand members, distribute cocaine and crack to forty-four cities out of the Los Angeles area alone. While the message that a person should not mix alcohol and drugs is frequently given, the truth is that the two are very often used together. The number of people who use both is too great to ignore.

In *The Myth Of Separation (Church & State)*, David Barton develops a strong correlation between the removal of prayer from schools and an explosion of crime, under-age pregnancies, and drug addiction. Barton cites the United States Supreme Court decision of Engel vs. Vital, 1962:

> This was the first case in which the Court applied its innovation of misapplied separation to overturn the longstanding tradition of school prayer. The controversy in this case was whether it was Constitutional for New York students to offer a simple prayer. The court found prayer to be unconstitutional. Barton shows that after God was effectively removed American

schools in 1962; violence, drugs, crime and teen pregnancy skyrocketed. Scores on SAT test plummeted. (145)

## Is America Doomed?

As Billy Graham once said, "If God does not punish the United States, he will owe Sodom and Gomorrah and apology." Why hasn't God punished the United States? There are two things that have preserved this nation; 1) There are still God fearing people in the United States. 2) The United States protects Israel with military technology. In Genesis 18, Christ appeared as the Angel of the Lord, and told Abraham that God would no destroy Sodom and Gomorrah if ten righteous men were found. Because two angels, sent by God, failed to find ten righteous men, they told Lot and his family to leave Sodom. God has spared the United States, and is waiting for the church to be removed at the Rapture. Once believers are removed, and only the wicked are left, judgment will eventually fall on America. In addition, Genesis 12:3 states, "I will bless those who bless you, and I will curse him who curses you." This is the unconditional covenant God made with Abraham. Anyone who blesses Israel will be blessed. Anyone who curses Israel will be cursed. Currently, many Bible-believing Christians support Israel as they are persecuted by the Muslims and various anti-Semitic countries. Once Christians are removed from the United States, America will join the ranks with the rest of the world and to a large extent become anti-Semitic. At this time the United States is locked in a cultural war between those who believe in Judeo-Christian absolutes and humanistic relativism. Once believers are removed from the battle, the war will be over.

## Where Is the United States in Prophecy?

America is not mentioned by name in the Bible. When Russia and her allies invade Israel, Ezekiel 38:13 states, "Sheba, Dedan, the merchants of Tarshish, and all their young lions will say to you, 'Have you come to take plunder? Have you gathered your army to take booty, to carry away silver and gold, to take away livestock and goods, to take great plunder?'" Sheba and Dedan refer to Saudi Arabia.

Some try to link the United States with the young lions of Tarshish. Charles Feinberg, in his book *The Prophecy of Ezekiel*, makes the following comment: "Tarshish has been identified with Great Britain, but not on good grounds. It may be either Spain or Sardinia, for there was a Tartessus in both areas. Some interpreters have inferred from verse 13 that these nations will befriend Israel and come to her defense, but this cannot be maintained with certainty" (223).

This does, however, raise another question: Why is America not mentioned as a key player in the events of the end-times? At the close of World War II, the United States was undoubtedly the greatest nation in human history in terms of political, economic, and military might. It seems strange that the United States would not merit at least some passing mention in the biblical passages where end-time events are described. Of course, most modern nations are not mentioned in the Bible; therefore, it could just be that God has chosen not to mention America. However, if the United States was the world's number-one power when the end-times arrive, how could it not be mentioned? Did the United States catch God by surprise? How does one explain this deafening biblical silence about America's role in the final years of this age?

## Will the Military Power of the United States Be Destroyed?

Many now believe that the reason America is absent from Bible prophecy is that there will be some natural or nuclear destruction that will remove the US from power. We can only speculate as to the means, but some things are certain:

1. America is not mentioned in the Bible.
2. America is Israel's main defender in the last days prior to the Rapture.
3. America may not be pro-Israel after the Rapture.
4. Israel will have Moses and Elijah to protect her for the first three-and-a-half years.
5. The invading Russian army with her allies are destroyed in the beginning of the Tribulation.
6. World power in the end-times is centered in the Roman Empire Confederacy.
7. European prominence can only be explained in the light of United States and Russian decline
8. Something will cause a cataclysmic decline in the United states after the Rapture.

## Who Opposes the Magog Invasion?

When Russia, Iran, Germany and their allies wage war, who do they oppose? Naturally, they will be invading Israel. Christ said, however, that this will be "nation against nation and kingdom against kingdom" (Matt. 24:7). The arch-nemesis to Communist Russia has been the United States. This is because Russia has been a Godless, oppressive, socialistic, anti-Semitic nation. The United States has been Christian-influenced, democratic, and pro-Israel. Things have changed in the United States. Christians will be removed by the Rapture, but the United States will still be a super-power with a desire to protect its interest in Middle East oil. The world is currently consuming one thousand barrels of oil per second. Consumption of world oil is at about the same rate of production. The level of spare capacity is about 2 million barrels a day. The oil industry is at 97.5 percent of capacity. This leaves almost no margin for error for things such as natural disasters, accidents, terrorist attacks, or war. Russia's invasion of the Middle East will be a definite threat to the United

States. Approximately 75 percent of the world's known oil reserves are located in the Middle East.

Iran's two chief enemies are the United States and Israel. Mahmoud Ahmadinejad has stated he wants to destroy the United States and Israel. Mark Hitchcock's book, *Iran: The Coming Crisis* makes the following observation:

> On October 26, 2005, at a conference titled "A World Without Zionism," Ahmadinejad addressed a gathering of about four-thousand students. Standing in front of a huge banner that read, "A World Without Zionism," he dropped several verbal bombshells: "They (ask), 'Is it possible for us to witness a world without America and Zionism?' But you had best know that this slogan and this goal are altogether attainable, and surely can be achieved. This regime that is occupying Jerusalem must be wiped from the map." The only bit of good news for Israel in these statements is that at least Ahmadinejad has recognized that Israel is on the map. No Arab or Islamic nation up to this point has even recognized the existence of the Jewish state or included Israel on any map of the region. (71)

The Western media insists on calling terrorists extremists. However, they are not extremists, they are orthodox Muslims. Any country that has a Muslim majority is anti-Semitic and anti-Christian. The Qur'an clearly teaches death to all Christians and Jews who do not accept Allah as the only God. Saudi Arabia is pouring hundreds of millions of oil dollars into the United States in an effort to evangelize Americans.

## Who Is the Twelfth Imam?

Within Shiite Islam, which dominates Iran, an Imam is a spiritual leader who is a bloodline relative of the prophet Muhammad. There is a prophecy in Islam about the coming of the twelfth Imam—Imam Muhammad Abul Qasim. It is believed by the Twelver sect that he disappeared in AD 878 in the cave of the great mosque of Samara without leaving any descendants. It is also taught that the twelfth Imam was still active and communicated with the outside world by messengers until AD 941 when all communication and contact with this world was cut off. According to Islamic teaching, he will return near the end of the world. According to their end-time view, when the returns, he will rule the earth for seven years. He will bring about the Final Judgment and the end of the world.

In *Iran The Coming Crisis*, Mark Hitchcock makes the following observation, "...Ahmadinejad is close to the messianic Hojatieh society that is led by Ayatollah Mesbah Yazdi. This spiritual leader frequently appears with the new president in public. The Hojatieh believe that only great Tribulation, increased violence, and conflict will bring about his coming. They believe that the 'creation of chaos on earth' can accelerate the Imam's return. Ahmadinejad believes that the Mahdi will appear when the globe is in utter chaos. This kind of end-of-day theology is what drives and compels Ahmadinejad" (78). When Israel and the United States destroy Iran's nuclear capability, this will force Iran to join with Russia against the Zionist United States and Israel.

## Is the United States Mentioned in Prophecy?

The United States is not mentioned in the Bible by name. The problem is the deafening silence. In Revelation 13:4, the earth dwellers ask the following question during the second three-and-a-half-year period of the Tribulation: "Who can make war with the head of the ten-nation Revived Roman Empire?" It appears that the ten-nation Revived Roman Empire of the Antichrist fills in the role of dominant world power after the demise of Russia and the United States. If the Rapture occurred this year, the United States could be devastated by a pre-emptive nuclear attack within a relatively short period, and clearly within three-and-a-half years.

This would mean that the United States would rise and fall within approximately 200 years. Any industrial power which survives the Seal Judgments will face the devastation and destruction in the seven trumpets and the seven bowl judgments. Each series of judgments become progressively more severe. Mountains, cities, factories, and homes will be destroyed. Nuclear, volcanic, and meteorite fallout will affect weather patterns and hinder normal rain and sun cycles. Famines, plagues and natural disasters will be the order of the day.

If Christ did not come to earth to rule, the human race would be utterly destroyed. What is sad is that while Judgment Day is at the door, few people know or care. Many people say, "That is what my Grandfather said." The fact is many Christians in the nineteenth and twentieth centuries were on the mark. Many people studied the Bible, understood end-time events, and were involved in evangelism and missions. America was a prosperous, God-fearing country. Today, unfortunately, much of the church has become lukewarm and apostate. Instead of end-time, evangelism and missions, we are concerned with divorce, drug recovery, and financial prosperity. Church golfing, baseball and networking are the order of the day. The ingredients for politically correct methodology are seeker-friendliness, being non-confrontational, and being non-judgmental. If you cannot conform and be non-confrontational, you will be confronted and removed. The New Age has arrived, and the old, narrow–minded, conservative hail, fire and brimstone is out. Unfortunately, nothing could be further than the truth. Hail, fire and brimstone is at the door. The United States is doomed. Once the church is removed, many of those left behind will not reach the end of the seven-year Tribulation. Many may die within months of Rapture, which could occur at any time. We as Americans love our country and do not desire to see its destructions. The important thing to remember is that our founding fathers realized they were mere pilgrims on their way to the New Jerusalem, a new city, where God will tabernacle with man forever. We have the hope of eternal life. All we can do is worn others that Judgment Day and the destruction of the United States is at the door.

## What Are the Four Things that Could Cause a Cataclysmic Deadline in the United States?

1. A large number of Christians will be removed at the Rapture. Eighty-five percent of Americans claim to be Christians. Forty-one percent of Americans claim to be "born-again Christians." Seven percent are identified as "evangelical Christians." This group is a subset of the born-again group. The main factor of the "evangelical Christians" is a belief that salvation is by faith in Christ alone, without human works. According to Barna, this represents about 14 to 16 million American adults. When one adds in children, the number could easily climb to 25 to 30 million. With a total population of 290 million, possibly 10 percent or more will be removed. A large number of these Christians are in America's heartland and produce large amounts of food for the nation.

2. High density population on the Eastern, Western and Gulf seaboards. There is a high density of population and economic power concentrated along the coastal areas of the United States in what has been politically called the blue states. During the first part of the Tribulation, the sixth seal is described as, "I looked when he opened the sixth seal, and behold, there was a great earthquake and the sun became black as sackcloth of hair, and the moon became like blood. And the stars of heaven fell to the earth, as a fig tree drops its late figs when it is shaken by a mighty wind. Then the sky receded as a scroll when it is rolled

up, and every mountain, and island was removed out of its place"
(Rev. 6:12–14). This is a period of worldwide cataclysmic disaster greater than anything previously recorded. Although Noah's
flood was worldwide, the number of people affected was much
smaller than the world population of billions that we have today.
Apparently, meteorites made out of other material from space
will impact the earth. If every mountain and island are affected
we can be sure the earth's oceans will be rift with giant tsunamis
greater than anything modern man has seen. This means large
amounts of destruction will occur on American coastlines both
in human lives and economic loss. In Acts 2:19, Peter quotes Joel
and states, "I will show wonders in heaven above and signs in the
earth beneath: blood and fire and vapor of smoke." This refers
to not only asteroids and meteorites, but also earth quakes and
volcanoes. It would not be surprising to see dormant volcanoes
such as Yosemite go off and discharge ash and smoke into the
atmosphere above the United States. This could cause a small ice
age and affect farm crops for year.

3. Moses and Elijah will have the ability to stop rain for three-
   and-a-half years. This will cause tremendous loss of agricultural
   production in the United States.

4. If Russia, Germany, Iran and their allies move into Israel and the
   Suez Canal, the United States may get militarily involved. The
   United States may not be pro-Israel, but self-interest will cause
   the it to protect its interest in Middle East oil. There has not
   been a weapon made that was not eventually used. It appears
   to be only a matter of time until World War III ends up in a
   nuclear exchange. Revelation 6:8 states that one-quarter of the
   world's population (1.75 billion people) die as a result of World
   War III. Since the United States loses its significance in world
   history somewhere around this time, one can only wonder if
   some of Russia's nuclear power is not unleashed on America.

## How Do We Know The United States Will Fall?

According to Bishop Usher's examination of the genealogy tables in the Bible, man has been on earth for approximately six-thousand years. At this time, the United States and Russia are the two dominate military powers. However, it appears that both these world powers will be destroyed during the first three-and-a-half years of the Tribulation. Revelation 13:4 states, "…Who can make war with him?" This is referring to the Antichrist and the European Confederation. This means that the military might of the United States, Russia, China, and Israel are reduced, which will allow the European Confederation to gain world supremacy. At this time Israel ranks fourth as a military power, but is merely a proxy for the United States in the Middle East. As goes the United States, so goes Israel. China is apparently decimated during the Sixth Trumpet Judgment in Revelation 9:13–21. From Ezekiel 38–39 we know that Russia, Iran and their allies will be destroyed during World War III and their invasion of Israel.

It appears that during this world war the United States will be destroyed. In Matthew 24:7, Jesus says, "For nation will rise against nation and kingdom against kingdom. And there will be famines, pestilences, and earthquakes in various places." Revelation 6:8 states, "And I looked, and behold, a pale horse. And the name of him who sat on it Was Death, and Hades followed with him. And power was given to them over a fourth of the earth, to kill with sword, with hunger, with death, and by the beasts of the earth." At the beginning of the Tribulation, war will break out, nation against nation, and kingdom against kingdom. This is not simply Russia, Iran and their allies attacking Israel. This is a world war with over 1.7 billion casualties. We can only assume the United States will not stand by and allow Russia to control the oil in the Middle East. It appears that the United States will be attacked during the Magog invasion and will be decimated. No conventional war has ever had this many fatalities. This war is different from any previous war. This war is unconventional. It is unfortunate that man has never made a weapon that was not used. It appears World War III will be a nuclear war.

# CHAPTER 10

# THE SEVEN TRUMPET JUDGMENTS

## What Are the Trumpet Judgments?

The book of Revelation has seven seals, seven trumpets and seven bowls judgments. The seven seals represent wax seals being broken off as the deed to the universe is opened and claimed by Jesus Christ. Only the Lamb of God, who is the God-Man kinsman redeemer, is qualified to open the seals and take possession of the earth. The seventh seal includes the next series of judgments, the trumpet judgments.

The seventh trumpet judgment includes the last series of judgments known as the bowl judgments. The seal judgments are found in Revelation 6 and 8. The trumpet judgments are found in chapters nine and eleven. The bowl judgments are found in chapter 16. There are technically twenty judgments since the fifth seal is not a judgment, it is actually memorializing the prayers of the saints and their petition for the kinsman redeemer to avenge the blood of those that were martyred.

The judgments are sequential and become progressively more intense as a new series of sevens begins.

The first seal judgments are partially the result of war. The result is death and destruction to one-quarter of the earth's population. The seven trumpet judgments are intense and cause death and destruction to one-third of the remaining world population. The first six trumpet judgments result in the destruction to one-third of the plant, animal life, and the destruction of one-third of the fresh and salt water. The seventh trumpet includes the seven bowl judgments and results in almost total destruction to life as we know it.

The book of Revelation loosely follows a pattern or type shown in the book of Joshua. Jesus Christ was the commander of the army of the Lord, not Joshua. "And it came to pass, when Joshua was by Jericho, that he lifted his eyes and looked, and behold. A Man stood opposite him with his sword drawn in his hand, and Joshua went to Him and said to Him, 'Are You for us or for our adversaries?' So he said, 'No but as commander of the army of the Lord I have now come.' And Joshua fell on his face to the earth and worshiped, and said to Him, 'What does my Lord say to his servant?' The Commander of the Lord's army said to Joshua, 'Take your sandal off your foot, for the place where you stand is holy.' And Joshua did so" (Joshua 5:13–15).

The battle plan was to send two spies into the land to save Rehab the harlot and her family. They would then dispose usurpers and recover the land to its rightful owner, God and his chosen people Israel. The method of attack would be to silently march around Jericho for six days, then seven priests are to blow seven trumpets and the walls of Jericho are to fall on the seventh day. A confederacy of eleven kings are to be destroyed. In the book of Revelation the battle plan is to send in two spies, Moses and Elijah, to save Tribulation saints, who were former prostitutes, in that they were in apostasy, from the coming judgment. Seven trumpets are blown. After seven years the walls of Babylon will fall down. A ten-nation confederacy with ten kings is joined by another king. They will be destroyed. Jesus will dispose the usurpers and take rightful possession of Canaan, and return it to the nation of Israel. Once again, God uses real events from the Old Testament as a pattern for real events in the future.

## What is the Significance of Trumpets?

Trumpets played a major part in the national life of Israel, finding use in ceremonial processions, in assembling people for war, journeys, and special feats, in warning of the coming day of the Lord, and in announcing the new year. Trumpets were also a signal for war, or the announcement of a new king. The seven trumpets in Revelation announce all of the above.

Following the pattern of the seal series, the first four trumpets are different in kind from the last three. These four set in motion the forces of nature to achieve their destructive effects on natural objects. Of the fifteen items affected by the plagues of the first four trumpets, one-third receives injury or destruction in twelve instances. God uses the world of nature to punish mankind. In the last three trumpets the earth's godless inhabitants face demonic onslaughts.

Like the bowls that follow, the trumpet series are reminiscent of the Old Testament plagues against Egypt. The first trumpet parallels the seventh Egyptian plague. The second trumpet resembles the first plague. The fourth trumpet recalls the ninth plague. The fifth trumpet parallels the eighth Egyptian plague. Both series are judgments against the enemies of God's people and comprise steps toward deliverance of the saints and the overcoming of an evil force. During the seven seals and the seven trumpet series, Moses and Elijah are forward observers of the heavenly artillery fire falling on the earth and the earth's inhabitants.

Moses and Elijah have some input on the placement of fire. "These have power to shut heaven, so that no rain falls in the days of their prophecy: and they have power over waters to turn them to blood, and to strike the earth with all plagues, as often as they desire" (Rev. 11:6). This fact is not lost on unbelievers, who hate them and blame them for God's wrath. "Now when they finish their testimony, the beast that ascends out of the bottomless pit will make war against them, overcome them, and kill them. And those who dwell on the earth will rejoice over them, make merry, and send gifts to one another, because these two prophets tormented those who dwell on the earth" (Rev. 11:7 and 10). The two witnesses will have ministry during the first three-and-a-half years of the Tribulation. During the short duration of their ministry they have total authority and fire power from God almighty to protect Israel and the temple. In the middle of the Tribulation they will be killed by the Antichrist. Their dead bodies will be seen live on satellite television on CNN. People will be so excited they will give each other presents like Christmas. Unfortunately, the two men will stand up and great fear will come on those who see them alive. Then they will be raptured to heaven as the earth dwellers watch in disbelief. Then an even more intense series of seven bowl judgments will follow.

## What Is the First Trumpet Judgment?

And the first sounded; and hail and fire mixed with blood came, and were cast into the earth; and the third part of the earth was burned up, and the third part of the trees were burned up, and all green grass was burned up. (Rev. 8:7)

Hail, fire, and blood will be cast upon the earth and a third part of the trees and all green grass will be burnt up. This will be a fulfillment of Joel 2:30–31. This is a repetition of the seventh Egyptian plague. Just as the Egyptian plague was literal, this will also be literal. A judgment such as this will have an enormous effect upon the quality of life and available food supply. Trees not only produce food, they are essential protection from violent storms and flooding. This verse predicts one-third of all trees on the planet are destroyed by this judgment. It is difficult to conceive what this will mean for human survival. Looking at the earth today makes this hard to imagine. However, just because we take God for granted does not mean he cannot withdraw his protection from earth dwellers who hold Him in open contempt.

This judgment is similar to one of the plagues of Egypt involving hail and fire. This plague adds that the hail and fire were "mingled with blood." This could be the result of death to humans and animals, or it may be part of the plague or the plague's effect on the water. Red tides can be caused by too much oxygen in the water, and result in the destruction of living organisms in water.

This combination resembles the results of local volcanic activity in Asia Minor that John may have witnessed. However, his constant use of Old Testament idioms argues for duplication of historical events. Hail and stones fall in showers of blood as hail and/or volcanic fireballs commonly falling in a shower of rain. Also, hot lava from within the earth's surface is red hot and flows like water until it cools.

It is also possible that these trumpet judgments which include flowing blood, pelting hail, and consuming fire describe what would happen in a nuclear holocaust. Keep in mind, history verifies that weapon systems have never been developed which have not been used. However, the military action seems to be limited to the seven seal judgments. The seven trumpet judgments seem to be delivered directly by God, and/or called in by Moses and Elijah.

## What Is the Second Trumpet Judgment?

And the second angel sounded; and (something) like a great mountain burning with fire was cast into the sea; and the third part of the sea became blood, and the third part of the creatures which were in the sea, which had life, died, and the third part of the ships were destroyed. (Rev. 8:8)

The mountain-like mass may be a meteoric chunk, ablaze with fire. The operative phrase is "As it were." The text does not refer to a literal mountain, but something which looked like a mountain. It could be from space or it could be the mushrooming of a nuclear cloud. In either case, the effect on the earth will be cataclysmic. Astronomers have spotted about 800 asteroids—solid rocky celestial bodies with a diameter of over one-thousand meters—moving along circumsolar elliptical orbits. However, there may be as many as two-thousand large asteroids. An asteroid measuring over one-thousand meters in diameter is potentially capable of destroying human civilization.

If a large meteorite struck the earth, the results would cataclysmic. The dust cloud would create acid rain which would poison the rivers and oceans, and the dust cloud would cut off sunlight. An asteroid will collide with earth, the only question is when. Many astronomers predict a collision happening millions of years from now to alleviate fears, but Bible believers sense a meteorite could be waiting at the door.

Water covers three-fourths of the earth, one-third being the Atlantic Ocean. One-third of the ships afloat today are in the Atlantic region. This passage may refer to one specific site or portions of several oceans.

## What Is the Third Trumpet Judgment?

Then the third angel sounded; and a great star fell from heaven, burning like a torch, and it fell on a third of the rivers and on the springs of water; and the name of the star is Wormwood; and a third of the waters became wormwood; and many men died from the water, because it was made bitter. (Rev. 8:10–11)

We get the word "asteroid" from the Greek word *aster.* The Greek word *apsinthos* means "undrinkable." Many believe this "great star" from Revelation 10 is a meteorite. That may be, but the results of this tragedy affect one-third of the rivers and springs of the water. It is certainly an unusual meteorite if that is in fact what it is.

The star is called Wormwood, which is an obscure, bitter substance. The wormwood plants in Israel are named after the Biblical name Wormwood. In the Old Testament, wormwood was the symbol for bitterness and sorrow. Lamentations 3:13 reads, "He has filled me with bitterness, he has made me drink wormwood." Amos 5:7 states, "you who turn justice to wormwood, and lay righteousness to rest in the earth." Jeremiah 9:13–16 uses it to describe God's judgment on those who disobey him. "Wormwood" is God's judgment upon the wicked who disobey. Man takes water for granted, but God does not have to provide natural clean water to those who deny he even exists, and who hold his laws in disrespect.

## What Is the Fourth Trumpet Judgment?

Then the fourth angel sounded; and a third of the sun was struck, a third of the moon, and a third of the stars, so that a third of them were darkened; and a third of the day did not shine, and likewise the night. (Rev. 8:12)

The sun, moon, and stars have been consistently used by pagan religions as objects of worship.

The sun, moon, and stars receive the immediate brunt of the fourth trumpet. God shows us in this one judgment that he alone is to be worshiped. As with the first trumpet judgment, this judgment reminds us of one of the plagues in Egypt.[56] This trumpet has no mention of the instrument used to strike the heavenly bodies, the idea perhaps being that the instrument should not receive as much attention as the plague itself.

Together with disease, the next ice age ranks as the biggest danger we as individuals are vulnerable to. The next ice age is not necessarily to be considered in the far off future, but could possibly be at the door.

The last ice age occurred in the Middle Ages and was a direct result of volcanic activity, which caused volcanic ash to block the sun's rays and to cause a devastating impact on weather and the resulting lack of agricultural production. People in weakened, undernourished conditions that are exposed to unseasonably cold weather became susceptible to the black plague—an epidemic which was spread by rodents and lice.

## What Is the Fifth Trumpet Judgment?

Then the fifth angel sounded: and I saw a star fallen from heaven to the earth. And to him was given the key to the bottomless pit. And he opened the bottomless pit, and smoke arose out of the pit like the smoke of a great furnace. And the sun and the air were darkened because of the smoke of the pit. Then out of the smoke locusts came upon the earth. And to them was given power, as the scorpions of the earth have power. And they were not given authority to kill them, but to torment them for five months. And their torment was like the torment of a scorpion when it strikes a man. In those days men will seek death and will not find it; they will desire to die, and death will flee from them. (Rev. 9:1–3 and 5–6)

In the original Greek text, the word "fall" is in the past tense. Thus the star fell previously to this time. This is not a literal star, because of the use of personal pronouns such as "him" and "he." This is an idiom for Satan. We know in Revelation 12:4 that Satan not only fell, but he took one-third of the angels with him: "His tail drew a third of the stars of heaven and threw them to the earth. And the dragon stood before the woman who was ready to give birth, to devour her Child as soon as it was born."

Jude 6–7 tells us that fallen angels are now held captive in the abyss in the center of the earth: "And the angels who did not keep their proper domain, but left their own habitation, he has reserved in everlasting chains under darkness for the judgment of the great day; as Sodom and Gomorrah, and the cities around them in a similar manner to these, having given themselves over to sexual immorality and gone after strange flesh, are set forth as an example, suffering the vengeance of eternal fire." II Peter 2:1–10 refers to the fact that God "did not spare angels when they sinned, but sent them to Tartaros, putting them into gloomy dungeons to be held for judgment." These are the angels who cohabitated with women to corrupt the human race at the time of Noah. This is one of the reasons for the flood. All but Noah and his family were destroyed. The angels involved crossed the line and were placed in prison. God allows Satan to let them out during the Tribulation. Their authority is limited to causing intense pain to earth dwellers for five months, but they are not given the power to kill. The leader of this demonic crew is called *Abaddon* in Hebrew and *Apollyon* in Greek, which means "destruction" or "destroyer." This leader is either Satan himself, or one of his Generals.

## What Is the Sixth Trumpet Judgment?

And the sixth angel sounded, and I heard a voice from the four horns of the golden altar which is before God,

Saying to the sixth angel which had the trumpet, Loose the four angels which are bound in the great river Euphrates.

And the four angels were loosed, which were prepared for an hour, and a day, and a month, and a year, for to slay the third part of men.

And the number of the army of the horsemen were two hundred thousand thousand: and I heard the number of them.

And thus I saw the horses in the vision, and them that sat on them, having breastplates of fire, and of jacinth, and brimstone: and the heads of the horses were as the heads of lions; and out of their mouths issued fire and smoke and brimstone.

By these three was the third part of men killed, by the fire, and by the smoke, and by the brimstone, which issued out of their mouths.

For their power is in their mouth, and in their tails: for their tails were like unto serpents, and had heads, and with them they do hurt.

And the rest of the men which were not killed by these plagues yet repented not of the works of their hands, that they should not worship devils, and idols of gold, and silver, and brass, and stone, and of wood: which neither can see, nor hear, nor walk:

Neither repented they of their murders, nor of their sorceries, nor of their fornication, nor of their thefts. (Rev. 9: 13–21; King James Version)

These four angels are evil angels because they are bound. God limits the authority of all angels, but the word bound is an idiom for fallen angels. The Euphrates River is a boundary between the East and the West. The real issue is whether the 200 million army is demonic or John's attempt to define a modern military. Most scholars believe it is a demonic army because they are led by four fallen angels, and the description of the mounted horsemen seems so bizarre. Whether this army is demonic or literal mounted Calvary with helicopter gun ships is uncertain, but the end result is that one-third of the world's population is destroyed. This puts the running tally at over one-half of the people of the world—or over 3.5 billion.

At the end of the church age, with the sound of the Four Horsemen of the Apocalypse approaching, the world has four military powers. The first is the United States, the second is Russia, the third is China, and fourth is Israel. Between the beginning of the seven-year period of the Tribulation and the beginning of the second three-and-a-half years, the United States, Russia, China, and Israel appear to be militarily decimated and the Revived Roman Empire Confederacy of the Antichrist becomes the undisputed world military power. Revelation 13:4 states, "Who is able to make war with him?" This is speaking of the beast rising up out of the sea and becoming a worldwide dictator. The Antichrist is killed, goes to the center of the earth, and comes back with one bad eye and one bad arm. He is now possessed by Satan and forms the eighth world empire and reigns as the number one military power. "Woe to the worthless shepherd, who leaves the flock! A sword shall be against his arm and against his right eye; his arm shall completely wither, and his right eye shall be totally blinded" ( Zech. 11:17).

"I saw one of his heads as if it had been mortally wounded, and his deadly wound was healed. And all the world marveled and followed the beast" (Rev. 13:2). Something happens to the military capabilities of the four super powers during the first three-and-a-half years of the Tribulation. The sixth trumpet appears to be the most likely place for the destruction of the Chinese military force. Only a Chinese-led coalition could possibly muster 200 million troops. China is eliminated, and this army sounds a lot like the type of modern military described in the Russian invasion of chapter 2 of Joel. This is not to say this is the same invasion as Joel, it only appears Joel was doing his best to describe modern warfare tactics in Joel. He is clearly describing the battle of Armageddon in chapter 3 of Joel.

"I will also gather all nations, and bring them down to the valley of Jehoshaphat; and I will enter into judgment with them there" (Joel 3:2).

If we look closely at the mounted cavalry, they sound a lot like the modern warfare described in the Magog invasion depicted in Joel 2:

Blow ye the trumpet in Zion, and sound an alarm in my holy mountain: let all the inhabitants of the land tremble: for the day of the LORD cometh, for it is nigh at hand;

A day of darkness and of gloominess, a day of clouds and of thick darkness, as the morning spread upon the mountains: a great people and a strong; there hath not been ever the like, neither shall be any more after it, even to the years of many generations.

A fire devoureth before them; and behind them a flame burneth: the land is as the garden of Eden before them, and behind them a desolate wilderness; yea, and nothing shall escape them.

The appearance of them is as the appearance of horses; and as horsemen, so shall they run.

Like the noise of chariots on the tops of mountains shall they leap, like the noise of a flame of fire that devoureth the stubble, as a strong people set in battle array.

Before their face the people shall be much pained: all faces shall gather blackness.

They shall run like mighty men; they shall climb the wall like men of war; and they shall march every one on his ways, and they shall not break their ranks:

Neither shall one thrust another; they shall walk every one in his path: and when they fall upon the sword, they shall not be wounded.

They shall run to and fro in the city; they shall run upon the wall, they shall climb up upon the houses; they shall enter in at the windows like a thief.

The earth shall quake before them; the heavens shall tremble: the sun and the moon shall be dark, and the stars shall withdraw their shining: (Joel 2:1–10; King James Version)

Joel is describing modern infantry supported with helicopter gun ships firing forward and behind, with guided missiles and rapid-fire military weapons. China is capable of forming a 200 million-man army. China's population has exceeded 1 billion people. Based upon the first four trumpet judgments, China would have no grass and would be lacking trees and water. Starvation and the leadership of fallen angels might be the hook that brings an Asia army West in seek of oil, water and food. Whether the army is human or demonic, it has a 200-million-man mounted cavalry bent on destruction. One-third of mankind will die as a result.

Those earth dwellers not killed by the plagues so far do not repent of their idolatry, murder, sorceries, sexual immorality, or thefts. Idolatry can be pagan gods, or anything man can worship such as cars, sports, or women. The word "sorceries" is *pharmakia* in Greek, from which we get our word "pharmacy." Marijuana, alcohol, cocaine, and prescription drugs are both a physical and spiritual issue. From a physical standpoint they can destroy one's health. From a spiritual standpoint, they blunt one's conscience and self-control and open people up to demonic influences. They even open people up to demonic possession in which demons can even gain control of the body. Sexual promiscuity, lying, and stealing are the result of the flesh or one's desire for gaining pleasure and control. People can become controlled by lust rather than the spirit of God or even their conscience. Stealing is a common occurrence when authority breaks down, because of crisis. Once lawlessness takes over, police authority loses control unless the police are prepared to use extreme measures. Normally, if lawlessness continues, a strong man will come to power with an authoritarian regime prepared to stop at nothing to eliminate anarchy. Unfortunately, the results can sometimes result in dictatorships which themselves become ruthless. This is the case in this instance, because the Antichrist soon moves into total world domination.

## What Is the Seventh Trumpet Judgment?

Then the temple of God was opened in heaven, and the
ark of his covenant was seen in his temple. And there were
lightning's, noises, thundering, an earthquake, and great
hail. (Rev. 11:19)

The sounding of the seventh trumpet, as in the days of Joshua,
brings a great heavenly celebration over the anticipated establishment of God's kingdom on earth and the victory of good over evil.
It is amazing that some people bet on the losing team when the victory has already been settled. The earthly temples are only replicas
of God's holy temple in heaven. The Seventh Seal includes the Seven
Trumpets. The Seventh Trumpet includes the Seven Bowls. The last
seal, trumpet and bowl all end alike with "voices," "thundering,"
"lightning's" and an "earthquake." This remarkable display of supernatural power is clearly a sign that God's judgment has come. Artillery attacks are coordinated from God's command post in heaven,
at the end of seven years of devastating bombardments, the final
ground game in consummated in the battle of Armageddon, where
Christ destroys the armies of the world with his spoken word. To
describe it as a battle is a slight overstatement.

# CHAPTER 11

# IS ISRAEL JUST DIRT?

## Is Israel Just a Piece of Dirt?

Today, many people say, that they like to focus on Jesus Christ and heaven. They think that Israel is just a piece of dirt. They like to stick to basics and say that prophecy is not that important to everyday Christian life. This type of statement shows either Biblical illiteracy or wickedness. Unbelief is a sin. Failure to study God's word is a sin. Jesus said man does not live by bread alone, but by the word of God. "But he who prophesies speaks edification and exhortation and comfort to men" (I Cor. 14:3). One who understands prophetic promises of God has the power to edify, exhort, and comfort man. When you understand the faithfulness of God, you have the assurance that God has the veracity, integrity, and power to do what he has promised. Understanding history from beginning to end gives us that assurance. When we discover Jesus is the hero, and he has all the answers, we have the hope, assurance and the knowledge that all is well. The Bible has over one thousand prophecies. Over five hundred have already been fulfilled. One hundred nine prophecies refer to signs of the first coming of Christ. Three hundred twenty-one prophecies refer to signs of the second coming. Without an understanding of prophecy, the origin and destiny of Israel, and the origin and destiny of the church, the Bible becomes unintelligible, the prophets lose their prophecies, and Christians become disoriented and disillusioned. The closer we get to Jesus Christ the closer we get to the truth, because he is the truth. We need to get smaller and Christ needs to become larger. If we make ourselves important, we make the mistake of saying that we, as the church, replaced Israel as the heirs of Abraham's Covenant with God. If we make ourselves even more important, we accept Satan's deception that we can be like gods. Those who buy into Satan's lie become deceived, and eventually believe the coming World Leader is actually God in the flesh, and worship the beast, and become separated from God forever.

First of all, Jesus Christ is not his name. This is a Greek translation of "Yeshuah Messiah." *Yeshuah* means "salvation is of God." The Apostle Paul wrote a trilogy of three epistles—Romans, Galatians, and Hebrews—showing that "The just shall live by faith." Messiah is the anointed one. The second coming of Christ will be a rescue operation in which Israel will turn to their Messiah and ask for help. "I will bring the one-third through the fire, will refine them as silver is refined, and test them as gold is tested. They will call o my name, and I will answer them. I will say, "This is My People"; and each one will say, "The Lord is my God" (Zech. 13:9). If Augustine had just looked at the name of Jesus Christ in Hebrew, he may have avoided two major errors of religion: 1) Salvation is of God, not human works or sacraments, and 2) The Messiah is the Anointed King of the Jews, and the church was grafted in as a wild branch, and did not replace Israel.

Secondly, God gave an unconditional covenant to Abraham, Isaac and Jacob, in which he gave the promised land to them forever. "For all the land which you see I give to you and your descendants forever" (Gen. 13:14). "And as for Ishmael, I have heard you. Behold, I have blessed him, and will make him fruitful, and will multiply him exceedingly. He shall beget twelve princes, and I will make him a great nation. But My covenant I will establish with Isaac, whom Sarah shall bear to you at this set time next year" (Gen. 17:20–21). God promised that Ishmael would produce a large race, however, they did not inherit the land or the Covenant. The Jews are the people of the Covenant. Someday, God will establish a New Covenant with Israel. The New Covenant promised to Israel was stated in Jeremiah 31:31–34:

> Behold, the days come, says the Lord, that I will make a new covenant with the house of Israel, and with the house of Judah: Not according to the covenant that I made it their fathers in the day that I took them by the hand to bring them out of the land of Egypt; which my covenant they brake, although I was an husband unto them, says the Lord: But this shall be the covenant that I will make with the house of Israel; after those days, says the Lord, I will put my law in their inward parts, and write it in their hearts; and will be their God, and they shall be my people. And they shall teach no more every man his neighbor, and every man his brother, saying, Know the Lord; for they shall all know me, from the least of them unto the greatest of them, says the lord: for I will forgive their iniquity, and I will remember their sin no more.

If we cannot trust God to keep his covenant with Israel, how can we trust in Him for salvation. The church does not have a covenant with God. Romans 11:24 states the church was a wild branch grafted into the olive tree, but Israel is a natural olive branch and will be grafted back into the olive tree. We will participate with Israel and the new covenant as adopted children when Christ comes to the world to establish the kingdom of God.

Dwight Pentecost quotes John Darby in his book *Things to Come*:

> He presented the view that there was one and only one new covenant in Scripture, made with the houses of Israel

and Judah and to be realized at a future time, to which the church bears no relationship whatsoever. He writes: "This covenant of the letter is made with Israel, not with us; but we get the benefit of it…Israel not accepting the blessing, God brought out the church, and the Mediator of the covenant went on high. We are associated with the Mediator. It will be made good to Israel by-and-by…The Gospel is not a covenant, but the revelation of the salvation of God. It proclaims the great salvation. We enjoy indeed all the essential privileges of the new covenant, its foundation being laid on God part in the blood of Christ, but we do so in spirit, not according to the letter." (121–122)

Thirdly, the Kingdom of God will be established on earth when Christ comes to rule in Zion. In the call of Abraham, God took the first step toward the setting up of his kingdom on earth. From the Exodus generation until the judges, God reigned through Moses, Joshua, and the Judges. At the time of Samuel there was a revolt against the "Theocracy," and Saul was chosen by the people as King. But the misrule of his successors and the idolatry of the people caused the cessation of the Theocratic reign in 606 BC and the "Times of the Gentiles." After approximately 630 years of the "Times of the Gentiles," God again made the attempt to set up his kingdom on the earth. But the king was rejected and crucified, and the setting up of the kingdom postponed. At the Rapture of the church, living believers will be taken to heaven. However, in seven years will come back with Christ and he takes his rightful place on the throne of David, and rules in Zion.

Fourthly, what some people refer to as dirt is professed by God to be a special holy land. It is where Jesus Christ was born, lived, died, and rose again. As the Lamb of God, Christ paid for the sins of the world. Grace is God's riches at Christ's expense. Only God exists outside the time zone. Only God knows the future from the end.

Prophecy is what delineates false prophets from prophets who speak for God. The Antichrist will come with false signs and miracles and will recover from a mortal wound, but prophecy is what proves that Christ was the son of God. The fact that Christ would be born of a virgin, would be of the line of Judah, would come 283 years after the command to rebuild Jerusalem, and would die for the sins of the world and rise again show that only Christ is the Messiah and the Golgotha and Jerusalem is Holy ground.

Not just a patch of dirt.

Last of all, Israel will be dispersed, but they will be re-gathered. The scattering and return of Jews to Israel after two-thousand years is a miracle, and is the major sign that we are in the end-times. To say that Israel is only dirt shows one is either biblically illiterate or wicked. "And he said, 'Go your way, Daniel, for the words are closed up and sealed till the time of the end. Many shall be purified, made white, and refined, but the wicked shall do wickedly; and none of the wicked shall understand, but the wise shall understand.'" (Daniel 12:9–10)

## Did Replacement Theology Lead to Sin?

When Augustine formed church doctrine and stated that the church replaced Israel and inherited the covenant and blessings of Abraham, he encouraged the persecution of Jews and the resulting shedding of the blood of God's chosen people. When Frederick the Great asked the court priest for an unanswerable proof, in one word, of the inspiration of the Bible, he replied "the Jew, your Majesty." The emblem of the Jewish race is a bush-burning that isn't consumed. Other than the veracity of God and his covenant with his people, there is no other way to account for the preservation of the Jewish Race. For two thousand years (1921 BC to AD 30), no other people but the Jews believed in the unity of God, or taught it. The Jews have been the teachers of monotheism to the nations. No Gentile nation, untouched by the Jewish influence, ever became Monotheistic. Even Muhammed was influenced by Judaism when he began to teach of the one god Allah. The Jewish Race has been the writers, preservers and transmitters of the Holy Scriptures. To them were committed the "Oracles of God" (Rom. 3:1,2).

After the death of Solomon in 975 BC, the Kingdom was divided, his son Rehoboam retained possession of the Judah and Benjamin tribes, and with the retention of them he retained Jerusalem and the Temple. An usurper named Jeroboamruled over the remaining ten Tribes and set up his capital as Samaria. This division of the Kingdom, known as "Israel," rapidly declined, and in 721 BC the Ten Tribes were carried captive to Assyria. The two Tribes, known as "Judah," survived more than another 100 years, but in 606 BC they were carried in captivity to Babylon, and Jerusalem was destroyed by Nebuchadnezzar in 587 BC Thus ended a period of deadly tribal wars which was made illustrious by the ministry of noble succession of great prophets. The captivity of Judah and the destruction of Jerusalem began a long period which still continues, known in the scriptures as "The Times of the Gentiles." This period is fully outlined and described in the book of Daniel. When seventy years of the captivity ended as prophesied in Jeremiah 25:11, some forty thousand of those from the captivity returned to Jerusalem to rebuild the City and the Temple.

While the Jews were permitted to return to their own land, they never again secured supremacy. They remained subject to the different conquerors of their land, though for the most part were governed by rulers of their own race. This was in fulfillment of the prophecy that the scepter or the right of rulership should not depart from Judah until Shiloh or the Messiah came. "The scepter shall not depart from Judah, nor a lawgiver from between his fee, until Shiloh (the Messiah) comes" (Gen. 49:10).

Contrary to popular opinion, there are no silent years. The period of history from Malachi to Christ was covered by the book of Daniel in chapter 11. Daniel 11 chronicles the wars between the Ptolemy's and the Seleucids. Chapter 11 culminates in a mention of Antiochus Epiphanies and the Maccabeus revolt. "Those who do wickedly against the covenant he shall corrupt with flattery but the people who know their God shall be strong, and carry out great exploits. And those of the people who understand shall instruct many; yet for many days they shall fall by sword and flame, by captivity and plundering" (Dan. 11:32–33). The period from Acts to the Rapture is described in Revelation 3–4, and the period of the seventieth week of Daniel is described in Revelation 6:19. There are no silent years that aren't covered by the Bible.

## Is It the Diaspora or a Scattering?

With the Crucifixion of Christ, the sorrow of the Jewish race began. Their cry, "His Blood Be on Us and Our children," (Matt. 27:25) has become prophetic. (Matt. 27:25). While the scattering of the Jewish nation was prophesied by the prophets, the church should not condone the persecution of the Jews. God's covenant still applies. "Those who bless Israel will be blessed, and those who curse Israel will be cursed."

In April of AD 70, the one hundred thousand men of the Roman army marched against Jerusalem. The city was surrounded by a triple wall, defended by ninety towers. The siege lasted four months. Josephus says that over 1 million people perished in the siege, while 97,000 survived as captives. This fulfilled the prophecy of Daniel that "the people of the Prince that shall come (Antichrist) shall destroy the City and the Sanctuary". (Dan. 9:26). After the destruction of Jerusalem by Titus, Jews were scattered far and wide. Sixty-five years later, in AD 135, the Jews sufficiently recovered to revolt again under Roman power. Hadrian then completed the work of Dispersion. In a war lasting three-and-a-half years, he devastated Israel, killed five hundred eighty thousand, and changed the name of Israel to Palestine.

## How Has Replacement Theology Affected the Jews?

Replacement Theology is the established doctrine of the Roman Catholic and Reformed Protestant Church. This teaches that the church replaced Israel as to her covenant blessing and her place in the Kingdom of God on earth. As a result of this false teaching, Canute banished all Jews from England in AD 1020. In AD 1096, the holy war was begun when the Roman Catholic Church attempted to murder all Jews in Europe who would not submit to baptism. Up to the time of Edward I in AD 1272, the Crown claimed to own the Jew and all he possessed.

In AD 1306, all Jews in France were stripped of their possessions for the benefit of the royal treasury and cast out of the land. It was not until AD 1723, when Louis XV gave the Jews permission to hold real estate in France, that the tide began to turn there. In AD 1492, Ferdinand and Isabella issued an edict of banishment against all the Jews in Spain. The long night of persecution came to a close. Anti-semitism began to be curbed when England passed the Naturalization Bill in AD 1752 and received its greatest restriction when our own Declaration of Independence was signed in AD 1776, declaring that all people have the God-given right to pursue happiness. However, despite much progress, Replacement Theology resulted in much anti-Semitism in the Roman Catholic and Reformed Churches. Anti-Semitism continues in the form Lutheranism, Calvinism, Nazism, and the Roman Catholic Church today. The majority of the world's professing "Christians" believe that the church replaced Israel and the Holy Lands are just dirt, like any other land.

## Are We Floating Through Space with No Purpose?

Naturalists would have us believe we are floating through space on a spinning planet with no purpose and no plan. However, the scriptures state that man has a purpose, God has a plan, and that plan has been revealed in the scriptures. One characteristic of mental illness is failure to make future plans and disregard one's own personal safety. What is more insane than to ignore where one will spend eternity and to not investigate God's plan for man's future? History started with man in a garden and ends in a city. Man fell through the sin of Adam. But Christ atoned for sin by his death on the cross. This atonement is appropriated by faith. This first coming, death, burial, and resurrection was prophesied down to the last detail. For every prophecy about the First Coming, there are seven prophecies on the Second Coming.

Some people say they are not interested in doctrine or prophecy, and they are instead focusing on Christian living. What many are really saying is that they are mainly interested in themselves, their family and material prosperity. Many people do not have the discipline to comprehend a systematic understanding of the scriptures so they can defend the church against heretics and be able to recognize false teaching. The influence of today's media–driven, entertainment-oriented culture results in many people not having the patience to study God's word and look for signs marking the end-times. They are therefore unable to warn a dying and doomed world. In the dark ages, only one in twenty five hundred people could read. Today, most people in the United States can read, but they chose not to. They prefer other people to do their thinking for them. Many people rely on pastors or Christian television personalities to blindly lead them. Unfortunately, many contemporary Christian leaders and television personalities are Biblically illiterate. Many do not know the original languages of Hebrew and Greek.

Many have never studied the Old Testament verse by verse. Many Christians today cannot distinguish between God's plan for Israel and God's plan for the church. The Rapture of the church and the future salvation of Israel have more to do about ecclesiology than eschatology. In other words, if one understands the Old Testament scriptures on the future of Israel, then one will have a better grasp of end-time events. One who has never studied the Old Testament verse by verse and does not understand God's plan for Israel will most likely be ignorant of end-time events.

Jesus said, "Not everyone who says to me, 'Lord, Lord,' shall enter the kingdom of heaven, but he who does the will of My Father in heaven" (Matt. 7:21). What would he say about a soldier's wife or fiancée who was not eagerly awaiting her husband's return from war, and was not waiting for news about the possibility of the war ending? It is interesting that God revealed the most information on end-time events to two people, Daniel and John. The Bible says God loved these two men. "At the beginning of your supplications the command went out, and I have come to tell you, for you are greatly beloved, therefore consider the matter, and understand the vision" (Dan. 9:23). "Now there was leaning on Jesus' bosom one of his disciples, whom Jesus loved" (John 13:23). The reason John was at the mount of transfiguration, was at the Olivet Discourse, and received the vision of Revelation was because John loved Jesus and Jesus loved John.

There seems to be only one person who understood the purpose of the First Coming. "Now a certain man was sick, Lazarus of Bethany, the town of Mary and her sister Martha. It was that Mary who anointed the Lord with fragrant oil and wiped his feet with her hair, whose brother Lazarus was sick. ...Let her alone, she has kept this for the day of My burial" (John 11:1–2; John 12:7). John the Baptist and the apostles were looking for a Messianic kingdom, but only Mary was anticipating Christ's death and burial. Jesus loved Mary and Mary loved Jesus. She listened, she had ears. Many people today do not listen to what Christ told the church, "He who has an ear, let him hear what the Spirit says to the churches" (Rev. 3:22). "But you, brethren, are not in darkness, so that this Day should overtake you as a thief. You are all sons of light and sons of the day. We are not of the night nor of darkness. Therefore let us not sleep, as others do, but let us watch and be sober" (I Thes. 5:4–6). Israel is not just a piece of dirt. It is the holy land where Jesus was born, died, rose again, and will rule for eternity. That is why it is holy ground. Let us all be named with the ones who loved Jesus, and Jesus loved.

# CHAPTER 12

# THE REVIVED ROMAN EMPIRE

## How Will the Roman Empire Revive Itself?

The book of Daniel lays out the history of the world until the second coming of Christ. God gave Daniel special powers to interpret dreams and receive dreams which told history in advance. This prophetic revelation of history was not only specific in every detail, it was also specific to time. Daniel gave the exact date when the Messiah would come. We know there was a gap in Daniel's dreams because each one had a specific gap in it from the time of Christ until the Rapture. These dreams chronicle four world empires: Babylon, Medo-Persia, Greece and Rome. At the time of Christ, the Roman Empire was divided into two portions. After Christ, there is an absence of dreams, and they then resume during the last seven years of human history during the Day of the Lord. Unknown to Daniel, the Holy Spirit inserted the church into history, during the time of Jewish Diaspora. When Israel is re-gathered, the church will be removed by the Holy Spirit. The time of the Jews will resume for seven years. During this time, Rome is revived, but in a different form. It is in the form of a ten-nation confederacy, which comes under the control of a world ruler commonly known as the Best, or Antichrist. This form of Revived Roman Empire will be crushed and destroyed at the second coming of Christ.

## What Is the History of the Jews?

The scriptures speak of three classes of people on earth: the Jew, the Gentile, and the church. The church is made up of both Jew and Gentile. Outside of the church all who are not Jews are Gentiles. Up to the call of Abraham, all people on earth were Gentiles. Abraham was the first Hebrew. The name of Jacob, the grandson of Abraham, was changed to Israel. Jacob had twelve sons, which became the heads of twelve tribes. After Solomon, ten of the tribes became known as Israel, and two tribes, Judah and Benjamin, became Judah. In 721 BC, Israel was carried captive to Assyria, and in 606 BC Judah was carried captive to Babylon. The prophet Jeremiah gave a time-specific prophecy that Judah would be in captivity for seventy years. After the seventy years a fair representation of the whole twelve tribes returned to land of Israel. However, from this time until the time of Christ, the nation of Israel was under a series of world empires.

## Daniel, Chapter 2

In the second year of Nebuchadnezzar's reign, he had a dream but refused to tell the priests and prophets. He knew if he told them his dream he would have no way of knowing who had the correct interpretation. These religious gurus rightfully complained that only God could read someone's mind. After much prayer, God revealed to Daniel not only the dream, but the interpretation:

> This image's head was of fine gold, his breast and his arms of silver, his belly and his thighs of brass,
>> His legs of iron, his feet part of iron and part of clay.
>> Thou sawest till that a stone was cut out without hands, which smote the image upon his feet that were of iron and clay, and brake them to pieces.

Then was the iron, the clay, the brass, the silver, and the gold, broken to pieces together, and became like the chaff of the summer threshingfloors; and the wind carried them away, that no place was found for them: and the stone that smote the image became a great mountain, and filled the whole earth…

Thou, O king, art a king of kings: for the God of heaven hath given thee a kingdom, power, and strength, and glory.

And wheresoever the children of men dwell, the beasts of the field and the fowls of the heaven hath he given into thine hand, and hath made thee ruler over them all. Thou art this head of gold.

And after thee shall arise another kingdom inferior to thee, and another third kingdom of brass, which shall bear rule over all the earth.

And the fourth kingdom shall be strong as iron: forasmuch as iron breaketh in pieces and subdueth all things: and as iron that breaketh all these, shall it break in pieces and bruise.

And whereas thou sawest the feet and toes, part of potters' clay, and part of iron, the kingdom shall be divided; but there shall be in it of the strength of the iron, forasmuch as thou sawest the iron mixed with miry clay.

And as the toes of the feet were part of iron, and part of clay, so the kingdom shall be partly strong, and partly broken.

And whereas thou sawest iron mixed with miry clay, they shall mingle themselves with the seed of men: but they shall not cleave one to another, even as iron is not mixed with clay.

And in the days of these kings shall the God of heaven set up a kingdom, which shall never be destroyed: and the kingdom shall not be left to other people, but it shall break

in pieces and consume all these kingdoms, and it shall stand
for ever. (Dan. 2:32–35, King James Version)

Nebuchadnezzar's dream revealed a metallic man, which represented the historical succession of ruling world empires: Babylon,
Medo-Persia, Greece, and Rome. At the time of Christ, Rome was
in the form of two legs, an Eastern and Western empire. However, it
never became a ten-nation empire, portrayed as ten toes. The dream
had a gap in it at the ankles. If there was no gap, the legs would be
out of proportion. In addition, the Roman Empire will be in existence, according to this dream, at the time of the Second Coming.
The two limbs of the metallic man did not appear until AD 364, and
by then the ten toes had not yet developed. The time when "Stone"
falls on the image is distinctly state as "in the days of those kings,"
that is, in the days of the kings represented by the "Ten Toes." This
will be a ten-nation confederacy in the end-times.

## What Is the Iron Mixed with Clay?

It is important to note there are only four kingdoms. The final period of history is the fourth kingdom of Rome in the form of a ten-
nation confederacy, with the Antichrist as the world leader. What we
have here is the deterioration from one kingdom to the other. Each
is inferior to its predecessor. The quality of the metals drops from
gold, silver, brass, iron and iron mixed with clay. Nebuchadnezzar,
as the head of gold, was an absolute ruler with no opposition to his
authority. The Media-Persian empire had two arms and was subject
to boundaries of authority. The Greco-Macedonian Empire began
as one empire, but was soon divided into four. Rome has two legs of
iron, but it eventuates into ten toes which are composed of both iron
and clay. Today, the United States is not a democracy, but instead
is a representative government or republic. However, the final form
of world government appears to be a democracy or a confederation

of the European Union, which is controlled by the public and also by a world leader. This form of government is represented by both the clay of democracy and the iron of a dictatorship. It also contains several ethnic groups. It never totally comes together. It is interesting that the Romans conquered with iron weapons, and the latest military weapons today are made of a composite of iron and clay compounds. The final form of government will be partly strong and partly broken.

## What Is the Seed of Men?

And whereas thou saw iron mixed with miry clay, they shall mingle themselves with the seed of men: but they shall not cleave one to another, even as iron is not mixed with clay. (Dan. 2:43)

We can all agree the final form of government will be a loose coalition of people who do not come together as one ethnic nation with mutual customs and traditions. What is controversial is the phrase "seed of men."

In Matthew 24:37, Jesus said, "But as the days of Noah were, so also will the coming of the Son of Man be."

In Genesis 6:2 and 4, we find that during the time of Noah the sons of God saw the daughters of men and they took wives for themselves and their children were Nephilim. *Nephilim* is a Hebrew word translated in the Authorized King James version as "giants." They were larger than normal people, however, the word does not mean "giants," it comes from the root *naphal*, meaning "fallen ones," and most modern versions of the Bible have left the word "Nephilim" untranslated.

In the Old Testament, the designation "sons of God" (*bene Elohim*) is never used of the progeny of men, but only of beings created by God. Angels were called the "sons of God" in Job 1:6. In the New Testament, Adam is called the son of God in Luke 3:38 because he was not born but created. Jesus Christ, as the kinsmen redeemer, is the only son of man and son of God. He was the son of God because of his virgin birth, and he was the son of man because of his human mother. However, he was God, because of his eternal nature. In Volume Two of his book *Systematic Theology*, Lewis Sperry Chafer states, "In the Old Testament terminology angels are called sons of God while men are called servants of God. In the New Testament this is reversed. Angel are the servants and Christians are the sons of God." The Greek Septuagint translated *Nephilim* as *gergenes*, which means "earth born."

Ancient rabbinical sources as well as early church fathers understood Nephilim to refer to an odd hybrid offspring of fallen angels and human women. These bizarre events were also echoed in the legends and myths of every ancient culture upon the earth: the ancient Greeks, the Egyptians, the Hindus, the South Sea Islanders, the American Indians, and virtually all cultures. In the fifth century, the worship of angels and the focus on celibacy caused the "angel" view of Genesis 6 to come under scrutiny. Substantial liberties were taken in the text to propose that the "sons of god" were the Godly line of Seth that married the "daughters of Cain." However, this interpretation has no sound basis.

Peter discusses the issue in II Peter 2:4–5 as follows, "For if God spared not the angel that sinned, but cast them down to hell (Tartarus), and delivered them into chains of darkness, to be reserved unto judgment; and spared not the old word, but saved Noah the eight person, a preacher of righteousness, bringing in the flood upon the world of the ungodly."

Verses six and seven of the Epistle of Jude states, "And the angels which kept not their first estate, but left their own habitation, he has reserved in everlasting chains under darkness unto the judgment of the great day. Even as Sodom and Gomorrah, and the cities about them in like manner, giving themselves over to fornication, and going after strange flesh, are set forth for an example, suffering the vengeance of eternal fire."

## Nephilim and Sodom and Gomorrah

Genesis 6:4 states there were Nephilim on the earth during the time of Noah and afterward. After the flood, there was a second eruption of these fallen angels, evidently smaller in number and more limited in area, for they were for the most part confined to Canaan. Genesis 14:5 states, "In the fourteenth year Chedorlaomer and the kings that were with him came and attacked the Rephaim in Ashteroth Karnaim, the Zuzim in Ham, the Emin in Shaveh Kiriathiam." *Rephaim* is translated as "giants" in the King James Bible. They were descendants of Nephilim through Anak (Numbers 13:22–33). These were to be cut off, driven out, and utterly destroyed, as stated in Deuteronomy 20:17 and Joshua 3:10, but Israel failed.

The Rephaim were mixed up with the five nations, which included Sodom and Gomorrah, and were defeated by the four kings under Chedorlaomer. Their principal locality was "Ashtaroth Karnaim," while the Emim were in the plain of Kiriathiam. Anak was a noted descendant of the Nephilim; and Rapha was another, giving their names respectively to different clans. Anak's father was Arba, the original builder of Hebron. The Palestine branch of the Anakim were named after Anak. They were great, mighty and tall. In Numbers 12:33, they inspired the ten spies with great fear. Og king of Bashan is described in Deuteronomy 3:11.

## Joshua As an Anticipatory Model

The book of Joshua appears to be an anticipatory model of the Day of the Lord. In the book of Joshua, the Captain of the Lord's Host (Jesus Christ) redeems the land to its rightful owner from the usurper kings. Some of the opposition during the time of Joshua were Nephilim. David killed a descendant of the Nephilim.

The book of Isaiah says that the Nephilim and their descendants will not participate in a resurrection as the portion of ordinary mortals. Isaiah 26:14 reads: "They are dead, they shall not live; they are deceased, they shall not rise." The original Hebrew translation of "deceased" is the word *Rephaim*. It is interesting that the Antichrist and the False Prophet go straight to the lake of fire and do not appear before the great white throne judgment. Revelation 19:20 states, "…These two were cast alive into the lake of fire burning with brimstone."

## Can Angels Have Sex?

Jesus said angels neither marry nor are given in marriage. Because of the fall of man and the introduction of death, man needed to produce offspring. Angels, on the other hand, do not die and do not need to produce offspring. However, this does not preclude the possibility that angels can act contrary to the will of God. In Genesis 3:15, God predicted , "And I will put enmity between you and the woman, and between your seed and her seed; he shall bruise your head, and you shall bruise his heel." It is interesting how Jesus is the Son of God, and the Antichrist is called the son of perdition.

In *The Spirit World,* Clarence Larken makes the following comments:

> It says they do not marry in Heaven, not that they do not have the power of procreation, but that it is not the nature of "Holy angels" to seek such a relationship. But it does not follow that if they have the power they will not exercise it in a fallen state. What these passages teach is that angels do not multiply by procreation. Angels as far as we know are created "en masse," as they are immortal, and never die,

there is no necessity for marriage among them. Marriage is a human institution to prevent the extinction of the race by death. (27)

The only thing we can say for certain is, "For we know in part and we prophesy in part. But when that which is complete has come, then that which is in part will be done away. For now we see in a mirror, dimly, but then face to face. Now I know in part, but then I shall know just as I also am known" (I Cor.13:10 and 12). When Christ comes, we will receive our glorified bodies and we will learn many answers to our questions.

## Daniel, Chapter 7

Daniel spake and said, I saw in my vision by night, and, behold, the four winds of the heaven strove upon the great sea.

And four great beasts came up from the sea, diverse one from another.

The first was like a lion, and had eagle's wings: I beheld till the wings thereof were plucked, and it was lifted up from the earth, and made stand upon the feet as a man, and a man's heart was given to it.

And behold another beast, a second, like to a bear, and it raised up itself on one side, and it had three ribs in the mouth of it between the teeth of it: and they said thus unto it, Arise, devour much flesh.

After this I beheld, and lo another, like a leopard, which had upon the back of it four wings of a fowl; the beast had also four heads; and dominion was given to it.

After this I saw in the night visions, and behold a fourth beast, dreadful and terrible, and strong exceedingly; and it had great iron teeth: it devoured and brake in pieces, and stamped the residue with the feet of it: and it was diverse from all the beasts that were before it; and it had ten horns.

I considered the horns, and, behold, there came up among them another little horn, before whom there were three of the first horns plucked up by the roots: and, behold, in this horn were eyes like the eyes of man, and a mouth speaking great things. (Dan. 7:2–8)

This vision again shows the successive empires of Babylon, Medo-Persia, Greece and Rome. It culminates in a description of the ten-nation confederacy. Then a little horn, the coming world ruler, plucks out three horns. Then becomes the leader of the Revived Roman Empire. This is explained to Daniel: "The fourth beast (Rome) shall be a fourth kingdom on earth, which shall be different from all other kingdoms, and shall devour the whole earth, trample it and break it in pieces. The ten horns are ten kings who shall arise from this kingdom. And another shall rise after them; he shall be different from the first ones. And shall subdue three kings. He shall speak pompous words against the Most High, shall persecute the saints of the Most High, and shall intend to change times and law. The saints shall be given into his hand for a time, and times and half a time" (Dan. 7:23–25). The Antichrist will subdue three kings, and then become a world ruler who rules for three-and-a-half-years.

## Daniel, Chapter 9

Seventy weeks (70 x 7= 490 years) are determined for your people and for your holy city, to finish the transgression, to make an end of sins, to make reconciliation for iniquity, to bring in everlasting righteousness. To seal up vision and prophecy, and to anoint the Most Holy. (Dan. 9:1)

The total length of this prophecy is 490 years. The total prophecy has not been fulfilled, because there has not been an end to sin and the Kingdom of God is not yet ruling on earth with everlasting righteousness. However, the first sixty-nine weeks has been completed. We know the weeks are units of seven years, because exactly sixty-nine weeks later (69 x 7= 483), Jesus Christ came as the Jewish Messiah. This leaves a balance of one week, or seven years. This is called the seventieth week of Daniel and continues after the Rapture of the church.

"And the people of the prince who is to come shall destroy the city and the sanctuary. The end of it shall be with a flood, and till the end of the war desolations are determined. Then he shall confirm a covenant with many for one week; but in the middle of the week he shall bring an end to sacrifice and offering. And on the wings of abominations shall be one who makes desolate, even until the consummation, which is determined, is poured out on the desolate" (Dan. 9:26).

"The people of the prince who is to come" are the Romans who sacked Jerusalem in AD 70 and destroyed the temple. The prince who is to come is the Antichrist, the future world leader.

## Who Is the Antichrist?

The beast that you saw was, and is not, and will ascend out of the bottomless pit and go to perdition. And those who d well on the earth will marvel, whose names are not written in the Book of Life from the foundation of the world, when they see the beast that was, and is not and yet is. Here is the mind which has wisdom: The seven heads are seven mountains on which the woman sits. They are also seven kings. Five have fallen, one is, and the other has not yet come. And when he comes, he must continue a short time. And the beast that was, and is not, is himself also the eighth, and is of the seven, and is going to destruction. And the ten horns which you saw are ten kings who have received no kingdom as yet, but they receive authority for one hour as the kings with the beast. (Rev. 17:8–12)

The beast who "was and is not" ties him to the beast with the death-wound who was healed in Revelation 13:3–14. This is the Antichrist who is killed, and comes back to life. God grants Satan the power to resuscitate this pseudo-Messiah, to deceive the world. The words "is not" refer to the beast's death, and his ascent from the abyss means he will come to life again. This is the same as his reappearance as an eighth king. The beast can refer to either an empire or the ruler of that empire. Each head of the beast is a partial incarnation of satanic power that rules for a given period, so the beast can exist on earth without interruption in the form of seven consecutive kingdoms, but he can also be nonexistent at a given moment in the form of one of an empire's kings. The nonexistent beast in verse eight is a temporarily absent king over the empire that will exist in the future.

The seven mountains symbolize seven kings. The seven kings represent several literal Gentile kingdoms that follow one another in succession. The kings and kingdoms are interchangeable, showing that a king can stand for the kingdom ruled by that king. The seven kingdoms are the seven that dominate world scene throughout human history: Neo-Babylon, Assyria, Babylon, Persia, Greece, Rome and the future kingdom of the beast. The five fallen empires are Neo-Babylon, Assyria, Babylon, Persia, and Greece. The one "which is" is the Roman Empire which was in power at the time of John. The "one which has not yet come" will be the future kingdom of the beast. As one of the seven, the best is a kingdom, but as an eighth, he is the king of that kingdom who sustains the wound and ascends from the abyss after his wound. When this occurs, he is king over an eighth kingdom because his reign following his ascent from the abyss will be far more dynamic and dominant than before. This is the sense in which he is one of the seven, but also an eighth. His eighth kingdom will last for three-and-a-half years. The eighth is an eighth king or world ruler, and not a distinctly different kingdom from the seventh head. He is distinct from his predecessors in that he subsequently has received supernatural powers from Satan at his resuscitation. Yet he is also one of the seven, the seventh which has not yet come, in that he takes the shape of an emperor in charge of an empire. This makes the eighth king a fusion of the raised beast and the empire over which he rules.

"The ten horns which you saw are ten kings" refers to the ten kingdoms who will join in a confederacy under the leadership of the beast in the final Gentile world empire. They will rule simultaneously with one another and with the beast. The Antichrist takes over three of the nations, and the others voluntarily join the confederacy of nations to form a Revived Roman Empire, with the Antichrist as a world ruler. The harlot is an ecumenical world religion that becomes the state church and goes along with the world empire and participates in ruler ship in the form of false religion.

## Who Is the World Leader?

In the Scriptures, the Antichrist is given many names: King of Babylon, the Little Horn, A King of Fierce Countenance, The Prince that Shall Come, The Willful King, The Man of Sin, Son of Perdition, and The Beast. He comes in the place of Christ as a false Messiah. Christ came from above (John 6:38), Antichrist ascends from the Pit (Rev. 11:7. Christ came in his father's name (John 5:43), Antichrist comes in his own name (John 5:43). Christ Humbled Himself (Phil. 2:8), Antichrist Exalts himself (II Thes. 2:4). Christ despised (Isa. 53:3), Antichrist admired (Rev. 13:3–4). Christ came to save (Luke 19:10), Antichrist comes to destroy (Dan. 11:36). Christ is the truth

(John 14:6), Antichrist is the lie (II Thes. 2:11). Christ is the son of God (Luke 1:35), Antichrist is the son of perdition (II Thes. 2:3).

While the Antichrist emerges in a political environment and functions initially as a political leader, he will gradually acquire religious connotations. Eventually he will require those subject to him to worship him when he sets up his image in Israel's temple.[57] He will require that everyone receive his mark on their arm or forehead.

### Revelation, Chapter 12

And war broke out in heaven, Michael and his angels fought against the dragon; and the dragon and his angels fought, but they did not prevail, nor was a place found for them in heaven any longer. So the great dragon was cast out, that serpent of old, called the Devil and Satan who deceives the whole world; he was cast to the earth, and his angels were cast out with him. Then I heard a loud voice saying in heaven, "Now salvation, and strength, and the kingdom of our God, and the power of his Christ have come, for the accuser of our brethren, who accused them before our God day and night, has been cast down." … Now when the dragon saw that he had been cast to the earth, he persecuted the woman who gave birth to the male child. But the woman was given two wings of great eagle, that she might fly into the wilderness to her place, where she is nourished for a time, and times, and half a time from the presence of the serpent. (Rev. 12:7–10 and 13–14)

In the Book of Job we learn that as an angel Satan has access to heaven. In this passage, we learn he is always bringing accusation to God about the failings of believers. However, our defense counsel is none other than the judge's son, who uses the fact that our sins have been paid for on the cross as our defense. In the middle of the Tribulation, Satan and the fallen angels are kicked out of heaven and they are no longer welcome. They have three-and-a-half years left to do what they can to stop the plan of God and the sealing of their doom. They turn on Israel, the woman who gave birth to the male child, who is forced to flee to the desert in Jordan. This is the period Satan empowers the Antichrist who kills Moses and Elijah and desecrates the temple in Jerusalem with an image of himself.

## Revelation, Chapter 13

And I stood upon the sand of the sea, and saw a beast rise up out of the sea, having seven heads and ten horns, and upon his horns ten crowns, and upon his heads the name of blasphemy.

And the beast which I saw was like unto a leopard, and his feet were as the feet of a bear, and his mouth as the mouth of a lion: and the dragon gave him his power, and his seat, and great authority.

And I saw one of his heads as it were wounded to death; and his deadly wound was healed: and all the world wondered after the beast.

And they worshipped the dragon which gave power unto the beast: and they worshipped the beast, saying, Who is like unto the beast? who is able to make war with him?

And there was given unto him a mouth speaking great things and blasphemies; and power was given unto him to continue forty and two months.

And he opened his mouth in blasphemy against God, to blaspheme his name, and his tabernacle, and them that dwell in heaven.

And it was given unto him to make war with the saints, and to overcome them: and power was given him over all kindreds, and tongues, and nations.

And all that dwell upon the earth shall worship him, whose names are not written in the book of life of the Lamb slain from the foundation of the world.

If any man have an ear, let him hear.

He that leadeth into captivity shall go into captivity: he that killeth with the sword must be killed with the sword. Here is the patience and the faith of the saints.

And I beheld another beast coming up out of the earth; and he had two horns like a lamb, and he spake as a dragon.

And he exerciseth all the power of the first beast before him, and causeth the earth and them which dwell therein to worship the first beast, whose deadly wound was healed.

And he doeth great wonders, so that he maketh fire come down from heaven on the earth in the sight of men,

And deceiveth them that dwell on the earth by the means of those miracles which he had power to do in the sight of the beast; saying to them that dwell on the earth, that they should make an image to the beast, which had the wound by a sword, and did live.

And he had power to give life unto the image of the beast, that the image of the beast should both speak, and cause that as many as would not worship the image of the beast should be killed.

And he causeth all, both small and great, rich and poor, free and bond, to receive a mark in their right hand, or in their foreheads:

And that no man might buy or sell, save he that had the mark, or the name of the beast, or the number of his name.

Here is wisdom. Let him that hath understanding count the number of the beast: for it is the number of a man; and his number is Six hundred threescore and six. (Rev. 13, King James Version)

The Antichrist or false Christ of the last times personalizes the beast. He bears 666, the number of man. The dragon, the beast and the false prophet make a pseudo-trinity or a false parallel to God the Father, the Son and the Holy Spirit. The beast is identified with one of its heads who is slain and given a new life and authority, and having power over the whole world. The ten horns represent the ten kings or kingdoms of the ten-nation confederacy of the Revived Roman Empire in the final form of the beast. The seven heads stand for seven successive world monarchies: Babylon, Assyria, Neo-Babylon, Medo-Persia, Greece, Rome and the regime represented by the ten simultaneous kingdom. This pattern follows the pattern of Daniel's visions where a horn represents either a king or a dynasty of kings. Rome, in its restored form, will have the agility, the vigilance and craft of a cat, the fierce cruelty of a leopard, the feed of a bear to crush her enemies, and the roar of a lion. This is what the Tribulation saints will face in the last days.

The fact that the head of the beast was slain points to the violent death of the head. After the false Christ is restored to life he suffers from a bad arm and lack of vision in one eye. At the beginning of the Tribulation, the Antichrist brokers a peace treaty with Israel, but after three-and-a-half years, he breaks the treaty and persecutes Israel: ending in the battle of Armageddon and the Second Coming of Christ to rescue Israel.

# CHAPTER 13

# THE SEVEN BOWL JUDGMENTS

## What are the Seven Bowl Judgments?

Revelation 15 and 16 bring the chronological events of the Book of Revelation to a conclusion; events that precede the Second Coming. As previously discussed, the structure of Revelation depends first on the seven seals which are broken in Revelation 6:1–17 and 8:1 and the seventh seal includes the seven trumpets in Revelation 8:1–9:21 and 11:15–19. The seven bowls of the wrath of God being introduced here are all included in the seventh trumpet. The order of events involves rapid increase in severity and in frequency of the judgments of God with the emphasis being on the seventh seal, the seven trumpets, and the seven bowls of the wrath of God. Parenthetic sections which intervene frequently in the Book of Revelation had to do with prophetic revelation concerning individuals and situations, but they do not advance the narrative chronologically.

Though the seven bowls of the wrath of God are similar to the judgments of the trumpets, notable differences are mentioned. The trumpet judgments extend to only one-third of the earth while the bowl judgments generally extend to the entire earth. The judgments appear to be repeated, but in actuality they become increasingly worse and occur in more rapid succession. The seven bowls occur one after the other in rapid sequence and immediately introduce the situation of the Second Coming of Christ. A series of judgments beyond anything ever mentioned before is revealed in Revelation 16.

### The First Bowl Judgment

"Then I heard a loud voice from the temple saying to the seven angels, 'Go and pour out the bowls of the wrath of God on the earth.' So the first went and poured out his bowl upon the earth, and a foul and loathsome sore came upon the men who had the marks of the beast and those who worshipped his image" (Rev. 16:1–2).

The first angel went and poured out his bowl on the land, and ugly and painful sores broke out on the people who had the mark of the beast and worshiped his image. In the first bowl judgment, the wrath of God causes painful sores and afflictions to be experienced by all those who worship the beast. This is an experience similar to the Egyptians in Exodus 9:9–11. This is an increase in judgment over the first trumpet which only affect one-third of the earth dwellers.

### The Second Bowl Judgment

"Then the second angel poured out his bowl on the sea, and it became blood as of a dead man; and every living creature in the sea died" (Rev. 16:3).

Prophecy Scholars are divided as to whether water is turned to real blood or what is called the "red tide." Red tide is a common name for an occasional occurrence where algae grow very fast and accumulate into dense, visible patches near the surface of the water. Certain phytoplankton species contain reddish pigments and bloom such that the water appears to be colored red. The term "red tide" is thus a misnomer because they are not associated with tides. They are caused by dormant cysts buried in sediment on the ocean floor becoming active due to increased amounts of oxygen. Regardless of the cause, the effect is that living creatures in the sea are killed. The earth-dwellers lose a valuable source of food and receive a stench of rotting fish. It is interesting that one of the Babylonian gods is Dagon, the fish god. This second bowl judgment destroys all fish, where the third trumpet judgment only killed one-third. This judgment is a repetition of an Egyptian plague.

### The Third Bowl Judgment

"Then the third angel poured out his bowl on the rivers and springs of water, and they became blood" (Rev. 16:4).

Some expositors tend to explain the judgment on the rivers and springs of water as something not actually blood. Of course nothing is impossible. We do know that Christ is the kinsman redeemer. One of the Levitical functions of a kinsman was to avenge the blood of a family member. The significance of this judgment is explained by an angel thus, "You are righteous, O Lord, the One who is and who was and who is to be, because your have judged these things. For they have shed the blood of saints and prophets, and you have given them blood to drink for it is their just due" (Rev. 16:5–6).

### The Fourth Bowl Judgment

"The fourth angel poured out his bowl on the sun and the power was given to him to scorch men with fire. And men were scorched with great heat, and they blasphemed the name of God who has power over these plague; and they did not repent and give Him glory" (Rev. 16:8–9).

Why do we fail to give God the glory he justly deserves? Why do we become preoccupied with our plans, or importance and ignore God almighty? We as Christians often make the mistake of setting our priorities out of order. The earth-dwellers, however, do not even acknowledge the existence of God or at least do not acknowledge an accountability to God. Instead, men worship nature or God creation rather than the creator. The Fourth Bowl is God's response for unbelief.

The sun was given power to scorch people with fire. They were seared by the intense heat and they cursed the name of God, who had control over these plagues, but they refused to repent and glorify him. The wicked ignore God. When God's wrath comes, they grudgingly acknowledge him and ask for pain to stop. When pain continues, they curse God. However, they fail to repent from their wicked ways, which is why they received God's wrath in the first place.

### The Fifth Bowl Judgment

"Then the fifth angel poured out his bowl on the throne of the beast, and his kingdom became full of darkness; and they gnawed their tongues because of the pain. And they blasphemed the God of heaven because of their pains and their sore, and did not repent of their deeds" (Rev. 16:10–11).

Babel, or Babylon, was built by Nimrod.[58] This was the seat of the first great apostasy. Here the Babylonian cult was invented, which was a system claiming to possess the highest wisdom and to reveal the divine secrets. The city of Babylon was the seat of Satan where he rules as the prince of darkness. When Babylon fell, Satan moved his throne to Pergamos in Asia Minor, where, according to Revelation 2:12–13, he was in John's day . When Attalus, the Pontiff and King of Pergamos, died in 133 BC, he bequeathed the headship of the Babylonian priesthood to Rome. The Antichrist will become the leader of a ten-nation confederacy known as the Revived Roman Empire. However, in the second half of the seventieth week of Daniel, the Antichrist will move his throne to Babylon.

Then the angel who talked with me came out and said to me, "Lift your eyes now, and see what this is that goes forth." So I asked, "What is it?" And he said, "It is a basket that is going forth," he also said, "This is their resemblance throughout the earth; here is a lead disc lifted up, and this is a woman sitting inside the basket"; then he said, "This is Wickedness!" and he thrust her down into the basket, and threw the lead cover over its mouth. Then I raise my eyes and looked, and there were two women, coming with the wind in their wings; for they had wings like the wings of a stork, and they lifted up the basket between earth and heaven. So I said to the angel who talked with me, "Where are they carrying the basket?" And he said to me, "To build a house for it in the land of Babylon; when it is ready, the basket will be set there on its base. (Zech. 5:5–11)

In this obscure passage in Zechariah, it appears that an evil woman, world religion, is moved back to its point of origin in Babylon. It is interesting that the United Nations is purported to be currently looking for a new sight for its facilities. New York City is very expensive land and provides little opportunity for the growth of UN facilities and staff support. In time we will find that Babylon will become a center of commerce, religion, and political power. Babylon, as the new throne of the Beast and the Beast's Empire, will become darkened. This judgment is a repetition of the ninth plague of Egypt. This darkness will prevail for some time on the earth. "That day will be a day of wrath, a day of distress and anguish, a day of trouble and ruin, a day of darkness and gloom, a day of clouds and blackness" (Zeph. 1:15).

This is the first mention of the beast's kingdom. It refers to a concrete kingdom with geographical extend, not to an abstract ruler ship of the beast. This plague puts the realm in a lasting condition of darkness, and is a retaliation against the Beast's attack on Israel in the second half of the Tribulation.

## The Sixth Bowl Judgment

"Then the sixth angel poured out his bowl on the great river Euphrates, and its water was dried up, so that the way of the Kings from the East might be prepared. And I saw three unclean spirits like frogs coming out of the mouth of the dragon, out of the mouth of the beast, and out of the mouth of the false prophet. (This is the false trinity, Satan, beast and false prophet.) For they are spirits of demons, performing signs, which go out to the kings of the earth and of the whole world, to gather them to the battle of that great day of God Almighty. Behold, I am coming as a thief. Blessed is he who watches, and keeps his garments, lest he walk naked and they see his shame. And they gather them together to the place called in Hebrew, Armageddon (Revelation 16:12–16).

The sixth angel poured out his bowl on the great river Euphrates, and its water was dried up to prepare the way for the kings from the East. Chronologically, the time of the Second Coming is very near. One of the major features of the period just before the Second Coming is a world war in which various parts of the world rebel against the world ruler who has taken power as the dictator some time before. In the light of this military conclusion to the Great Tribulation, the sixth bowl makes its own contribution in preparing the way for the kings of the East to cross the Euphrates.

Few portions of Revelation have called for more varied interpretations than this verse. Scholars have divided opinions on who the "kings from the East" are. Many believe the drying up of the Euphrates River will prepare a path for military invasion by the rulers of China and other countries. The implication from the text is that the Euphrates River is dried up by supernatural means such as an earthquake, or drought, although the method is not revealed. Though this passage does not connect directly with the sixth trumpet, apparently the river is dried up in order for the great army of 200 million to cross it as indicated in the sixth trumpet (9:14–16).

The two events are chronologically close together even though they belong to different series. Though no further information is given about the sixth bowl, John records a small parenthetic section, giving the overview of Armageddon.

*The Battle of Armageddon.* If the world was a chess board, Israel would be the center. Israel lies along the fertile crescent which acts as a land bridge between Africa, the Middle East, Europe, and the Far East. In the final war of history the world's armies come together with the intent of controlling Middle East oil, the Suez canal, and eliminating Israel as a problem. What they are actually doing is fighting against God.

The term "Armageddon" comes from the Hebrew tongue. *Har* means "mountain" or "hill." *Mageddon* is likely the ruins of the ancient city of Megiddo, which overlooks the Valley of Esdraelon in northern Israel—the place where the armies of the world will congregate. The campaign of Armageddon will actually take place in Jerusalem and southern Israel. Despite the huge armies involved, it will not be much of an epic struggle between good and evil. Christ will speak and the enemy will be destroyed. Zechariah predicts the battle will end when the Messiah returns to earth and his feet touch down on the Mount of Olives. This battle concludes with the Second Coming of Jesus to earth. No matter how mighty someone on earth is, they are not a rival to the power of God.

The armies from all over the world are gathered geographically to the Holy Land to fight it out for power. The local of the war is described as Armageddon. The term "Armageddon" geographically refers to the area east of Mount Megiddo in northern Israel and includes the large plain of Esdaraleon. Megiddo, in Hebrew, corresponds to the title in Greek, Armageddon. This area has been the scene of great battles in the past, including that of Barak and the Canaanites and the victory of Gideon over the Midianites. Saul and Josiah also were killed in this area. The valley is rather large, being fourteen miles wide and twenty miles long. Large as this area is, it obviously cannot contain the armies of millions of men, and it seems to be the marshaling point.

Actually, the armies are scattered up and down the Holy Land for a length of some 200 miles. Both World War I and World War II were identified by some as Armageddon, but subsequent history prove that they were wrong. The enticement of the demons is apparently effective because the armies of the world assemble to fight it out in the Holy Land. The fact that the demons, including the efforts of the dragon, the world ruler, and the false prophet, openly invite a world war, seems to be a contradiction because in Revelation 13 the world government is put together by Satan in order to fulfill his imitation of the millennial world government. The answer to this puzzle is found in Revelation 19 as the Second Coming of Christ is revealed. What Satan is doing is gathering all the military power of the world in a vain effort destroy Israel, to prevent the second return of Christ, and to indirectly contend with the army from heaven. It, of course, is futile because Christ speaks the word and the armies and their horses on both sides of the conflict are instantly killed in the actual judgment that occurs at the Second Coming.

The Euphrates River is one of the most prominent rivers in the Bible, as it has stood as a natural barrier between East and West since the dawn of human history. The booming population explosion of the nations of the East has produced a new interest in Bible prophecies concerning "the kings from the East." Actually, there is little information on the subject. The literal rendering of the expression is the quote, "kings from the sun rising," which is a reference to the kings from the Oriental nations of the world. Since it refers to them en masse, it indicates that they do not amalgamate or lose their identity (for they are "kings"), but instead form a massive Oriental confederacy. This confederacy may be preparing to oppose Antichrist, whose capital lies in Babylon, but because of the lying tongues of the demons we are about to study, they will be brought across the Euphrates River on the side of Antichrist in opposition to Christ. Sixty years ago, China would have lacked the technology and infrastructure to mount a massive movement of people. However, in recent years, China has made a leap in technological progress and God is not staging events that will lay a foundation for a massive invasion from the Far East.

The second part of the sixth bowl judgment reveals the three unclean, froglike spirits that will come from the mouth of the devil, the Beast, and the False Prophet. These deceiving spirits, by working miracles before the "kings of the whole world," will trick them into coming to gather for the "battle on the great day of God Almighty." After the five preceding judgments of God, the earth will be in such a chaotic shambles economically, socially, and religiously that kings of the earth will not be prepared to do battle with anyone. Only by this supernatural sprit of deception on the part of Satan, the Antichrist, and the False Prophet will they be able to summon the kings and the armies of the world to find conflict against God and his Christ. The time of this event must be the very last days of the Tribulation, since the next bowl concludes the Tribulation with the destruction of Babylon.

According to God's divine purpose, Armageddon will be the event in which he will judge the wicked. Both satanic and human opposition will be focused on God's elect nation of Israel, and God will bring them to that location to bring down their foolish schemes of rebellion. The psalmist records God's response of laughter at the puny human plans to overthrow God himself at Armageddon: "Why do the nations rage and the people plot a vain thing? The kings of the earth set themselves, and the rulers take counsel together, against the Lord and against his Anointed, saying, let us break their bonds in pieces and cast away their cords from us. He who sits in the heavens shall laugh; The Lord shall hold them in derision. He shall speak to them in his wrath, and distress them in his deep displeasure; Yet I have set My King On My holy hill of Zion" (Psalms 2:1–6). "For behold, in those days and at that time, when I bring back the captives of Judah and Jerusalem, I will also gather all nations, and bring them down to the Valley of Jehoshaphat; and I will enter into judgment with them there on account of My people, My heritage Israel, whom they have scattered among the nations; they have also divided up My land" ( Joel 3:1–2).

And I saw heaven opened, and behold a white horse; and he that sat upon him was called Faithful and True, and in righteousness he doth judge and make war.

His eyes were as a flame of fire, and on his head were many crowns; and he had a name written, that no man knew, but he himself.

And he was clothed with a vesture dipped in blood: and his name is called The Word of God.

And the armies which were in heaven followed him upon white horses, clothed in fine linen, white and clean.

And out of his mouth goeth a sharp sword, that with it he should smite the nations: and he shall rule them with a rod of iron: and he treadeth the winepress of the fierceness and wrath of Almighty God.

And he hath on his vesture and on his thigh a name written, KING OF KINGS, AND LORD OF LORDS.

And I saw an angel standing in the sun; and he cried with a loud voice, saying to all the fowls that fly in the midst of heaven, Come and gather yourselves together unto the supper of the great God;

That ye may eat the flesh of kings, and the flesh of captains, and the flesh of mighty men, and the flesh of horses, and of them that sit on them, and the flesh of all men, both free and bond, both small and great.

And I saw the beast, and the kings of the earth, and their armies, gathered together to make war against him that sat on the horse, and against his army.

And the beast was taken, and with him the false prophet that wrought miracles before him, with which he deceived them that had received the mark of the beast, and them that worshipped his image. These both were cast alive into a lake of fire burning with brimstone.

And the remnant were slain with the sword of him that sat upon the horse, which sword proceeded out of his mouth: and all the fowls were filled with their flesh. (Rev. 19:11–21; King James Version)

Behold, the day of the Lord is coming, and your spoil will be divided in your midst. For I will gather all the nations to battle against Jerusalem; the city shall be taken, the houses rifled, and the women ravished. Half of the city shall go into captivity, but the remnant of the people shall not be cut off from the city. Then the Lord will go forth and fight against those nations, as he fights in the day of battle. And in that day his feet will stand on the Mount of Olives, which faces Jerusalem on the East. And the Mount of Olives shall be split in two. From East to West. Making a very large valley; half of the mountain shall move toward the north and half of it toward the south. Then you shall flee though My mountain valley, for the mountain valley shall reach to Azal. Yes, you fled from the earthquake in the days of Uzziah king of Judah. Thus the Lord my God will come, and all the saints with You. (Zech. 14:1–5)

At the time of the end the king of the South shall attack him; and the king of the North shall come against him like a whirlwind, with chariots, horsemen, and with many ships; and he shall enter the countries, overwhelm them, and pass through. He shall also enter the Glorious Land, and many countries shall be overthrown; but these shall escape from his hand; Edom, Moab, and the prominent people of Ammon. He shall stretch out his hand against the countries, and the land of Egypt shall not escape. He shall have power over the treasures of gold and silver, and over all the precious things of Egypt; also the Libyans and Ethiopians shall follow at his heels. But news from the East and the North shall trouble him; therefore he shall go out with great fury to destroy and annihilate many. And he shall plant the tens of his palace between the seas and the glorious holly mountain; yet he shall come to his end, and no one will help him. (Dan. 11:40–45)

No world power will be able to stand against the Antichrist. Once the United States, Russia, Iran, Germany, and China have been militarily decimated in the first three-and-a-half years of the Tribulation, no super power will be able to match the power of the revived Roman Empire of the Beast. In time the balance of the world governments are faced with the ultimatum of surrender or annihilation.

Those who support him will be rewarded with wealth, honor, position, and subordinate power. He will carve up the land of Israel and apportion it to his most trusted followers. Israel itself will be of great importance to him, not only because of its strategic geographical location as the hinge of three continents but also because it will be the centerpiece of his false religion and his total disregard for the holiness of God's temple in Jerusalem. Control over an administrative district in Palestine will be a choice political plum and a measure of his apparent power.

So far, everything will have gone his way. But then he has to deal will revolution. Two old rivals, Egypt, the king of the South, and Syria, the king of the North, will come back onstage in the last days, united in a hatred of the Antichrist. The military strength of the Antichrist will be spread thin as he attempts to police the whole world in one world system. The Antichrist's monolith will begin to disintegrate. We learn from the Book of Revelation and the prophets Isaiah and Jeremiah he will begin to lose his grip on his universal empire. From the Apocalypse we see the early vials of God's wrath will be directed at the power structure of the Beast.

Once Egypt and Syria see their opportunity to break free from his rule, these two countries will join against the Antichrist. The country of Palestine (Israel), occupied by the Antichrist, seems to be the focal point of this joint military venture. The Antichrist will be at Babylon, one of his capital cities, when this new insurrection breaks out in an attack on his garrison in Israel. This combined attack will provoke a swift response. The Antichrist will mobilize and hurl his forces against Egypt, committing both land and sea forces to secure his vital interests in that strategic corner of his empire. Egypt and Syria, bitter enemies of Israel, will meet their retribution as a result of this final onslaught on that land.

The Antichrist's line of march will lie through Israel. At this time, he probably will make the onslaught on Jerusalem mentioned in Zechariah 14:2. By now Jews will be thoroughly awakened to the character of the Antichrist and will seize this opportunity to revolt and fight against this attack. Their efforts will be largely unsuccessful.

Three peoples, Edom, Moab, and the children of Ammon—historically the bitterest enemies of Israel—will escape his fury. On a modern map, we would identify these countries with the country of Jordan. We are not told why these countries escape the Antichrist's wrath other than through God's provision and the remoteness of the area.

The Antichrist will deal firmly with the countries he overthrows on his Westward march. He will receive bad news from home. While he is invading Israel, God destroys Babylon. When it is most vulnerable, news is received that the Kurds from the North have invaded the Tigris-Euphrates valley and the capital of the Beast's empire. In addition, news is received that the Far East is mobilizing against him. The Antichrist will be all the more infuriated by these insurrections in the West and will hinder his preparation for dealing with the new Oriental alliance of the "kings of the east." They will imperil all of his holdings in the West.

Finally, he will reach Egypt, where he will deal summarily with the king of the South. He will systematically plunder Egypt of its wealth. He will loot the museums containing the treasures of the pharaohs to pay for the growing drain of his military. Egypt's allies, Libya and Sudan, will prove to be untrustworthy and will quickly submit to the army of the Antichrist. The Antichrist's mighty, monolithic, worldwide empire is beginning to show major cracks. It was built on treachery, war, terror, lies and every form of wickedness. It was energized by Satan, but it now becoming more difficult to hold together. The kings of the Far East, taking advantage of the Antichrist's troubles in the Middle East, will march in search of power and control of the Middle East oil. They will cross the Euphrates and rapidly deploy on the plains of Armageddon. An alliance of mountain Kurds also attack from the North.

Infuriated and enraged, the Antichrist will mobilize his Western European Confederacy. The enormous military and industrial resources of the West will be rapidly harnessed for war. The stage will now be set for the Battle of Armageddon.

Somewhere between the Mediterranean and the Jordan, in the vicinity of Jerusalem, the Antichrist will plant his command post. With what armies he can gather from the West, he will prepare for the final confrontation with the East. But his number has come up. The handwriting is on the wall. His doom is sealed. The divine clock of seven years, which began with the signing of his treaty with Israel, has come to the end. Now, the clock on the wall chimes the final hour.

When Israel is totally surrounded by the world armies with no hope in sight, the remaining one-third of the population will finally turn to their Messiah as their only hope. At the stroke of seven years, the heavens will open. The Lord of Lord and King of Kings will appear, followed by the armies of heaven and accompanied by his bride.

The demented human perspective leading to the final march to Jerusalem appears to be motivated by the effort of earth dwellers to solve what they believe to be the source of the world's problems, the Jews. The persecution of Israel builds up and culminates in the worldwide gathering of armies in Israel. The Armageddon conflict is the last major event on the prophetic timeline before the establishment of Christ's millennial kingdom.

*What Are the Stages of Armageddon?* Although no single bible passage provides a sequence of all the events of Armageddon, it is possible to construct distinct stages. When combined, these stages provide a complete picture. The stages are as follows:

1. The assembling of the allies of the Antichrist. (Ps. 2:1–6; Joel 3:9–11; Rev. 16:12–16)
2. The attack of the king of the South and the North. (Dan. 11:40)
3. The destruction of Babylon (Isa. 13–14; Jer. 50–51; Rev. 17–18)
4. The fall of Jerusalem (Mic. 4:11–5:1; Zech. 12–14)
5. News from the East and the North. (Dan. 11:44)
6. The armies of the Antichrist at Bozrah (Jer. 49:13–14)
7. The national regeneration of Israel. (Hos. 6:1–13; Zech. 12:10; 13:7–9; Rom. 11:25–27)
8. The Second Coming of Jesus Christ. (Isa. 34:1–7; Hab. 3:3)
9. The battle from Bozrah to the Valley of Jehoshaphat (Jer. 49:20–22; Joel 3:12–13)
10. The victory ascent upon the Mount of Olives (Joel 3:14–17; Rev. 16:17–21; 19:11–21)

The primary biblical reference to the battle of Armageddon is Revelation 16:12–16, which says the Euphrates River will dry up to prepare the way for the "kings of the east," whose ultimate destiny is Har-Mageddon. The assembling of the armies begins at the same time as the divine judgment poured out with the sixth bowl. While the Antichrist is gathering his armies in northern Israel for the purpose of attacking Jerusalem, God causes the destruction of Babylon, the capital of the Antichrist's kingdom.

Although the Antichrist's capital will have been destroyed, the major portion of his forces will be with him, in his invasion of Israel. While he has been occupying Jerusalem and the temple, for the last half of the Tribulation, in the end he brings his army not to occupy but to destroy the Jews. Although Zechariah 12:4–9 and Micah 4:11–5:1 describe a temporary resurgence of Jewish strength and stiff resistance, one half of Jerusalem will fall. The losses on both sides will be enormous, but the Antichrist's forces will begin to prevail. The battle will become desperate for the surviving Jews.

The campaign will shift into the desert and mountains, probably to a location about eighty miles south of Jerusalem to the area of Bozrah and Petra. At the beginning of the second half of the Tribulation, many of the Jews will flee into the desert for safety. After Jerusalem is captured, the Antichrist will move south in an attempt to destroy those who are hiding in Petra. This area is about thirty miles south of the lower end of the Dead Sea. When all seems hopeless, the remnant of Jews will turn to their Messiah in desperation. The heavens will part, and the King of Kings and Lord of Lords will appear on the clouds.

### The Seventh Bowl Judgment

"Then the seventh angel poured out his bowl into the air, and a loud voice came out of the temple of heaven, from the throne, saying, 'It is done!" and there were noises and thundering and lightning's; and there was a great earthquake as had not occurred since men were on the earth. Now the great city was divided into three parts, and the cities of the nations fell. and great Babylon was remembered before God, to give her the cup of the wine of the fierceness of his wrath.

Then every island fled away, and the mountains were not found. And the great hail from heaven fell upon men, every hailstone about the weight of seventy-five pounds. And men blasphemed God, because of the plague of the hail since that plague was exceedingly great" (Rev. 16:17–21).

With the announcement of the seventh bowl, the final judgments preceding the Second Coming on earth are revealed. No earthquake like this event has ever occurred. Christ is rearranging the furniture for his new Kingdom. He is leveling mountains and cities and raising up Zion to be the focal point and the highest point on the face of the earth.

Earthquakes have plagued the world throughout history. With an increase in population and a building of cities, earthquakes now affect populous areas with increased casualties and destruction of property. This final "big one" earthquake is the last and largest one before the Second Coming. The topographical nature of the world will be dramatically changed as the aftermath of the earthquake. Islands and mountains will disappear resulting in loss of life and property. A huge wave in the ocean created by these changes will bring total destruction that is beyond description.

In addition to the earthquake, however, there will be a tremendous supernatural hailstorm with huge hailstones, weighing between seventy-four and a hundred pounds each. Whatever is left from the earthquake in terms of building monuments of men will be beaten into pulp by these hedge blocks of ice. As with previous judgments from God, however, it does not bring repentance or confession of sin, but instead recognizes that the judgments came from God and curse God because of it.

The world is now set for the Second Coming of Christ, but before this occurs, a parenthetic summary section expands on a description of the fall of Babylon. Chapter 17 reviews the destruction of the Babylonian world religion. Chapter 18 describes the literal fall of the Antichrist's capital city.

# CHAPTER 14

# THE DESTRUCTION OF BABYLON

## What Is Ecclesiastical Babylon?

Ecclesiastical Babylon consists of the amalgamation of the world religions into one corrupt world system. John was invited by one of the angels who had the bowls of divine judgment to witness the punishment of ecclesiastical Babylon. By using the term "ecclesiastical," it is not meant that Babylon is the true church in any sense of the term, but it is Babylon from a religious standpoint. An extensive study of the religions of Babylon demonstrate that many of them were carried over in part into Roman Catholicism and formed the background for some of the ceremonies. The Babylonian influence, however, is always contrary to the truth, and her final hour is described in this chapter.

> "So he carried me away in the Spirit into the wilderness. And I saw a woman sitting on a scarlet beast, which was full of names of blasphemy, having seven heads and ten horns. The woman was arrayed in purple and scarlet and adorned with gold and precious stones and pearls, having in her hand a golden cup full of abominations and the filthiness of her fornication. And on her forehead a name was written; Mystery, Babylon the Great, the Mother of Harlots and of the Abominations of the Earth. And I saw the woman, drunk with the blood of the saints and with the blood of the

martyrs of Jesus. And when I saw her, I marveled with great amazement" (Rev. 17:3–6).

The harlot's position as one "who sits beside many waters" represent "peoples and multitudes and nations and tongues." The "many waters" interestingly corresponds to Babylon's situation on the Euphrates, with its canals, irrigation trenches, dikes and marshes surrounding the city and contributing to its protection and wealth. The harlot has committed fornication with all levels of society, from the kings of the earth to the rest of earth's inhabitants. This mainly refers to selling forgiveness of unrepentant wickedness for money. Religious prostitution occupies the forefront in Chapter 17 and the closely-related economic harlotry in Chapter 18. The Babylonian system gains international influence and even domination in both religious and political realms through its cooperation with the beast in his political domination. Religious compromise necessitated in this kind of association is totally incompatible with the worship of the one true God, and so amounts to spiritual prostitution. Prostitution is the selling of physical gratification without true love. Religious prostitution is telling people they are wonderful and spiritually wealthy in exchange for money, without regard to the true worship and love for God. The harlot thrives on spreading her filthy vices from her beautiful, but contaminated cup.

The great prostitute described in these verses is a portrayal of apostate Christendom and the World Ecumenical Movement in the end-time. When the Rapture occurs, all true believers will be caught up to be with the Lord, but those who claim to be Christians or who were religious but were not born again will be left behind. This second grouping constitutes the apostate church, which will dominate the political and religious scene during the seventieth week of Daniel.

The apostasy, called adultery and fornication in Revelation 17:3–6, of course refers to spiritual unfaithfulness and is not limited to physical adultery. The church, devoid of any redeeming influence, has now become completely united with the world. As the passage indicates, it is working hand in glove with the political powers.

John saw a woman on a scarlet-colored beast with seven heads and ten horns. The beast is the political empire described in Revelation 13:1–10. The fact that she is seated on the beast indicates that she is working with the beast to attain common ends, that is, the subjugation of the entire world to their authority and allowing the political power to support the apostate church. The woman wears the trappings of ceremonial religion in which purple and scarlet are prominent and which is often enhanced with precious stones. From the title written on her forehead, she is linked with the mystery of Babylon the Great.

Babylon is the title that covers all forms of false religion. Babylon represents the rebellion against God and the attempt to build a tower in recognition of the worship of heathen deities, man, and man's abilities. Ecclesiastical Babylon refers to its religious power and not its secular political power. Nimrod's wife was the founder of the Babylonian religion. She was given the name Semiramis, and according to the adherents' belief, she had a son named Tamuz who was miraculously conceived. Tamuz was portrayed as a savior who fulfills the promise of deliverance given to Eve. This was, of course, a satanic description which permeates pagan religions. The concept of woman and child was incorporated in various religious rites which were conducted by a priestly order. This order worshiped the woman and the child and is the background for the tendency in Roman Catholicism to glorify Mary the mother of Jesus.

As Christianity came in contact with the Babylonian religion, it created turmoil and confusion for the church. Through the centuries, there has been a tendency for the church to be anchored in the world instead of in God, and modern liberalism has gone further yet in its departure from the Scriptures. This prophecy concerning Babylon, as well as other allusions to religion in the Book of Revelation, demonstrate how the apostasy will have its final form in the Great Tribulation through its worship of the world ruler and Satan.

In the period of the first half of the seven years leading up to the Second Coming of Christ, Babylon, combined with Romanism, will become a world religion. This world religion will be Christian in name, but not in content. Those who do come to Christ will be subject to the persecution of the woman on the scarlet beast, and the woman will be "drunk with the blood of the saints." The apostate church has been unsparing in its persecution of those who have a true faith in Christ. Those who come to Christ in the end-time will have the double problem of avoiding martyrdom at the hands of the political rulers and at the hands of the apostate church.

The purpose of the alliance between the woman and the beast is that both are seeking world domination. When this is finally achieved, as the end of this chapter indicates, the political power will no longer need the religious power to support it.

The confusion of the seven heads of the beasts with the seven hills of Rome, however, arises from the inattention to the details of the passage. The seven heads are kings or kingdoms. A further statement is made, "Five have fallen, one is, the other has not yet come; but when he does come, he must remain for a little while." This refers to the great nations of the past who were empires. This would include Babylon, Assyria, neo-Babylon, Medo-Persia, Greece, and ancient Rome. Rome is the sixth kingdom, but later in history Rome is revived and becomes a seventh king. The Revived Roman Empire is considered the seventh king. This is what John refers to when he stated, "the other has not yet come" (Rev. 17:10).

The years will progress towards the Second Coming of Christ. As this happens, however, the ten-nation kingdom, which will be revived by Rome, will become a world empire. With its ruler, this ten-nation kingdom is the eighth king. This is stated thus, "The beast who once was, and now is not, is an eighth king" (Rev. 17:11). Based on a study of Daniel 7 and Revelation 13, the ten horns represent ten kingdoms which will band together to form the nucleus of the Revived Roman Empire and which will have power during the first half of the last seven years.

The next development, however, is a tremendous additional revelation. "The beast and the ten horns you say will hate the prostitute. They will bring her to ruin and leave her naked; they will eat her flesh and burn her with fire. For God has put it into their hearts to rule, until God's words are fulfilled" (Rev. 17:16–17).

The same ecclesiastical apostate church, typified by the woman that was supported and brought into being with the help of the scarlet beast or political ruler, is now destroyed. In the first half of the seven years, this woman, representing the world religion, will have power. This power is a continuation of the world church movement in the present world from which the true church was raptured in the earlier sequence of events. When the head of the ten nations takes over as world ruler at the midpoint of the seven years, the apostate church will no longer be useful and, as a matter of fact, is in the way. Accordingly, then ten nations will destroy the woman and terminate her power and position. This is similar to Adolph Hitler using the Roman Catholic Church to gain power in Germany. Once he was in power, he did not need the church, and prior to his death was in the midst of creating a religion to worship man, and ultimately to worship himself.

The coming world ruler will claim to be God himself. For the final three-and-a-half years, the world religion will worship the world ruler and will worship Satan—the power behind the world ruler. The whole religious system, originating in ancient Babylon, is brought to its close. This happens because the worship of the world rulers, the final form of religion, is atheism and does not need this support. Revelation 17:18 states, "The woman you say is the great city that rules over the kings of the earth." This quote refers to the fact that the Vatican and the World Ecumenical Movement establish their seat of authority in Babylon. The Babylonian religion will be characterized by the mystery of darkness, incense burning, superstition, ignorance, immorality, priesthood, nuns, sprinkling, idolatry, and many other forms of Babylonian mysticism. After the Rapture, the world religious leaders will bring all Babylonian-based religions together into one global, idolatrous religion.

Whenever in control of a country, Roman Catholics, Muslims, Hindus, and Buddhists have prevented the spreading of the Gospel. The Roman Catholic Church has been the main offender. Rome's frantic opposition to the Reformation (caused by her pagan indulgences and corruption of the true faith) is a good example. It is stated that in the thirty years between 1540 and 1570, no fewer than nine hundred thousand Protestants were put to death. This was the Pope's call for the extermination of the Waldenses. The inquisition is the most infamous event in church history. It was devised by the popes, and was used to maintain their power for five hundred years. In seventeenth century Bohemia, approximately 3 million Protestants were killed. During the Spanish Inquisitions that took place between 1481 to 1808, there were at least one-hundred-thousand people killed and 1.5 million people banished.

Since the religions of the world all have idolatry in common, it will be simple for them to amalgamate into a common basis. However, God will bring judgment on the world's religions and avenge the blood of the martyrs.

## The Destruction of the City of Babylon

Chapter 18 of Revelation starts out by saying, "After these things." This is an idiom for a change in subject matter. The destruction of Ecclesiastical Babylon, or the Headquarters of the World Religion, was just described in Revelation 17. After these things, or after the destruction of the world ecumenical religion, the destruction of the city of Babylon is described in chapter 18. This attack is a response to the attack by the Antichrist of the city of Jerusalem and the desecration of the Holy of Holies in the Middle of the seventieth week of Daniel.

> After these things I saw another angel coming down from heaven, having great authority, and the earth was illuminated with his glory. And he cried mightily with a loud voice, saying, "Babylon the great is fallen, is fallen, and has become a habitation of demons, a prison for every foul spirit, and a cage for every unclean and hated bird! For all the nations have drunk of the wine of the wrath of her fornication, the kings of the earth have committed fornication with her, and the merchants of the earth have become rich through the abundance of her luxury."
>
> For in one hour such great riches came to nothing. And every shipmaster, all who travel by ship, sailors, and as many as trade on the sea, stood at a distance and cried out when they saw the smoke of her burning, saying, "What is like this great city?" And they threw dust on their heads and cried out, weeping and wailing, and saying, "Alas, alas, the great city, in which all who had ships on the sea became rich by her wealth! For in one hour she is made desolate." (Rev. 18:1–3; 9, 19)

In Chapter 17:16, the Beast and the ten leaders of the confederacy turned on the world religion and destroyed her. The Antichrist only uses religion to gain power, and once he gains power he does not need religion and he destroys it as a possible competitor to his insatiable lust for this position over others. People who purchase sexual favors or religious approval for money have little respect for God or their Para-moors. They are more interested in themselves and their lust for others and power. However, when God causes the destruction of the Antichrist's capital city of Babylon, the world weeps with sorrow. Many ship captains and men of international trade are depressed and shocked at the loss of their wealthy client.

In Isaiah 13 and 14, we are told that God will punish the world and move the earth out of its orbit. God will stir up the Medes to destroy Babylon and it will never be inhabited again (verse 19). Babylon was overrun by Media-Persia, but it was not destroyed as Sodom and Gomorrah. In Jeremiah 50:9, we are told, "For behold, I will raise and cause to come up against (Babylon) an assembly of great nations from the north country." Jeremiah 51:27–28 and 31 state, "Set up a banner in the land. Blow the trumpet among the nations! Prepare the nations against her, call the kingdoms together against her. Ararat, Minni, and Ashkenaz. Appoint a marshal against her; cause the horses to come up like the bristling locust. Prepare against her the nations, with the kings of the Medes, its governors and all its ruler, all the land of his dominion. And the land will tremble and sorrow; every purpose of the Lord shall be performed against Babylon, to make the land of Babylon a desolation without inhabitant. One runner will run to meet another, and one messenger to meet another, to show the king of Babylon that his city is taken on all side."

The Medes were an ancient people who lived in the mountains in what is now part of Iran, Iraq and Armenia. Some believe they were the ancestors of modern Kurds. Ararat, Minni, and Ashkenaz are mountain ranges in modern Turkey.

This is a double fulfillment. Babylon was taken by Cyrus in 539 BC, but he spared the city by damming the Euphrates river and going under the walls. Isaiah 13–14 and Jeremiah 50–51 are primarily speaking of the destruction of Babylon in the last days, from which it will never recover.

Tim LaHaye and Ed Hindson, make the following comments in their book, *Bible Prophecy Commentary*:

Jeremiah's most extensive prophecies are against Babylon. As with Isaiah 13–14, some commentators view Jeremiah 50–51 as having been fulfilled against ancient Babylon, but the details simply do not fit the Babylon of the past. The passage can only be true of the Babylon of the future, which will be the capital of the world under the authority of the Antichrist. The description Jeremiah gives here fits that of a destruction of Babylon in the course of the war of Armageddon. (166)

Isaiah 13–14 and Jeremiah 50–51 describes the destruction of the future Babylon of the Antichrist for the following reasons:

1.  It will never be inhabited again (Jer. 50:3, 13, 39)
2.  Walls and building material destroyed (Jer. 50:15, 26)
3.  Earth knocked off its axis (Isa. 14:13)
4.  Babylon never to be remembered (Isa. 14:23)

These descriptions do not fit ancient Babylon.

As mentioned above, the city of Babylon was captured by Cyrus, who was mentioned in prophecy by name 125 years before he was born. There was no destruction of the city or the walls at that time. The enemy went under the walls. In 331 BC, Alexander the Great approached the city. The people surrendered and opened the gates. In 25 BC, the famous geographer Strabo visited Babylon. He described the Hanging Gardens as one of the Seven Wonders of the Ancient World. He also described the bountiful crops of barley produced in the surrounding country. On the day of Pentecost, as mentioned in Acts 2:8–10, there were Jews in Jerusalem from Babylon. According to I Peter 5:13, the Apostle Peter wrote his first epistle from Babylon.

In AD 917, Ibu Hankel mentions Babylon as an insignificant village, but still in existence. In approximately AD 1100 it was enlarged, fortified, and its name was changed to Hillah, or "Rest." In AD 1898, Hillah contained about ten thousand inhabitants, and was surrounded by fertile lands. Saddam Hussein spent millions of dollars restoring Babylon.[59] It is clear the prophecies of Isaiah and Jeremiah have not been fulfilled. There is even a blog on the Internet by an atheist pointing out how these prophecies have not been fulfilled. He uses their lack of fulfillment to discredit Isaiah's, Jeremiah's, and God's word, not knowing that they these will be fulfilled shortly.

Babylon the Great will be an immense city, the greatest in every respect the world has ever seen. It will be a typical city, the London, New York, or Paris of its day. It will become the center of worldwide commerce. Its merchandise will be of gold, silver, precious stones, pearls, silk and costly woods. Its fashionable society will be clothed in the most costly raiment and decked with the most costly jewels. Homes of the rich and famous will be filled with the most costly furniture of precious woods, brass, iron, and marble. The fastest cars, boats and planes will be on parade. They rich and famous will traffic in the "souls of men." Women will sell their bodies and men their souls to gratify their lusts and passions. The markets will be crowded with cattle and sheep. The wharves will be piled with electronic and mechanical devices of all kinds. Business men and promoters will give their days and nights to scheme how to make big money fast. There will be riotous parties and extreme luxuries with ceaseless social activities. However, in one day it will all go up in smoke. The end will come to the shock of the whole world!

# CHAPTER 15

# THE RESURRECTION

## The Resurrection

The concept of future bodily resurrection is found throughout the Bible. John 5:28–29 places resurrections into two general categories: the resurrection to eternal life and the resurrection of judgment or eternity in the lake of fire.

The first resurrection includes the redeemed of all the ages. These resurrections do not occur at the same.

The timing of the resurrection of these individuals depends upon the category of dispensation to which they belong.

> "But now Christ is risen from the dead, and has become the Firstfruit of those who have fallen asleep. For since by man came death, by Man also came the resurrection of the dead. For a as in Adam all die, even so in Christ all shall be made alive. But each one in his own order; Christ the First-fruit, afterward those who are Christ's at his coming. Then come the end, when He delivers the kingdom to God the Father, when he puts an end to all rule and all authority and power. For he must reign till he has put all enemies under his feet. The last enemy that will be destroyed is death" ( I Cor. 15:20–26).

The scriptures delineate four resurrections: Christ, church age believers, Old Testament and millennial believers.

1. The resurrection of Jesus Christ is the first fruit of many to be raised. (Rom. 6:9; I Cor. 15:23). It is no accident his resurrection was on the Feast of First Fruits.
2. The resurrection of the church age believers at the Rapture. (I Thess. 4:16)
3. The resurrection of Old Testament believers and Tribulation martyred at the Second Coming (Jews and Gentiles). (Rev. 20:3–5; Dan. 12:2)
4. Resurrection or the provision of glorified bodies of all millennial believers after the millennium.

The second resurrection is the resurrection of unbelievers at the great white throne judgment and their subsequent sentence to the lake of fire for eternity.

> "Then I saw a great white throne and Him who sat on it, from whose face the earth and the heavens fled away. And there was found no place for them. And I saw the dead, small and great, standing before God, and the books were opened. And another book was opened, which is the Book of Life. And the dead were judged, according to their works, by the things which were written in the books. The sea gave up the dead who were in it, and Death and Hades delivered up the dead who were in them. And they were judged, each one according to his works. Then Death and Hades were cast into the lake of fire. This is the second death. And anyone not found written in the Book of Life was cast into the lake of fire" (Rev. 20:11–14).

Almost all religions teach the immortality of the soul; but the Bible teaches the redemption of and the survival of the total person:

spirit, soul and body. The ancient Greeks believed in the life after death for the soul, but since the body was the source of all evil, release of the soul from the body was desirable. A heretical Christian sect called Gnostics share this concept derived from Greek philosophy. The Bible does not teach that the physical body is the source of evil; the Pauline term "flesh" refers to man's sinful and selfish nature which, while it manifests itself through actions of the body, derives from a "carnal mind" (Rom. 8:6–7). Christ, by his Incarnation, Death, and Resurrection, redeemed the total person who is in Christ, giving him a hope of a bodily resurrection which will occur at the Rapture of the church for Christians. We will have a new body not subject to death, and a new heart not subject to lusts and evil desires.

## What is the Purpose of the Great White Throne Judgment?

The purpose of second resurrection or the great white throne judgment is not to determine the spiritual state or destination of unbelievers. These are settled during man's earthly life. Romans 2:6 states that all people who reject Christ's payment for their sins must answer for their works and receive their dues. The unsaved will be judged according to the contents of certain books. These books seem to include those that have a full, accurate record of their works and their shortcomings.

The great white throne judgment may rightly be called the "final judgment." It is clearly indicated to take place after the expiration of the millennial reign of Christ. This judgment takes place neither in heaven nor on earth, but somewhere in between the two. "And I saw a great white throne, and Him that sat on it, from whose face the earth and the heaven fled away; and there was found no place for them" (Rev. 20:11).

This judgment is for those called "the dead." The only ones left unrestricted at this time are the unsaved. Contrary to popular opinion, the judgment is not to determine whether or not they are saved. It is rather a judgment on the evil works of the unsaved. The sentence of the "second death" will be passed upon them. The second death is the confirmation and the making of that eternal separation from God which the first death entailed. God does not send anyone to the Lake of Fire. Instead they choose to go by rejecting the redemption freely offered by Christ as savior.

## How Do We Know God Exists?

By definition, mistakes are caused by wrong thinking. Right thinking will avoid mistakes.

Practicing logic equates to putting one's thoughts in order. Avoiding logic is, by definition, irrational. Some say logic does not apply to God. However, that statement is self-refuting. Theology is logic (logos) applied towards God (theos). While it is the Holy Spirit, not logic, that reveals truth about God, logic is capable of confirming theology. Otherwise, theology would be illogical. The basis of all logic is that no two contradictory statements can both be true and at the same time false. This means that some statements are true and some are false.

The Bible states, "Now faith is the substance of things hoped for, the evidence of things not seen" (Heb. 11:1). If something could be seen it would not require faith. However, this is not to say that faith is based upon the illogical. Can we prove the existence of God with logic? Romans 1 states that creation clearly reveals God and that man is without excuse for disregarding the very existence of God. Unbelief is a state of the soul and is sin. The historical basis of man's sin is not from ignorance. It comes from rebellion in the presence of clear light. Romans 1:18 states, "For the wrath of God is revealed from heaven against all ungodliness and unrighteousness of men, who hold the truth in unrighteousness." There is a continuous revelation of the wrath of God in contemporary society.

## What if There Is No God?

If there is no God, then man and the universe are doomed. Like prisoners condemned to death, we await our unavoidable execution. If there is no God, and there is no immortality, life has no purpose. Life is absurd. It means that the life we have is without ultimate significance, value, or purpose. In a world without God, who can say what is right and what is wrong? It is well documented that Adolph Hitler read Charles Darwin's book *The Origin of Species by Means of Natural Selection or the Preservation of Favored Races In the Struggle For Life*. If there is no God, and man is an animal, and life is improved through survival of the strongest, then Hitler was right. However, since there is a God, man is born with a conscience, and the Holy Spirit convicts all men of sin and righteousness, all men instinctively know there is a God and are ultimately accountable to Him.

Does logic establish that there is a God? Logic establishes that no effect can be produced without a cause. Following this idea, we eventually come to an uncaused cause, who is God. Some may ask, who caused God? However, God is outside, time, space and matter. God is not an effect. He does not require a cause. In studying matter, we know that energy cannot be created or destroyed. Only its form can be changed. Logic tells us that something outside of this universe created energy. Something designed DNA, the software of life. Software does not design itself.

Following the 1931 publication of Edwin Hubble's *Law of Red Shifts*, proving the universe is, indeed, expanding, Albert Einstein grudgingly accepted "the necessity for a beginning" and stated that he had made the greatest mistake of his life to deny that the universe had a beginning.[60] Einstein was eventually forced to logically accept "the presence of a superior reasoning power, but did not accept the doctrine of a personal God to the day he died. However, once we pass into the next life there will be no unbelievers. Many who have clinically died and returned have said that when their soul left their body, they immediately knew there was a God and has a sense of guilt and wrong doing.

## Is Evolution a Religion?

Evolution is a belief system through which faith follows a process of self-transformation, without any outside agency as a creator or master designer. Evolution believes that an act of chaos generated the cosmos and disorder was transformed into order. Darwinism believes that all design and complexity that can be observed in the universe can be traced back to an initial explosion. This is difficult to logically embrace since explosions, by their nature, bring chaotic disorder. The laws of physics teach us that systems allowed to naturally proceed go from order to disorder.

Evolution alleges that over the course of millions of years, single-celled organisms developed into complex organisms by natural selection. However, there is no such thing as a simple cell. Single cells are very complex organisms. Plants and animals cannot typically reproduce hybrids, and can only reproduce like kind. One can cross a male donkey and a female horse and get a mule. However, the mule cannot reproduce. This is because a donkey has sixty-two chromosomes and a horse has sixty-four chromosomes. However, horses and donkeys are both in the horse family. One cannot cross a horse and a tiger.

If the earth is billions of years old, and the layers of the earth have been laid down gradually over millions and millions of years, the fossils embedded in the crust of the earth should show the record of the transition of life forms from the past. We should be able to identify living things in the process of change from one kind to another. However, no intermediary fossils exist.[61] In fact, the geological column exists only in texts books. Fossils in the middle states of development between fish and bird, or mammal and man, have never been discovered. Charles Darwin himself said that the fossil record was "perhaps the most obvious and serious objection" to his theory. The truth is that evolution is not scientific, it is only a hedonistic pseudo-science created to justify the lack of accountability to God. The evolutionary theory cannot explain where laws of physics came from, what is the power source of energy, or where matter originally comes from. And in fact if the universe is not billions of years old, the entire evolutionary belief system collapses into thin air. The whole argument for evolution is based upon the premise that if given enough time, chaos can create complexity. Without billions of years, evolution crumbles into witchcraft and black magic. Logic and facts support the truth that, "In the beginning God created heaven and earth" (Gen. 1:1). There is right and wrong and man is accountable to God. There is a purpose for life. Without God as a creator, we have purposelessness, hedonism, and sociopaths without conscience. We have nothing but the living dead.

## Is the World Billions of Years Old?

Contrary to evolutionary thesis, we have a growing body of evidence showing that dinosaurs did not live millions of years before man. In fact, drawings in caves and footprints show man and dinosaurs lived together until fairly recent time. Approximately four-thousand years ago, the earth experienced a major shift in climate. Prior to that time, large tropical forests existed in the north and south poles. The atmospheric pressure was over twice the pressure it is now. A canopy of water or ice surrounded the earth and blocked ultraviolet rays. Under these conditions, plants, animals, and humans lived up to ten times longer and dinosaurs grew to extremely large sizes.[62]

We have uncovered skeletons of humans and animals much taller than they are today. Reptiles lived hundreds of years. Dinosaurs are merely large lizards or reptiles that grew for many years under different weather conditions. Approximately four-thousand years ago, this environment changed. The canopy covering the earth dissolved and flooded the earth. Mountains were formed. Millions of dinosaurs were killed. The life span of man and animals was dramatically shortened.

Today, only in our deepest oceans do we have conditions similar to the prior living conditions. Sea life grows to extremely large sizes under increased pressure and greater ultraviolet screening. Large sea creatures have been discovered over a hundred feet long in recent times. Today, the hedonistic science community fights with a vengeance to prove the earth is billions of years old. State-run schools will not give scientists tenure unless they conform to the popular misconception that the earth is billions of years old. This is because America has gone from a Bible-believing country to a godless nation of relative truths. Today's scientists believe in uniformatarianism. They reject the fact that God intervened in world history and created the Noaic Flood, altering today's geologic columns. Naturalists worship the concept of time. They believe that if we have enough time, life can come from a rock or inanimate material. However, without sufficient time their cause is hopeless and they must face the consequences of accountability to their maker. God says, "The fool has said in his ear, 'There is no God.' They are corrupt, they have done abominable works, there is none who does good" (Ps. 14:1).

## Is the Bible God's Word?

How do we know the Bible is the infallible word of God? Deuteronomy 19:22 states that when a prophet speaks for God, the thing comes to pass. In other words, only God is outside time. No other religious book outside of the Bible is capable of dogmatically providing time-specific prophecies and citing names hundreds and thousands of years ahead of time. False prophets and pseudo fortune tellers deal in generalities and give many predictions. Once in a while they are correct. However, the Bible is specific and is never wrong. Anyone who ever gives wrong prediction does not speak for God. God is not near perfect, he is absolute perfection.

Nebuchadnezzar, the king of Babylon, had a dream. He asked the wise men of his day to interpret his dream. However, to prove they were telling the truth he would not tell them the dream They told him only God could give an interpretation, without knowing the dream. God gave Daniel the dream and the interpretation, which became the history of the world. The dream was a large statue of a man. His head of gold represented Babylon. His chest and arms of silver represented Medo-Persia. Its belly and thighs of bronze represented Greece. The legs of iron represented the Roman Empire. The feet of iron and clay represented the ten-nation European confederation of the Antichrist during the Tribulation or the seventieth week of Daniel.

Daniel also gave a time-specific prophecy providing the exact day the coming Messiah would present himself as king to the nation of Israel. Joshua Messiah presented himself as king on that very day. The Bible proves it is from God because it gave over 300 prophecies about Jesus Christ that were fulfilled. Jesus was born of a virgin, in Bethlehem, of the house of David. He died for our sins, was buried, and rose again.

## Do Non-Christians Go to Hell?

One law of logic is the law of the excluded middle. A proper premise must be one way or the other with no middle ground. If Christianity is true, then all other religions are false. They cannot all be true at the same time. Aristotle remarked that he could not see how God could forgive evil. The answer is that God could not forgive sin. The wages of sin is death. "For all have sinned and fall short of the glory of God, being justified freely by his grace through the redemption that is in Christ Jesus" (Rom. 3:23–24). God's solution to the problem of the penalty of sin was to send his son to become a human, to become a kinsman redeemer, and to pay the penalty of sin. "Most assuredly, I say to you, unless one is born again, he cannot see the kingdom of God. For God so loved the world that he gave his only begotten Son, that whosoever believes in Him shall not perish but have everlasting life" (John 3: 3, 16). Jesus said, "I am the way, the truth, and the life. No one comes to the Father except through me. For God did not send his son into the world to condemn the world, but that the world through him might be saved. He who believes in him is not condemned; but he who does not believe is condemned already, because he has not believed in the name of the only begotten Son of God" (John 3:17-18,14:6).

## Judaism

What about Jews who do not become Christians? Judaism requires a blood sacrifice as an atonement for sin. Where are the blood sacrifices? Judaism says that the scepter will not depart from Judah, nor a lawgiver from between his feet, until the Messiah comes" (Gen. 49:10). If Jesus was not the Jewish messiah, how does Judaism explain their loss of a national existence after the time of Christ? Where is the monarchy of Judah during the Diaspora? Judaism states that the Messiah was to come riding on a donkey in AD 33. Where is the Messiah? Judaism without Joshua Messiah is not true Judaism. One day soon, all Israel will be redeemed!

## Hinduism

There is no single God in Hinduism. Hindu concepts of deity can include any of the following: Monism (all existence is one substance), pantheism (God is in creation as a soul is in a body), animism (God or gods live in nonhuman objects such as trees, rocks, etc),. polytheism (there are many gods), and monotheism (there is only one god). Hinduism believes in reincarnation. However, the Bible states that man is appointed to die once, but after that judgment. Hinduism and Christianity cannot both be right. One must be wrong.

## Buddhism

Buddhism has many good ideas. It encourages brotherly love and opposes selfishness. However, early Buddhism rejected the idea of a personal God. Mahayana worships many Gods. Buddhists believe in reincarnation. Both Buddhism and Christianity cannot both be true. They are mutually exclusive.

## Islam

The Muslim religion denies the deity of Jesus Christ. Muhammad was an illiterate pseudo prophet who borrowed oral traditions from both the Old and New Testaments. Many events in the Koran are not in chronological sequence. The Qur'an encourages war, rape and plundering: "Fight against such of those who have been given the Scripture as believe not in Allah nor the Last Day, and forbid not that which Allah hath forbidden by His messenger, and follow not the religion of truth, until they pay the tribute readily, being brought low" (Surah 9:29). In *Behind the Veil*, Joseph Abd El Shafi states, "Muhammad, though he claimed to be the best prophet and apostle of God, was a hideously violent and bloodthirsty man. He tortured and mutilated prisoners, killed those who surrendered and took their women and children. How could this be the prophet of mercy?" (76). Both Christianity and the Qur'an cannot be true. They are mutually exclusive.

## How Can a Loving God Send People to Hell?

It is God's desire that all men be saved. God does not send anyone to hell. Men who reject Christ as the payment of their sins must accept the results of their choice. God gives man free choice, and he will respect each individual's choice. Some accept Christ as their personal savior. Some reject God, and choose to be separated from God for eternity.

## What about People Who Have Never Heard the Gospel?

Romans 1:20 states, "For since the creation of the world his invisible attributes are clearly seen, being understood by the things that are made, even his eternal power and his divine nature, so that they are without excuse." Proverbs 1:3–5 states, "...If you cry out for discernment, and lift up your voice for understanding, if you seek her as silver, and search for her as for hidden treasures; then you will understand the fear of the Lord." If we can mail a letter to anyone in the world, certainly God can reach anyone with the Gospel. During the Tribulation there will be 7 billion people alive. There will be more people alive at the end-times than have ever lived since the beginning of man. Moses, Elijah, the 144,000 Jewish believers, and angels will all proclaim the mercies of God and the coming judgment. Many will become saved, but many will choose to reject God and will suffer the consequences of their fatal decision. God is righteous and holy. Man without Christ is lost.

## What Does it Mean to Be Born Again?

Being born again is something God does supernaturally. It is not something man does. Becoming a Christian is not accomplished through cleaning yourself up and making yourself presentable to God. Being born again is not physical birth. It is spiritual birth.

When Adam sinned, he spiritually died. Through Adam, all humans are born spiritually dead. Being born again is something God does to people who believe in Jesus Christ as their Lord and Savior. A child born into the best Christian family cannot get to heaven upon the merits of his father or mother. Christianity is not transmissible. It is not cultivation. It is not training. New birth is a divine change. "To as many as received him, to them gave he the power to become the sons of God." Mercy is when a judge lets something slide. Grace is when a judge pays the penalty, invites the guilty party home, and adopts them with full family privileges. Grace is God's riches at Christ's expense.

## Why Do We Need the New Birth?

First, our own nature required it. By nature, we are the children of wrath. We are disobedient. We are aliens to the holiness of God. Every one of us has sinned. We are not fit for God or heaven. Something has to happen to turn us from sinners into saints. Compared to some of our pagan neighbors, we may not look so bad. However, compared to God, we all lack God's perfect righteousness.

The second reason we have to be born again is because God's nature requires it. God is holy, without spot, without sin, without stain. He cannot countenance sin. He cannot pass over sin, cannot accept, receive, or take sin into heaven. You may be a fit subject of the best of society on earth, but that does not make you acceptable to heaven.

Thirdly, the work of Christ requires it. If there were any other way to be saved except by the washing of regeneration through the blood of Jesus shed on the cross, then Jesus would never have had to die. If God forgive man of sin in any other way, Christ would not have been required to die. However, Jesus said, "I am the way, the truth, and the life; no man comes to the Father by me" (John 14:6).

Lastly, the word of God requires it. John 3:3 boldly states, "Except a man be born again he cannot see the kingdom of heaven."

## What Will the New Birth Do For Us?

First, it will take care of the past by the pardon of every sin. Second, the new birth will give us a new heart. Only the power of God can free us from slavery of the passions of our own desires. There is no man, no matter how strong or self-righteous, who can overcome temptation and the lusts of the flesh. Lastly, we are promised an eternal future with God. In John 14:2, Jesus said, "In My Father's house are many mansions. If it were not so I would have told you. I go to prepare a place for you. And if I go and prepare a place for you, I will come again, and receive you unto myself, that where I am, there you may be also."

## What if You Are Not a Christian?

If you are not a child of God, a dreadful pit of glowing flames of the wrath of God lies beneath you. Only the hand of God is keeping you out of Sheol. Sheol is a holding tank in the depths of the earth where unbelieving souls are kept until Judgment Day. On Judgment Day, if your name is not written in the book of life, you will be sent to hell for eternal pain and suffering. Unbelievers attribute their current state to things such as the health of their body, the care of their life, and the means they use for their own preservation. However, these things are nothing; if God should withdraw his hand, they would avail no more to keep from falling than the thin air can hold up a person who is suspended into it. The unseen, unsought of ways and means by which people suddenly go out of the world are innumerable and inconceivable. Unconverted men walk over the pit of Sheol on rotten covering, without sensing they are one moment away from a horrible end. There are currently sinners who have already gone into the next life of pain and suffering. God is less angry at these sinners than some unbelievers alive today. In other words, there are people alive today who are worse than some people already in hell. The only reason they are alive is because of God's mercy and because they were born more recently.

Do not tempt God by continuing as you are. Will you accept him as God and as the lord of your life? You are not promising to be perfect, or to turn over a new life. You are confessing that you have sinned, you need forgiveness, and you are identifying with the death of Christ. You are confessing that he paid for your sins on the Cross. Jesus is pleading. His pierced hands are stretched out to you in love. God wants you to become part of his family. Will you, right now, from the very depths of your heart, say to Jesus, "Lord, you loved me enough to die for me. I love you enough to live for you. Here is my life at your feet to prove it. I do accept Christ as my Savior. I do give my life into his service. Praise God! If you expressed this prayer you are born again and are a member of God's family. This is not based on how you feel, but upon God's word. There is no higher power. However, if you do nothing, you are lost!

# CHAPTER 16

# THE MILLENNIAL REIGN OF CHRIST

## How Long Will the Millennial Reign Last?

Revelation 20 declares that Christ will return to earth and establish himself as King in Jerusalem and reign for one thousand years. During this period, Satan will be bound. It states the following:

"Then I saw an angel coming down from heaven, having the key to the bottomless pit and a great chain in his hand. He laid hold of the dragon, that serpent of old, who is the Devil and Satan, and bound him for a thousand years; and he cast him into the bottomless pit, and shut him up, and set a seal on him, so that he could deceive the nations no more till the thousand years were finished. But after these things he must be released for a little while. And I saw thrones, and they sat on them, and judgment was committed to them. And I saw the souls of those who had been beheaded for their witness to Jesus and for the word of God, who had not worshiped the beast or his image, and had not received his mark on their foreheads or on their hands. and they lived and reigned with Christ for a thousand years. But the rest of the dead did not live again until the thousand years were finished. This is the first resurrection. Blessed and holy is he who has part in the first resurrection. Over such the second death has no power, but they shall be priests of God and of Christ, and shall reign with him a thousand years…Now when the thousand years have expired, Satan will be released from his prison and will go out to deceive the nations which are in the four corners of the earth, Gog and Magog, to gather them together to battle, whose number is as the sand of the sea. They went up on the breadth of the earth and surrounded the camp of the saints and the beloved city. And fire came down from God out of heaven and devoured them. And the devil, who deceived thee, was cast into the lake of fire and brimstone, where the beast and the false prophet are, and they will be tormented day and night forever and ever. Then I saw a great white throne and him who sat on it, from whose face the earth and the heaven fled away, and there was found no place for them. And I saw the dead, small and great, standing before God, and the books were opened. and another book was opened, which is the Book of Life. And the dead were judged according to their works, by the things which were written in the books. The sea shall give up the dead who were in it, and Death and Hades, delivered the dead who were in them. And they were judged, each one according to his works. Then Death and Hades were cast into the lake of fire. This is the second death. And anyone not found written in the Book of Life was cast into the lake of fire. Satan is bound not by the Lord, not by a host of angels, not even by Michael the archangel, but by a single, unnamed angel. We often imagine a huge cosmic struggle going on constantly between God and Satan. This is not the true picture. Satan is a created being. God is all powerful, all present and all knowing, thus Satan is not a counterpart or a rival to God.

"How you are fallen from heaven, O Lucifer, son of the morning! How you are cut down to the ground, you who weakened the nations! For you have said in your heart, 'I will ascend into heaven, I will exalt my throne above the stars of God; I will also sit on the mount of the congregation, on the farthest sides of the north; I will ascend above the heights of the clouds, I will be like the Most High.' Yet you shall be brought down to Sheol, to the lowest depths of the Pit. Those who see you will gaze at you, and consider you, saying, 'Is this the man who made the earth tremble, who shook kingdoms, who made the world as a wilderness, and destroyed its cities, who did not open the house of his prisoners?'" (Isa. 14:12–17).

## What Will the Millennial Kingdom Be Like?

The conditions during the millennium will depict a perfect environment both physically and spiritually. It will be a time of peace, joy, comfort and without poverty, as stated by Micah 4:2–4,; Isaiah 32:17–18, and Amos 9:13–15. Only believers will enter the Millennium, it will be a time of righteousness (Matt. 25:37); obedience (Jer. 31:33); holiness (Isa. 35:8); truth (Isa. 65:16); and fullness of the Holy Spirit (Joel 2:28–29). Christ will rule as king (Isa. 9:3–7), with David as regent (Jer. 33:15). Jerusalem will be the center of the world, rising physically to reveal its prominence (Zech. 14:10). Prior to the Second Coming, mountains will be leveled, making Zion the highest point on earth.

At the end of the Millennium, the unsaved dead of all ages are resurrected and judged at the great white throne. They will be condemned and cast into the lake of fire, their final abode. The devil will join the Antichrist and the false prophet in the lake of fire, where they will be tormented forever and ever. Once a person is born, our soul is like software: It has no mass, and is not subject to time. It lasts forever. God does not send anyone to the lake of fire, they chose to go by rejecting god's plan for their life.

## What Will Be the Form of Government?

The government of the Millennial reign will be a theocracy, and Christ will rule as the King of Kings and as God with absolute authority. "...One like the Son of man, Coming with the clouds of heaven! He came to the Ancient of days, and they brought him near before him, then to him was given dominion and glory and a kingdom, that all people, nations and languages should serve him" (Dan. 7:13). "...yet I have set My King on my holy hill of Zion. I will declare the decree: The Lord has said to me, "You are my son, today I have begotten you. Ask of me, and I will give you the nations for your inheritance, and the end of the earth for your possession" (Ps. 1:6–8). "The Lord said to my Lord, sit at my right hand, till I make your enemies your footstool" (Ps. 110:1).

Although the throne of Christ will be established in Jerusalem, his dominion will not stop at the border of Israel. It will extend throughout the entire earth, with every Gentile nation falling under his domain. The resurrected David, who is given both titles of king and prince, will be directly under Christ, having authority over all Israel. He will be a king because he will rule over Israel, but he will be a prince in that he will be under the authority of Christ. The twelve apostles will have authority over the twelve tribes.

"...and Jesus said unto them, verily I say unto you, that you who have followed me, in the regeneration when the son of man shall sit on the throne of his glory, you also shall sit upon twelve thrones, judging the twelve tribes of Israel" (Matt. 19:28). The millennial kingdom the father appointed for the son was extended by Christ to the twelve apostles. Christ's domain will be over all the world, David's rule over all Israel, while the apostles' jurisdiction will be over particular tribes. The twelve are promised two privileges with this appointment. The first is that they will be continually with

Christ and eating and drinking at his table throughout the kingdom period. The second privilege is to have their own thrones from which they will rule over the tribes of Israel.

Along with the Jewish branch, there will be a Gentile branch, which will co-reign under Christ. The church and the tribulational saints will be lead by twenty-four elders. Revelation 20:4 describes the saints that are to co-reign under Christ. First, there are those to whom judgment has been given. This would be a reference to the church saints who were raptured prior to the Great Tribulation. The judgment spoken of is that of the judgment seat of Christ, the judgment of the believer's works. In fact, it is the outcome of this judgment that will affect the position of each church age saint in the kingdom. A second group of saints who are to co-reign are those who had been beheaded for the testimony of Jesus. These are the believers who will be martyred during the first part of the Great Tribulation and were mentioned under the fifth seal. A third group are those who did not worship the Antichrist or his image, nor received the mark of 666 on their forehead or on their right hand. Since these things were initiated only at the middle of the Tribulation, this third group of saints are those from the second half of the Tribulation. The church and the tribulational saints will co-reign over the Gentile nations. They will be the King's representative authority and will carry out his decrees to the nations.

## What Will Be the Worship in the Millennium?

The restored theocracy is marked by the adoration given to the Lord Jesus Christ. A temple will be built by God in Jerusalem and animal sacrifices will be offered as a memorial to shed the blood of Jesus Christ. Fresh water will flow out of the temple and bring life to the dead sea. The millennial kingdom will be a wonderfully spiritual time. First and foremost, the risen, glorified Lord Jesus, Himself, will be present. With the removal of Satan comes the removal of his demonic forces and his world system.

Christ's reign is characterized by righteousness. Men will feel safe and free of oppression and persecution. There will be a full knowledge of the Lord and a fullness of the Holy Spirit. There will be a universal worship of the Lord Jesus, centered in the magnificent new temple in Jerusalem.

Worship will be of quality and depth never before seen on earth, as righteous Jews and Gentiles gladly come to Jerusalem to praise the great Savior King, as is prophesied in Isaiah 2:2–4, Ezekiel 20:40–41, and Zechariah 14:16. With the glory of the Lord once again present in the temple, the sense of worship will be best described by the word "awesome." Jerusalem will be a spiritual magnet drawing people to worship and praise the Lord.

According to Ezekiel 43:13, Zechariah 14:16–21, and Isaiah 66:20–23, animal sacrifices will be connected with the worship of Jesus Christ in the millennial kingdom. That animal sacrifices are mentioned in connection with millennial worship has troubled some because they appear to be a throwback to the outdated Levitical worship and diminish the work of Christ on the cross. But these sacrifices do not mean that there is a return to the Levitical worship system, and they do not detract from the cross. Like the Old Testament temple that revealed the character of God through its rituals and provided a place for sinful men to approach God, the millennial temple will perform the same basic function for those under the new covenant. We who are in our resurrected bodies will apparently not need these sacrifices, but there will be sinful men in non-glorified bodies who will. These people (even if they are believers) can and do sin because of the presence of the old sinful flesh. This inspires the need for cleansing and purification exists. Afterward, in the eternal kingdom on the new earth, there will be no sacrifices and no temple, because there are no longer any non-glorified people. There are only resurrected people living in a new and glorious environment.

## The Physical Characteristics of the Millennial Kingdom

The curse that was placed on the creation at the time of the fall of man will be lifted. Peace will come to the animal kingdom, which has been characterized by violence and death. All animals will once again be plant eaters, as they were in the original creation. Wolves and lambs will live together and lions and oxen will graze together. "The wolf also shall dwell with the lamb, the leopard shall lie down with the young goat, the calf and the young lion and the fatling together; and a little child shall lead them. The cow and the bear shall graze; their young ones shall lie down together; and the lion shall eat straw like the ox. The nursing child shall play by the cobra's hole, and the weaned child shall put his hand in the viper's den. They shall not hurt nor destroy in all my holy mountain, for the earth shall be full of the knowledge of the Lord, as the waters cover the sea" (Isa. 11:6–9).

The reversal of the curse will also enable the earth to once again be amazingly productive, being freed from thorns and thistles. Much of the present earth is unproductive because it is desert, but the millennial kingdom will be characterized by an abundance of water, the desolate, dry areas of the earth will blossom as the rose. Jesus Christ will remove disease and physical deformity from the earth. This will result in long life spans, such that if someone dies at the age of one hundred they will be thought of as being cut off prematurely. The life span of those in their earthy bodies will rival those who lived in the days of Noah. We as members of the raptured church age will have our glorified bodies and will not be subject to death or sin.

With the earth being freed from the curse and becoming universally fertile, and with disease on earth being almost nonexistent, we can understand why peace, prosperity, and a sense of well-being will characterize the Messiah's kingdom. However, when Satan is let lose at the end of the one-thousand-year reign, some people will join him in open revolt against God—hard though this may be to believe. This only shows that some people have negative volition and even under a perfect environment they are determined to revolt and receive their assignment in the lake of fire with eternal torment.

# CHAPTER 17

# ETERNITY

## The New Jerusalem

And I saw a new heaven and a new earth, for the first heaven and the first earth had passed away. Also there was no more sea. Then I, John, saw the holy city, New Jerusalem, coming down out of heaven from God, prepared as a bride adorned for her husband. And I heard a loud voice from heaven saying, "Behold, the tabernacle of God is with men, and he will dwell with them, and they shall be his people, and God himself will be with them and be their God. And God will wipe away every tear from their eyes; there shall be no more death, nor sorrow, nor crying; and there shall be no more pain, for the former things have passed away. (Rev. 21:1–4)

And he carried me away in the Spirit to a great and high mountain, and showed me a great and high mountain, and showed me the great city, the holy Jerusalem, descending out of heaven from God, having the glory of God. And her light was like a most precious stone, like a jasper stone, clear as crystal. Also she had a great and high wall with twelve gates, and twelve angels at the gates, and names written on them, which are the names of twelve tribes of the children of Israel; three gates on the east, three gates on the north, three gates on the south, and three gates on the west, now the wall of the city had twelve foundations, and on them were the names of the twelve apostles of the Lamb. (Rev. 21:10–14)

And the city is laid out as a square, and its length is as great as its breadth. And he measured, the city with the reed; 1,500 miles. Its length, breadth, and height are equal. Then he measured its wall: 216 feet...And the twelve gates were twelve pearls: each individual gate was of one pearl. And the street of the city was pure gold like transparent glass. But I saw no temple in it, for the Lord God Almighty and the Lamb are its temple. And the city had no need of the sun or the moon to shine in it, for the glory of God illuminated it, and the Lamb is its light. And the nations of those who are saved shall walk in its light, and the kings of the earth bring their glory and honor into it. Its gates shall not be shut at all by day (there shall be no night there). (Rev. 21:16–25)

And there shall be no more curse, but the throne of God and of the Lamb shall be into it, and his servants shall serve him. They shall see his face, and his names shall be on their foreheads. And there shall be no night there: They need no lamp nor light of the sun, for the Lord God give them light. And they shall reign forever and ever. (Revelation 22:3–5)

The Scriptures do not give us a great deal of information about the future eternal kingdom of God. Perhaps this is because we would not be able to really comprehend what it will be like, since it will be so far beyond our present experiences. People who claim to have had outer body experiences and traveled to heaven or the center of the earth, claim that one's senses are magnified many times over. While these claims are not inspired and may be an illusion or distortion of sensory perception, we can be sure that the eternal state will far exceed our expectations and experiences in our current temporal bodies. Revelation 21 tells us that such things as sin and death will be removed. There will be no more pain, sorrow, or tears.

## New Heavens and a New Earth

One of the final judgments following the millennial kingdom will be the destruction of heaven and earth, as stated in II Peter 3:10–13: "But the day of the Lord will come as a thief in the night, in which the heavens will pass away with a great noise, and the elements will melt with fervent heat; both the earth and the works that are in it will be burned up. Therefore, since all these things will be dissolved what manner of person ought you to be in holy conduct and godliness, looking for and hastening the come of the day of God, because of which the heavens will be dissolved being on fire, and the elements will melt with fervent heat? Nevertheless we, according to the promises, look for new heavens and a new earth in which righteousness dwells."

When these have been destroyed, God will call into existence new heavens and a new earth. In the eternal kingdom, therefore, these new heavens and earth are not simply a renovation of the old heavens and earth but are, rather, the result of a definite act of creation. The word "new" (*kainos*) denotes something that is fresh or new in quality but not something that is strange or uniquely different. This would suggest that the newly created heavens and earth will strongly resemble the previous ones that were destroyed by fire. Apparently the new earth will resemble the old with the main exception that there are no oceans on the new earth. Our present oceans are a result of God's judgment, and there will be no evidence of judgment in the eternal kingdom.

The new earth will be the dwelling place of God's people. God is going to do in the eternal state what he originally intended to do in the first creation. Mankind was created to dwell on this earth in fellowship with God. In the eternal kingdom, man will be involved in various kinds of meaningful activities, learning and serving the Lord. The church will dwell on this new earth because the scriptures teach that the church will be wherever Christ is, and he will be ruling in this eternal kingdom.

"And if I go and prepare a place for you, I will come again and receive you to myself; that where I am, there you may be also" (John 14:3). Israel will dwell on this new earth since the promises in the covenants guarantee an eternal dynasty, kingdom, throne, and blessing. "By faith Abraham obeyed when he was called to go out to the place which he would afterward receive as an inheritance. And he went out, not knowing where he was going. By faith he sojourned in the land of promise as in a foreign country, dwelling I tents with Isaac and Jacob, the heirs with him of the same promise; for he waited for the city which has foundations, whose builder and maker is God" (Heb. 4:8–10).

After the creation of the new heavens and earth, the Apostle John is told the beautiful holy city, the New Jerusalem, will descend from heaven to the earth. The city is of incredible size and beauty. It measures 1,500 Roman miles long, 1,500 miles wide, and 1,500 miles high. It is built like a mountain.

"And he carried me away in the Spirit to a great and high mountain, and showed me the great city, the holy Jerusalem, descending out of heaven from God" (Rev. 21:10). Some scholars say the city is a square and some say it is a pyramid. However, if it is square that is 1,500 miles high, why would it need a 216-foot wall? If it is a pyramid, it would not seem to be very practical. John said he was taken to a mountain. Normally, a mountain has a large base with width and depth and height. This would explain why there are only three dimensions given, and why it appears to reach to heaven. Some say the New Jerusalem descends from heaven, but does not land on earth and hangs in space. If this is so, it would not be a mountain, it would be more like a space ship. However, man can only speculate, because the scriptures do not provide much in the way of specifics. We are strictly on a need–to-know basis. We do not need to know at this time. God is God, and we are but flesh.

A time line would show four-thousand years from Adam to Christ. We would show approximately two-thousand years from Christ until the Second Advent. If Christ was in paradise in the center of the earth for three days, he would have possibly been 3,900 miles beneath the surface of the earth. Some Jewish sages believe heaven is directly over Jerusalem in another dimension. If it was 3,900 miles above the earth, this would in effect make a cross. If Zion is 1,500 miles high, it would appear to reach to heaven.

It is interesting that dates before the death of Christ on the cross in Zion are BC and after the cross are AD. Many of the languages east of Zion or Jerusalem, such as Arabic, Chinese, and Japanese read right to left. Latin languages West of Zion read left to right. The Exodus generation in the Old Testament marched in the form of a cross with the tabernacle surrounded by the twelve tribes and moved towards Zion or Jerusalem. In the New Testament we are to take up our cross and go to the utter most parts of the world. During the day of the Lord, the emphasis returns back to Jerusalem.

The New Jerusalem is not only declared to be beautiful, like the bride adorned for her husband, but it is said to have gates of pearl, buildings of pure gold, and foundation stones of precious gems. Pearls are caused by agitation, gold must be refined, and precious gems are caused by tremendous pressure applied to inexpensive coal. The believers in eternity will have gone through much agitation, purification and pressure, but we will be made beautiful by God through the shed blood of Jesus Christ and the work of the Holy Spirit.

The quality of life we will have is something that we cannot fully appreciate now. "For I consider that the sufferings of this present time are not worth to be compared with the glory which shall be revealed in us. For the earnest expectation of the creation eagerly waits for the revealing of the sons of God. For the creation was subjected to futility, not willingly, but because of him who subjected it in hope; because the creation itself also will be delivered from the bondage of corruption into the glorious liberty of the children of God. For we know that the whole creation groans and labors with birth pangs together until now" (Rom. 8:18–22).

Judgment Day is at hand! Maranatha! Our Lord Come!

# NOTES

1 Chiliasm is Greek for 1,000 years. Millenarianism is from the Latin mille, meaning 1,000 and anni, meaning years.
2 Matthew 24:22.
3 Arnold Fruchtenbaum, Th. M., Ph.D.
4 Genesis 3:15.
5 Psalm 148:3, 6; Daniel 12:3.
6 Jude 9.
7 Matt. 17:3.
8 Daniel 9:1.
9 Luke 16:27–31.
10 Matthew 24:22.
11 Romans 11:2.
12 Romans 11:25.
13 Benwar, Paul, "Understanding End Times Prophecy", p.122.
14 Ezekiel 11.
15 Ezekiel 40–48, Isaiah 56:6, Zechariah 6:12–15.
16 Acts 2.
17 I Thessalonians 4:16.
18 Matthew 13:24–30.
19 Revelation 13:16–18.
20 Matthew 16:18.
21 Genesis 10:8–10.
22 Acts 11:26.
23 Revelation 3:17.
24 Revelation 19:1–10.
25 Matthew 17:3.
26 Clark, *Darwin: Before and After.*
27 Phillips, *Exploring the Future*, 227.
28 Lindsey, *The Late Great planet Earth*, 84.

29  Barton, *The Myth Of Separation.*
30  Bloom, *The Closing of the American Mind.*
31  Barnett, *The Universe and Dr. Einstein,* 106.
32  Blunden, *Works of Fredrich Engels,* 1.
33  Ezekiel 38:8.
34  Psalm 22, Isaiah 53.
35  Josephus, *War of the Jews, Book VI, Chapter V.*
36  Ephesians 3:3.
37  Genesis 7:4.
38  Daniel 9:24–27.
39  Phillips: *Exploring the Book of Daniel,* 202.
40  Revelation 6:8.
41  Revelation 9:18.
42  Revelation 16:16.
43  Hitchcock, *Iran The Coming Crisis,* 82.
44  Barton, *The Myth of Separation,* 21.
45  Ibid.
46  Ibid.
47  Ibid., 24.
48  Ibid., 39.
49  Ibid., 22.
50  Washington, George. First inaugural address, April 30, 1789.
51  MacArthur, General Douglas. Farewell speech to cadets at West Point, May 12, 1962.
52  Lamont, *The Philosophy of Humanism,* 10.
53  Reagan, *One Nation Under Man,* 42.
54  *Journal of American Psychological Association,* March 2003.
55  Cottrell: *Roger Nash Baldwin and American Civil Liberties Union,* 86.
56  Exodus 10:21–23.
57  II Thessalonians 2:4.
58  Genesis 10:8–10.
59  Dyer, *The Rise of Babylon,* 23.

60  Ross, *The Fingerprint of God,* 59.
61  Gish, *Creation Scientists Answer Their Critics,* 127.
62  McLean, G. S., Roger Oakland, and Larry McLean, *The Evidence For Creation,* 49.

# BIBLIOGRAPHY

Appelman, Hyman. *Ye Must Be Born Again.* Grand Rapids: Zondervan Publishing, 1934.

Bauman, Louis. *Russian Events in the Light of Bible prophecy.* Philadelphia: Balkiston Co., 1942.

Beckwith, Francis J. and Koukl, Gregory. *Relativism.* Grand Rapids: Baker Books, 1998

Benware, Paul. *Understanding End-Times Prophecy.* Chicago: Moody Publishers, 2006

Blackstone, William. *Jesus Is Coming.* Grand Rapids: Kregel Publications, 1989.

Bork, Robert. *Slouching Towards Gomorrah.* New York: Regan Books, 1996.

Courson, Jon. *Tree of Life Bible Commentary, Revelation: Volume 1 & 2.* Jacksonville, OR: Tree of Life Publications, 1998.

Chafer, Lewis Sperry. *Systematic Theology: Eight Volumes.* Dallas: Dallas Seminary, 1969.

Charles, R. H. *The Book of Enoch.* San Diego: The Book Tree, 2006

Feinberg, Charles. *The Prophecy of Ezekiel.* Chicago: Moody Press, 1970.

Fuchs, Daniel. *Israel's Holy Days.* Neptune, NJ: Loizeaux Brothers, 1985.

Fruchtenbaum, Arnold. *The Footsteps of the Messiah.* Tustin, CA: Ariel Press, 1990.

Hitchcock, Mark. *Iran The Coming Crisis,* Sisters, OR: Multnomah, 2006.

Hitchcock, Mark. *Seven Signs of the End-Times.* Sisters, OR: Multnomah, 2002.

Hitchcock, Mark. *101 Answers To The Most Asked Questions About the End-Times.* Sisters, OR: Multnomah, 2001.

Hindson, Ed. *Approaching Armageddon.* Eugene, OR: Harvest House Publishers, 1997.

Hocking, David. *The Coming World Leader.* Tustin, CA: Hope for Today Publications, 2000.

Hocking, David. *Moral Catastrophe.* Tustin, CA: Hope for Today Publications, 2001.

Hoehner, Harold. *Chronological Aspects of the Life of Christ.* Grand Rapids: Academic Books, 1975.

Ice, Thomas & Timothy Demy. *Fast Facts on Bible Prophecy.* Eugene, OR: Harvest House, 1977.

Ice, Thomas & Timothy Demy. *When the Trumpet Sounds.* Eugene, OR: Harvest House, 1995.

Ironside, H. A. *Revelation.* Neptune, NJ: Loizeaux Brothers, 1930.

Jeffrey, Grant. *Armageddon Appointment With Destiny.* Toronto: Frontier Research Publications, 1988.

LaHaye, Tim. *Revelation Unveiled.* Grand Rapids: Zondervan, 1999.

LaHaye, Tim & Ed Hindson. *Popular Bible Prophecy Commentary.* Eugene, OR: Harvest House, 2006.

LaHaye, Tim & Jerry Jenkins. *Are We Living in the End-Times?.* Carol Stream, IL: Tyndale House, 1999.

LaHaye, Tim & Thomas Ice. *The End-Times Controversy.* Eugene, OR: Harvest House, 2003.

Larkin, Clarence. *Dispensational Truth.* Philadelphia: Rev. Clarence Larkin Est., 1918.

Lindsey, Hal. *The Late Great Planet Earth.* Grand Rapids: Zondervan, 1970.

Missler, Chuck. *The Magog Invasion.* Palos Verdes, CA: Western Front Ltd., 1995.

Morris, Henry. *The Genesis Record.* Grand Rapids, MI: Baker Book House, 1989.

Morris, Henry. *The Revelation Record.* Wheaton, IL. Tyndale House, 1983.

Morey, Robert. *The Islamic Invasion.* Eugene, OR: Harvest House, 1992.

Pember, G. H. *The Great Prophecies.* London: Hodder and Staughton, 1881.

Pentecost, Dwight. *Things To Come.* Grand Rapids: Dunham Publishing Co., 1966.

Phillips, John. *Exploring The Book of Daniel.* Grand Rapids: Kregel, 2004.

Phillips, John. *Exploring The Future.* Neptune, NJ: Loizeaux Brothers, 1992.

Price, Randall. *The Coming Last Days Temple.* Eugene, OR: Harvest House, 1999.

Price, Randall. *Jerusalem In Prophecy.* Eugene, OR: Harvest House, 1998.

Rosenberg, Joel. *Epicenter.* Carol Stream, IL: Tyndale House, 2006.

Strauss, Lehman. *God's Prophetic Calendar.* Neptune, NJ. Loizeaux Brothers, 1987.

Schaeffer, Francis. *The God Who Is There.* Downers Grove, IL: Inter Varsity Press, 1968.

Scofield, C. I. *Scofield Reference Bible.* New York: Oxford University Press, 1967.

Thomas, Robert. *Revelation An Exegetical Commentary: Two Volumes.* Chicago: Moody Press, 1995.

Walvoord, John. *The Rapture Question.* Grand Rapids: Academie Books, 1979.

Walvoord, John. *Major Bible Prophecies.* New York: Haper Paperbacks, 1991.

Walvoord, John. *The Nations, Israel and the Church in Prophecy.* Grand Rapids: MI: Academie Books, 1988.

Unger, Merrill. *Biblical Demonology.* Wheaton, IL: Scripture Press Publications, 1952.